2S/6
£1

Thank you for buying my book.
I hope you enjoy reading it.
Best wishes
Madeleine Orrick.
March 2009

GW00372717

Maddie was born in Hampshire and has lived there all her life. She has a close-knit family of one son, two daughters, six grandchildren and three great-grandchildren.

She has been a widow for eight years and since then has lived alone enjoying many other pastimes as well as writing, which include: spending time with her young granddaughter; walking her German Shepherd with the family and their dogs; gardening; home improvement and craft work.

ANDERS FOLLY

Madeleine Orrick

ANDERS FOLLY

Vanguard Press

VANGUARD PAPERBACK

© Copyright 2009
Madeleine Orrick

The right of Madeleine Orrick to be identified as author of
this work has been asserted by her in accordance with the
Copyright, Designs and Patents Act 1988

A CIP catalogue record for this title is
available from the British Library.

ISBN 978 184386 436 3

*Vanguard Press is an imprint of
Pegasus Elliot MacKenzie Publishers Ltd.*

www.pegasuspublishers.com

First Published in 2009

**Vanguard Press
Sheraton House Castle Park
Cambridge England**

Printed & Bound in Great Britain

Acknowledgements

My grateful thanks go to my daughter Debs for her patience in helping me to master the computer and for being my best critic. Thank you Treasure. Also my granddaughter Lisa for giving me the computer; my niece Sue for her typing skills and my granddaughter, Nastya, for her photography.

The rest of my children and family I thank for their faith and support. I love you all to bits. Special thanks go to my brother, Dave, and his friend Jim, for putting me in touch with Pegasus Elliot Mackenzie, who have shown me kindness, patience and courtesy. Thank you David, Mary, Sarah and all of your colleagues.

List of Characters

David Anders	Father
Marie Anders	Mother
Gerald Anders	Son
Philip Anders	Gerald's Dead Twin Brother
Pamela Anders	Gerald's First Wife
Robert Anders	Gerald and Pamela's Eldest Son
Alexander Anders	Gerald and Pamela's Youngest Son
Charles Hughes	Gerald's Friend
Felicity Hughes	Charles's Wife
Sophie Hughes	Charles and Felicity's Daughter
Darren	Gerald's Grandson
Samantha and Timothy	Darren's Children
Francesca	Darren's Half Sister
Mike Jennings	Francesca's Ex Fiancée
Lawrence Harcott	Solicitor and Family Friend
Celine Edyvean	Robert's Wife
Adam Wesley	Solicitor Partner to Charles Hughes
Ronald and Jane Wesley	His Parents
Melissa Wesley	Sister to Adam
William Jessop	Doctor at London Clinic
Marcia Roberts	Gerald's Second Wife
Tamara	Her Daughter
Bob Johnson	Groom at Anders Folly
Simon Hall	Manager at Southampton Factory
Matthew Willard	Violinist at Academy with Sophie
Clare and Joseph Willard	His Parents
Ann and Roy Murrey	Hotel Owners
Colin Murrey	Their Son
Abigail Spence	Nanny to Robert and Alexander
Lorna Pennington	Cook at Anders Folly
Maisie	Housemaid
George Watts	Gerald's Manservant
Jake and Jed	Odd Job Men
Edward	Their Father

CHAPTER ONE

1992

The long, hot day had lengthened into a balmy evening, and the scorching sun that had drenched the vast, sandy beaches of the Cornish coast from early morning had all but disappeared, leaving a glowing red arc in the fast gathering dusk of the mid-summer evening. Music drifted hauntingly on the still night air, mingling with echoing laughter and softly lapping waves, crossing the calm expanse of water to the rambling stone-built house on the shore to reach a lone figure seated in a wheelchair. Gerald Anders frowned deeply and thumped the padded arm of his wheelchair with a frail fist, cursing strongly, reluctantly aware the music was quite bewitching, but was this what he had spent his lifetime restoring the family fortune for? To leave it in the hands of this middle-aged, pleasure-seeking son of his who would fritter it away on wild orgies. He was aware of what went on at Alexander's 'yacht parties' and it certainly wasn't what he had bargained for, when he had agreed to him anchoring a boat in the bay.

It had seemed an innocent enough request at the time; there was no mention of size, so it had come as something of a shock when the sleek, fifty foot *yacht*, had sailed into view and dropped anchor. He thumped the arm of his chair again glowering balefully at the scene in front of him. *Two* sons. Both disappointments. Robert clearing off – was it really twenty-six years ago? His glower deepened. And now, Alexander, still behaving like an addle-brained schoolboy when he should be producing heirs. It was Pamela's fault – *she* had ruined them. The glower turned sulky. Robert had always been the steady one – the rightful heir to Anders Folly. The bitterness he had lived with over the years welled up afresh. Little fool! Giving up all of this.

His eyes dwelt proudly on the well-appointed room with its high, ornate ceiling and oak panelled walls, lined with antique furniture and works of art, before returning to the wondrous view, overlooking the Atlantic Ocean.

"Just to marry that dreadful girl who was already pregnant with another man's child," he reflected bitterly. It rankled, how Pamela had given up trying to reconcile them; in hindsight it was as if she hadn't cared, but that couldn't be right. No, she realised that *he* was right in his refusal to make the first move. Reluctantly he allowed himself to wonder about Robert. Had he got sons of his own? A ray of hope pierced his gloom. It went without saying that he wouldn't have anything to do with *the mother*, but grandsons? Heirs, for the family business? He sat up straight, fresh hope surging, turning swiftly to determination as floodlight bathed the calm water of the bay, etching the yacht against the deep blue velvet sky. Loud splashes and shrieks of wild laughter followed as party guests dived or jumped overboard. The light, he had been informed, was Alexander's signal for 'SANI' to begin or, Swim as Nature Intended. It was called skinny-dipping in his day.

He gave a grunt and pressed the button to close the tall French doors; another button closed the heavy brocade curtains with a barely audible swish, then he jerked his chair to the side table, where George would place his supper and a nightcap of brandy, any time now.

He had hardly settled before George appeared. George always drew the curtains, before the yacht's light came on, but tonight it was earlier than usual. He remarked on the smoked salmon sandwiches, which Lorna had laid out on a small, silver platter.

"Just as you like 'em," he said cheerfully, hiding his concern.

His blood boiled at Alexander's lack of consideration. He had asked him once to anchor in a neighbouring bay for his father's sake and he had answered, "None of your damned business George; do you good to let *your* hair down sometimes – metaphorically speaking of course," he had added, giving a sly grin at George's bald pate before dismissing him with a flamboyant flick of a well-manicured hand.

Invitations to Alexander's yacht parties were much sought after, but George knew his escapades went unpunished under his father's cloak of respectability. And although tormented by the parties, Sir Gerald, based on bitter past experience, recognised Alexander was better where he could keep an eye on him, but George had suspected for some while that something illegal was going on. A powerboat slipped away on the dark side of the yacht when the light came on, to rendezvous with a fishing vessel, anchored some way out; on its return, parcels were hoisted on board. Why under cover of darkness if it was legal? George had observed it through the powerful telescope in the attic and knew that the light was more than just a signal for the bathing to begin, it was to alert the other boat. If he ever had proof of contraband, he would take the utmost pleasure in informing the authorities, except that his frail employer would never forgive even the slightest hint of scandal brought on the family. That was how Alexander got away with so much.

Gerald spoke, breaking into his thoughts and he turned from where he was pouring brandy from a decanter into a cut glass goblet.

"I need to find someone I lost touch with a long time ago, George. No publicity of course so a private investigator is out of the question."

George placed the goblet on the table beside him half suspecting what was in his employer's mind. Dare he break the strict rule? Lorna had said it was taboo. He decided not to risk it, saying instead in his broad cockney dialect: "Why not ask Mr 'ughes? 'e would know, like as not – and 'e knows the family better than anyone." George waited while Gerald drummed the arm of his wheelchair with blue veined fingers and stared intently at the wall opposite.

"Mm. I'll ring him tomorrow morning." He took a sip of brandy and started on his supper. George left the room, smiling gleefully. If he was guessing right, Alexander could be in for a few well-deserved shocks. As Gerald's personal manservant, he was privy to most family concerns but this was something that happened before his time and for some reason the subject of his first wife and eldest son was forbidden. Lorna, his usual source of information, became *very* tight lipped if she even *thought* he was going to ask questions.

"No point in gossipin' and guessin'. Only he knows the reason behind his change of heart. All I know is he was devoted; something happened after she died. And if you value your job, you won't ask questions," she had warned, when he first joined the household. It didn't stop him from being curious though.

He hurried back to the kitchen where Lorna was making their bedtime cocoa.

"Master Alexander could be in for a few shocks – if my guess is right."

"We can always hope." She put two mugs of cocoa on the kitchen table and sat down.

"Aren't ye goin' ta ask why?"

"No need. You'll tell me anyway. Never knew such a man for guessin'." Lorna gave a wry smile, folded her arms and listened with growing interest to his interpretation of Gerald's question.

"Possible I suppose, but ..." She shook her head sceptically, afraid to hope.

"I'm right. I know I am."

"Well if you are, it will be the savin' of Anders Folly – and Mr Gerald." Lorna clasped her hands together. "Please let it happen."

"I'll drink ta that." George raised his mug of cocoa and they looked at each other hopefully.

*

The sleek, white yacht named after, its owner's historical namesake, Alexander the Great, lay hidden from public gaze, and at two o'clock in the morning, revelries were at their height.

Alexander sprawled languidly, a trident by his side, a model dolphin at his bare feet, filling a massive rococo throne, set on a raised plinth at one end of the yacht's spacious lounge. A guilt crown rested on his wispy, grey hair, a voluminous, lavishly gold trimmed white toga enveloped his rotund form. From this elevated position he directed his weekend 'Feasts', as he liked to call them.

15

He saw himself as king to the loyal followers who clamoured to be his guests. They loved his style; he gave them excitement.

Each week the theme was different. Tonight he was 'Poseidon', Greek god of the sea. The lounge was draped with artificial seaweed and colourful crustaceans, with huge sea monster couches, amongst low, shell shaped tables littered with exotic fruits, luscious delicacies and ornate wine goblets, and the young people wore white, Greek style robes; the girls had twisted, gold cords spanning their tiny waists.

Next week was to be another 'Trinidad feast'. He recalled the wildness of those nights and smiled in anticipation. Bongo drums, calypso rhythms, youngsters swaying to softly strumming guitars, then the mood would change becoming fast and frantic, among palm trees, mango dishes exuding wonderful Caribbean fragrances; aromatic oils, coconut scented candles, brilliantly coloured costumes, dusky make-up; everything had to be right; the one thing all of these nights had in common, was the intoxicating atmosphere. The air always hung heavy with exotic, heady perfumes, designed to send the youngsters into a frenzy of excitement or stupefy them into forgetfulness.

Alexander liked young people. They were so receptive to his ideas – and also received excellent allowances, with no questions asked providing nothing rocked their wealthy parents' comfortable lives. The 'yacht set', as they liked to call themselves were totally indifferent to how dearly they paid for entertainment, as long as they were part of the 'In crowd'.

He would *really* show them when the old man died.

Ideas raced through his mind of the changes he would make to the house and its surrounding hundred acres. It was really infuriating that his best plans were on hold; the whole place was absolutely wasted on the old man. He ignored the fact that he was still very much in awe of the power that his father wielded, in spite of his disability. As a boy, he learnt to stay out of his way. Mother had always been far more accommodating.

A statuesque, deeply tanned young woman in her mid-twenties, drifted over and sat at his feet. He reached out and stroked her shining dark hair, which hung loose to her bare waist. Unlike the other girls, she was dressed in a brief suede skirt that sat neatly on her slim hips, barely reaching the top of her incredibly long legs, while an equally brief one shouldered top, barely covered her high firm breasts, where a solid gold crescent moon medallion, suspended on a long gold chain rested. A wonderful piece of jewellery for any occasion, but for portraying 'Diana' the Huntress and Goddess of the moon it was perfect. Her, only other adornment was a sheaved hunting knife, clasped to her narrow waist by a deerskin belt.

The necklace was a gift from Alexander. Tamara was his stepsister. He felt very protective towards her and they had an affinity which defied his understanding. Considering her mother was *that detested* woman, who had married his father. What a shock that had been, on his return from Europe. Encouraging her teenage daughter into wild ways had started out as a vendetta against Marcia, until it turned into a very lucrative partnership. Recognising her theatrical talent he had taught her the art of creating his feasts. He had allowed Marcia to believe that he had tired of aggravating *her* and saw her daughter as nothing but an irritating child, whilst guiding Tamara into not drawing attention to herself, as she had done previously by throwing tantrums, running up huge clothes bills and purposely getting parking fines in an effort to get attention from her mother. He taught her how to take control and get what she wanted, by using easily available means. The name Anders opened many doors if you knew which buttons to push. That was how to deal with having an all-powerful father; use some of the power to further one's own ends. Tamara had learnt quickly and even improved on his methods. He left practically all of the arrangements to her now. Yes, she was a great inspiration when it came to flamboyant themes. He gave a contented sigh and took a quaff of wine. And to think he had once coveted, above all else, a seat on that stuffy board of directors that his father set such great store by – probably because it was a privilege reserved for Robert. Life had certainly been a lot less irritating since Robert had ceased to be the blue-eyed boy. He smothered a hiccup, having imbibed too freely; the youngsters must never see him anything other than 'in command'.

Tamara touched his hand, pointing to his gold wristwatch where he noted with some surprise that the hands showed four o'clock. Lost in thought, he had missed everyone settling down for the night, as always, in any comfortable spot they could find. Some preferred the deck on hot, airless nights. He rose stiffly, following Tamara between recumbent bodies, heading for the main cabin, with its king-sized bed and rich, blue satin hangings. From his doorway he watched her disappear in to her own cabin, followed closely by an almost too handsome, well-built young man with Italian looks. Fabian and Tamara! He wanted better for her. Things would change when the house was his. An hour later, his door opened.

"The packages are ready," Fabian said.

He gave a sleepy grunt. Dawn was already breaking.

By ten o'clock, Fabian was organising the small staff that had arrived onboard to clear up the debris. Brunch would be served at twelve o'clock. As always, it consisted of everything, from full English to Continental breakfast. Cheeses, meats, croissants and crusty rolls covered the table with an array of different preserves, fruit juices and cereals. Fabian was in charge of the food which was always excellent and plentiful, as Alexander was confident it would

17

be, having head-hunted him from his favourite restaurant seven years ago when the feasts were small gatherings of close friends. Two years later, Tamara had joined them and things had really taken off. Her drive and energy had stimulated Alexander into making bigger, untraceable profits for them. To all intents and purposes, the youngsters were just partying at his expense but all of them were sworn to secrecy, which made them feel part of a very elite circle

Everyone had to be completely sober before departing in the evening by motor launch, which would take them along the coast to where their cars were parked.

Each week six of them were handed smart, black shopping bags and keys to individual lockers in Waterloo Station, with strict instructions to deposit the package at the earliest possible moment, place the key in the addressed envelope and post it back to him.

Alexander had used this method of transporting his illegal merchandise for over seven years. His couriers were warned not to ask questions, and Alexander was always very generous.

Incredibly, Tamara was unaware of Alexander's lucrative sideline. It was something to do with the childlike trust she had in him that made him want to keep it from her. He had this need to make her happy and he had never felt like that about anyone before. Her very presence gave him peace. Since childhood he had never sought for or valued the opinion of any woman. They were, and always had been unnecessary to his happiness, with the exception, perhaps, of Abigail Spence, but that was years ago.

*

Charles Hughes replaced his telephone receiver and pressed the intercom button. His secretary's voice answered.

"Janet, I have to go out; cancel appointments for the rest of the day and ring my wife to say I won't be in to lunch, please. I shall be at the Anders' home and not to be disturbed, except for an emergency."

He grimaced, viewing the pile of folders balanced precariously on the large kneehole desk but it was a long time since Gerald had asked for his help – and he had sounded terrible.

He arrived at the house promptly at ten o'clock and was shown into the study, where Gerald was waiting anxiously. Having made up his mind to find Robert he had to get things started. If only he wasn't stuck in this damned wheelchair he cursed again and again.

Charles took his outstretched hand. "Gerald, a pleasure to see you." He was shocked at his appearance and eyed him anxiously as he drew a chair up to the side of the desk, saying, "You sounded worried when you telephoned."

"Yes, I am." He waved his hand, dismissing George. All he could think about was putting Charles in the picture; the door had hardly closed before he blurted out:

"I must find Robert. Someone must look after everything when I'm gone. Alexander will destroy Anders Folly within a year. Robert must be found. When can you begin?"

Gerald's over-bright eyes sought reassurance whilst Charles found it difficult to believe his ears. Why this incredible about turn? Even the accident hadn't changed his attitude towards Robert, but this was a desperate man, afraid that time was running out. Why the sudden panic though? He had never seen him like this in all the years they had known each other and Gerald had been adamant that he would *never* contact Robert, under *any* circumstances. What had changed his mind?

Charles looked at him with quiet grief, remembering their early days when they had been inseparable.

"Let me make a few notes," he said calmly drawing a note pad from his brief case, relieved to see Gerald relax a little. He wrote 'Gerald' at the top of the page, searching for something reassuring to say, and looked up to find Gerald with closed eyes. A brief moment of panic gripped him, before realising Gerald was asleep. Taking a deep breath he rose and crossed to the wing chair beside the fireplace.

CHAPTER TWO

Fran ran agitated fingers through her short, chestnut hair, staring unseeingly out of the open window, her eyes clouded with unhappiness.

Her first floor flat overlooked the park where trees and shrubs were ablaze with colour. She often marvelled that she was in the heart of London with its throbbing life a short distance away, but on this summer's evening the ever-changing view failed to capture her, she felt robbed of its peace at the thought of Mike not being there.

A wall divided them for the first time. She thought wistfully of their plans, asking herself at the same time how she could let her brother's three-year-old twins go to strangers, while she left for a new life in America. How would she be able to put Samantha's sad little face out of her mind and tell Timothy that she wouldn't be there when he was afraid? Mike's voice broke into her thoughts making his own feelings abundantly clear.

"I want to marry you Fran but I won't take on two children; they would completely wreck our plans."

They were sitting at the table and he leant forward, putting his hand over hers. "Sorry," he added gently, hating her stricken look. "If you change your mind…" he started to say with a helpless shrug, as Fran interrupted.

"They need me. How can I leave them?" she pleaded miserably, tears springing to her eyes.

"They *have* got a father," her fiancé pointed out referring to her younger brother Darren. "They are *his* responsibility, not *yours*," he added quietly.

Darren was a pilot, stationed in Germany with the RAF and Zara; his wife had been flying out to join him with their three-year-old twins when she was taken ill on the plane. The pilot had radioed ahead and a waiting ambulance had rushed her to hospital but she died of food poisoning before there was time to treat her.

Darren had flown home immediately with his two badly frightened children, automatically taking them to Fran. Sam couldn't accept she wouldn't see her mother again but Tim understood, because when his hamster died, daddy explained that Fudge had gone to live with Jesus in Heaven.

"If Jesus has got Fudge, why does he need Mummy as well and how long will it be before he wants Sam and Daddy to go to live with him – and then you, Auntie Fran?" His eyes had grown wide, imagining himself all alone, and holding him tightly she had promised everything would be all right and every night when she crept in for a last peep at the two heads on the pillows, she desperately hoped it would.

Mike had been patient at first, expecting Darren to make arrangements for them to be with him, but soon began to suspect that he was happy to leave the problem in his sister's willing hands. Sure enough, at the end of his compassionate leave, Darren returned to his unit. Mike broached the subject bearing in mind their wedding was only six weeks away. Uncertainly she had assured him that Darren must have something in mind, but it came as no surprise when a letter arrived begging Fran to take care of the children.

Dear Fran,

I have realised in the last two weeks that I would find it impossible to settle down to civilian life and look after the children as I first intended. Without my lovely Zara, there is no meaning to anything; the only thing keeping me sane is the routine of service life. I know you love the children and they adore you; I can't think of any other situation where they would be even remotely happy. Will write more soon.

He had signed himself your loving brother.

No mention of their wedding plans or Mike's views. Fran's heart had plummeted. Realising she should have said something before he returned to Europe. Mike's new job in America was due to start as soon as they were married. How could Darren ask this of her?"

Mike had listened patiently to her loyal excuses, then said with an edge to his voice, "You obviously feel you can't refuse even though it will ruin our plans."

"Couldn't we look after them for just a little while, until he gets his head together and the children settle down?" she asked miserably realising what she was asking of him, yet still needing to. Before he could answer, Sam cried out in her sleep, as she had done every night.

He waited nearly an hour for her to settle down, but when it became evident that she had no intention of going to sleep until she had Fran's undivided attention, he went, promising to get in touch the next day.

A hurried call later, saying he would be away all week didn't raise any questions in her mind, because as journalists they were accustomed to last minute assignments.

Now as he faced her across the table again, she realised he had put that week of space between them for time to think. He never made rash decisions.

His tall rangy frame tense with emotion, he said, "Your brother has no right to use your feelings for his children in this way, and what about me, don't I matter anymore?" He leant on the table and glared straight into her troubled face.

21

Fran returned his gaze pleadingly. She had never seen him really angry before.

"Of course you matter," she said in a despairing whisper. "Can't you see having to choose is tearing me apart, I love you."

"Not enough it would seem." Mike fixed her with his steady gaze again and she could see the hurt in his eyes. She looked away unable to bear the thought of making a decision. She couldn't remember a time when he hadn't been there for her. Since her first day at *The Echo* six years ago, fresh from college, Mike had been there – encouraging, protective, teasing her into laughing at herself when silly mistakes seemed like the end of the world. She made up her mind.

"I'll telephone Darren tonight and explain that he must have the children out there with him. I should have got it sorted before he left; but it wasn't an easy subject to broach under the circumstances. I am as much to blame."

"Very well," Mike agreed, his tone softening. "I really don't think he should need it spelt out, but perhaps he just hasn't given enough thought to the strain two youngsters put on our relationship – let alone our marriage." He pulled her gently to her feet. "I need you to myself until we are ready to start our own family."

She nodded wordlessly and raised her face; he claimed her lips possessively and the familiar surge of warmth filled her as she relaxed against him, drawing comfort from his nearness and thinking wistfully of their past Sundays. Lovely days spent getting to know one another, leading to whole weekends when they came to the decision that they wanted to spend the rest of their lives together. She moved in the circle of his arms as a loud bump followed by a howl of pain came from the adjoining room, where the twins had been sent to play whilst she and Mike talked.

He loosened his hold as she drew away saying, "I had better go and see." His hands moved to her slim shoulders and held her firmly for a moment, forcing her to look into his eyes again, then quietly and seriously he said, "The final decision is yours. I have to go to the Middle East and I'll be away for two weeks; if I don't hear from you then, I will assume that you have decided to stay with the children and avoid any painful goodbyes."

She stared at him shocked to realise how final his decision was; how thoroughly he had thought things through. A second howl made her glance towards the door and he released her with an impatient gesture.

"I'll telephone Darren this evening," she promised earnestly, edging towards the door as she heard Sam calling for her in pain. "I'll be back in two minutes," she called over her shoulder as she left the room. He had gone when she returned less than five minutes later. Through the open window she could see him leaving the building. "Mike, Mike wait, don't go – not yet," she ended in a whisper. He looked up as if he had heard, raised a hand in salute then, unsmiling, turned away.

Fran watched him walk through the park, with the long loping stride so easily recognisable from a distance, waiting for him to turn as he always did to give a last wave, but his figure disappeared from sight without a backward look and she turned away, with a lump in her throat and her stomach in a tight knot. Fighting back the tears, she busied herself collecting their coffee mugs as the children burst into the room.

"Can we come in now Mike's gone?" they chorused, blissfully unaware of the anguish they were causing her.

When they were in bed and asleep, the evening stretched endlessly in front of her. They always spent Sunday night with a takeaway, in front of the television – their favourite night of the week.

She sat at the big roll top desk, disconsolately rehearsing what she would say to Darren, making notes and scribbling them out, before hesitantly picking up the receiver and dialling the number in Germany.

*

Fran was angry; amber flecks glinted in her green eyes and she ran agitated fingers through her already tousled hair. Why hadn't Darren phoned straight away, as her message left on his answering service had urged, stressing importance. A full week had passed; it wasn't like him but she could *not* think of another single excuse to tell herself. "It's too bad," she muttered throwing a pencil on the littered desk, slumping in the chair and staring moodily in front of her, abandoning any further attempt at clearing up her backlog of work. She went to the kitchen to prepare lunch and was filling the kettle as the front door bell rang.

"I'll go, I'll go," Sam shouted excitedly, feet clattering, auburn curls dancing, paying no heed to Fran's protests as she dumped the kettle on the stove and followed.

"Sam how many times must I tell you not to open the door to strangers?" she asked crossly.

By this time Sam was holding the handle, saying precociously, "It might not be a stranger," as the door swung inwards to reveal a tall figure standing in the dimly lit hallway, briefcase in hand. Sam stepped back, overcome with shyness and Fran gave her a little push in the direction of the bedroom, saying firmly, "Go and play in your room," before facing the caller.

"Good morning, I am trying to contact Mr Anderson on behalf of my firm." He handed her a business card and she read: 'Adam Wesley, in association with Charles Hughes. Solicitor.'

"He left this as a forwarding address with his estate agent. I understand he is away at present."

Fran nodded. "Mr Anderson is in the RAF."

"So you are Mrs Anderson?"

"No, but perhaps if you tell me what this is about, I can help you."

"Is there a Mrs Anderson or children? The little girl obviously belongs to you."

Fran began to feel uneasy and instinctively went to close the door, eyeing him up and down, taking in the long, belted, raincoat with the collar turned up and the trilby hat pulled well down over his forehead. He seemed quite young but it was hard to say because he kept his head down and she could only just see a pair of luminous dark eyes, and a small dark moustache, also his voice was strangely gruff. She wasn't of a nervous disposition but there was something definitely odd about him and she was suddenly very aware of being alone with two small children. "If you have any further questions, I suggest you come back in a short while; I'm expecting Mr Anderson's friend any minute – he is a policeman and will answer any questions you have."

It was all she could think of on the spur of the moment, but it worked because the stranger instantly appeared nervous as he heard the lift approaching, and turned on his heel, pulling his hat even further down over his face and headed for the stairs. Fran closed the door and slipped the safety catch on, chiding herself for not keeping it on and annoyed with herself, thinking of the questions she *should* have asked. 'Call yourself a journalist?' she muttered.

The incident was forgotten in the event of the overdue telephone call from Darren in the evening. He was full of remorse, blaming himself for being so blind to her predicament.

"I only got your message half-an-hour ago – I've been away from the base. Sorry, Love, I just wasn't thinking straight."

A lump rose in her throat making it difficult to reply. She pictured her brother's face and her heart went out to him. "I understand," she managed after a small pause. She had always been there for him and things don't change just because you grow up.

"You've been a brick, Sis, and I've found a nice couple, willing to look after Tim and Sam until I find a housekeeper and rent a house."

Fran spirits lifted as he went on, "There is a service flight leaving in a week's time, which would get me home by six-thirty next Friday and we would return on the Sunday. Will that be OK?"

"Of course – and Darren – I'm really sorry."

"Don't worry. You aren't to fret; we will be fine. It wasn't fair of me to ask and I can only say again that I wasn't thinking straight. Chin up and I will see you a week today. Shortly after that I will dance at your wedding, eh? Love to the kids."

Fran was smiling broadly as she replaced her receiver. Now she could write to Mike; the letter would be waiting for him on his return. Her thoughts were happy as they walked through the park the next day. She strode out cheerfully, Mike's letter in her hand ready to post. At last after the long weeks of misery since Zara's death, things looked brighter. By Friday, the laughter that had been missing from their lives was partly restored and there were great preparations for the evening. She compared the solemn little faces of a week ago and felt guilty that some of it had been due to *her* mood. By six o'clock they were changed and ready. Fran was in the kitchen, putting finishing touches to Darren's favourite roast lamb, whilst Sam was rearranging the table yet again. Tim, although apparently transfixed to the television, was obviously waiting as eagerly and was the first one to the door when the bell rang. Sam was trying unsuccessfully to barge him out of the way and Fran followed smiling in anticipation. Darren was early. The children's faces fell at the unexpected sight of a woman in RAF uniform standing in the doorway and Fran's heart gave a sickening lurch as the uniformed figure asked, "Miss Francesca Anderson?"

"Yes," she breathed.

"Could we have a word? Alone would be best," she added her gaze flickering towards the children.

"Wait in your bedroom, children," Fran said quietly ushering the woman into the lounge and hardly waiting to close the door before turning to search her sympathetic face, a terrible sense of foreboding rendering her speechless.

"Sit down my dear, I'm afraid I have come with some very terrible news."

Long after she had gone and the children had cried themselves to sleep, Fran sat in the gathering darkness, dry eyed and motionless. Words kept running disjointedly through her numbed mind. Presumed dead. Test flight. Plane crashed early this morning – when they were happily preparing dinner for him. *"How could God let this happen?"*

Eventually she roused herself, heedless until that moment of how chilled she had become and rose stretching her stiff limbs, then with slow, heavy movements began to clear away the untouched meal, wondering despairingly how she was going to cope with the future. She would have to write to Mike again. There was no question what she had to do now. The prospect of a future without Mike was devastating, but without Darren too – intolerable.

A long determined ring on the front doorbell woke Fran out of a deep sleep and she quickly slipped out of bed noting with surprise that the hands of the clock pointed to nine-thirty. How had she slept until this time? And no sound coming from the children's room either. How odd! Hurriedly throwing on her blue cotton housecoat, she ran to answer it, running a comb through her tousled hair on the way, and came to a halt at the door, thinking her ears must be playing tricks. The twins voices seemed to be coming from the other side; panic made her turn the lock and throw it back so suddenly that she startled the two children waiting to be let in. They stared at her apprehensively, realising that her look of amazement boded no good. Then Sam said boldly, "Jaffa was barking and scratching the door so we had to take him out. Josie's dog does that when he wants the toilet." She nodded her head and gave what Fran had come to know as her challenging look.

"We just took him for a little walk," Tim said sheepishly.

Fran's eyes narrowed and she pursed her lips, returning his wide-eyed look, well aware he didn't believe in the make believe spaniel any more than she did.

"Jaffa really enjoyed his run in the park, didn't you boy?" Sam bent down and smoothed the air while Fran swallowed hard and sat down with a bump on a nearby chair, her legs suddenly refusing to support her as she pictured all of the things that could have happened to them, then in a shaky voice she said, "Never – I repeat – never – do that again. Do you understand? You are never to leave the flat without me – ever."

She lent force to her words by flinging her arm in the direction of the kitchen. "Now go and wait for breakfast."

They scampered past her and she heard a whispered exchange. "I think she's cross."

"So do I."

"I wonder why? Mummy always let us play outside."

Fran shuffled back to her bedroom, her fluffy, pink mules making a plopping sound as she went. A flat is no place to bring up children, she told her worried looking reflection, sitting with elbows on the dressing table. They need a garden, a swing, a playhouse – and grass to play on. It was two weeks since that dreadful Friday and she hadn't made a single decision that made any sense for their future. While she dressed she considered Darren and Zara's house on the outskirts of London. It was spacious with a big garden. It hadn't sold yet and there was nothing to stop them from moving in she supposed, dismissing the idea immediately as memories surfaced.

Tears stung her eyes and she brushed them away impatiently. Mike said he wouldn't get in touch for painful goodbyes, but she felt sad and rejected that he hadn't even sent condolences; it felt as if he had written her off without another thought. Pride made her square her shoulders and sit up straight. This was no time for self-pity. She had three weeks to make positive arrangements.

First and foremost, was to withdraw her resignation. Until now, one-parent families, were something she had read about, but it was becoming reality with a vengeance. New mothers had time to prepare; new babies stayed put for a year; *she* needed eyes in the back of her head and be able to run in two directions at the same time. It came home also, just how alone they were. Both of her parents had died in a car crash nine years ago and Zara had been an orphan, so the children had never known grandparents or relations – in fact she was their only family. Still debating with herself she made her way to the kitchen, where Sam and Tim, having helped themselves to cereal, were munching in a very subdued way. Her heart cried for them, and on the spur of the moment suggested, "Why don't we take a trip to the zoo today?"

They ran to her flinging their arms round her legs and she held their small bodies closely.

"We're sorry Auntie Fran," they chorused.

She ruffled their hair. "Come on, let's make a picnic and get going." Whatever the problems they wouldn't be solved by the three of them being unhappy.

It was late when they returned home, weary after the long day tramping around the zoo, stopping to eat their picnic in the friendly shade of a huge spreading oak, then riding home on an open-air, double-decker bus. The twins had squealed with delight and Fran knew whatever the difficulties, she would manage somehow.

While she was preparing supper, the doorbell rang. Her heart leapt as she hurried to answer it, still half expecting Mike to call; her disappointment wasn't altogether lost on the tall, well dressed stranger, who apologised for calling so late, explaining he had called twice, earlier in the day.

"What can I do for you?" she asked acutely aware of her bare feet, wishing she had retrieved her shoes from under the kitchen table, where she had kicked them off, to feel the cool, tiled floor.

"I am trying to contact Mr Darren Anderson, on behalf of a client."

It was dim in the hallway but as the caller reached into his inside jacket pocket, he turned slightly and his clean-shaven profile was etched sharply against the fading light from the window behind him.

He held out a card. "I am Adam Wesley."

Her outstretched hand halted between them. "Who?" she questioned blankly.

"Adam Wesley," he repeated.

"But…"

Still proffering the card, he raised his eyebrows quizzically.

"Are you sure?" As soon as she asked she wished she hadn't.

The caller gave an amused smile and reached into his pocket again, producing a wallet. "Well yes, I'm pretty sure. Let's see now, driving licence, bankers card. He handed them to her along with the calling card. "I'm afraid I don't carry my passport," he apologised and she could see he was trying to keep a straight face.

She gave a swift glance and reassured, handed them back with a flustered explanation. "I'm sorry, but some very odd person called three weeks ago – giving the name Adam Wesley, also wanting to see my brother; it just seems too much of a coincidence."

He frowned. "Can you describe him?"

She didn't have to stop and think, she had gone over the incident many times in her mind and also had the safety lock moved to the top of the door, out of the twins' reach.

"Nothing like you. Tall, very, very slim, dressed in a dark, belted raincoat and dark trousers: he wore a trilby hat pulled well down, dark glasses, small dark moustache," she see-sawed her right hand, "mid thirties maybe – oh, and he carried a black briefcase and wore gloves." She paused for a second before adding, "Extremely light on his feet, I noticed when he ran towards the stairs."

Adam's mouth had dropped open slightly. "So you couldn't really give a good description, then?"

She looked at him, realised he was laughing at her again and relaxed with a sheepish grin. "I'm a journalist."

"Aah!" Then seriously he asked, "Why did he run to the stairs?"

"He heard the lift coming, and I had just told him I was expecting a policeman friend of Darren's who would answer his questions."

"And were you?"

"No, but I was in the flat, alone with two small children and it was all I could think of at the time."

"Quick thinking, good job you were on the ball." His eyes twinkled admiringly and she noticed how startlingly blue they were in his suntanned face as he continued. "It really is important that I contact your brother; perhaps you have an address where I can reach him?" he asked hopefully.

She hesitated fractionally, before inviting him in.

"Make yourself comfortable. I will just settle the children."

Returning a few minutes later, after taking the sleepy-eyed Sam and Tim their sandwiches and a hot milk drink in bed, she found him sitting at the table where Mike so often sat. He looked up as she entered carrying a tea tray.

"What a pleasant view you have."

"Yes, I love it, but a flat is no place to bring up children, I'm discovering."

"How old are they?" he asked noticing the absence of a wedding ring.

"The twins are three. They belong to my brother," she said quickly seeing his glance.

She poured tea into the cups, leaving him to help himself to milk and sugar, while she told him of Darren's plane crash and found herself pouring out other problems, whilst he listened attentively and asked the occasional question. It wasn't until there was a pause, quite some time later that she realised he had produced a small tape recorder and was recording their conversation. She started to her feet.

"Why are you doing that?"

"Please don't be alarmed. This could be imperative to your future. I'm certain my client is unaware of your brother's death – and I will have to take further instruction before I say more, but you can expect to hear from me tomorrow."

His blue eyes looked steadily into hers and she amazed herself by nodding. She who prided herself on being so reticent about her private life, had just confided her innermost worries to this man, who, until two hours ago she had never set eyes on.

He stood up to leave, his athletic figure seeming to fill the room and those eyes held hers in a magnetic look as he clasped her hand and said goodnight, promising again to be in touch the next day.

*

It was quiet in the lobby of the hotel where Adam booked himself a room for the night. The receptionist had just come on duty and while he checked which rooms were available Adam looked around, his gaze resting fleetingly on the revolving door as a young man stepped out.

"If you would just sign the register, sir." The receptionist held out a pen, and he signed, before taking the key.

"Room two hundred and ten, sir. Have a pleasant stay."

"Thank you. Good night."

"Good night sir."

The young man was waiting for the lift, engrossed in his newspaper. When it came he stepped in, retreating to the far corner, leaving Adam to press the button.

"Which floor?" Adam asked, glancing over his shoulder.

"Two," came a gruff reply from behind the newspaper.

The lift stopped and the man followed him, as he stepped out of the lift onto the thickly carpeted landing. Conscious of footsteps keeping pace with him, Adam turned sharply, sensing the stranger was unusually close, and taken unawares, bent double as a knee caught him in the groin and a practiced hand chopped the back of his neck. Dazed and in pain, he felt the key wrenched from his fingers and while still reeling was barged roughly through the now open, bedroom door and sent sprawling to the floor where he hit his head on the bedpost. He tried to rise and defend himself but a well-aimed kick in the ribs sent him crashing and before he could try again a blow to the side of the head rendered him unconscious.

He came to, feeling as if he had been hit by a truck, and lying there with only the light from the street lamp to relieve the darkness he fought to control the nausea that rose in his throat as he tasted blood on his lips. His mind cleared and memory flooded back. There had been something distinctly familiar about his attacker, which he couldn't focus on at that moment. Rising painfully, he lurched towards the light switch and steadied himself against the door. Of course! Tall. Slim. Raincoat. Trilby. Miss Anderson's description of the other Adam Wesley. Well she was certainly right about one thing – he *was fast on his feet.* A glance at his watch showed it was eleven-fifteen; he must have been out for half an hour.

The bathroom mirror told him his appearance would without doubt cause comment. A cut lip and a rapidly closing eye gave him the lopsided look of a boxer, and he certainly hadn't bargained for what felt like a couple of broken ribs when he left home that morning. He debated whether to report the matter and decided not to, a decision that he was glad of ten minutes later when he discovered that his briefcase was missing. The one thing that Charles Hughes had stressed was no publicity. He would just have to wait for a reasonable hour and telephone for further instructions. The family wasn't the only thing he had made contact with, he thought ruefully, touching his eye.

Having bathed his face and cleaned himself up, he gingerly laid his aching body on the bed and lay staring up at the high, old-fashioned ceiling. Going over the case, which until two days ago had been strictly in the hands of his senior partner, but when a trip to London was necessary, Charles had thankfully handed the mission over to him – and what a good job he did. It would have been far more serious if Charles had been attacked so savagely.

It was a strange case and he wondered, not for the first time, why contacting this Darren Anderson was so urgent and why it had been so difficult to track him down. The hours dragged by; sleep was out of the question. The sound of a milk float humming along made him look at his watch. Ten past five. He knew Gerald Anders to be an early riser, but he decided to wait another twenty minutes before calling and use the tea making facilities, wishing he had noticed them tucked away behind a screen before. The hot tea was soothing and made him realise how hungry he was, but the notice on the wall over the electric kettle said that seven o'clock was the earliest breakfast. He groaned, but reminded himself that it *was* London and *somewhere* would be open.

He put the call through on the telephone beside the bed, and the receiver was picked up very quickly. Gerald's deep, imperious voice answered at once, almost as if he had been expecting the call and as briefly as possible, Adam outlined the events of the previous evening, ending with the attack on himself and the theft of the briefcase.

Gerald was excited to hear about the twins, but Darren's death just seemed like another part of the curse that was dogging the family.

"Sorry to hear you caught the thin end of things, m' boy, but I just wonder, who the devil this feller can be and what it is he wants, to go to such lengths?"

"I have no idea and I'm sure Miss Anderson hasn't either. How would you like me to proceed, sir?"

There was a lengthy pause before Gerald, sounding less assured than usual said, "In view of what has happened, go back, and ring me in half an hour – whatever you do don't leave them until we have spoken again."

"What shall I say to Miss Anderson? She is bound to think it an intrusion."

"I can't help what she thinks – my concern is for the children's safety." His tone was suddenly brisk, obviously anxious to finish their conversation and get on with arrangements.

Adam replaced his receiver, collected his jacket and left the room, startled into assuring himself of Fran and the children's safety. Could they really be at risk? Sir Gerald seemed to think so. Perhaps he did suspect who the attacker was, after all.

Down in the lobby, the receptionist, weary from his night's vigil, hardly gave the departing guest a glance as Adam paid the bill, and thankfully no comment was made. It was only a short walk back across the park to the block of flats. As he drew near, in spite of the pain in his ribs he hastened his step anxiously, seeing a figure at the window where he judged her flat to be. Fran, sitting at the table drinking a cup of tea, was amazed to see Adam Wesley heading across the park at that hour, with the obvious intention of calling. Even

31

from that distance she could see he was walking badly and holding his side. She met him at the door to avoid waking the children and exclaimed in whispered horror as she saw his bruised face.

"Whatever happened to you?"

He was breathing heavily with his arms folded across his stomach and she led him into the lounge, helped him to lower himself into a comfortable chair then poured a cup of hot sweet tea from the pot on the table.

"I have to call my client back, then I will be able to tell you more. This happened soon after I left you, and my attacker matched your description of the man who called on you."

"What on earth is going on?" she asked frantically, picturing the figure in the dimly lit hallway again. She shuddered, hugging herself, remembering how Sam opening the door had in all probability been face to face with the same violent character. She recalled her feeling of apprehension – it hadn't been fanciful after all.

She looked up to find Adam watching her intently and pulled herself together. They sat and drank tea, watching London stir to life, until Adam said it was time to make the call. She brought him the telephone from the desk, then, piling everything onto the tea tray took it to the kitchen. Almost straightaway the shrill bell of the telephone broke the silence and woke the twins. Bare footed and in their pyjamas they pattered out to the kitchen, agog at the sound of a strange voice coming from the lounge.

Fran put their breakfast on the table, listening to the one-sided telephone conversation with one ear, whilst coping with a bombardment of questions from the now thoroughly wide-awake youngsters, but they fell silent when Adam entered the kitchen.

"Hello," he greeted them with a lopsided grin.

Their mouths dropped open as they studied his bruised face, then together they slid from their chairs and edged round the table to Fran.

"It's alright, darlings; this is Mr Wesley and he has had a nasty accident now I want you to sit and finish your breakfast and then get dressed for me." She gave them each a little push towards their chairs and they went, still watching Adam, wide-eyed. He motioned Fran into the lounge, shutting the door.

"Sir Anders has instructed me to invite you and the children to visit him in Cornwall. He is sending a car for us in two hours' time. I would seriously suggest you go," Adam advised.

After a long pause she found her voice. "But why? And why the hurry?"

Adam hesitated not wanting to frighten her. "He is afraid for your safety, after last night."

He watched her eyes fill with alarm.

"It's all to do with this client you can't tell me about, isn't it? And now this *thug* knows where we live. Why did you come? I've got enough troubles already," she cried.

"I believe it's more to do with the other Adam Wesley, who found you before I did," he reminded her gently.

Fran stared at him, realising what he said was true.

"Seriously, accept the invitation; it could be of considerable advantage to you and the children, anyway what have you got to lose? If you don't like it when you get there, you can turn around and come back. At the worst you will have a couple of days away," he reasoned logically.

"I need time to think," she said with a worried look.

"By the way, if you are wondering why the phone rang, Sir Anders called me back because it was long distance – just thought you would like to know."

Suddenly he gave her a pleading look. "And while you're thinking, you couldn't rustle me up a bite to eat could you? I haven't eaten since four o'clock yesterday and I'm absolutely starving." He continued to look at her pleadingly and suddenly she laughed.

"Bacon sandwiches OK?"

"Fantastic!" He followed her and watched as she arranged rashers on the grill tray, willing them to cook quickly. Fifteen minutes later he was contentedly tucking into well-filled sandwiches and another cup of strong tea. Fran smiled in spite of her worrying thoughts and left him to eat while she went to check on the children. When she returned he had finished eating and was feeling his swollen eye. She went to the cupboard and fetched witch hazel and cotton wool.

"In the absence of a piece of steak, this will have to do."

She soaked the cotton wool and dabbed gently at the bruise then stood back surveying her handiwork.

"I have decided we will come with you." She still wasn't sure why she was agreeing to this ludicrous plan, except that curiosity had got the better of her and it appealed to her sense of adventure.

"Good!" Adam breathed a sigh of relief, thankful to be able to carry out his instructions, which far from being the *invitation* he had extended on Sir Gerald's behalf, had amounted to a royal command. Once she was there though he was convinced it would be to their advantage.

CHAPTER THREE

Charles settled himself more comfortably in the big wing chair, noting with relief that Gerald was breathing rhythmically, chin sunk deep into his chest. He gazed around the familiar room recalling the many happy hours spent there. Theirs had been a long and close friendship until Gerald remarried, he reflected sadly. Slumped in his wheelchair behind the huge rosewood desk, that had been his father's and his father's before him, he was a shadow of the upright, dynamic figure he had once been.

He gave a deep sigh as memories of David and Marie flooded back. He and Felicity still grieved for them: the only parents they had ever known – Marie, with her gentle, loving ways and David, brilliant businessman, caring father. They had shaped *his* life from when he left university at twenty-one. That was when Gerald had first introduced him to his father, in the spring of 1939, convinced they could be of help to one another.

1939

David Anders had been in the throes of setting himself and his son up in business: a car manufacturing plant on the outskirts of Southampton. He was a dynamic character and Gerald was a younger edition of him. Anders and Son made a good team.

Charles was considered, according to his tutors, to have a promising career ahead of him, but to say that David, an immaculate man himself, was not impressed by the young law student, was the understatement of all time, as he regarded him from behind his desk with growing dismay wondering why Gerald was so certain he would be an asset to them. How could he possibly allow anyone looking like that to represent them? The *awful* Harris Tweed sports jacket with leather patches on the elbows; baggy unpressed trousers, shirt with curling collars, down-at-heel shoes with laces that didn't quite match; and to top it all the untidy brown thatch of hair. It only took the horn-rimmed spectacles, held together with sticking plaster, to complete the perfect stereotype picture of an absent-minded professor. A good meal wouldn't go amiss either, he guessed. What was his son thinking of? Against his better judgment, he agreed to a trial, on the understanding that Gerald took his friend along to their tailor and barber.

"Thanks, Dad. You won't be sorry. You'll see."

David tossed his eyes heavenwards and waved Gerald away, but within weeks, he was admitting he shouldn't have judged the book by the cover.

"Charles knows what I'm going to say before I say it," David told a smug Gerald.

In September of that year, Britain went to war with Germany and David joined the war effort by turning out army transport vehicles on a government contract. Gerald and Charles had call up papers and were both highly incensed when rejected. Gerald with asthma and Charles with fallen arches. They soon realised, however, there were many duties they *could* fill, and threw themselves fiercely into whatever was needed. Such as fire fighting on the factory roof during the inky black nights, when shells whistled, incendiary bombs fell all around and search-lights sent giant beams sweeping across the sky to pin point droning enemy aeroplanes, or distributing and organising the building of Anderson shelters for civilians to take refuge in during the sleepless nights, endured by young and old, rich and poor alike – war did not discriminate.

Gerald gave his time unstintingly, scouring the countryside for large properties, which owners were glad to sell, and turning them into convalescent centres for the wounded and maimed servicemen, returning from 'The Front'. Salving his conscience to a small degree, for not being amongst the wounded himself.

It was during the opening of the fourth home, deep in the heart of the New Forest, that he met Pamela, the newly appointed matron of Forest End. Until then, women hadn't figured very largely in his life, but with her red hair, and green eyes that flashed when she thought her authority was being challenged, was a challenge in itself to Gerald. Her fieriness excited him and at the same time endeared her to him. He fell head over heels in love, and of course dealt with it in the same way as everything else. He bombarded her with presents and flowers, telephoned her daily and at the end of a month, proposed marriage. Her blunt, "You must think I'm completely mad, I hardly know you," astounded him, but characteristically made him even *more* determined to make her his wife. Pamela, knowing instinctively that anything he attained *easily*, would pall *quickly*, bided her time, intending to give in eventually with gracious reluctance, because she had never met a man like him before.

Charles, in the meantime, was beginning to appreciate the wholesome roundness of his secretary, Felicity. Felicity was a natural blonde with deep violet blue eyes and a peaches and cream complexion.

"She's built like a woman should be built," Charles claimed, referring to her generous curves, in what Gerald called, his slightly pompous courtroom manner.

"Give me a tall, willowy, long-legged, red-head with flashing green eyes," Gerald had teased, anticipating his more sober minded friend's look of disapproval, with a good humoured grin.

Charles had moved into the Anders' home, a three-storied Victorian semi, on the out-skirts of Southampton, six weeks after war broke out.

"It makes sense," Gerald had pointed out. "They will only billet a stranger on us in the spare room, so you would be doing *us* a favour really."

"Well if you put it like that," Charles had readily agreed.

Gerald was well pleased with himself, not only had he made his mother happy, now she could, 'feed the poor boy properly', but he had done it without making Charles feel a charity case.

Charles had spent the first sixteen years of his life in an orphanage, having been abandoned as a baby and had therefore never known anything like the comfort of the Anders' home. His gratitude to Marie knew no bounds. He thanked her constantly for washing and ironing and cooking tasty meals, which she managed in spite of rationing.

"She will expect a pay rise if you keep this up," David joked, when having wiped the last little drop of gravy with the last morsel of herb dumpling, Charles laid down his knife and fork, with a deep sigh of contentment and looked up to find them watching him with amused affection.

He grinned sheepishly. "Dumplings didn't taste like that in the orphanage; you could have shot planes down with them." He stood up and started to collect the plates.

"Leave that, dear," Marie said.

"No, you have been on voluntary service all afternoon, you put your feet up and rest."

There were cries of dismay from David and Gerald, but they both got to their feet, stealing anxious glances. She was such a tower of strength they took how much she did for granted. Gerald put both hands on his father's shoulders and guided him to the armchair opposite his mother's. "Keep Mum company; we promise not to break everything."

They settled down in the flickering firelight. The room was warm and cosy. David reached for his pipe and tobacco pouch and Marie watched the familiar ritual, as he teased the tobacco and filled the round rosewood bowl. Tonight it seemed even more comforting than usual and when she said, "It feels almost like having the family complete again," he just nodded wordlessly, knowing that her thoughts, like his own, were perhaps happier than they had been since the death of Gerald's twin brother, Philip, four years ago. Philip had constantly been hunched over some reference or textbook. He dreamed of becoming an archaeologist. It wasn't the wisest choice, in view of the asthma that both he and

Gerald suffered from. He would go from college to the town library, where he would leaf through heavy, dusty tomes and stagger home under the weight of another to read in the evening, whereas Gerald spent his spare time playing cricket or tennis. In hindsight, they all three blamed themselves for not encouraging him to exercise more, then his heart might have stood up to the last fatal attack; but as Gerald, even in his own grief, fought to help them with theirs, said, "He was doing what he loved best. He hated the sweatiness and rowdiness of sports, so let's remember him reading his books and playing the piano."

The clatter of dishes had ceased and David could hear the kettle whistling for the cup of tea that always followed the evening meal. Marie had nodded off and the familiar theme music, heralding 'Dick Barton. Secret Agent', came over the radio. He watched her fondly, puffing on his pipe. Soon the air raid siren would sound as it always did some time every evening, then they would have to leave the comfort of the fireside and go down to the shelter. And Gerald and Charles would go on fire watch duties.

In 1944, daily reports of the allies' advancement into Europe brought optimistic hopes for peace.

"It's a time to cautiously celebrate," David declared one Saturday evening when the six of them were seated around the dining table.

Felicity and Pamela had become regular visitors much to Marie's delight, however, it had to be said, that although she and Felicity shared many of the same interests and liked each other from the start, she found Pamela worrying, until Pamela put her mind at rest by saying, "I can't do the wonderful housewife and mother bit, it just isn't me. I love my job and I'm good at it, but Gerald will always come first."

From the sitting room Gerald heard them chatting and sighed thankfully, he worried about how his mother would cope with Pamela's modern thinking, but the war *had* changed everybody, even mothers. Gone was the idea that women only ran the home and raised children. Now they made munitions, farmed the fields, drove buses and coped single-handed, whilst their men were away fighting.

In response to David's 'cautious celebration', Gerald turned to Pamela.

"That reminds me, I haven't proposed this week." It had become a standing joke, even though he was in deadly earnest. "Can we name the day yet, my darling?"

He missed Pamela's quiet "Yes" as he continued, "Put my poor mother out of her misery, take me off her hands." Everyone else gave a delighted whoop!

"You may laugh, but one day she will say—"

"Yes," Pamela repeated loudly, as Gerald's mouth dropped open.

Recovering he jumped up. "Mother, Dad. She said yes, she actually said *yes*. We've got to celebrate. How? Er – er." He looked blankly at everyone in turn, before grabbing Pamela and kissing her soundly, just as David, who had slipped out quietly, returned carrying a magnum of Champagne.

"Get some glasses, Mother, our son is getting engaged."

Marie returned minutes later, carrying six glasses and a brown leather cube shaped box, which she placed in front of Gerald.

"This belonged to Dad's mother. Don't be afraid to say if you don't like it, Pamela dear."

Gerald opened the case to reveal an exquisite half-hoop of diamonds and they all heard Pamela's sharp intake of breath, as she looked from the ring to Gerald and back to the ring again.

"I've never seen anything so lovely," she managed, through happy tears. "Are you sure you can bear to part with it?" she asked Marie.

Marie's face was wreathed in smiles. "I'm happy you like it as much as I do. And I know Dad will like to see you wearing it, won't you, dear?"

David beamed and nodded. "It's very generous of you dear. The ring is yours to do with as you wish of course. Mother left it to *you*." They raised their glasses and the conversation turned to, "Where on earth did you find Champagne and how long have you been holding out on us?"

David tapped the side of his nose. "It's not *what* you know, but *who*," he quoted. At that moment the lights flickered and plunged them into darkness.

"I'm nearest." Charles pushed his chair back and rose unhurriedly, reaching behind him for the two silver candlesticks that always stood ready for the next power cut. Having lit them he placed one at each end of the dining table, where they threw out a myriad of soft reflected light.

"Why didn't we think of this before?" Gerald exclaimed, captivated by the soft radiance of the candlelight, shining on Pamela's hair. "Happy, sweetheart?" he asked adoringly and she nodded, eyes shining, lips parted in a doting smile.

"Bet you can't believe you caught me at last," he teased.

Pamela returned his banter imperturbably. "If I had known this wonderful ring came with you I'd have said yes *straight* away."

"Back to normal," David reassured Marie, patting her hand. *He* was thinking how pretty *she* looked in her dusky pink twin set and single strand of pearls. It was good to see her looking so happy. He had thought never to see it again, after Philip's death. No one could replace him but Charles had helped to fill the gap. His very presence had eased the pain that they were all locked in and he was also very like Philip. Always pouring over books and files *and* he played the piano even though he had never had a lesson and couldn't read a note of music, but he only had to hear a melody to be able to play it.

Gerald, looking decidedly merry, was refilling the glasses with Champagne, when Pamela realised how quiet Felicity had gone and never one to hesitate, raised her glass.

"Here's to Charles and Felicity, may they decide to tie the knot soon, as well."

David and Marie looked at each other and then at Felicity, who blushing furiously took a larger mouthful of Champagne than she intended and choked. Charles jumped up patting her clumsily on the back as Pamela, still holding her glass aloft, hiccupped and gave an owl-like blink. Charles, who had been about to sit down again, remained standing and picked up his glass, chuckling good-humouredly.

"I'll drink to that but woe betide you when you are sober, Madam," he warned Pamela.

"Propose. Propose," Pamela insisted, hiccupping again.

"Pamela, you are embarrassing Felicity," Marie scolded affectionately, picking up her glass hopefully. And then, much to everyone's delight, Charles turned to Felicity, who hadn't said a word and asked with an enquiring frown, "Does the idea of marrying me make you choke, m' dear?"

Eyes shining, Felicity gazed up at him and shook her head.

"Then will you make me and everyone here very happy, and say you will be my wife?" He took her hand in his and she stood up.

All she could say was, "Oh, Charles!" He kissed her gently on the lips and they sat down still gazing happily at each other.

Pamela broke the silence. "So we can take that as a yes?" she enquired, picking up her glass again as everyone laughed and Marie surreptitiously wiped away a tear.

"Well done, Charles!" Gerald raised his glass. "And well done to you, my love," he whispered in Pamela's ear, whilst bestowing a kiss.

Marie had yet another surprise and after a whispered conference with David and Gerald, she picked up one of the candles and left the room, returning a few minutes later with another ring box and placed it in front of Charles.

"This was intended for Philip's wife and we would all like you to have it, if Felicity likes it. This one belonged to *my* mother."

Felicity and Charles could only stare, first at each other and then at Marie, David and Gerald in turn. "We can't possibly let you do that," they echoed each other.

"Just have a look at it," Marie urged, her motherly face creased with smiles again.

Charles passed the box to Felicity and she passed it back. "No you," she murmured shyly.

This time the box concealed a beautiful dark blue sapphire surrounded by smaller diamonds. Felicity gasped, unable to take her eyes away from the shining gems, then with a reluctant shake of her head she closed the box, slid it back across the table and looking at Charles repeated, "We can't possibly; it wouldn't be right." Raising her eyes to Marie and David, she said, "I have never received such kindness and generosity in my whole life and I don't just mean the ring. You have made me welcome in your home and shown me what it must be like to have a family. I can't tell you how much that has meant."

Everyone listened intently to the unusual event of Felicity saying so much.

"It makes me very ashamed of the lie I have let you all believe." She hurried on afraid of losing courage and anxious everything should be set right. Her voice shook as she continued. "The aunt and uncle I said brought me up, don't exist. I was raised in a children's home. My first job at fourteen was office junior. I made tea, ran errands, filled inkwells, etc. By the time I was sixteen and had to leave the home, I was a filing clerk, saving every penny to pay for typing and short hand lessons and eventually came out top for speed and efficiency. I lived in a hostel because it was cheap." She paused and allowed herself a wry smile. "It's amazing how desperation concentrates the mind. I got promoted to head of the typing pool, then to private secretary and then I saw your advertisement, Charles. I couldn't believe the wage you were offering and even more unbelievable, I suited you, but if you want to change your mind about marrying me I will understand." She finished in a whisper, searching his face with wide, troubled blue eyes that matched the sapphire ring.

They had all listened sympathetically to her outpouring, but Charles nearly exploded with excitement.

"That is totally amazing; wish I'd known before, but of course I have never told *anybody* else, that I also grew up in an orphanage. I would have asked you to marry me ages ago but I was too embarrassed about my background. It's so amazing, I can't believe it." He caught her to him in a bear hug and then, as the thought struck him, he released her and chuckled, "It will be the smallest wedding party on record."

"Let's make it soon. You *will* all come won't you? You are the only family we have."

"All the more reason for accepting the ring. You can't upset your adopted family," Gerald insisted, sliding the box back to Charles.

Pamela whispered in Gerald's ear. "Fine with me, but are you sure? It's your day."

"I can't think of anyone nicer to share it with, can you?" In reply, he looked at his parents and then Charles and Felicity.

"Pamela's had what we think is a lovely idea and, hope you will feel the same. Go on, dear."

"How do you two feel about sharing a double-wedding? It's quite fashionable these days, so apart from making it very special, it's practical and economical as well, don't you think?" She waited expectantly, as they looked at each other in speechless amazement.

"Is there no end to incredible surprises tonight?" Charles asked, completely overwhelmed by the good heartedness of this loving family. "I don't know how we will ever repay your kindness."

"Start by putting the ring on Felicity's finger and making Mother happy," David suggested.

It had certainly been a night to remember. And the wedding that followed three months later was another shared occasion that lived on in all of their memories.

A year later the war ended and David's factory returned to making cars. Machinery had to be restored, new accounting systems set up, all providing valuable employment for men returning from the war, but the need for convalescence was also at its height and Gerald worked tirelessly in aid of the war wounded. Their plight of living without limbs, and suffering dreadful nightmares, when longed for sleep brought not oblivion, but shell-shocked screams of horror to their tormented minds, tore at his very soul. He raised money in every way possible and opened another three homes, this time on the coast; two of them for the many orphaned children. He and Pamela bought a cottage in the New Forest to be nearer to her work.

His good works might possibly have gone unnoticed but for the death of his grandfather, who at the age of seventy-eight, declared his intention of designing a flying machine and launching it and himself from the cliff top, east of his home – Anders Folly. He would take on all comers and a prize of twenty-five pounds would go to the machine staying airborne the longest, which he fully expected to win. 'Please collect your entry forms from the Smugglers Arms.' Of course the newspapers printed the story of his life, including the good works of his grandson and raised the prize money to fifty pounds, so in spite of David and Gerald's plea to give up this madness, he went ahead – and spent six weeks in hospital with a broken leg afterwards. His next exploit, three months later, was to take off in a hot-air balloon from the same cliff top. It appeared he enjoyed the limelight. However, the balloon plummeted into the sea and as they reached him, he just had time to say, "That's the way to go!" clutching an empty whisky bottle.

Afterwards they were to discover he had been given six months to live and was determined not to end his days in misery. They also discovered he had gone though all of his assets leaving him with a last recourse, of selling the house – something he couldn't contemplate. The newspaper had paid him enough to settle his debts, so William Anders died a happy man.

As a result, Gerald's name was put on the honours list and he was awarded the MBE.

"Only thanks to Grandpa William," Gerald said ruefully. "The way he bulled me up, I should be St Gerald, and wearing a halo. I really don't deserve it."

"I can't agree entirely," David said, trying to keep a straight face and failing completely. "But perhaps the old reprobate redeemed himself in a small way, eh, Mother?" Marie pursed her lips, conceding reluctantly, "I suppose so."

After the funeral, they went to Anders Folly to make sure the house was securely locked. They were horrified at the state of the lovely property, especially David, who had boyhood memories.

"To be fair, this isn't his doing," he mourned sadly. "The Ministry Of Defence took it over during the war for RAF Headquarters. The furniture was moved out and he gradually sold it, I presume. He lived in the Smugglers Arms for the duration, so that's where the money went, no doubt."

Marie took up the story. "We asked him to come and live with us, but he said he couldn't stand our small lives, in a box, in a narrow street." Even now she couldn't keep the hurt out of her voice.

"You must know it wasn't that, dear," David said patiently. "He was a Cornishman, and couldn't live anywhere else."

"Then why couldn't he just say that?"

"Because he was old and cantankerous and Grandma had just died." Gerald came to his father's aid. "Now come on, Mum, let's decide what is to be done. Any ideas, Dad?"

David shook his head mournfully, looking around at the peeling paintwork and dirty walls. The once smooth floor boards were scratched and scored by heavy boots which would never have been tolerated in his mother's day. They went from room to room and each one told the same story.

"Let's look on it as Grandpa's war effort. After all it was home to a lot of very homesick fighter pilots and aircrew. I bet these walls could tell a few stories – and it's all part of Anders Folly history now, isn't it? I can just imagine them sitting here playing cards, reading – or playing darts," Gerald enthused, pointing to some small holes on the wall in the alcove beside the fireplace.

"And bombing operations would have been planned in the study," David rejoined, his imagination fired. "The walls would have been covered with maps and there would have been huge tables, with maybe a Waaf or two, moving whatever they move on maps to show the position of the planes on bombing raids."

"They would have written to loved ones and opened parcels of homemade cakes," Marie reminisced.

"It would have been warm on winter nights, with a big log fire burning in that enormous fireplace and thick blackout curtains at the windows," Felicity added dreamily.

"And there would have been dance-band music and Vera Lynne singing on the radio, and a record player there." Pamela pointed to a corner, where broken pieces of a seventy-eight record were scattered. Charles was silent, realising Gerald had achieved his purpose.

Later, when David was dreaming in the study and the women were in the kitchen, discussing the merits of the huge Aga cooker, Charles went with Gerald to inspect the outside of the property and asked, "How do you do it? Every time the parents are feeling down about something you find exactly the right thing to say."

Gerald grinned. "Practise, old boy. Got to keep them happy."

"They are lucky to have you."

"They are lucky to have *us*. And *we* are lucky to have them," he corrected.

"I don't know of another person alive who would share their parents so generously," Charles mumbled gratefully.

Gerald stopped in his tracks, turned to look him straight in the eyes and said earnestly, "When Philip died the three of us could hardly bear to sit in the same room as each other. *Their* grief was harder to cope with than my own."

"But I can't take his place."

"Of course you can't," Gerald agreed. "No one is expecting that, but you have helped to fill a huge void that could have gone on forever. And anyway," he grinned suddenly, "Mother enjoyed rescuing you from your own dismal attempts at cooking and ironing." His face straightened. "Seriously, Charles, they think of you as a son and that is fine with me. It sort of makes us brothers. Eh?"

He held out his hand and Charles grasped it, too overcome to speak, but from then on he called them mum and dad, with touching pride.

"What was that all about?" Pamela asked, when they went back in to the house. "It looked serious." She had witnessed their conversation from the kitchen window and at first thought that they were arguing, something she hoped never to see.

"Just brother talk," Gerald answered, punching Charles playfully on the shoulder. "Anybody come up with what we are going to do with this impressive property? It can't stand empty for too long. All those in favour of selling?" Looks of dismay greeted him. "A children's home?" Gerald raised a finger.

"This needs serious thought," David decided, "Mother and I have had enough for one day and my stomach says it's dinner time."

Driving back to the local hotel, in David's maroon Austin, they all made suggestions of what could be done. All except Charles, who was, Gerald noticed, deep in thought.

David and the ladies went straight to their rooms and Gerald and Charles made for the bar, where Gerald ordered two large whiskey and sodas and took them to a table in the window, where when they were settled he demanded, "What's on your mind then? Come on, out with it," he insisted as Charles hesitated.

"I'm not sure that it should come from me."

"We settled all that. Get on with it," Gerald warned.

"Well, I would like to see the folks in that lovely house. Felicity has noticed Mum tires quickly these days and wants her to see a doctor, but Mum insists she is all right. Now don't get upset."

"No. No, I won't," Gerald said, his brisk manner disappearing.

Charles continued, aware of the stillness that had come over Gerald. "What if we got the essential rooms liveable and persuaded her to have a holiday there. If she thought she was doing it for Dad?" He raised his eyebrows.

"You *are* learning fast," Gerald commented dryly.

"I have a good teacher." They looked at each other seriously.

"Good thinking. We will put it to them over dinner." He looked desolate as Charles went to get another drink. The thought of his mother being ill terrified him.

A week later no persuasion was needed. Marie was forced to see the doctor with palpitations and was ordered plenty of rest and fresh air. No more fund raising, cooking for the elderly, or WVS duties – 'time to give someone else a turn,' the doctor ordered, well aware of Marie's reputation.

The decision was made. David, Gerald and Charles returned to Cornwall to arrange for a firm of decorators to start work. Pamela was on duty and Felicity stayed to look after Marie.

The main part of the house was made comfortable and the wings were shut off. The work took a month to complete, and then curtains were the main worry. The original ones had been heavy enough to provide good blackout and six years had left them in tatters.

"Well there are more urgent things to concentrate on," Gerald pointed out, wondering what the fuss was about. "I'm sure we can run to some new ones, can't we?"

"Only if you can suggest where we get them from, even supposing we had enough coupons. In case you haven't noticed, the war hasn't exactly left us in plentiful supply of anything," Pamela said sharply. There was only a week to go before Marie and David would move in, and she wanted to dress the freshly painted windows for them with rich, red velvet. Frustration was making her short tempered. And there were so many other things she wanted, but without coupons, money was useless. Clothes were gradually filtering into the shops, but you had to be on the spot, with your coupon allowance and queue for ages to even have a chance of buying anything half decent and she desperately wanted something other than the short, straight skirts they had been restricted to. She went off in an exasperated huff leaving Gerald and Charles to look at each other with a 'what brought that on' expression.

"It's a blessing these chandeliers were left. Can't think how we would replace *them*; and probably they only remained because nobody could face taking them down," Gerald groaned as he and Charles restored them to the lofty, newly distempered ceilings. It had taken two full days, using extremely high ladders, borrowed from the decorators, and they were exhausted.

"Why didn't the decorators do this?" Gerald asked curiously, having just put the last screw in place.

"Because it would have cost as much as whitening the ceilings and I considered it an unnecessary extravagance," Charles said practically.

"Remind me to have a word with you on that, before we do the rest of the rooms," Gerald rejoined, as they finally stepped down to the hall floor.

Marie appeared in the kitchen doorway. "You boys have earned a beer. Come along, dinner won't be long."

Felicity had prepared piles of fresh vegetables to serve with Marie's crispy roast potatoes, and well-risen Yorkshire pudding; It all looked mouth watering sitting on top of the newly scoured Aga cooker, in the best willow pattern serving dishes. Best of all though, was the wonderful aroma of roast beef that had been pervading the house since early morning – a rare and special farewell treat from Marie's butcher. Many people had been sorry to see the family leave Southampton; probably a little envious as well, because the war years had left the whole nation feeling the need to get away from it all.

"My very favourite part of the weekend," Charles said appreciatively as he sat down rubbing his hands together, making everyone smile. His love for Marie's cooking was becoming a legend.

David said grace. Not something they did regularly, but it seemed fitting at this time, to thank God for delivering them all safely to this warm, peaceful world far away from the suffering and deprivations that others were still enduring – a free world where they could pick up the pieces of their lives again.

They drank a toast with another of David's mystery bottles of Champagne.

"Peace in our time." David held his glass aloft.

"And for the rest of the world very soon," Marie added.

It was a simple, homely scene in spite of their grand surroundings and not one of them could have envisaged the changes there would be over the next two and a half decades, as they shared the first of many happy times at Anders Folly.

*

The removal van bringing all of their worldly goods had departed, and as Marie and the girls feared, the furniture was inadequate and completely out of place. Even the men remarked that it looked a bit sparse in the large rooms.

"It's too small," Charles said stating the obvious to Gerald, who just looked blank. "Perhaps it will look better when some carpets are down."

"It won't," Pamela said bluntly, ignoring her husband's frown. Marie had sat down on the settee which had seemed large in the other house. She looked despondent.

"Well, Rome wasn't built in a day," David said briskly. "Let's get started, while Mother and Felicity organise some lunch, then we'll take a look around the town and pick up some supplies. A short break will do us *all* good. That was a long drive." They had set off at 5 o'clock that morning, and the furniture van had been waiting for them, having loaded up the day before.

Gerald declared his intention of inspecting the attics.

"I want to know the roof is sound before we leave you on your own," he told David.

Charles said he would help.

A walled staircase led up to the roof space and they were amazed to find a suite of quite sizeable rooms with sloping ceilings. In the largest one there were a number of, what looked to be, long bulky rolls of thick, brown paper, which, on closer inspection proved to be carpets. Charles and Gerald's jaws dropped, then, together they raced eagerly downstairs to fetch the others.

David's face was a picture. "I never thought to see these again. They are the original carpets my great, great grandfather brought back from his travels in China. How on earth did they get here? And so well wrapped."

"Let's get them downstairs," Pamela tried to pick up one end and pulled a face.

"This job is too big for us. We need some serious help," David laughed, his excitement mounting.

"Let's get someone right now." Marie smiled happily.

David bent and kissed her cheek. What a fright it had given him, when the doctor had been so grave about her heart. He would do anything to keep that smile on her dear face and as it turned out, it was to be a day full of smiles. Felicity called it 'Serendipity day'.

46

On the edge of the small town, away from the souvenir and teashops and tourist attractions, they happened on a smallish second-hand furniture store. It was packed to the ceiling with all kinds of solid, pre-war pieces but the piece that caught Marie's eye was a headboard.

"Look at that wonderful old wood, David. How it shines." And then she realised it was a four-poster. David had walked on, so she called to him to come and look. He strolled back half-heartedly, wondering why his wife, who always liked everything spotless, was so interested in a dilapidated old shop. The others had walked on to watch the local fisherman hauling their catch on to the quayside. "Far more interesting," he was suggesting, until he saw what she was pointing to. He looked hard, then pressed his nose against the window, then stood back and stared for a full minute.

"What do you think?" Marie asked curiously. He was behaving very strangely.

"I think I am going to buy it," David answered in a dazed voice and without more ado, strode purposefully into the dusty interior of the shop.

Marie looked along the narrow street with its tiny, Cornish stone houses either side and could see four figures leaning on the sea wall. She wished they would turn so that she could beckon them back, but they didn't so she followed David into the shop where he was already deep in conversation with the owner.

"Oo ar," the man was assuring him, "if not 'ere then in the storeroom out back."

"Marie, believe it or not, you have found my mother and father's bed. See if you can catch the children's attention."

As she stepped outside again they were sauntering back, wondering what was keeping David and Marie. She beckoned them excitedly and they hurried their steps.

The storeroom at the back of the shop was a regular Aladdin's cave. Not only did the old man have the rest of *that* bed, but seven more from Anders Folly, as well as the wardrobes and dressing tables, a huge long sideboard, two matching seven foot long settees and numerous side tables and china cabinets. They couldn't believe their eyes. William had sold it piece by piece, as he needed cash and even the old man hadn't realised quite how much he had bought.

"It's nearly *all* there. Too big for most houses and nobody wants the old fashioned stuff anymore. Sugar-boxes, that's all the modern stuff is. Pah!" he said with disgust. "Only thing I sold was the dining table, to some tourist and even *he* didn't want the chairs."

"How much do you want for all of it?" Gerald enquired and saw the old man's eyes light up. He prided himself on being a judge of character and this was a genuine trader he decided.

"There is also a big carpet moving job to do; can you help?" he added.

The old man promised to let them know in the morning, when he had worked out a fair price and also promised to get help to move the carpets.

"I would say we did a very good afternoon's work," Gerald claimed triumphantly, as he put the car in gear and turned towards home.

"*If* he turns up and *if* the price is genuine," Pamela warned.

"*He* will and *it* will be," Gerald assured them with confidence. And sure enough, Edward, as he introduced himself, was as good as his word. His van pulled into the drive as they were finishing breakfast and he and his two strapping sons Jake and Jed climbed out.

"Guess you'll want the carpets laid first," Edward drawled in his slow Cornish accent. "You boys start on them while I talk a bit o' business with the boss."

Edward had arrived at a very fair price for the furniture, happy to get it all sold at once and also pleased that William's 'bits' were back where they belonged.

"'E were an 'ansome fella, were William. We 'ad a lot o' good times together 'im and me." He blew his nose noisily. David was touched by the affection in his voice.

"Do you know, 'e very often sold a piece o' furniture, just to buy a drink for our boys up 'ere, when they was fed-up like, when a plane got lost, or a mate died. Ar 'e did. Just like that." He snapped his fingers and trundled off to help with the carpets, leaving David to stare after him, thinking they might just have to reconsider their opinions of his father's, rumbustious ways.

By the end of the week the furniture was in place and Marie's treasures sat compatibly amongst the larger pieces. The carpets, with their soft, muted colours looked wonderful on the newly restored wooden floors and the only thing missing were the curtains, but the weather was good so it didn't matter too much yet.

David took particular pleasure in entering the house through the thick oak double doors. They led into the spacious hallway where a highly polished, round table filled the forefront, which must, Pamela insisted, always have a huge bowl of seasonal flowers in the centre. Five sets of double doors gave way into a large square sitting room, a long dining room, a study and the east and west wings. A green baize swing door, hidden by the stairs, led into the large square kitchen, with its quarry-tiled floor and white distempered walls. There was a room sized walk-in larder with a marble shelf for fresh food on one wall and more shelves from floor to ceiling on the other three. Two other doors led from the kitchen, one into the kitchen garden and the other into a passage, where one large room and four smaller ones formed the servants' quarters, according to Pamela.

"There are a lot of similarities to Forest End," she informed them.

The broad oak staircase rose to a wide semi-circular landing with four ornately carved doorways facing, and as it curved back, double doors either side led into wide corridors, each with two more bedrooms, and bathrooms, so forming the east and west wings.

Edward had come up with a very likely answer to the mystery of the carpets. The MOD, realising their value, had avoided responsibility for replacing them, by storing them.

"Thank goodness for that," Marie said thinking about the state of the floors.

Edward was a mine of information about almost everything and came to their aid frequently, which was a great comfort to all of them. It was Edward who sent his boys along to clear a fallen tree and chop it into logs for winter and it was Edward who, with the help of Jake and Jed, could tackle plumbing, electrics or even sweeping the great tall chimneys.

"What would you expect?" Felicity would ask whenever Edward was able to fix a problem. "We met him on 'Serendipity Day'."

After that first week, they visited as often as they could but Felicity suddenly developed travel sickness and five weeks passed before she and Charles could return. In the meantime, Pamela had solved the problem of the curtains. For obvious reasons, the curtains at Forest End had been removed and stored in one of the huge linen cupboards, and being a large property, the windows looked roughly the same, she thought. Without raising hopes she measured the windows, found them to be the same size and on their next visit, she and Gerald bundled them onto the hall floor.

"They aren't exactly the shade of red that I planned but they will do for the time being I think." She put her head on one side and looked mischievously at Marie, who was cradling her face with a rapt expression. "Won't they be needed?" she asked.

"Not allowed. We have washable, government issue."

The sheen on the pre-war velvet had dulled with being stored for so long, but David hastily strung a clothes line, from one big apple tree to another, in the orchard and after several hours the creases had dropped out and they looked perfect. The burgundy looked rich and rather splendid dressing the sitting room, dining room and study windows.

"But who do they really belong to?" Marie worried.

"Gerald. He bought the house. Don't worry, we haven't stolen them," Pamela laughed delightedly.

Gerald nodded, grinning proudly at Pamela.

The following week, Felicity was able to travel, even though she was still feeling very sick but the exciting news was she was pregnant. Charles wanted her

49

to give up work straight away, but she wouldn't hear of it. After three more weeks though, she telephoned Marie and confessed to how awful she was feeling, but she hadn't told Charles because he worried so. Without more ado, Marie rang him, suggesting Felicity stayed with them until she was feeling better.

"In three months she will feel fine," she assured him.

"I would love to believe so, but her just being with you will be a relief for both of us."

Felicity arrived armed with wool, needles and patterns, begging to be shown how to knit. She was a quick learner and soon mastered the art, much to Pamela's astonishment.

"Why don't you just buy them?" she asked, completely unimpressed by the pile of little coats and bootees that Felicity and Marie produced in a few weeks.

Marie loved both of the girls but she knew Pamela would never need her in the same way as Felicity did. Pamela had a mother, albeit they didn't keep in touch, but then she was such an independent person, and Gerald was her world. She had no need of mothering. David, however, was a different matter. Pamela adored him. He was the father that she had lost. And Felicity was the daughter that Marie had always yearned for.

CHAPTER FOUR

At the end of three months Felicity was well, and ready to return home, but Charles decided she would be happier living near Marie and approached Gerald, in his office, one morning.

"I want to buy a suitable property down there, that I can turn into offices downstairs and live above. I would travel on set days and still be totally committed to the firm of course. Would that be agreeable with you?" he asked earnestly. Gerald leaned back in his upholstered chair and put the tips of his fingers together, regarding him thoughtfully for several long minutes, until Charles wished he would say something.

"You've obviously given the matter a lot of thought, but why buy? Mum and Dad would be thrilled if we did up a part of the house for you – then you could rent an office and see how things go before you commit yourself."

Charles looked embarrassed and guessing his thoughts, he added quickly, "Purely selfish on my part of course. I haven't had to worry about the folks while Felicity has been around. I just can't wait to ask Mum and Dad."

Charles looked alarmed. "I haven't talked to Felicity yet – didn't want to get her hopes up until I had things sorted."

"She will be tickled pink, and you are a brother in all but name. The baby will be born at *home*," he said jubilantly.

Charles was quite overcome. "She will *know* where she comes from," he said emotionally.

"It's a girl then."

"Definitely."

*

Marie and Felicity burst out laughing.

"How does the east wing sound?" David asked. "These two have already picked the wallpaper. It was only a case of running it by you Charles, but other than that, it has all been planned down to the last detail. Why they aren't on the board of directors – I'll never know." He gave a resigned grin and placidly continued to tease tobacco into his pipe.

One week before Christmas Day, Felicity gave birth to a girl. It was a difficult birth and they were told more children would be out of the question but Felicity was well and little Sophie was a healthy six and a half pounds.

"I wouldn't let you go through that again, anyway," Charles vowed.

That was the best Christmas ever. They gathered around the piano singing carols, with Charles accompanying them, played games, walked along the shore when the tide was out and ate too much. All too soon it was over and Pamela and Gerald had to leave.

Although nicely settled in their wing of the house, Felicity and the baby spent a lot of time in the big, warm kitchen with Marie who could hardly bear to be parted from little Sophie.

Charles reconsidered his original idea and instead applied for a position in a well-established practice, belonging to Laurence Harcott, an elderly bachelor with a sharp eye for detail, and a reputation for getting things right, which suited Charles admirably and the fact that the position only called for three days a week was almost unbelievably convenient.

The premises consisted of a wide hallway running between two large rooms, which at present, was being transformed into a reception, leaving the other room, which had been the reception, free for Charles's office. A small kitchen at the rear gave the secretary, Jessica Lewis, (a widow in her mid-forties, who occupied the flat above), facility to make coffee and afternoon tea. Laurence Harcott himself lived in a detached house ten minutes walk away, where his only companion was a white Persian cat called Isadora. His housekeeper came in daily to clean and cook for him. He was a genial man, not yet ready to retire but ready to forego long days in court and the more complicated cases, he explained looking over the top of his glasses at Charles; his short rotund figure all but hidden behind the mound of files piled on his desk.

"He is a real Dickens character," Charles told Gerald, describing his employer. "A real gentleman. And I shall learn so much from him."

"Really?" Gerald sounded surprised, and Charles went on to explain.

"I have learnt as you and Dad have grown, to deal with business and government contracts, industrial insurances, and officials who frightened me to death at first. I even did my first house conveyances on your nursing homes. Nobody could have had a better beginning. Now I have the chance to round myself off, with ordinary people's problems, more general law work and the experience of court cases."

He had an eagerness that Gerald envied; he loved the thrill of the chase himself. Everything in *his* world was going so smoothly. The factory ran on oiled wheels and the nursing homes were well under control with excellent staff. *He* could do with branching out, and how long was his father going to be content now that Mother had been given a clean bill of health? He said as much to Charles.

"What have you got in mind?"

"Don't know – just need a new challenge."

Charles gave a thoughtful, "Mmm. I may know of something. Would you be prepared to go to the Midlands?"

Gerald pulled the corners of his mouth down. "Depends on what it was," he said without much enthusiasm.

"Let me dig deeper, before I say more," Charles advised, and they left it like that until a few days later, when Charles was on his usual visit up country, and staying overnight with Gerald and Pamela. He had news of a steel manufacturing firm that was on the verge of bankruptcy.

"The way I see it, you have two options if you are interested. One, you just take over because the bank are in the process of putting it in the hands of the receiver, or you go to their rescue, making sure you are the majority share holder. They have excellent trading records and are…"

Gerald interrupted him. "So why are they in trouble and which option would you advise?"

"They are in trouble because they tried to expand too quickly – an easy mistake to make. Personally I would go for option two. There would be no takeover problems like staff and management, which can cause a lot of grief when an outsider moves in. And they *have* been doing a good job, hence the over confident expansion. More a boardroom misjudgement, I would guess. But you will have to move quickly."

Feeling the old rush of adrenaline, Gerald rose quickly from his armchair opposite Charles and without a word went to the telephone in the hall. Charles and Pamela, hearing him speaking to his father in a cautiously excited voice, looked at each other with a knowing smile.

"He's off again," Pamela said, in a resigned voice.

"You love it! Admit it!" Charles teased.

David travelled up the next day, his dark eyes so like Gerald's gleaming in the same way. The three of them threw the idea about well into the night and decided that financially they could manage the venture, but it would drain their resources for a time. It was time to find out more, they agreed.

The following day they went to Sheffield and contacted the bank and the owners of the firm, leaving with all the relevant data after having had a thorough look around. The new extensions were a good investment but also the cause of the financial trouble that the company was in. It took them three days to investigate and another to negotiate. Charles was clear and concise when dealing with the details that David, Gerald and he had worked out and the board of directors were extremely relieved to learn that they were not going to lose the company all together. It proved to be a good merger.

*

Then Pamela announced that she was expecting a baby at the end of the year. She hadn't had a single day's sickness and was wondering what all the fuss was about. Indeed the whole pregnancy *and* the birth gave her no reason to think otherwise.

"It makes me feel a real ninny," Felicity confided to Marie.

"No need, there aren't many as lucky."

Robert came into the world at Anders Folly, on Sophie's first birthday. Marie couldn't believe how lucky she was to have two such beautiful babies in the house and dreaded the day when he left, but motherhood does strange things and Pamela had a change of heart. She pictured bringing Robert up in this warm, family home, with the advantage of having Marie and Felicity to help, and that was when they moved into the west wing permanently.

Pamela was a devoted mother, even surprising herself with the intense love she felt for her small son. They were halcyon days for all of them. Weekends were particularly lively when Pamela and Gerald were always in high spirits. Shrieks of laughter and squeals of delight could be heard coming from the west wing at all hours, especially when they had been to the yacht club for the evening. Gerald had joined for the social life and on calm days they even managed to get David and Marie to join them in sailing round the bays. Charles was also becoming quite proficient under Gerald's guidance and he and Felicity went along to the club-house with them occasionally, where Pamela was always the belle of the ball, in her fashionable, 'New Look' dresses which suited her tall, slim figure so well. She and Gerald made a handsome pair, Gerald, tall and dark, in his evening suit, and Pamela in emerald green, cream, sapphire blue, or plain black. She wore them all to devastating effect.

Charles and Felicity were always modestly dressed and Felicity had a womanly serenity that gave her an air of good breeding. Charles was very proud of her. He loved Pamela like a sister but turned white at the thought of being married to a woman like her. Two years later Pamela gave birth to their second son Alexander, and *he* was to be the *last,* she vowed, repentant of everything she had said and thought previously, when nine months of nausea followed by a breach birth resulted in stitches.

"Never again!" she warned Gerald.

But there was worse to come. Alexander was the complete opposite of the other two babies. He cried all night, cat napped through the day and kept up a lusty yelling that drove everyone to distraction.

After two months he began to settle down, except on weekends when Gerald was home and he was robbed of Pamela's undivided attention. They kept him up late, crept around in the dark, hoping desperately for a good night's sleep but the minute their heads touched the pillows, the wailing started.

"You would think he had X-ray vision or something," Gerald complained to Marie as he sat at the kitchen table waiting for breakfast.

"Poor boy," Marie sympathised. "It was too much to hope that you would get two alike. Good job he wasn't twins!"

Gerald stared at her with new respect. "How did you manage?"

"You just did. I was on my own a lot. Dad was always chasing some scheme or another to turn one pound into two. There weren't many luxuries but we had you and Philip; that was enough. This phase doesn't last forever, son."

But nothing in Gerald's orderly, and one might even say charmed, life had prepared him in the remotest way for the invasion of Alexander, and that night when the same thing happened again his patience snapped.

"All I ask is a good night's sleep. That child is an abomination," he could be heard roaring from the west wing, followed by a short silence before a door opened and Pamela's worried voice called along the landing asking for help.

Marie padded across and opened their door. "What is the matter, dear?" she asked sleepily, awake instantly at Pamela's next words.

"Gerald is having an attack. Sorry to disturb you but Alexander's woken Robert and they are both crying." Marie could hear that she was near to tears herself as she grabbed a dressing gown and ran along the landing, calling to David to come.

Gerald was in a fair amount of distress, sitting on the side of the bed, breathing into a paper-bag, which Pamela always kept handy.

Marie went to him and told Pamela to see to the children. She had dealt with so many attacks over the years with both Philip and Gerald and saw his look of relief as she stood in front of him, encouraging him to breathe and relax. He was soon breathing normally again and full of apologies.

"It was my fault, I got het up."

She brushed the apology aside and helped him back to bed.

"It might be better if Pamela stayed in the children's room for the rest of the night," she suggested looking across at Pamela who was white faced and ready to burst into tears. She would have taken the still screaming Alexander with her, but he wouldn't settle for anyone but his mother. David had already taken Robert back and tucked him in the middle of their bed where he was asleep.

They were a very subdued party the next day and for Pamela it was almost a relief to see Gerald drive off; she was so tired and really couldn't cope with anything other than the baby.

The following weekend Gerald telephoned to say that he couldn't get home because he had a business meeting and Pamela was shocked. She flounced into the kitchen, where Marie and Felicity were preparing the evening meal and after announcing that Gerald would not be joining them, burst into tears, which she quickly wiped away and asked David, "Can Gerald afford a nanny?"

"If you need a nanny, my dear, you must have one and I have to say that I think it is a good decision."

Pamela threw her arms around him and flew out of the kitchen again, sobbing.

David himself drove down to the village and placed an advertisement in the local paper and another in a national paper. Several candidates applied, but the minute they set eyes on Abigail Spence, they knew that she was the one. She was seventeen, with dark hair and merry brown eyes that twinkled when she laughed and a soft, Scottish brogue, but more to the point Alexander was quiet from the minute she picked him up.

"When can you start?" David asked, trying not to sound too eager.

"Well I sort of brought my belongings and haven't anywhere to stay, so now would be a good time I'm thinking?"

From then on life returned to normal. Abigail could constantly be heard, talking to Alexander and singing Gaelic lullabies, and there was only the occasional, lusty yell, when he was hungry.

Gerald arrived on the Friday evening, looking sheepish and apologetic. "Sorry," he mumbled burying his head into Pamela's neck and hugging her tightly. "God how I missed you. Serves me right for telling a lie, but you guessed; I should have known you would. I'll do better," he promised.

She kissed him lightly on each corner of his mouth then full on the lips, and gave a secret little smile.

"No need."

"Why? What have you done? You haven't had him adopted have you?" He asked with mock enthusiasm as she gave him a playful punch. "I must say it's mighty quiet – except for – what *is* that?"

Abigail was singing as she put the boys to bed and he followed the sound, his curiosity fully aroused. Pamela gave a little smile as he hesitated and looked at her, before opening the bedroom door.

The room was warm and dimly lit. Robert's brown curls could be seen peeping above the bedclothes; he was already asleep and Abigail, unaware of her audience rocked back and forth singing softly, as she fed Alexander his bottle, her tiny figure almost lost in the big old-fashioned rocking chair. Pamela whispered her name and she looked up with a smile, nodded and continued singing. They went downstairs again and made for the sitting room, where the rest of the family were having a pre-dinner drink and waiting for his reaction to Nanny Spence.

"*She* is worth gold dust. How does she do it?"

"I think the trick is not to let them get a word in edgeways," Charles remarked dryly. "She talks to him non-stop." He spread his hands. "So it works. Don't knock it."

"I think it is the Scottish lilt in her voice," Marie said warmly.

At bedtime Gerald had another surprise, as Pamela led him upstairs to the main landing. "We are sleeping here. Abigail has got our room. That should suit my Lord and Master," she teased,

"Not 'arf, me lovely," he said, dragging her into the bedroom.

"Now not too much noise you two. Remember we are next door," David complained in a long-suffering tone, knowing with certainty that his words fell on deaf ears less than a minute later.

"Well we know who Alexander takes after for noise anyway," David commented wearily. "Will those two never grow up?" he tutted, turning off the bedside light and thumping his pillow.

"When Gerald was ready to leave on Sunday evening and they were all gathered to wave him off, he wagged his finger at each one in turn.

"Now whatever you do don't let that girl escape, if she gets fed-up – double her wages, or even treble them. Just hang on to her. I hold you all responsible for my future sanity."

"I think we did the right thing," David and Pamela chorused shaking hands as he drove away.

Abigail came up with the idea that the rooms at the top of the house would make an ideal nursery floor and give Pamela and Gerald back their bedroom. David promptly agreed and volunteered to organise the changes. Five of the rooms would be needed; the largest one already had a fireplace and would make a nice living room, leaving three bedrooms and the smallest one to be turned into a bathroom. Within a month they were comfortably installed, and David's peace was restored.

Marie couldn't help comparing *her* life when her boys were small, but she knew given the choice she wouldn't have had it any other way.

The years slipped by quickly. Laurence Harcott's brother died and his widow went to live with her sister, which meant that at Christmas he was on his own and Charles asked Marie if they could stretch to one more.

Laurence was an immediate favourite with everyone. He had the children in fits of laughter with his rendering of 'Old Macdonald' and had everyone passing the parcel, making sure that the music stopped at the children. He did conjuring tricks which brought gasps of wonder from Sophie and Robert and left Alexander gaping as he produced sweets from behind his ears, then to everyone's surprise he disappeared behind the curtain and re-appeared as Father Christmas, carrying presents tied up in a sack.

When it was time for him to leave and Marie tried to thank him, he replied graciously "My dear lady, money can't buy what you brought to my life this Christmas."

He was automatically adopted as Uncle Laurie and included on every occasion from then on, and was to have great bearing on everyone's future.

*

Time came for Sophie to start school and Pamela drove her to the local kindergarten where a year later, Robert joined her. Pamela enjoyed the morning run, realising how she missed the bustle of working and getting up in the morning with a purpose; so when a vacancy for a school nurse arose, she applied and got the job. It was hardly demanding, as there were only two schools in the area but having whetted her appetite for nursing again, she quickly went on to take a refresher course in midwifery. This quite soon led to full-time employment. Pamela was in her element and Gerald was complacent, as long as it didn't interfere with their social life. However, David spoke his mind when extra work fell to Marie and Felicity.

Pamela was shocked. David had never pulled her up before.

"I'll give it up if you really want me to," she said with a crestfallen look. "But I think I know how to help."

David gave her a wary stare and Marie and Gerald looked intrigued, knowing she could twist David round her little finger and wouldn't give up that easily.

"I'm listening," he said sternly, already melting at the forlorn look in her green eyes. She spoke very quickly, in one breath.

"Well, if I pay Abigail we can afford a cook and that would help mum and Felicity a *lot*. What do you think?" she asked brightly. "I was never any help in that department anyway," she observed wryly as Gerald collapsed laughing and David and Marie looked nonplussed.

"Mother, we need to talk." Hand in hand they went to the study and shut the door.

"What do you think?" Pamela whispered.

"Have patience," Gerald advised, realising his mother would be reluctant to relinquish the kitchen to a stranger.

David was actually all for it. Marie *should* have more time to enjoy the house and the grandchildren. "But I don't want you thinking that you aren't in charge; I like our home run just the way *you* do it." Marie wasn't sure though.

But of course, Pamela kept her job and two weeks later Lorna Pennington, a tall, capable woman in her mid-twenties, with a broad Cornish accent was hired.

"Talk about united nations," Gerald tutted, "I've only just mastered Scottish."

Marie found if difficult to stay out of the kitchen, but after a while enjoyed being able to spend more time gardening and reading to the children. Robert and Sophie would sit one either side of her, on the big settee, after their night-time bath. She introduced them to all of the well-known fairy stories and as they got older, 'Gulliver's Travels', and 'Robinson Crusoe', and 'The Water Babies' were added to the shelves. There were so many books; eventually they wouldn't fit in the big bookcase in the alcove, where Philip's photograph, and a vase of fresh flowers always stood.

Robert was very intrigued that Uncle Philip looked exactly like his Dad, and wanted to know why didn't twins die at the same time if they were born at the same time?

It saddened Marie that she was unable to visit Philip's grave, and for some while had been toying with the idea of creating a library in his memory, where she could spend quiet time remembering him – the question had been where? Yesterday, she had finally decided on the perfect place and put the idea to everyone on Saturday evening when they were gathered round the dining table.

She half expected they might think it was too sad, but they all understood, and Gerald said his and Pamela's contribution would be to install the shelves.

"So where is this library going to be?" Pamela asked.

Marie looked apologetic. "Well, Philip always loved sunsets, which means it has to be in the west wing. Would you mind *very* much giving up one of your downstairs rooms? It would make the perfect place with its view over the countryside."

Pamela's eyes filled with tears. "It's a lovely idea; as you say the room will be perfect. I never knew Philip but I wish I had. He must have been very special."

"Here, here," Charles and Felicity echoed.

"So what can we give?" Charles asked Felicity,

"How about one of those tall ladders on wheels?" she suggested.

"I would like to do it for the anniversary of his death, in three months' time. Would that be possible, dear?" she asked David.

"If that is what you want, we will make it possible," he assured her, burying his nose in his glass of wine, suddenly.

Lorna Pennington came in to clear the dishes, and was surprised to see the solemn faces.

"Was the dinner not to your liking, Mrs Anders?" she asked in a worried voice.

"Everything was perfect, as usual, thank you, Lorna."

"Marvellous!" Charles added.

"Now *that* is the royal seal of approval," Gerald assured her, as her face shone with pride and the solemn moment passed.

"I'll help Lorna to get finished; she will need to get home," Felicity offered.

"Me too," Marie said, with a contented smile, as Pamela wrinkled her nose.

"You bring Sophie and Robert down for their story." Pamela escaped with alacrity as Marie shooed her away.

The library was duly finished and Marie invited the local vicar to bless the room, with a family service in memory of Philip.

Laurie arrived with a huge box containing a complete set of Charles Dickens novels. They were beautifully bound, in red leather with gold leaf embossed lettering and raised bands on the spines. On the flyleaf of 'Pickwick Papers' he had written: To my dearest friends, on this memorable occasion. He had signed his name and in brackets (Mr Pickwick).

Charles flushed, as he read it.

Laurence grinned and nodded towards Sophie who was admiring the books, unaware of her father's discomfort. "Little pitchers etc., but I find it flattering. Thank you, m' boy."

The big decision was which shelf they should go on.

"That's a hard one," Pamela remarked dryly, waving to the rows of empty shelves, where only the children's books occupied one of the lower ones.

The piano had been placed in the window, where the light was good and Philips's photograph had place of honour, next to the usual bowl of fresh flowers. His music was placed neatly in the music stool and Sophie who had been showing great interest, was to have a weekly lesson from a local teacher who would come to the house. This was to be her eighth birthday present from Marie and David.

Then the time came for Alexander to leave the comfortable nursery world – and Abigail, whom he had grown so attached to, that he screamed every morning when they were parted.

"We should have seen this coming," Gerald thundered when he was told.

Everyone else had of course, but in view of the fact that he was so unresponsive had left him to Nanny, who was never absent, because as she explained, "Anders Folly is my world. There is nowhere I want to go."

The spinster aunt, her only living relative, who had taken her in with great reluctance when her parents were killed in a London air-raid, had asked her to leave on her sixteenth birthday, and they had not communicated since.

"We lame dogs seem to find you." Felicity said when she and Marie were alone.

"I don't want to hear you speak like that again. How can you even think it? Look how much richer you make our lives," Marie said knitting furiously.

"The wool will catch fire," Felicity said and as usual they ended up laughing together.

Every morning, Alexander was bundled screaming into the car with Robert and Sophie, who after trying unsuccessfully to console him, gave up and put their hands over their ears. And then he stopped for no apparent reason. Months later it transpired that Robert, on hearing a distressed Abigail say, "He will make himself hoarse if he keeps on," told Alexander that he would turn into a horse if he didn't stop.

As the years went by, it became obvious to Marie that Robert was not interested in becoming a member of the firm as his father and his grandfather expected. Robert's idea of a wonderful day was to go around bookshops with her, where they would spend many happy hours, stocking the library shelves. Increasingly, he would spend time reading in the library, or if peace escaped him there, hidden amongst the rocks in the cove, where Sophie would often join him to share their dreams.

It worried him that he was expected to follow in his father's and grandfather's footsteps. That was what sons did he had been told for as long as he could remember. He adored Sophie, she was the only one apart from Grandma, that he could really confide in and with her long, blonde curls and wide blue eyes, he thought she was the most beautiful girl in the world and although a year older, she looked up to him and felt safe when he was there. Alexander could be frightening when the adults weren't around. He would pull the bow off her long hair and lift her skirt, shrieking with delight at the sight of her knickers, and sometimes he seemed to aggravate her just to upset Robert.

Once, when she was practising, Marie had caught him swinging the music stand so that the music fell to the floor. She had remonstrated with him, whereupon he lashed at the piano keys with both hands and banged the lid shut, narrowly missing Sophie's fingers. Then he gave Marie a defiant look shouting, "I want to play the piano. Tell her to get off. I can do it better than her anyway."

For the first time in her life, Marie had raised her hand to a child. She stopped herself, when his eyes grew big with fear and ran from the room bawling that Grandma had hit him. Hearing his shouts Abigail came running from the nursery, where she was ironing.

"What is all that noise about?" she demanded.

"Grandma hit me," he yelled. "She did, she did," he insisted, seeing the disbelief in her eyes.

"Then you must have done something really terrible."

"Didn't, didn't do nothing," he sulked going to her and putting his arms round her minute figure.

"Anything," Abigail automatically corrected him as she took his hand and led him back downstairs saying, "Come along."

Marie was in the act of closing the library door as they approached her.

Sophie, unnerved by the incident, had run to her mother. "My fingers wouldn't work and I've never seen Grandma really angry before," she told her tearfully.

"Alexander has come to apologise Mrs Anders. He must have upset you badly." There was a pause whilst Alexander stood, stiff and silent.

"Alexander, I'm waiting," Abigail warned.

"Shan't."

Marie held up her hand, as Abigail would have insisted.

"I won't tolerate behaviour like that Alexander. Especially in Uncle Philips's room. It is a place where we can all go when we want to be peaceful, but you have lost that privilege, so until you know how to behave, that room is out of bounds to you. Now, are you at least going to tell the truth? You told Nanny I hit you."

"It's true," he shouted, eyes full of hatred and Marie shook her head sadly as she walked away.

"Well I think that calls for no television after tea, don't you?" Abigail could be heard saying on their way back upstairs.

Some time later when Marie was in the garden tending her roses, Alexander came out and walked towards her. Her heart gave a little lift thinking that he had repented and she wouldn't need to tell Pamela, but he stood feet astride, scowling, chin stuck out in a pout.

"You upset Nanny. You made her *angry* with me. She is *never* angry with me. *And* you have made me miss television tonight."

She answered quietly, "No dear, *you* made her angry with you."

He stared at her, his eight-year-old mind rebelling, then turned on his heel with a parting shot of, "I hate you."

She was very disturbed and decided not to let the incident drop as she had in the past. She told David and he said Gerald should be told as well; Pamela would just sweep it under the carpet to avoid punishment.

Consequently, as much as she hated to, Marie told them of the incident and Alexander was called to the study where his father was waiting, with a face like thunder, while his mother tried to calm him down.

"How dare you speak to your Grandmother and bully Sophie in that way," he roared.

"I'm sure he didn't mean it, did you, darling? Tell Daddy you didn't."
Pamela stood behind him running loving fingers through his thick crop of curly, auburn hair, looking imploringly at Gerald, who shot her a look of complete exasperation before turning on Alexander again.

"What have you got to say for yourself? The lie about Grandma hitting you, what about that?"

"'Tisn't a lie," Alexander pouted.

Gerald turned to Pamela. "Ask Abigail to come in."

Alexander looked relieved. Everything would be all right if Nanny was here.

"I thought as Alexander had apologised, everything would be alright, sir."

"Apologised? When is this supposed to have happened," Gerald asked ominously.

"I saw him from the window, sir. He went to his grandmother, in the garden and she said he was a good boy... and there was... no need to punish him," she petered out lamely, looking at Alexander in dismay as tears began to run down her cheeks.

"You've no right to make Nanny cry," Alexander shouted, running to her and throwing his arms around her waist. "Alright. She didn't hit me, but she wanted to. She hates me, that's why she told."

"Grandma loves you," Gerald said quietly. "And I want you to go and say sorry to her."

He looked rebellious, but his mother drew him away from Abigail, gave a gentle push towards the door, and they followed.

When facing Marie, he said in a loud voice, "I'm sorry, Grandma."

Unknown to them, his gaze was fixed somewhere above her head, then slowly lowering his eyes he stared her out before turning to Abigail. "Can we go upstairs and watch television now?"

Gerald intervened. "No. The punishment that you avoided by lying stands. See to that please, Nanny."

Alexander got up, shot a black sideways look at his grandmother and followed Abigail upstairs.

"He hates me," Marie said to David as they got ready for bed that night.

"Because you dare to discipline him," David replied with a sigh. "Gerald has got a lot of trouble to come with that boy."

*

Eight years later, Laurie said the same to Charles, when he voiced his concern about Alexander's increasingly worrying behaviour towards Sophie.

63

On her eighteenth birthday the whole family bought her a 'Steinway' baby grand piano. She had exceeded all expectations and they thrilled to her music. Her ambition was to become a concert pianist and Uncle Laurie had written away to the London School of Music, where she had been enrolled for the next term. He would pay all expenses.

"An old man's pleasure. What else will I do with my money?" he asked when Charles demurred.

Laurie was all for bringing Alexander's behaviour to Gerald's attention, but Charles and Felicity argued that it would cause a rift between them and Pamela.

A year after Sophie went away, Robert won a place at Oxford University. He was to read English Literature and History. Laurie again wanted to foot the bill, for the books and any private tutorials.

"I really want to do this. It makes me feel included. My sister-in-law just about manages the odd Christmas card."

"Well, why not?" David looked around for agreement "Laurie has been one of the family for years, hasn't he?"

Robert had spent sleepless nights, worrying that he wouldn't be allowed to take up his place at Oxford. Gerald's first reaction was: where will the two subjects get him in the firm? But Charles had spoken up saying that it was pity not to take the wonderful opportunity when he had worked so hard to get it.

"I wouldn't have missed my university days for anything, even though I was so hard up. Would you, Gerald?" he asked quietly.

"I never could win an argument against you." Gerald gave in gruffly. "I still can't see what good the subjects will do him though."

"Plenty of time for the firm, son. He is only eighteen, let him have his youth." David spoke up unexpectedly.

"I wasn't quite twenty when I started," Gerald argued.

"So give him his two years," Charles urged.

"They *are* right, dear," Marie said gently.

"You too Mother? Well never let it be said that I deprived my own son. But in two years' time, I shall expect you to knuckle down to a responsible life," he said seeing Robert's anxious face relax with relief.

"Thanks Dad."

Later, he sought Charles out. He and Felicity were in their sitting room.

"Thanks for your support, Uncle Charles. I'm grateful."

"What are godfathers for?" Charles replied sympathetically, adding seriously, "you are going to have to tell him sooner or later you don't want to join the firm, you know."

"You know?"

"Call it an educated guess."

"I really want to please Dad – and Granddad, but I have this burning need to be with books. I *will* do my best to settle down in the firm but I just need this chance first. You understand don't you?"

Charles nodded. "Your Uncle Philip would have as well, I imagine."

Felicity gave an encouraging smile. "And Grandma. She agonises for you, but would never go against your father's wishes. Sophie would say enjoy it while you can."

"She's enjoying her music," Robert said fondly.

"You keep in touch then?" Felicity asked innocently, knowing happily they did. Robert was very special to her. After all he had probably spent more time with her and Sophie than he had with his mother, and she had an unspoken hope for her treasured girl.

*

With Robert and Sophie gone, and all three men away for days on end, Alexander changed. He would sit in David's special chair: a wine coloured, leather wing chair that had been a gift from Marie on his sixtieth birthday, and surreptitiously give her hostile looks with those cold slate-grey eyes, challenging her to object. He also took to sitting at the head of the dining table in David's place. None of the boys had ever taken liberties like that, but it would just sound petty she thought if she voiced her objection. And annoyingly, Pamela found it very amusing.

"Thinks he is in charge with all the men away, I suppose."

Marie hadn't a single doubt that that was what he thought. At sixteen he was tall and well built. He wore his auburn hair too long but it was the fashion she was told. He had his mother's flair for clothes and wore them well. In fact he was an extremely attractive young man. And although friends were never invited home he appeared to be quite popular at the local college and indeed he *could* be very amusing. His mimicry of well-known personalities and his grasp of dialects was both inspired and witty and there could be no doubt that his future lay in the entertainment world, much to his mother's admiration and his father's disgust.

David asked him out of interest one day if he thought there was a living to be made from entertaining. His glib answer was, "I don't have to worry about that with all of this to fall back on, do I, Granddad?" And he waved his arm theatrically, encompassing the room.

It was supposedly said in fun, but David had serious misgivings about the boy he confessed later to Marie and was shocked when she owned up to her own feelings.

"My dear, you can't tolerate feeling intimidated in your own home, especially by your own grandchild."

"Perhaps I'm imagining things," she said hastily regretting that she had said anything, but tears sprung readily to her troubled eyes as she tried to deny it and he could see her trembling.

"Please don't say anything to Gerald," she begged, "it will only make things worse, like it did before. Promise me?"

He promised, but from then on he refused to go away at the same time as Charles.

"I would just rather that one of us was here at all times," he eventually had to explain to a puzzled Charles, refusing to be drawn further.

Not satisfied, Charles got David away from the house by suggesting a walk along the cliffs, where he tackled him gently.

"I can tell that something is worrying you, Dad."

"It's nothing. Mother is feeling shaky that's all. She would hate me mentioning it; get Felicity to keep an eye on her and be here when I'm not will you?"

"Of course. But should she see a doctor?"

David was silent.

"It's Alexander isn't it?" Charles challenged him. "Felicity mentioned he is throwing his weight around and lording it when we are away. Mum maybe feels he is too big to be told off, but she mustn't be *afraid* to."

He gave a small laugh, purposely making light of his words, knowing that if his suspicions were right, David would find it embarrassing but he knew how Alexander had taunted Felicity and himself and *they* had said nothing. It seemed ridiculous now, but the threat seemed real enough at the time. There had been real malice in Alexander's eyes when he had leered at Sophie.

David's head had jerked round and their eyes met.

"Ah! I thought so. He actually had us afraid he was going to harm Sophie. His problem is he feels left out and doesn't realise it's his own doing. I mistakenly didn't take the boy to task because, like you, I didn't want to upset Pamela."

David's silence said everything. "He must be taught a lesson," Charles said angrily.

They walked on in silence, following the coastline with the sea on their left. A steep grassy incline led up to where the ground levelled and they found themselves looking down on the neighbouring bay. They had never explored this far before and the view was magnificent. The Atlantic ocean stretched as far as the eye could see and today it was wild and rough with white, foam topped, giant waves dashing and swirling around the rocks far below.

They were both puffing by the time they reached the barren, wind swept cliff top and stopped to get their breath. Charles tried to speak but the wind took his voice so he pointed instead to a house standing well back from the edge of the cliff, raising his eyebrows questioningly. David raised his eyebrows and nodded. With one accord they made in that direction and as they got closer became aware of its derelict state. They sheltered on the lee-side, glad to be able to hear themselves speak.

"It must be on your ground," Charles said, peering through a grimy window.

"I imagine so, I had completely forgotten about it. It was always occupied by the gamekeeper when I was a boy. I know it is remiss of me, but I have never actually studied the deeds in great detail. The house passed to me. I didn't have to buy it."

"Understandable. It will be interesting to find out though. I can't believe we haven't found it before now, but with two avid readers and one television fan, our children are not exactly enthusiastic explorers, are they?"

They stayed for a while longer trying doors and windows, but all were securely locked, so frustrated and intrigued they turned for home.

On reaching the house they dragged Gerald out of the sitting room where he was dozing in front of the television and the three of them went into the study, dug out the deeds and went into a huddle over the desk.

After much deciphering of solicitors' jargon, there appeared to be no doubt that the dilapidated cottage was the original smallholding. It dated back to well before Anders Folly was built. David had been rummaging in his desk and straightened up with a triumphant. "Aha!" holding aloft a tin box.

"I remembered this old box of keys. It was on the top shelf of the larder when we first arrived. I stowed it away and forgot about it. If there *is* a key it would seem a likely place."

"If anyone can tell us its history, I would think Laurie or Edward could. They and their families have lived here all their lives," Marie said later as they sat around the table in the warm kitchen drinking tea, the box of keys spread out in front of them. Outside, the wind was gusting round the house and at three-thirty it was already dark.

"Why don't we walk up and see it tomorrow. Laurie might be interested in going with us," David suggested. "Providing we can find an easier route that is."

It had become a regular custom for Charles to drive down and bring Laurie back for Sunday lunch and the next day the main topic of conversation was the old cottage. Disappointingly he didn't have much to add except that at one point, Anders Folly was signed over to a certain Rebecca James.

"I don't know the ins and outs, only that it was willed back to Jeremiah Anders some years later – well before my time."

Edward was also able to add a little to the story that had been passed down to him by his father. Apparently, Jeremiah Anders had lived in the cottage for years, after losing Anders Folly in a card game. It was let as holiday accommodation for a good many years before the war and when the war came it was commandeered as a lookout post with its panoramic sweep of the Atlantic Ocean, and the English Channel."

"So, it was probably the original property," Gerald said, trying to imagine the house as it had been. It was really a large cottage, with three quite impressive bedrooms and a bathroom upstairs and two large rooms and a kitchen down, but even in his wildest imagination he wouldn't have come close to who its next occupant would be or what part the old property would play in his future.

*

Charles still hadn't decided what to do about Alexander, when a call came through the following Saturday at ten-thirty pm. He and Felicity were watching television with Marie and David in the sitting room. Gerald and Pamela were on their usual visit to the yacht club and wouldn't be home until the early hours.

"Just have to pop out – problem at the police station. Won't be long." He was gone before awkward questions could be asked.

It was a very relieved and white-faced Alexander who greeted his arrival. He had expected his father.

"Get me out of here, they are treating me like a common criminal," he demanded indignantly.

"If you behave like one, you must expect to be treated like one," Charles observed coolly, placing his briefcase on the table and taking out an official looking form, before slowly uncapping his fountain pen, and sitting opposite.

"There are questions you need to answer."

"What's all that for? Just get me out of here." His voice rose shrilly.

"The formalities have to be followed for police records. Fortunately for you, your father was out and I answered the telephone, so my immediate advice is watch your manners, because I could have you kept in, and brought in front of the Magistrate on Monday morning. Do I make myself clear?" he demanded.

"You wouldn't dare."

"Try me."

"You are enjoying this, aren't you?"

"Not really, Alexander, but then unlike you, power to frighten isn't my idea of enjoyment."

Alexander's eyes narrowed and his chin went up.

"So that's what this is all about?"

"I will just go and see what can be done about these charges."

Charles got to his feet his face void of expression, gathered up the completed form and his briefcase and left the room. Less than half a minute later a police constable took Alexander along to a cell; he was obviously in total shock. Charles, with a good view of his face from where he was sitting in the office nearly had second thoughts. This was Gerald's son, his own godson, but his heart hardened at the sergeant's next words.

"There *were* drugs on the premises, sir, so if he is caught again he will have to face the music."

"Thank you, sergeant. Keep him for an hour and I will come and take him home," Charles said in a dejected voice

"I think you are doing the right thing, don't feel too badly."

It was a very subdued Alexander that sat rigidly upright in the car an hour later.

"I suppose you are going to tell on me?" he said dispiritedly.

"Getting drunk in a nightclub is stupid, but being under-age is lunacy."

"He will ground me and stop my allowance *and* enjoy doing it," he said bitterly. "I won't go there again, I promise."

"Then this can remain between the two of us, but I shall expect better behaviour. I know you understand what I am referring to."

"Yes, and thanks for getting me out of that place."

When they reached the house, Abigail was hovering about the landing and yet again Charles thought how ludicrous it was for a seventeen-year-old boy to have a nanny.

"I have been worried sick," she greeted him, "you are never this late."

"He has been with me, Abigail. Sorry that you have been worried. Pop off to bed. We will just make a drink and Alexander will be up."

He led the way to the kitchen, dismissing any opportunity for further questions as Alexander shot him a grateful look.

"Are you serious about drama college?" Charles asked as he filled the kettle.

"Dad won't stand for it. He says I need a real job."

"He said yes to Robert. Give it a try, perhaps under the same two-year condition. Time you fended for yourself. It makes you feel good." They talked over cups of tea and Alexander boasted when he was old enough he would go to London and live his own life. Charles listened, concerned about the outcome if

Gerald denied him an acting career. He got to his feet and cleared the cups and saucers into the sink, unable at that moment to offer any suggestions.

"Plenty of time to think about London. Get school over first. Your father has your best interests at heart. I will help if I can. Right now it is time for bed."

CHAPTER FIVE

December arrived, bringing with it icy winds and hoarfrosts. The ornamental fishpond, David's latest addition to the front of the house, froze over and it was a daily task to break the four inch thick ice. Indoors, huge log fires were kept burning and damped down over night, ready to be stirred to life again in the morning; but everyone preferred the kitchen and Marie's warming breakfasts. Shortly afterwards Lorna would arrive and take over for the day. Her arrival by way of the kitchen door would bring with it a blast of cold air as, breathing heavily from the bicycle ride from her cottage, she would divest herself of seemingly never ending layers: coat, body warmer, scarf, woolly hat, gloves, boots, thick socks and lastly a thick cardigan, under which she still wore another cardigan, a jumper and more thick socks to work in.

"And a liberty bodice too no doubt," David commented one morning after watching the performance and marvelling that she could even move, let alone ride a bike.

December also brought Robert and Sophie home for the Christmas holidays. Robert had hardly changed, except to get taller, but Sophie stopped everyone in their tracks. Gone was the studious, slightly old-fashioned, well-rounded young woman and in her place was this beautiful waif-like creature, whose honey blonde, previously curly hair, now hung straight and silky to her slim waist. Her long skirts and turtle-necked jumpers just seemed to accentuate her thinness, causing Felicity and Marie to exchange anxious glances.

"It's just a fashion thing, along with the 'Beatles' and 'Flower Power'," Robert advised, trying to put Felicity's mind at rest. "She eats well enough. Costs me a week's allowance when I take her to dinner," he laughed.

"Do you get to see her often?" Felicity asked anxiously, just as Sophie, who had been practising in the other room ran in and went straight to the fire spreading her cold fingers to the blaze.

"I heard that Robert Anders. Take it back." Picking up a cushion she proceeded to pummel him.

"Alright, alright, I take it back. It takes two weeks' allowance," he said grabbing her hands and pulling her down beside him, giving a frown. "You're freezing. Let's get you warm." He rubbed her arms as she tucked her feet up underneath her and cuddled up to him on the settee. Felicity watched, her eyes shining, until Sophie caught her look.

"It isn't going to happen, Mummy, sorry!" she said gently. "We thought it would, didn't we Rob?"

He nodded and gave a rueful smile.

Felicity frowned, not convinced. "How can you be so sure?"

Robert looked uncomfortable but Sophie laughed. "We booked a room in one of the best hotels in London. We thought we would do it properly and it would be wonderful. We bought an engagement ring, had dinner sent up to the room, soaked in a Jacuzzi." She stopped and smiled softly at Robert who pulled her closer, saying with a helpless little shrug, "It would have been like sleeping with my sister; if that makes sense to anybody but us."

Felicity nodded. "You two have something very precious – true friendship."

"Anyway, we talked all night, had breakfast in bed, took the ring back and now that is out of the way we are just happy to have each other. Love you, Rob." She gave him a hug.

"Love you, Sophie." He kissed the top of her shining hair.

Felicity got up with a small sigh. "I'll see if Grandma wants a cup of tea, how about you two?"

"Mm lovely."

Returning with the tea twenty minutes later, she found them still curled up, sound asleep. Looking at them fondly she put another log on the fire and crept out, still nursing her regrets.

At dinner that evening the talk was all about their birthdays, in five days' time. Sophie would be twenty and Robert nineteen. One of his precious years was already up.

Gerald had arrived home that evening for a three week Christmas break and was obviously feeling tetchy.

"Are you giving *any* thought to your future, Robert?"

"I still have a year to go, Father. I shall be concentrating on exams first." He frowned down at his plate, pushing the food around.

"Huh. Waste of time if you ask me."

Gerald took a mouthful of food and chomped aggressively as Marie and Pamela exchanged a 'what's up' look.

Alexander, always nervous when his father was around, chose that very worst moment to make a bid for attention and Charles closed his eyes in dismay.

"Could I do a two year course at drama school, Father? There is an excellent one in Manchester and I leave college next Easter. Could I?"

Charles groaned inwardly. Did the boy have a self-destruct button or something?

Gerald glared. "Absolutely out of the question," adding as Alexander was about to speak again, "and I don't want to hear another word on the subject."

Actually his look alone, quelled any further comment, and there was complete silence whilst everyone concentrated on eating, until Marie said brightly, "Laurie is coming on Christmas Eve and staying until after the New Year. Dad and I thought it best, with the weather so bad."

"He'll love that. I think he gets quite lonely when the office is closed," Charles said, his face alight with pleasure.

Normally, dinner was happy and relaxed but it was a relief on this occasion to leave the dining room. Gerald sat on with a second cup of coffee, morose and silent, apparently oblivious to anything other than his own thoughts. He then went straight to the study and shut himself in.

"Is anything the matter? Gerald isn't at all himself," Marie asked Pamela as they went through to the sitting room.

"I keep telling him he is working too hard but he won't listen. Perhaps the break will do the trick." Pamela crossed her fingers and tossed her eyes heavenwards.

"Best ever time to have a birthday, with all the decorations up," Robert commented as he and Sophie dressed the Christmas tree later. Bad luck about drama school, Alex. Perhaps Dad will reconsider though. Catch him on a better day."

Alexander was slumped on the settee glowering into space.

"There aren't any better days where I'm concerned. He just hates me. I'll show him one day, you wait and see if I don't."

Pamela went to comfort him but he pushed her away and got up, kicking the box of decorations out of his way as he flounced from the room. Charles listened to him climb to the top of the house and slam the door shut, thinking with a resigned sigh: 'Back to Abigail.'

"Men! Clumsy creatures!" Sophie darted to rescue the fragile tree ornaments but they were well packed and unbroken.

"Oh, even the lovely Matthew?" Robert teased.

"Rob!" Sophie blushed and shot a look at Felicity and Marie, who were agog with curiosity, suddenly knitting in slow motion.

"Oops! Sorry, Soph!" He gave an unrepentant grin.

Sophie looped a garland of red tinsel around his neck and tugged. He stuck his tongue out and made his eyes bulge causing Marie and Felicity to go into fits of laughter and ask, "So who is Matthew?"

"Well, Matt is tall and skinny with long hair and pimples and he has a bath every month, whether he needs one or not. Let me see now, oh yes! He is American, plays the fiddle and only eats junk food. And if you think *he* sounds awful, you should see the two I got rid of." He shook his head in mock despair.

There was silence whilst Felicity and Marie grappled with alarm and Sophie gave him a withering look.

"Is he really American, dear?" Felicity asked anxiously.

"That is the *only* bit that *is* true. Take no notice. Matt and I started on the same day and we are good friends."

"Is he not tall and long haired?" Robert insisted.

"Well yes, but…"

"And does he not play the fiddle?"

Sophie put her hands on her hips and looked exasperated.

"Told you so." Robert folded his arms akimbo.

"Enough Robert, we want to hear Sophie's version *and* I want to know when you started shortening your names and why? You all have such lovely names."

"Well it's like this Gran." He eyed her mischievously as she gave him a warning look over the top of her glasses.

"It's friendlier. Charles would be Chas. Alexander, Alex and Dad would be Gerry."

Pamela, who had followed Alexander, returned in time to hear his last words and did a double take at the tinsel around his neck.

"Oh, very fetching I must say. And as for anyone calling your father Gerry, with its war time connotations, they would definitely have to have a very strong death wish, so don't even think it."

Charles, who had been sitting behind his paper, suddenly shook it closed, got up without a word and made to leave the room.

"Daddy, we were only joking." Sophie cried. He stopped and turned.

"What was that, Poppet?" he asked absently.

"Are you irritated by our silliness?" she asked anxiously, going up to him.

He kissed her forehead. "Got to do something. Won't be long."

"He wouldn't even have heard, dear. He wasn't reading. He has things on his mind." Felicity assured her.

"Are you sure?" Robert was also concerned.

"Even Uncle Charles can't read the paper upside down," she said simply.

Charles was already heading for the study. He had to help Alexander. He had promised.

Gerald was nursing a tumbler of whisky and the decanter was on the desk beside him.

"That bad eh?" Charles fetched himself a tumbler. "Drinking alone is bad for your health," he chided, pouring himself a drink.

"That would seem to be in the lap of the gods anyway," Gerald answered with a helpless shrug.

"Tell me," Charles demanded, his voice sharp with concern. This wasn't like Gerald.

"I don't want anyone else to know, least of all Mother and Dad."

"Right." The word came out slow and deliberate.

"As you may or may not know, I am a blood donor. Every year I get a check-up, only this year the blood test was not good. In a nutshell, they are testing for cancer and I'm terrified."

Charles could feel the hair on the back of his neck rising and all he could say was, "Christ almighty!"

Gerald poured himself another drink and held the decanter out to Charles, who nodded vigorously. They both took a large gulp before Charles recovered his speech enough to ask, "When will you know?"

"Within the week."

"Christ!"

They sat on, discussing what until now had been un-thought of matters; matters that suddenly seemed paramount with the looming possibility of one of them not being able to carry on as usual.

"I must make sure my affairs are in order. Pamela and the boys will be well provided for, but she is hopeless at paperwork. You will see to all of that for her?"

"Need you ask?" He sounded offended.

"I know, I know. Sorry. I'm not thinking straight."

"Hardly surprising, but as you have always said. Let's take things one at a time and if the worst comes to the worst, we will deal with it together."

"How would I ever have managed without you over the years?"

"Probably better than I would without you. It has always been very much a two way thing," Charles replied practically.

"What if I can't work? Dad can't be expected to do all that I do and you have your work cut out already. Laurie is pretty much a figure head these days, I imagine?" The fear had returned to his eyes.

"He still sees to the clients who have been with him for years. He gives them the old world courtesy that they are used to and they, quite rightly, have complete faith in his advice."

Charles's admiration for Laurie had never changed and he considered himself the fortunate one.

"If only Robert had started with us a year ago, he would have been well into things by now. University would have been fine if he had been taking realistic subjects." Gerald thumped the desk.

"Robert will come up trumps when the time comes," Charles soothed.

"And as for Alexander, well words fail me. He hasn't got an intelligent thought in his head."

Charles took the opportunity and ventured to say, "He might just do alright at acting, wouldn't it be worth letting him try?"

75

Gerald gave him a despairing look. "Please don't fight me on this. The thought of a son of mine, prancing about a stage pretending to be someone he isn't, just turns my stomach. It isn't that I *want* him to join the firm. God knows he will be little enough help there, but he must learn to appreciate what we have worked for and not think that it is going to be handed to him on a platter, just to indulge a frivolous lifestyle."

His utter abhorrence told Charles it would be unfair to interfere, even for Alexander.

"What position do you envisage for him?"

"Just learning the export side perhaps. He is presentable enough. I don't know what he would be like on paperwork, but we have an excellent manager at Southampton, who would be willing to train him. I had a word a couple of months ago."

"Where would he live?"

"Pamela would see to that. Probably send Abigail along as well, to hold his hand," Gerald joked, much to Charles's relief. At least his mind was off the big problem, for a while.

"How do you think he will take to the idea?" Gerald mused, emptying his glass again.

Charles got up to put another log on the fire and said over his shoulder, "Put in the right way, I think he will jump at the chance. Point out the advantage of earning a wage and being in control of his own life, as opposed to going on to further studies. It would give him something positive to tackle."

"What I can't understand, is why I haven't got the same working relationship with my boys as my Dad had with me. I can't communicate with Alexander and Robert isn't on the same wavelength at all, even though I *can* talk to him without feeling furious all the time, as I do with Alexander. Why do you think it is?"

"*Your* parents were hard up. If you or Philip cried in the night, your *mother* was there, not a nanny. They alone fed, clothed, cuddled and disciplined you. It may be as simple as that, who can say?"

At that moment the door opened and Marie's face appeared. She smiled as she caught sight of them slumped in their chairs, each nursing a half filled whisky tumbler and 'feeling mellow' as she delicately put it.

"I have a little scheme to run by you, if you are up to comprehending that is."

"Fire away, Mother." Gerald gave an inebriated wave of his glass and Charles, ever the gentleman, rose unsteadily and brought a chair forward.

"Thank you, dear. Well now, Sophie has an American friend, alone in London because his parents are touring, so we thought it would be hospitable, it

76

being the season of goodwill and so forth, to invite him down for Sophie's birthday as a surprise for her. On a scale of one to ten, Robert says he is eleven. What do you think?"

"I think you're match-making, Mother dear."

"Do I want an American son-in-law?" Charles asked Gerald, twisting his face.

"Robert says he is really suitable," Marie coaxed.

The two men looked at each other and gave resigned shrugs.

"And we will never hear the end of it if we don't agree," Gerald lamented.

"And I do have complete faith in – in…" He waved his hand in the air and snapped his fingers.

"Robert," Marie obliged on her way to the door.

She returned to the sitting room smiling, where flickering flames danced on the walls, red berries contrasted with mistletoe and green holly, and the tree where small lantern lights shining on tinsel and baubles, lit up the sparkling fairy on the top. In her silver dress and crown she seemed to be blessing everyone with her silver wand, and it was all reflected in the huge, gilt framed mirror hanging over the fireplace – a beautiful and quite magical scene – Marie sighed with contentment. Her life was so full and rich; she thanked God every day, even though she also asked him frequently why he had taken Philip from them.

"I think you might be carrying your husbands to bed tonight," she declared picking up her hot chocolate and settling back onto the settee with a satisfied little smile.

"Seriously?" they asked together. It was unheard of for Charles to over-indulge, and Gerald only on the odd occasion.

Marie nodded sipping her chocolate. "Do them good! They both work too hard. But it *is* funny to see them," she chuckled.

Half an hour later when they poked their heads round the study door, both men were snoring peacefully, their drained glasses on the desk next to the empty decanter. Pamela and Felicity raised their legs onto footstools and Marie fetched blankets. They slept the night away, oblivious for a short time to the trouble ahead.

They awoke early and took themselves for a much needed walk along the bay. It was still cold and damp but the wind had died and the sea no longer crashed against the rocks. Instead, grey and calm, the only sound was the cry of the gulls wheeling overhead. They walked in silence, hands dug deep in pockets, shoulders hunched against the cold, breath forming clouds in the air, each having much the same, 'if the worst comes to the worst', thoughts. After a while they retraced their footsteps, still deeply indented in the wet sand, and made their way back to the kitchen door, where Jed and Jake arrived as they were kicking off their wellingtons.

"Hello, what have they got you doing now?" Gerald greeted them.

They returned his greeting with a respectful touch of their caps. "Morning Mr Gerald, morning Mr Charles. 'Tis to move the piano, so Miss Sophie can play for you over Christmas." Jake always did the talking and Jed would just nod in agreement, his good-natured face shining.

The delicious smell of grilled bacon and sausages wafted towards them as they opened the kitchen door and Marie said, "Ah, just in time, boys!"

Jake and Jed waited eagerly to be ushered to the big table, which was already set with a blue check tablecloth and piles of toast and creamy butter. Two minutes later, Felicity put a huge plate of breakfast in front of each of them. Gerald and Charles sat opposite and David, who was already seated at the head of the table, put his paper down declaring as Marie and Felicity joined them, "I could eat a horse!"

"You will all certainly get as big as one," Pamela commented dryly, eyeing the piled up plates with disgust as she helped herself to black coffee and left the kitchen, shuddering with revulsion at the fast disappearing mountain of food. Even at this early hour she was dressed immaculately.

Sunday was Lorna's day off and Marie took back her kitchen, happily admitting she enjoyed her freedom the rest of the time.

Breakfast over and the piano moved, David took Jake and Jed into the grounds to discuss the building of a new hen house. "With the family growing larger we need more eggs. Don't you agree, Gerald?"

His father's hearty enthusiasm usually inspired him, but with the best will in the world he couldn't respond. "I'll catch up, Dad," he said touching his head, to which David gave an understanding grin and went off happily.

It was the longest weekend ever, trying to keep up with the cheerful banter around him.

Monday was Robert and Sophie's birthday and also when he would hear his results. He hung by the study telephone all morning, ostensibly waiting for a business call. It came at two o'clock, when Charles was still at the office, so he dragged his outdoor clothes on and practically ran from the house, making for the steep path to the top of the cliffs. Marie watched him from the window, wishing he would rest more and carried on putting the finishing touches to the birthday cake.

Lorna was dressing a freshly cooked salmon, Felicity was decorating a sherry trifle and Pamela was putting toppings on canapés. Abigail came in to say that she had made up the extra beds and was there anything else she could do to help?

Marie said a cup of tea would be a lifesaver. The kettle was already singing and tea was soon being passed round for the umpteenth time that day.

Sophie thought Robert was taking her to town, to pick up last minute items, but in fact, they were meeting Matthew from the four o'clock train. Alexander had gone with Charles to deliver two urgent documents for him. Charles could easily have delivered them on his way home, but he wanted to make the boy feel more wanted, whilst the only topic of conversation was Sophie and Robert's party.

Jessica was already at her desk when Charles let himself and Alexander into the office and she had the documents ready for Charles to check.

"Alexander is going to deliver these. *He* can telephone for a taxi."

"Certainly, Mr Hughes. Will that be all?"

"You could ring Mr Harcott and say I will pick him up at three o'clock if he prefers; he may like extra time, with tonight in mind. Oh, and book the taxi for half an hour's time Alexander; that will give me time to go through these." He waved the sheaf of papers as he disappeared into his office.

By the time the taxi arrived Alexander was feeling important. He knew the papers entrusted to him were for two of the biggest landowners in the area.

"Pity you can't drive, we could have saved the taxi fare," Charles joked as an idea dawned on him. "That's an idea for your seventeenth birthday. How about driving lessons?"

Alexander stared at him, for once speechless.

"Have to ask your Dad first of course – but I expect it will be alright," he said hastily, seeing his face drop.

Alexander spent the rest of the day in a state of nervous excitement in case his father said 'no' to the lessons.

"Can I ask him straight away?" he begged Charles.

"Let me have a word first," Charles advised, suddenly realising he should have chosen a better time than today of all days.

The study was empty. He tried the kitchen. No sign of Gerald but Felicity said, After his telephone call came he went racing up the cliff path as if his life depended on it and I haven't seen him come back yet, Charles." She called after him, shaking her head hopelessly as he headed out the door, all other concerns banished from his mind.

What if Gerald couldn't handle the bad news? He puffed his way up the steep slope, dreading what he might find and arrived at the top, heart pounding, gasping for breath. In the distance he could see Gerald sitting head in hands on the ancient seat outside the cottage. He ran as fast as his legs would carry him.

"We – will – see it – through – together," he gasped painfully, relief giving way to curiosity as Gerald raised a ravaged face, forcing a grim smile.

"It's alright!" he said brokenly.

Charles sat down with a bump and managed to gasp "He shortens my life by ten years and says it's alright! Tell me man! Preferably before I pass out."

"I've got high blood pressure, which is what made me pass out in the office, and –" Charles interrupted. "Oh! And is there anything else you just happen to have forgotten to mention?"

Gerald shrugged. "It was only the once, but I have been getting breathless spells. Apparently I have a breathing disorder and I have an appointment on Wednesday afternoon to sort out how much is due to the asthma."

They bear-hugged and clapped each other on the back.

"I'm coming to the doctor's with you; from now on, whatever happens – we do it together."

Gerald nodded, his face relaxing with the relief; everything was under control.

"Come on now, let's get back to the house, Laurie is there and the children will be back soon. Better be there to greet Matthew or we will be for it. The women have laid on enough food to feed the neighbourhood by the looks of things."

Charles put his arm along Gerald's shoulders as they made the steep descent, and Gerald said, "I would still like to keep this to ourselves until after Christmas."

"Even Pamela?"

"Especially Pamela. She is going to throw a wobbly for sure and won't be able to hide it from the others. Let them enjoy Christmas. We will know more on Wednesday anyway."

"Fair enough. We can say that we are going up on business. It won't be entirely untrue."

They braced themselves against the steepness of the path, talking earnestly of whether to travel up by car or train.

Train they decided, in case the weather changed to fog as it was doing at this moment. It had rolled in surreptitiously from the sea, as it had a habit of doing in the winter and everything was quickly being blotted out, as they scrambled the last few yards towards the shafts of light from the house, looking forward to being indoors. The eerie, muffled echo of a fog horn, sounding deceptively close, made them jump and laugh at themselves and at that moment Marie, who had been watching for them, tutted affectionately to Pamela and Felicity. "Look at them, will you? They're like two schoolboys sharing a secret."

"It would seem the end of the world isn't nigh after all," Pamela observed dryly, ladling punch from a crystal bowl and decorating the sparkling cups with slices of fruit.

"Oh, it probably was but they will have averted it single handed," Felicity said with a straight face, placing her hands over her heart and declaring, "Our Heroes." Whereupon, Pamela put her hands over her heart, "Our Heroes," they chorused, to raised eyebrows from Charles's and Gerald's, "How much of that stuff have you two had? I thought you were keeping an eye on them, Mother. Shame on you."

"Can anyone join in?" Laurie's plaintive enquiry came from the doorway. When Charles had gone dashing off, Marie had settled him in the lounge with a glass of wine and the newspaper; he was holding a glass, minus the wine.

"Laurie, old fellow. Forgive me." Charles went and took his glass. "How about sampling this excellent punch? Everyone else seems to be happy on it. Even Lorna and Abigail are quite flushed I see, and I don't think it is all to do with a hot stove."

Laurie joined in the laughter, accepting the drink somewhat tentatively. "I never quite trust punches," he said suspiciously.

"Rightly so! Anyone else?" Gerald asked, picking up two more glasses and handing one to Charles.

"How about you, sweetheart? Your glass is empty," Charles said turning to Felicity.

"I'll stick to my lemonade, thank you," Felicity giggled, pointing to a bottle on the dresser.

Charles gave her a quizzical look and murmured to Gerald, "My wife got like *that* on *lemonade*?" He reached for the bottle and caught Marie's look as she clapped her hand over her mouth, eyes alight with suppressed mirth.

"Why do I get the feeling that this isn't lemonade?" he asked suspiciously, holding up the nearly empty bottle, but before she could answer the kitchen door opened and Robert, Sophie and a tall, young man were framed in the doorway.

"What a hubbub! No wonder you didn't hear us arrive," Robert laughed.

"This is Matthew everyone." Sophie drew him forward, her face radiant, as she took him first to her parents. He shook hands with them and Charles noticed the firm, strong grip. He, like most men set great store by a man's handshake, but Sophie's smile and a firm handshake wasn't enough to convince him he was good enough for his girl. Like Felicity, he had always hoped she would marry Robert, who they liked and knew. It would all have been so straight forward, and comfortable. Why did this Matthew have to come on the scene and spoil things? For a moment he was seized with unreasonable jealousy, before sanity returned and he heard a softly spoken American accent thanking them for inviting him to stay and Felicity replying that although they were delighted to meet him, the idea was entirely Sophie's grandmother's.

"Then my grateful thanks are due to this lovely lady?" he said turning to Marie with a smile that won her over, instantly.

"Grandma, what an angel you are." Sophie launched herself at Marie and hugged her. "It was a lovely surprise, I couldn't have had a better present. Thank you. Thank you."

Quite overwhelmed, Marie could only murmur, "There, there, dear."

Matthew shook hands with everyone in turn, finally reaching Alexander who, Charles noticed, had taken up his defensive position behind Abigail.

Gerald heard his 'tut' and asked, "What's the matter?"

"We need to talk."

"Now?"

"Now."

They slipped out to the study where Charles hurriedly suggested the driving lessons.

"Do you think he is responsible enough?" Gerald asked dubiously.

"I think he will surprise you, and I would like you to tell him tonight, if you agree."

"Why the rush?"

"These joint birthdays make him feel left out. It would give him something to celebrate as well."

Gerald was touched. "Thank you for caring enough to do something about it." They clasped hands. "Come. I mustn't monopolise you with anymore of *my* problems."

"*Our* problems!" Charles corrected as they rejoined the party.

Gerald told Alexander of Charles generous offer immediately. Everyone applauded and to his embarrassment, Pamela hugged him, while David and Marie watched fondly.

Unfortunately, Alexander instantly swapped his attention from Abigail to Charles and never left his side all evening, which was gratifying but left Charles groaning when he bumped into him every time he turned round. The rest of the evening was a great success. Matthew was 'at home' with everyone and even Charles found him *very agreeable to talk to*, which was as far as he was prepared to commit himself at this moment in time, he told Felicity, when she kept pressing him for his opinion and whose unusually playful mood he had since discovered was due to the large amount of Marie's two-year-old, homemade Elderflower wine that she had consumed.

"Sorry, Charles. I remember now, I ran out of bottles and used that lemonade one; I had actually forgotten it was still in the pantry," Marie explained apologetically.

"Well, I forgive you," Charles began sternly, "but only if you make sure to keep a good stock in; it makes *me* laugh to see her having such a wonderful time. I only hope she doesn't have a headache in the morning."

Gerald and Charles rose very early the following morning, but in spite of the hour, Robert was already in the library, fitting in his new volumes. Books were always his favourite gifts and at this hour he could usually rely on being undisturbed – but not this morning.

"Fancy a walk along the beach?" Gerald called quietly, on their way out.

"That is the second invitation I have had already this morning. Can't you all stay in bed and give a fellow some peace?" he complained cheerfully, without interrupting his task.

"Good Lord! Who else?"

"Sophie and Matt. She is showing him the view from the cliffs – she says." He grinned as they left.

It was an incredible morning. One that comes out of the blue and then reverts back, just as unexpectedly. White fluffy clouds scudded across an otherwise clear blue sky and there was a hint of frost in the air.

High above them, Sophie and Matthew were unaware of being observed as they kissed.

"She will be alright. We are all disappointed she and Robert didn't make a match, but I think she has chosen well. I like him, don't you?"

"Yes, dammit."

Gerald smiled. "I know, and you are right of course. There isn't a man walking the earth good enough for her."

They continued walking and talk turned automatically to the two o'clock appointment at Southampton General Hospital the next day. The tickets were booked for the nine o'clock train.

By the time they returned to the house nearly two hours later, everything was astir. Breakfast was in the making with Felicity and Abigail helping, and Lorna's niece, Maisie, a girl in her late teens, was busy vacuuming the sitting room. David was insisting the help arrangement should be permanent, with the usual opposition from Marie when Gerald and Charles walked in.

"Now see what you have done," Marie scolded. They will think I am on my last legs."

"Your Mother doesn't need to work so hard. It isn't as if we can't afford help, now," David said, seeking their support.

"Dad is right. You will have help," Gerald said.

"Absolutely!" Charles agreed.

Maisie joined the household and in spite of Abigail's opinion, that the girl was a ha'penny short of a shilling, she did her work well and the house shone as it had never shone before. Unfortunately, Alexander overheard the remark and immediately took it that Maisie was mentally retarded, which gave him visions, picked up from a Victorian drama on television, of taking advantage of her when the opportunity arose. That is what sons of wealthy families did, according to history, he assured himself confidently.

Maisie, as it happened was just tongue-tied and completely in awe of the family, who lived in the 'Big House' and were only spoken of with reverence by Aunt Lorna. In fact, she was a spirited young woman with a very definite mind of her own – but that was something Alexander was to learn, to his cost, at a later date.

At breakfast Gerald broke the news that he and Charles had been unavoidably called to Southampton the next day, and apart from a few disappointed 'Ohs' no further comment was made.

CHAPTER SIX

Gerald's mind had been put at rest when they ruled out his worst fear, therefore he was not prepared for the grave words of Doctor Kennedy, the specialist who shook hands with them and invited them to sit down. It was a large room, with windows taking up the whole of one wall, making it *too* light Gerald thought. He wanted to hide this shaking fear that numbed his mind and blotted out everything except the words 'shadow on the lung'. Charles noted his vacant, ashen face and leaned forward.

"Is this anything to do with the asthma?"

"Nothing quite so simple I'm afraid. More tests are needed, but we are almost certainly dealing with the early stages of TB, which means hospital treatment, prolonged rest, and plenty of fresh air. I expected Mrs Anders to be here as well."

Charles realised for the first time how strange *his* presence must seem.

"She doesn't actually know. When cancer was ruled out, we thought we could spare the family until after Christmas."

He felt acutely embarrassed. How could he have agreed to this foolish situation? The fact they wanted to see Gerald again so quickly *should* have made him realise. It must have been the relief, mixed with everything else happening at once.

"I see," the doctor said not unsympathetically.

"I suppose we *wanted* to believe everything was alright," Charles confessed.

"I made him agree," Gerald blurted out, coming to earth with a jolt, on hearing his fumbling excuses.

"Well anyway, I have made a provisional booking for January 2nd, at a London clinic. We have caught it in its early stages, so with proper care and treatment I expect you to make a full recovery within the year."

Gerald and Charles looked at each other. "London? A year?" they chorused.

"Believe me. It's the best."

They left the consulting room and Charles waited in the reception area, whilst Gerald was taken to have further tests. It seemed like forever to Charles, although it was actually only half an hour. He watched people come and go with worried faces, the rich and not so rich with one thing in common. Ill health was a great leveller. And then, quite suddenly they were home, neither remembering much of the journey. Dream-like, they found the car where they left it that morning.

"I still don't want them to know until after Christmas."

"I don't know if that's wise."

"Do this for me, Charles. I promise to tell them on the day after Boxing Day."

"That is still a week away."

"I know, but it will give me time to come to terms with it, before helping Mother and Dad. It's going to bring Philip back, all over again. And then I can't bear to see Pamela unhappy – if I can spare her a week…?" His voice cracked.

With great misgiving, Charles bowed to Gerald's wishes again, but when they were all sitting around the dinner table, or swaying to the melodious Strauss music that Sophie played and he saw their happiness, he had to agree that perhaps Gerald had been right. His own heart was heavy though, with thoughts of what was to come. In the last twenty years they had all shared and known an idyllic life. He blankly refused to think of the passing of time and a future without any one of these dear people who had taken him and his family to heart, as he had taken them to his.

The seasonal ambience surrounding the house filled everyone with a sense of well-being and the festivities began early on Christmas Day. Fires burnt brightly in the wide fireplaces, the aroma of a thirty-pound turkey cooking slowly in the Aga overnight pervaded the whole house, and everyone was offering to help.

Pamela had taken great care in laying and decorating the snowy white tablecloths with gleaming cutlery; silver candlesticks, tall red candles; sparkling wine glasses and hand-made Christmas crackers – blue and gold for the ladies, red and gold for the men, each bearing a name, and placed across a silver table mat. Gracing the centre of the long table was a huge crystal bowl of deep red double-headed chrysanthemums.

There were twelve of them to sit down and it had been necessary to add a small table at one end, to make room for everyone.

"We will have to get a bigger table if our family keeps growing," Marie commented, admiring Pamela's handiwork.

"Well we aren't going to get any fewer, that is for sure," Pamela laughed, "you will have great-grandchildren before you know it."

Marie clasped her hands under her chin, her face alight with anticipation. "Won't it be wonderful?"

Pamela didn't look so sure. "What if they all scream, like Alexander?"

"What's that?" Gerald asked coming up behind them and planting a kiss on Pamela's neck.

She repeated their conversation, adding, "Of course that would make us grandparents. Bit daunting isn't it?"

"Lovely idea!"

"What? Grandchildren?"

"That as well, in about ten years from now. No, I meant the bigger table. I know just the one that would look fantastic in here, I'll see what I can do." And then he suddenly remembered that, in exactly a week's time he wouldn't be here for who knew how long. He turned on his heel abruptly to hide his distress and retreated to the study, where Charles found him, ten minutes later.

"How could I forget? And yet I did. I actually haven't given it a thought since first waking up this morning. Everything seems so normal, I know I'm going to wake up and find it has all been a bad dream."

"Come and join in, if you don't want them to guess something is wrong. We are waiting to sing."

Gerald followed him into the hall, looking about as if seeing it for the first time. He noticed the garlands of holly, ivy and mistletoe decking the walls and entwining the staircase, and the poinsettias and ferns that filled a huge copper bowl on the round table. He knew without doubt it was Pamela's handiwork and that he had never really taken it all in before. He had been so busy he had taken the ordinary things for granted. Nostalgia gripped him, enhancing the beauty of this wonderful home that they had been fortunate enough to inherit and he vowed in that moment to do everything in his power to make sure his sons continued what his father, Charles and he had restored, so that their children could enjoy the same. Never again must Anders Folly be allowed to fall into dilapidation. All of this passed through his mind in the short space of time it took to cross the wide hall and enter the sitting room.

It was a happy gathering, waiting to sing: 'Happy Birthday Baby Jesus' – a tradition they had started when the children were small and the meaning of Christmas had been explained to them. Matthew was bemused. What really impressed him was the closeness of the family, the way they all pulled together to make it good for everyone. Over dinner, he joined in the general chitchat, but couldn't help dwelling on the warmth and geniality between these people. In his world, Christmas had always been spent in a top class hotel, in whichever city his parents happened to be touring at the time and therefore amongst strangers to a great extent. There was a great void between the lavish parties of 'the celebrities', he had grown up with and the simple homely pleasures of this family. He asked himself how he was going to avoid that other lifestyle for Sophie and himself when they married. Would Sophie be happy amongst the rich and famous? Would it be fair to take her in to that world when, sadly and quite soon now, she was going to learn that although she played with considerable ability she lacked the brilliance necessary to become a concert pianist. He would give anything to be wrong, but knew he wasn't. He had tried to prepare her, without being the one to bring her world crashing. That had to come from the Academy – as it surely would. And to destroy her family's expectations would make it even harder for her.

After dinner, when everyone had lent a hand to clear away, a walk was suggested but the rain clouds that had threatened all morning, chose that moment to burst and it was out of the question. Instead, Charles and the young people went off to play table tennis. Charles had learnt to play as a youngster, and had recently installed a table in the music room with the intention of teaching Felicity to play, on long winter evenings. So far she wasn't doing well.

"I'm not built for speed," she would gasp, collapsing with laughter when, for the umpteenth time, the bat failed to make contact with the ball, therefore when Matthew turned out to be a good player Charles was delighted.

The Queen's speech ended and the firelight threw flickering shadows around the room in the twilight. Gerald stared moodily into the flames, glad of the silence that fell, as lulled by the warmth and good food, they all nodded off. Pamela's head rested on his shoulder. He kissed her hair and she nestled closer squeezing his hand as it lay in hers. He agonised at the thought of being parted. London was so far away and visits would be few and far between.

The rain lashed against the windows and the room grew darker; inside it was cosy and safe and gradually stillness crept over him. By this time next year, God willing, it would be behind him. Resolution took over from despair. He had to make a full and speedy recovery so that he could go on looking after his family. He drifted into a deep sleep and woke to find the curtains drawn against the wild night and everyone sitting quietly, drinking tea.

"You should have woken me," he said sheepishly, blinking the sleep from his eyes as Felicity handed him a cup.

"Daddy wouldn't hear of it. Said it would do you more good than any old cup of tea and we weren't even allowed to speak above a whisper," Sophie teased.

"Nonsense!" Charles ruffled her hair affectionately.

"Shall I do the honours, Grandma?" Robert asked, standing beside the tree. Marie nodded and motioned Alexander to lend a hand.

The pile of presents was larger than ever this year. Matthew had added his, after a last minute dash to the local wine merchants to purchase a bottle of best malt whiskey for each of the men and a huge box of chocolates for each of the ladies, not forgetting Abigail, who was quite overwhelmed to be included. "Ye really shouldna. I'll away and get my knitting needles out."

Matthew gave her a puzzled look, but she assumed he knew about her handmade, Aran or Fair Isle jumpers. And he turned away, wanting to watch Sophie's face.

"You didn't wrap that yourself," Pamela said, admiring the exquisitely wrapped gift with its swirls of gold ribbon.

Matthew pretended to look offended.

"I know Bond Street when I see it," she said admiringly.

Sophie was almost reluctant to undo the ribbon but it came off in one piece and she immediately caught her hair back with it, looking at Matthew as she did so. He relaxed back in to the corner of the settee, his long, supple frame looking extremely distinguished in well-cut navy blue slacks and wool shirt. Beside him Sophie looked very tiny in a dark red, ankle-length dress. Her eyes were sparkling and she had never looked lovelier. They all watched as she removed the gold wrapping paper and revealed a cream leather case. Inside, a chain bracelet with three gold charms attached, lay on a bed of rich brown velvet. She gave a cry of delight as she held it up to reveal a tiny gold violin, a grand piano and a small gold heart between the two, which opened to reveal a tiny diamond.

"A romantic way of proposing," Felicity said dreamily, as they were getting ready for bed that night.

"Mmm. I had better start asking some questions. We really don't know anything about him, except that he comes from America and plays the violin – and not a bad game of table tennis," he added almost to himself. "Seems to be alright for cash if the bracelet is anything to go by, unless he has been saving up." He rambled on, debating with himself whilst Felicity just smiled and continued brushing her hair. He had already accepted Matthew but he had to make all the right noises. She understood that.

There had been so many presents and each one was admired but the most admired was Laurie's gift to David and Marie. He had said for some time he wanted to teach them to play chess and now it was apparent why. They unwrapped the box together, mystified as to what it could be until one of the figures tumbled onto Marie's lap, then one by one the ebony and ivory, 'Knights of Old' chessmen were unwrapped and last of all, the heavy matching board, with its brass inlay, outlining the small squares. It was a wonderful antique piece and on the enclosed card it said: 'This has always been a very dear possession of mine, so it had to go to my very dear friends. Hoping you get as many happy hours from it as I have, and that I may share some of them with you. Your devoted, friend Laurie.'

For Gerald and Pamela there was a seascape oil painting by a local artist and for Charles and Felicity a Constable oil painting of 'The Haywain'.

"But these are your treasures, Laurie," Felicity said with concern when they were alone. She had seen and admired them on her visits to his home.

"Think what a pleasure it will give me to see them in this wonderful old house, knowing they will still be treasured long after I'm gone."

She nodded understanding, but a cold finger touched her heart; she had never heard him speak like that before. Even the children's presents were personal mementos, instead of the usual generous cheque. A Dresden china figurine for Sophie, a mahogany book rest for Robert and a silver-topped walking stick for Alexander. And for Matthew a leather bound book on the history of Cornwall, from Laurie's own bookshelf. Each item had played a part in his life and had happy memories he told them.

It took some time to finish opening all of the presents and by then it was time to get supper. Cold pork, ham and turkey were laid out with Lorna's homemade pork pie, with salad and homemade pickles and chutneys to accompany them. Matthew groaned that he had never eaten so much in one day, but it was all so lovely he couldn't resist.

"Sounds like a man after your own heart, Charles," Pamela teased, poking him in the ribs.

Charles got up and walked to the piano. "Just for that I will play your song first."

He started to play 'I'll never stop loving you', followed by 'Always'. "For Mother and Dad." Then, he went into 'You are my honey, honey suckle' and called for Laurie to come and sing. Laurie soon had everyone joining in, and then Sophie insisted on 'Old McDonald' – their childhood favourite.

"I know that one," Matthew said, reaching behind him for his violin case. They were all so entertained by Laurie's imitations and Matthew's dexterity on the strings of his violin that it just had to be repeated, and after that Charles said it was someone else's turn.

"Matthew and I have put something together," Sophie said shyly and together they played 'Cornish Rhapsody', 'The Moonlight Sonata' and Chopin's 'Polonaise in A'. Then Matthew played a haunting, Hungarian, gypsy melody, and it didn't take an expert to recognise his brilliance; everyone was entranced.

"Told you he played the fiddle, didn't I?" Robert said laughing at their awestruck faces.

Sophie had one last little surprise for them. She fetched two guitars from behind the piano and she and Matthew sat down and sang 'Edelweiss', persuading everyone to join in the second time.

"When did you learn to play?" Felicity asked, astonished.

"Just two weeks ago and that is her whole repertoire, as yet," Matthew laughed as they returned to their seats.

"Your turn, Robert," Matthew prompted.

"Sorry, I don't have a party piece."

"Not true. I remember you doing one at the end of term party."

"Yes, of course, Shakespeare's 'Soliloquy'. Come on Robert," Sophie urged.

"I'll get the lights," Alexander volunteered as Robert, trying to keep a straight face, donned Sophie's large, black velvet beret and picked up a book. By this time, it was obvious, this had also been rehearsed to great effect. A hush fell as he stood with the open book in both hands, with just the firelight and candles for lighting:

'To be, or not to be, – that is the question: –
Whether 'tis nobler in the mind to suffer
The slings and arrows of outrageous fortune,
Or to take arms against a sea of troubles.'

He performed the whole soliloquy. The recitation was excellent and the inflexion in his voice was worthy of Richard Burton, Marie claimed as he gave a sweeping bow and everyone applauded.

"And now Ladies and Gentlemen, for your further entertainment," Robert announced, "the one and only," at this point Sophie struck a cord on the piano. "Mr Noel Coward."

Alexander had slipped away after turning the lights off and now strolled in, complete with slicked back hair, a yellow Paisley cravat and a long cigarette holder.

One hand resting on the grand piano, the other waving the cigarette holder he waited for Sophie to finish the introduction, then, in clipped tones began to sing 'Mad dogs and Englishmen', followed by 'Mad about the boys'. Charles was sitting beside Laurie and whispered, "Good, isn't he?"

"Isn't he just," Laurie answered, the irony in his voice lost on him as everyone applauded the polished performance.

Everyone that is, except Gerald. It made him squirm. How could he *love* Alexander and yet dislike everything about him? He reminded himself how little he would be seeing him shortly and forced a smile in answer to Pamela's, "He really is very good."

"That's all, folks!" Robert took Sophie's hand and led her back to Matthew.

"Time for a cup of hot chocolate, I think," Marie said, glancing at the clock on the mantelpiece, showing midnight. "We didn't expect to be so royally entertained; it has been a thoroughly enjoyable evening. Thank you all. You certainly kept the rehearsals well hidden; we had no idea."

"I'm going to have a whisky night cap, from that very nice bottle I was given today." David bowed to Matthew. "Will anyone join me?"

"Mmm. Good idea," Gerald, Charles and Laurie agreed.

"I'll get them," Charles offered.

By twelve-thirty Marie and Felicity were both yawning. Charles heaved himself out of his chair saying there was another long day tomorrow and he was ready for bed. He and Felicity were at the door, when Sophie got up, went to the piano stool and began to sing very softly: "You're my everything." They stopped; it was their song; and it had never sounded lovelier. Unable to speak, they each blew a kiss.

"Night, Mummy, night, Daddy. Thank you for being the best."

Robert sat down beside her on the long stool and eased her over with his hips.

"You've got everyone weeping. How about our tune? Ready. Steady. Go." A lively rendition of 'Chopsticks' followed, with Sophie challenging him to play faster and faster, until they collapsed against each other laughing. Robert wasn't at all musical and it was his sole achievement, attained only with great patience on Sophie's part, over the years.

It all bemused Matthew who had never experienced such displays of affection. Laurie guessed what he was thinking. "Don't try and understand their generous hearts or question their sincerity. This family is unique and once you know them you have friends for life. I personally feel privileged to share their company."

"I would include you in that company, sir."

Laurie gave him a shrewd look and lowered his tone. "And I think you will fit the bill very nicely for our Sophie, but there is something bothering you, isn't there?"

Matthew's head jerked, his jaw dropping.

"I'm a good listener and I know how to keep things to myself when necessary. Right now though, I'm for my bed." He eased himself forward. "Goodnight m' boy. Don't forget."

"Goodnight, Mr Harcott, and thank you, I won't."

"Call me Laurie. Everybody does."

He said his goodnights and thanked them all for a very enjoyable evening.

"Time for us as well." David knocked his pipe out against the fireplace before assisting Marie out of her chair.

"I think we are *all* ready, aren't we?" Gerald started to damp the fire down.

It was actually more of a statement than a question but the young ones were ready anyway, all except Alexander, who bridled at being told when to go to bed, and would have argued had Abigail not noticed the indignant pose and given him a warning look. So, totally oblivious to his son's objection, Gerald continued attending to the fire.

Matthew observed the miming with interest; the first note of discord he had witnessed in the week of his visit.

Boxing Day morning dawned, if it could be said to have dawned. Dense fog shrouded the house like a thick, grey blanket making it impossible to see out.

"Looks like being another cosy day indoors," Marie said cheerfully as she rescued sizzling bacon and spooned hot fat over the newly laid eggs, frying in the pan. She was never happier than when all of her brood were around.

"A good day for your first chess lesson," Laurie said to David.

"Perfect," David agreed, reaching for a slice of toast and spreading it liberally with butter as Felicity put their breakfast in front of them. The peace that had reigned for the last hour was abruptly shattered, as Robert, Sophie and Matthew crowded in debating the merits of Tom Stoppard's new play, 'Rosencrantz, and Guildenstern are dead'.

"Who's dead?" Marie asked with concern, sending them in to fits of laughter, while Felicity just looked at her, equally mystified as to why someone dying should be so funny.

"It's a play, Mother," Gerald explained, entering at that moment and frowning reproachfully at the youngsters as he poured a cup of black coffee and handed it to Robert to take up to his mother.

Pamela and Alexander seldom put in an appearance at breakfast and only Pamela knew that Abigail gave Alexander his in bed, on the holidays.

"Quite the young gentleman, isn't he?" Pamela would smile indulgently.

Gerald was very quiet all day, but as sport was on the television, no one realised he was looking into the fire most of the time, sorting in his mind how to tell them the next day. It was important they should all feel everything was under control, although, heaven knows who would take over his workload.

The difficulty would be to stop his father from taking on too much. He had earned his retirement; not that he would ever fully retire, with his keen interest in the business, but his mother would need him here.

The day passed all too soon. Laurie was delighted at how quickly David picked up the rules and strategy of chess.

"Must be that brilliant business brain of yours," Marie joked. "I have no chance."

That didn't turn out to be the case though, she mastered the game just as quickly and surprised David with some astute moves, which he rather peevishly put down to luck, while Laurie looked on, highly amused.

"It couldn't have come at a better time," Charles said quietly, nodding towards the three of them, but deep in thought, Gerald wasn't with his train of thought.

"Sorry?"

"Chess. It will help to keep their minds occupied."

"Oh! Yes, yes of course." He gave an enlightened smile as David gave a triumphant cry of "Check!" and Laurie advised Marie to look carefully. Seconds later, David, groaned. He could see the opening and it only took Marie a little longer to spot it, much to his annoyance.

"Checkmate! I believe." She said gleefully, sitting back and looking very pleased with herself.

"Luck! Pure luck!" David grumbled.

"Wait until you are past the basics. Then you will have to look to your laurels. She is going to make a worthy opponent," Laurie warned, laughing at his discomfort, knowing that they would soon learn to love the game – not just winning. Experimenting with different moves was the absorbing part.

"Dinner smells good." Robert came in rubbing his hands together and made straight for the fire, sniffing the air appreciatively. He had been reading in the library since breakfast and was thoroughly chilled. "The library is like an ice box. If you run out of space, Grandma, you can use it as a meat store," he said, only half joking.

"Oh my goodness! I was so engrossed I quite forgot dinner." Marie practically ran from the room and Charles called, "Whatever you do don't burn my very favourite dinner, Mother."

"Which is?" Matthew asked curiously, who like Charles, loved every meal that was served up. "They are all so delicious, how can you choose?"

"Ah! You haven't tasted 'roast beef and Yorkshire pudding, á la Marie' yet," Charles assured him, rubbing his hands together in anticipation, as Laurie said, "Hear, hear."

"Why do we have to eat at lunch time on Sundays and Christmas? Why can't we stick to normal?" Alexander asked irritably. He had only just come down after having breakfast in bed, and certainly wasn't going to be ready for one of his grandmother's gigantic dinners.

"That is a very good question," David answered. "Just tradition I suppose."

"Stupid tradition if you ask me," he scowled.

"Well nobody did, so don't be rude to your grandfather," Gerald checked him, frowning heavily.

"Let's take the ladies a sherry," Charles intervened quickly. "Come with me Alexander," he ordered. Alexander followed him into the dining room where the drinks were set out on the sideboard and the table was laid ready for dinner. Pamela had been busy again, in spite of the fact that she never appeared to do much. Between them they managed to present a quality of living that normally took servants, he found himself thinking as he poured drinks. Glancing at Alexander's disgruntled expression, he sighed. The boy had never known anything less than this perfect life, why would he appreciate it? With this in mind, he said more tolerantly, "Try not to rock the boat. Your father is very tired and needs to relax. Don't rile him."

"If he's tired and irritable, why doesn't he go to bed early, as he would make me?"

The, truculent reply made Charles think of the confined months ahead for Gerald, and devastated by the thought, he snapped, "Take these to the kitchen, and for goodness sake try being pleasant for a change."

Alexander gave him a searching look as he took the tray of drinks. Uncle Charles was in a funny mood; no point in risking the driving lessons. With a lightning mood change he smiled radiantly. That always did the trick.

"Sorry, Uncle Charles. Of course I will do my best to keep Dad amiable, especially if it makes things easier for you. I know how difficult he can be."

He went, leaving Charles staring after him, asking himself how the conversation had swung round like that. The boy had twisted things to make it seem as if Gerald was the one at fault and that he, Charles, was complaining about him. He shook his head in disbelief. No! He could do without trying to work Alexander out at the moment. He picked up another tray of drinks and took them into the sitting room, muttering to himself that after tomorrow, there would be no further need for this awful secrecy.

CHAPTER SEVEN

Pamela awoke to find Gerald propped up on his pillows looking down at her. Their eyes met and she smiled sleepily as she slid her arm across him and held her face up to be kissed. This was always one of their favourite times to make love, but this time he resisted saying they must talk.

"Later," she murmured trying to pull him towards her.

"No. Please listen. It's very important," he insisted, reluctantly disentangling himself.

She realised that he was serious and sat up, shrugged her bare shoulders into a warm bed-jacket, plumped up the well filled pillows with their delicately embroidered slips, into a comfortable position and leant back, hands clasped.

"Ready," she said, blinking hard, to concentrate, and smothering an overwhelming desire to slide back under the soft sheets again.

Gerald hated to bring her carefree world crashing, but it couldn't be put off any longer. She sat motionless as he related the events of the last two weeks, her eyes never leaving him. He had expected anything other than quiet acceptance. Fear – anger – even hysterics maybe, because although a good nurse, when it came to family she panicked, but here she was saying matter-of-factly, "I have heard of this clinic; it is the best in the country. The sooner you can be admitted, the better."

"Can't wait to get rid of me, eh?" He gave a relieved smile.

"Something like that," she answered gently.

"Mother and Dad have to be told, and the boys, of course. Charles will have told Felicity by now."

She nodded realizing their anxiety in keeping it to themselves, so that everyone else could enjoy Christmas. Christmas seemed a million light years away now.

"Will you tell the boys? I'll tell Mother and Dad as soon as I'm dressed."

"Break it gently."

"Of course."

He met Felicity coming out of his parents' room. She took his hand and squeezed it, her blue eyes swimming with tears, as she shook her head to his questions.

"They don't know yet, do they?"

The clink of china and Marie saying, "Lovely cup of tea," reached him through the door. He knocked and saw his mother sitting up in bed balancing a tray on her lap, looking pretty and rosy from sleep; his father, tousle haired, rubbing his eyes was grumbling drowsily, "It's like Victoria Station in here this morning."

Gerald smiled in spite of himself. Memories were made of such scenes. It made him angry at being the one to spoil things. Their reaction was much as he expected, stricken looks, fear-filled eyes, but overall, concern for him. He left them sitting up in bed, staring at each other in wordless misery, his father's arm about his mother's shoulders. He closed the door behind him and slumped against it, his father's voice reaching him, comforting and encouraging.

"Come, dear, we have to be strong for Gerald. Pamela will be distraught, so we will have to help him with her – and the children. Charles must need to talk. It will have been hard on him."

Marie threw the covers back, dragging her thoughts from that other dreadful time when Philip was ill. They never thought he would die – but he had. An involuntary sob left her throat and David was at her side instantly.

"I know, I know, but it isn't the same," he said, his own face crumpling.

She leant against him for a moment then moved away with a determined, "Of course it isn't. I don't know why we are even thinking like that."

"That's my girl." He kissed her cheek.

She dressed with trembling fingers; David finally went to her aid and fastened the buttons on her dress, then poured her another cup of tea; (it was a bit stewed but still drinkable), then they composed themselves before leaving the room.

Downstairs the household was back to normal. Lorna was in the kitchen, Maisie was vacuuming the lounge and breakfast was laid in the dining room. Gerald was telling Laurie, who always arose early and Charles and Felicity were helping them all to porridge from a tureen on the sideboard. Charles held Marie's chair for her, his hands resting momentarily on her shoulders. Felicity kissed her then David, unable to speak. David just caught her hand and gripped hard.

"Should I go to Pamela?" Marie asked in a strained voice.

"She's with the boys. They will be down soon," Gerald reassured her.

Robert arrived first and went straight to his father. "Dad, how can I help?" He looked very scared and earnest. How could this happen to anyone as strong as his father?

"Thank you son. We will talk after breakfast, in the study."

Pamela arrived shortly after, looking extremely business-like, much to everyone's surprise. Her hand shook as she helped herself to the inevitable black coffee and orange juice, but other than that she was quite composed as she sat down and told Gerald that she had telephoned the London clinic, to ask about accommodation.

"What accommodation?"

"Apparently there is a small, family run hotel nearby that they are happy to recommend. I have booked a double room for Monday night, and confirmed that I can stay for as long as necessary. It's all arranged."

David and Marie looked relieved. Gerald stared. "But darling, I will be in there for months."

Chin up, eyes flashing, she said with quiet finality, "I know."

Gerald opened his mouth, closed it again and gave a reminiscent smile.

"What?" Pamela demanded.

"You reminded me then of that first day we met at Forest End and I had the temerity to question your orders. Those wonderful green eyes flashed and you shook your red head so hard, a lock of hair escaped from that starched, white cap. I thought you were the most enchanting thing I had ever seen and I fell for you in that moment."

"You caused me a lot of aggravation," she said sternly and then smiled into his eyes.

"What me?" he questioned innocently.

"Yes, you. How about when you set up a projector in the long ward and I went off duty, quite happily convinced they were all watching cartoons for three hours, when instead, you had brought along two, very, shall we say 'unwholesome' films? And to add to your sins, you laced their tea with whisky in the interval. The poor nurse was run off her feet, wondering why they kept on asking for more tea, but I suppose we should thank you for the quietest night we ever had on the ward, once we managed to settle them down that was." They both smiled at the memory and everyone else laughed loudly.

"Well the poor souls needed cheering up. That young Cockney boy went home that day. You remember, always cracking jokes. Great character. Lost an eye and wore a patch. Always taking off Nelson."

"Joe. Little Joe Watts," Pamela reminded him. "*He* had me tied in knots as well. It was a favourite send up of his. It went: 'What's your name?' 'That's right Miss.' 'No, I said what's your name?' 'Yes Miss. That's right Miss.' It took several more attempts, and I wasn't sure if he was deaf or daft, until I caught his mates laughing. Corny by today's standards, I suppose."

"Very poignant, sad and happy memories." Robert had been listening, fascinated. They had never shared wartime experiences. To be fair, perhaps he had never shown any interest in *their* personal war. Now 'The Second World War' by Winston Churchill – that was different. That was real history! For the first time, perhaps because things were in danger of changing, it registered they had actually met *and* lived through that era. Their lives hadn't always been as orderly as today. He looked at them with new eyes, trying to imagine his stern father as the instigator of such a prank, and picture his mother as anything less than elegant, living in less than their present comfort. How real could history get? A good subject for his essay!

Sophie and Matthew had slipped in and were also enjoying the story.

"It's like hearing a love story unfold," Matthew murmured, as Sophie begged for more.

Gerald and Pamela looked at each other, trying to think of something amusing. "How about the time I bribed a nurse to tell you the new doctor's car had broken down and he was phoning from the local pub, a mile away. Would you drive out and rescue him? That was the first time I asked you to marry me," he said sounding pleased with himself.

"I said you must be mad. I was absolutely furious at being dragged out of a warm bed, but no one else could drive. It was freezing cold, pouring with rain and of course, I wasn't informed for some strange reason that the doctor had already arrived and was, even then, tucked up in his own nice warm room. I had no choice – or so I thought," she glowered at him.

"I realised that too. I showed him his room," he admitted placidly.

"You didn't value your life much," Robert chuckled.

"Those were the lengths I had to go to. Your mother would never have forgiven herself if she had missed her big chance with me."

Pamela spluttered.

"Faint heart never won fair lady," Laurie said, shaking with laughter.

Gerald got up and went to the sideboard. "I'm ready for breakfast after all that; come on everybody."

Breakfast had been keeping warm on the hotplates. It had to be said that it was past its best; even so every last morsel vanished.

"He did it again," Charles murmured to Laurie. Laurie pursed his lips. "He is a great loss to the diplomatic service."

David was anxious to get down to business and they went to the study. "Care to join us Laurie?" Laurie was pleased to be included.

"I am going to the hospital to hand in my notice," Pamela told Marie. "Unless you need me," she added, slipping her arm through Marie's as they walked across the hall.

"You go dear, and – thank you." She gave Pamela's arm a squeeze, her eyes bright with unshed tears. "I am so relieved you are going with him."

"You mustn't upset yourself. He will be fine. They have wonderful new drugs these days; it isn't the deadly disease it used to be. The clinic is the best; I know that for sure, I wouldn't let him go otherwise. He will be fit and well before you know it." Marie was reassured. If Pamela could be so unflustered, that had to be a good sign. They parted at the foot of the stairs, as Alexander reached them.

"You took your time, Robert came down ages ago."

"What's the great rush? He isn't going for days yet," he said in a bored voice.

"You could show a little more concern."

He went towards the study, muttering, "Dear Robert," and blaming his father for, her bad mood.

As he entered, his grandfather, was saying, "I think we should opt out of the Sheffield company and let Brian and his sons take full control again. *They* are in a position to buy us out now, but more importantly it would cut *our* workload. I will take over for Gerald in the meantime. How say you?"

Gerald spread his hands in resignation. "What do you think Charles?"

"I'm in favour. You have done too much travelling. I wouldn't advise going back to as much, even when you are fit again. Southampton is doing tremendous business, and later, if you still need a new challenge, we will find something closer to home, perhaps." He looked at Gerald. "I know you will find it hard, but there is no need to work twenty-six hours a day to keep bread on the table any more."

"More time at home Dad, doing a bit of sailing and walking along the cliffs," Robert volunteered as Alexander groaned inwardly. He was leaning against a bookcase, listening indifferently. None of this was of slightest interest to him, and then his ears pricked up, as Gerald turned his attention to Robert.

"You asked if you could help. Well you can, *very* considerably. I need to know that Granddad isn't travelling alone. I want you to accompany him absolutely everywhere and lighten the load."

There was silence as his words sunk in, then Robert said haltingly, "You mean leave University?"

"You won't be sorry. In a year's time when you are twenty, you will have a seat on the board. Financially you will be independent. How about it, son? Are you with us?"

Put like that he couldn't refuse. "Of course, Dad. Anything you say."

"What about me?" Alexander demanded.

"You will finish college and get your 'A' levels. After that, I have in mind for you to start in the export department. You will *start* at the bottom and *learn* the business thoroughly. Later on, it could involve travel. It would depend on your aptitude really – and your behaviour of course," he couldn't help adding.

Alexander was impressed. A good second best to drama school, which he knew was out anyway, but he would show reluctance – there could be more perks that way. "Drama school is out then?"

"It was never an option," Gerald said coldly.

"When do I get a seat on the board?"

"All in good time," David chipped in, seeing Gerald's temper rising. "Any comments Laurie?"

"I think you are doing the right thing. It is obviously the time to regroup and I will do anything within my power to help."

"Nothing much can be done until the New Year, when everyone starts back to work, but you could put Brian in the picture," Charles said to David.

They talked on about matters far above Robert and Alexander's heads, until Pamela, calling to say she was back, broke the meeting up and David said, "We are neglecting the ladies. How about we suggest a walk? The sun is actually shining and it's time we had some fresh air."

The next four days flew by. Pamela packed and made preparations, leaving Abigail with a full set of instructions and a telephone number where she could be reached, with strict orders that Marie was not to be worried by any matters concerning the boys. Abigail knew she only meant Alexander.

New Year's Eve was unusually quiet, with Pamela and Gerald having departed that morning. Marie was subdued – David was restless. Laurie was afraid that he might be in the way but David persuaded him to stay, with Felicity adding sensibly, "The house will be cold, your housekeeper isn't expecting you back until tomorrow."

"I don't know why you don't just live with us," David said matter-of-factly. "Why doesn't he Mother?"

"It would make sense," Marie agreed, "you know you are welcome, Laurie."

"I may take you up on that after April." The enigmatic statement hung between them while they waited for him to elaborate, but he didn't and no more was said. That was one of the things he liked about them. Always interested never prying.

Sophie burst into the sitting room, bringing cold air with her. She and Matthew had been walking along the cliffs and she looked radiant, with windswept hair and rosy cheeks. Kneeling down beside Marie's chair, she asked seriously, "Grandma, would it be awful of us to go to the Yacht Club dance tonight?" The words came out in a rush as she looked from Marie to her mother, apologetically.

Marie touched the long, blonde hair, tenderly. "Not at all. Uncle Gerald would hate you to miss it, because of him; go and enjoy yourselves."

Felicity rested her fresh young cheek on hers and held her.

By seven-thirty the young ones were gathered in the hall. The boys were well groomed in suits and ties and Sophie looked delightful in a cornflower blue dress that exactly matched her eyes, and a piece of silver tinsel set in a crown on top of her hair.

"You look like the Christmas tree fairy." Charles frowned disapprovingly.

Robert leapt to her defence laughing. "It's New Year's Eve Uncle Charles."

"Well you three take care of her. That neckline is far too low as well," he said grumpily, as Sophie stood on tiptoe and kissed his cheek, with an airy "Bye, Daddy. Happy New Year."

"I assume that means don't wait up. Who is driving?"

"Taxi, sir," Matthew volunteered, just as the doorbell rang and Alexander opened the door with a sweeping gesture. *He* was positively overflowing with exuberance. His parents were away and he was going to enjoy himself.

"Mm. Well not too much drink and no noise when you come in," was Charles's parting shot. They were gone, leaving the hall silent and somehow empty.

Felicity took his arm and smiled up at him teasingly. "Why do I get the impression you wish she was still a little girl?"

"Rubbish! Although I tell you, raising a girl is a whole different ball game to raising a boy," he said gloomily.

"She won't come to any harm while she is with Matthew and Robert," Laurie said with a comforting pat on his shoulder. "Now come and enjoy this duck in orange sauce. It smells wonderful."

CHAPTER EIGHT

The driver edged forward in the line of taxies waiting to disgorge their passengers. In the general melee, Alexander spied a group of college lads and wound the window down, but they disappeared.

"Same class as you?" Matthew asked with interest. In the two weeks he had stayed at Anders Folly, none of Alexander's friends had visited and he hadn't moved out of the house, which struck him as odd for a boy of seventeen who gave the impression of being bored.

"Just people in the same year. Certainly not in the same class," Alexander replied in a disparaging tone.

Robert tutted, but the remark explained his lack of friends.

"Oh look, there's Diana. Who is that with her?" Sophie cried. "And there's Alison – and Jane. Oh, I haven't seen them for ages, I can't wait to introduce you," she said hugging Matthew's arm.

He groaned. "Just promise me I won't have to dance with them," he begged.

"There's only six," Robert teased as they alighted.

Inside the festively decorated clubhouse, people greeted each other whilst searching for their tables. Each round table was covered with a bright red cloth and held a tall, tallow candle in a holly-covered holder. The entire hall was hung with brightly coloured garlands and coloured lanterns, stretching from wall to wall. In front of the stage was a glittering Father Christmas, complete with reindeers, pulling a fishing smack, inviting guests to throw in their loose change for the local fishermen's fund. Covering the high ceiling an enormous fishing net filled with multi-coloured balloons, waited to be released at midnight.

Gerald's permanently reserved table was in the far corner of the spacious hall, not too close to the band, at Father's special request, Alexander told Matthew.

"Can't abide holding conversations in mime." he imitated as they sat down.

"Mother and Dad come here regularly and they like family and friends to join them," Robert explained to Matthew.

"Quite so. A good host always considers comfort."

Alexander looked up. His interest had already been aroused when he noted Matthew's evening suit, because if there was one thing that Alexander knew about, it was clothes and that jacket was top-drawer he assessed shrewdly. And now he sounded experienced.

"Even Mummy and Daddy come sometimes," Sophie laughed.

"And it has even been known for Grandma and Granddad to come, on special occasions." Robert pulled an awestruck face.

"Like when the Royal yacht berths," Matthew rejoined with easy humour. "Don't knock it. Home loving people are rare these days."

"The rarer the better for me," Alexander said getting up. "I'm going to ask that wicked looking girl over there for a dance."

They watched him make his way towards a girl wearing a strapless, scarlet dress, who was standing at the bar with a group of other, unaccompanied girls.

"Oops, I think he is out of his league. Marcia must be twenty-three." Sophie gave a worried frown, expecting a rebuff, fearing his reaction, but apparently her fears were needless, because the girl moved on to the dance floor with him.

"Would you take him for seventeen?" Matthew asked with amusement. "Come on let's dance. I can't wait to hold you," he whispered, smiling deep into her eyes. Alexander forgotten, she followed him on to the floor where he held her closely, as they shuffled to 'Bridge Over Troubled Waters'.

"You reach my heart in more ways than one," he murmured softly, bending to kiss the top of her head, as the music stopped and a girl's voice interrupted the moment.

"Sophie! Good to see you; where are you sitting?"

"Alison, good to see you too and didn't I see Jane with you? This is Matthew. Matthew this is Alison. We went to school together."

They shook hands and Alison flashed her eyes. "I can see why you have kept *him* to yourself. I'll find Jane and bring her over. I can see Robert at your table and *we* are on our own. We'll come and join you." Without waiting for an answer she went to find Jane.

"Nothing like waiting to be asked," Matthew murmured.

"Hope Robert won't mind," Sophie said as they made their way back to the table where, within two minutes, Jane and Alison joined them.

"This is jolly decent of you Sophie. Didn't think we would get a seat tonight, not having booked and it's lovely to see you again Robert. And this is the gorgeous Matthew, I hear." Jane turned a dazzling smile on Matthew, that didn't quite reach her eyes. She was medium height, medium brown hair and medium, Robert decided at a glance. How was it that no other girl measured up to Sophie?

Alexander came back with the girl in red, who was impressed that he had a table. He settled her in a chair, introduced her and then said, "How about some wine? Will you do the honours Robert? My round." With that, he disappeared to the gents. Robert smiled to himself and went to order the wine, amused by Alexander's wiliness. He would have been refused drinks; the bar staff all knew he was under-age. Oh well, where was the harm? It was New Year's Eve and he did look good in his evening suit, he thought proudly. Let him have some fun to make up for not going to drama school. Devastation at the thought of not returning to Oxford swamped over him. Those wonderful, quiet rooms, with a sense of history pervading every corner, where one could work for hours without interruption, and the learned Dons, always there to point the way. The thought of never seeing it all again left an unbearable ache that refused to leave. He came out of his reverie to find himself at the head of the queue, with the barman giving him an amused look and requesting his order for the third time.

"I thought you were stoned already Robert." He gave a cheeky grin.

"Sorry." Robert grinned back. "Haven't even *had* a drink yet. Send four bottles of wine to table fifteen, will you please?"

"Don't know what you will be like after you *have* had a drink then," the barman joked, writing down the order and passing it to a waiter.

The wine arrived at the table and Robert's jaw dropped as he saw Alexander pull out a roll of banknotes and carelessly toss two on to the tray, with an airy, "Keep the change," to the waiter. Sophie's eyebrows vanished in to her wispy fringe, as she first stared in amazement, then let out a giggle, as she caught sight of Robert's expression, but the others were unaware of anything unusual so it remained their private joke. Robert had hated being seventeen and uncertain. At least Alexander didn't suffer from that problem he observed – quite the opposite in fact. He was standing at the table holding forth with considerable success. The girls were giggling and flattering him with their admiration and the more they laughed, the wittier he seemed to become, until he had a crowd around him, including Robert who was also laughing.

Matthew and Sophie got up to dance and Marcia stood up. "I want to dance," she demanded, pulling Alexander towards the floor. A cheer went round the small gathering, as he was torn reluctantly away from his audience. He was slightly annoyed. People had been listening to him and it had given him a tremendous buzz. His good humour was quickly restored however, when he saw how the men were looking at her, and envying him.

The evening progressed with the usual novelty dances. 'The 'Twist', which was still relatively new to that part of Cornwall, created a big stir, with Marcia the centre of attention, performing expertly and encouraging everyone to have a go. Alexander quickly got the hang of it and was very excited by the attention they got as a couple. A buffet was served at ten o'clock, and after more dancing it was nearly midnight. Alexander and Marcia decided to go outside for a breath of fresh air before it struck twelve. At five minutes to twelve, Alexander returned to the table alone. He looked bright-eyed and was a little unsteady on his feet, but other than that was still full of life and went to join a group that he had been talking to earlier.

Robert found himself alone and looked around for Matthew and Sophie. Matthew's tall figure was nowhere to be seen, but catching sight of long, blonde hair he made his way over. She was standing with her back to him and he put both arms round her waist and said in her ear, "Come and dance with me."

She turned and Robert recoiled. It wasn't Sophie! He was looking into a pair of laughing, hazel eyes, which held as much surprise as his own. In that moment he thought he must be, dreaming – the girl was so like Sophie. The same hair, same height, same wide smile. Realising he was staring, and still had his hand on her waist, he snatched it away. "Sorry, I thought you were Sophie." He still couldn't take his eyes from her face.

"I believe you because I saw you with her," she laughed.

"Do you know Sophie then?"

"No. I'm new to the area but I noticed our hair is similar."

"Are you alone?" he asked, thinking in the next moment what a stupid question it was to ask a girl like this, but he couldn't think of anything else to say and he was desperate to keep her talking.

"My partner is on the committee and he has gone to help count the donations. I understand they announce the result at the end of the evening." She smiled up at him shyly. "If the offer is still on, I would love to dance though – as long as Sophie won't mind."

Robert drew a breath. Could this be happening? "No, Sophie won't mind," he said faintly. They swayed in silent unison to a dreamy waltz. He was acutely aware of her hand in his and the softness of her body as he held her. Her perfume was fragrant and she was as light as a feather in his arms. If only the evening wasn't nearly over. He had to see her again. What if she was engaged, or even married to this committee member? He knew them all; who was he? He searched desperately for something to say, but was completely tongue-tied. The dance ended; he escorted her off the floor, where her partner, Colin Deveral, a likeable, fresh faced, local farmer, claimed her. Robert's heart sank. She was laughing at something he was whispering in her ear and he realised he hadn't even asked her name. At the end of that dance, Colin just had time to announce they had collected two hundred pounds for the Fishermen's fund, before a ship's bell rang out for midnight and a loud cheer went up. The band started playing 'The Conga' and someone led the merrymakers outside, around the clubhouse, and back inside again. Robert saw her in the middle of the long line, with Colin behind her. And then again, on the other side of the circle for 'Auld Lang Syne', but he didn't get another opportunity to speak to her. Then just as the band finished playing 'God Save the Queen', she appeared beside him.

"Goodnight Robert, and I forgot to say Happy New Year." She reached up and kissed his cheek. "I hope we meet again."

Again he was lost for words, until she turned to leave. "I don't even know your name." It came out in a rush and she turned back. Their eyes met and held.

"Celina."

There was a moment's pause before he said, "Yes of course, it would be."

She gave him a quizzical look.

"It's Latin for heavenly."

She gave a slow smile, as she backed away with a small wave of her fingers. Sophie watched the little exchange and felt a stab of jealousy.

Matthew had also been watching. "This is the one; are you prepared?" His insight surprised and embarrassed her. She turned with an enquiring, "How do you know? They have only just met."

"Look at her. She is everything he has been looking for. You could be twins. Are you absolutely certain it wouldn't work between you? I would rather know now than have us all regret it in the future."

"I have never been more certain of anything. I am *in love* with you, but I do love Robert and I shall be happy for him, even if a bit of me doesn't want him to find anyone to replace me." She hugged him, laughing at her own foolishness.

On the way home in the taxi, Sophie suddenly remembered Marcia and asked Alexander where she had disappeared to.

"She had to leave."

"She didn't even say goodnight; that was a bit rude after spending the evening at our table."

"Don't make a big deal out of it; we will never see her again, anyway," he said offhandedly.

"It just wasn't like Marcia, that's all," Sophie insisted.

"How would you know?" he demanded.

"We went to school together."

"Will you shut up about it?"

"Steady on," Matthew said quietly.

Sophie was sitting between him and Robert on the back seat. Alexander was in the front, next to the driver. Robert was still thinking about Celina and really didn't want this conversation, but he could hear by Alexander's voice that it was going to get out of hand if he didn't intervene.

"You worry too much," he said gently, touching Sophie's hand. "I'm sure there is a perfectly simple explanation."

"Not that it is any of your business," Alexander retorted hotly, just as the taxi drew to a halt in front of the house. Flinging open the door, he jerked himself out on to the drive, and slammed the car door. Robert winced – so much for being quiet he thought, beginning to get a bad feeling about Alexander's aggression.

By the time he had paid the driver, Alexander had opened the door, and they made for the kitchen.

"I'll put the kettle on," Matthew offered. He didn't like the way Alexander had spoken to Sophie and was about to say so, when Robert confronted his brother.

"That was out of order in front of a stranger."

"He was only a taxi driver, for God's sake."

"What has happened? Why are you so upset?"

Alexander hesitated, glowered then seemed to make up his mind.

"If you must know, that little trollop stole my roll of money, jumped into her car and drove off, before I could stop her. I feel pretty silly, so let that be an end to all of the fuss."

They stood open-mouthed until Matthew said, "Aren't you going to inform the police?"

Alexander looked startled, but quickly recovered. "Have you got any idea what my father's reaction would be? He would go berserk at the merest hint of scandal and we can't afford to upset him now, of all times."

"You're right of course," Robert said slowly with a worried frown. "She shouldn't be allowed to get away with it though."

"Perhaps it would be better to let it drop. There are Grandma and Granddad to think about as well. They are worried enough as it is," Sophie said.

"Absolutely," Alexander agreed.

The incident had sobered them and they went to bed in a worried mood, all except for Alexander who was relieved that the incident was to be forgotten.

The following morning, they rose late and Sophie and Matthew went in the car with them when Charles took Laurie home. It was a week before their return to London, and Sophie needed new shoes. Matthew hummed and hawed and in the end, Sophie went to the shops on her own while he went to Laurie's house and it was agreed that Charles would pick them up at four-thirty. Matthew sighed with relief, as they dropped her off, confiding that shopping with Sophie for shoes was an experience not to be repeated. "She tries on every pair in town, and then buys the very first pair."

"Just like her mother. I think they do it purposely so that we will leave them to go shopping alone."

Matthew looked puzzled. "So why do they ask us to go in the first place?"

"Afraid they will hurt our feelings," Charles replied phlegmatically.

Laurie chortled. "So by asking you, their conscience is clear; then they make sure you don't enjoy it, so you won't want to go again? Is that what you are saying?"

Charles pondered for a moment. "That's about it."

Matthew gave a confused frown.

"Take no notice m' boy, women are the most unselfish creatures ever born."

"You haven't met my mother," Matthew mumbled inaudibly, as they arrived at the house.

Charles retrieved Laurie's suitcase from the boot and handed it to Matthew.

"Make sure to carry it upstairs for him, would you?"

"Of course."

Laurie had already made his way up the path to the front door, where he turned and raised his hand as Charles called, "See you later," and Matthew caught up with him. The house was warm and smelt deliciously of freshly baked scones.

"Ah, Peggy has made tea for us. She will have gone home by now. Make yourself at home," Laurie invited. They hung their coats on the old fashioned hallstand, situated at the foot of the stairs. It was dark oak, carved with laurel leaves, and had four brass hooks either side and a place for umbrellas with green painted metal drip trays. In the centre there was a glove box with a lid that opened upwards and an oblong mirror above it. Next to it, a wooden plaque with a picture of 'St Michael's Mount' held a clothes brush and shoehorn and next to that hung an antique barometer. Matthew imagined Laurie tapping it each morning, and smiled. It was all from a lovely, bygone era and he thought that it epitomised Laurie, with its place for everything and everything in its place, simplicity.

In the sitting room, a coal fire burned brightly in the brick hearth, and a wide bay with French doors overlooked a small garden, beyond which, the sea glistened tranquilly. A round table covered with a white cloth, held an appetizing array of sandwiches, scones, strawberry jam and thick clotted cream, set on Royal Albert china. Dark red, heavily fringed curtains, drawn right back, allowed watery shafts of sunlight to slant across a brown leather Chesterfield suite. It was comfortable and homely, with just the right amount of organised clutter to look lived-in, Matthew thought, as his attention, was caught by an ancient radiogram, with a variety of records in a rack on the wall above.

"Does it really still work?" he asked in wonderment.

"Like me, as old as it is, it still works," Laurie assured him.

"Some people never get old."

"True, true. It's mostly in the mind. Keep that active and you have a head start. I'll put the kettle on." Matthew followed him into the hall and picked up the suitcase. "Point me in the right direction."

"Top of the stairs on the right. Thank you m' boy."

He returned in seconds and whilst the kettle boiled, made friends with Isador (Issie for short), Laurie's overfed, white, Persian cat. When the tea was made, he carried the tray in and they sat at the table in the bay, watching the daylight fade.

After a while, Matthew said, "I would value your opinion, if I'm not taking advantage of your hospitality."

"My time is yours, and welcome."

He listened attentively, whilst Matthew poured out his concerns for Sophie.

"Our life is different in every way. Would it be fair?"

"Surely there will be advantages as well – her career for instance?"

"That is one of my main concerns. I am not convinced she will become a concert pianist."

"How come?"

He looked downcast. "Sophie plays beautifully, but not brilliantly. She will know for sure this coming year."

"You sound as if you know about these things."

Matthew gave a sigh. "I may as well tell you; it will come out eventually. Have you heard of Clare Windsor?"

"The famous pianist?"

"She is my mother." There was no joy in his voice.

"Is that a problem?"

"The lifestyle could be. There is no room for anything but music, and she plans for my life to run in the same pattern. Celebrity parties, no friends as such, just people who are useful to your career. Living in an overheated penthouse suite is all I have known, until now. There will be an almighty row when she hears about Sophie. I was allowed to come to England and study because she considered it safer than Paris – and it fits in with her current tour."

"She will be against the idea of marriage then?"

"Totally. In her mind, I must be dedicated to music. Until I met Sophie, I was content I suppose. I know now, there is so much more. Music will always be a major part of my life but not to the exclusion of a wife and proper home."

"You mean like Anders Folly?"

Matthew's expression relaxed. "*That* is my dream now."

"Understandable, but it takes special people to make a home like that. Sophie is one of them and you are doing her an injustice. She will cope with whatever life throws at her, as long as you love her. There is a very strong person under that gentle character, at least let her make up her own mind. We will all be sad for her if she doesn't achieve her ambition, but certainly not disappointed in her musical ability, and she will make the best of things. Just be there for her, as the family will be."

They ate in silence until Matthew glanced up and caught Laurie looking at him.

"Why haven't you told Sophie about your mother? I would have thought that you would be really proud."

"Oh I am, but I'm not ashamed of my feelings, because for the first time in my life I have a chance to be just plain Matthew Willard, and not Clare Windsor's son. If that sounds selfish, ask yourself if Sophie's family would have been so at ease with me, if they had known my background, or even Sophie herself. That is what is so wonderful: they accept me for me and not for who my mother is. It isn't even known at the school. If I make the grade in England, it has to be on my own merit."

Laurie gave an enlightened, "Aah."

"Now you will think I am paranoid."

"Not a bit. Your secret is safe with me."

"I knew it would be." He spread a scone thickly with jam and cream, as Laurie had and took a bite. Laurie smiled at his look of bliss, and was pouring them a second cup of tea, when the doorbell rang. He looked at his pocket watch and started to rise. "Too early for Sophie, who can that be?"

"Perhaps Charles finished early. Let me go," Matthew offered, getting to his feet.

"He has got a key, it can't be him."

As Matthew opened the door, a distressed Sophie shot inside and burst out, "Alexander has gone too far this time." Her cheeks red with anger and eyes full of tears she marched through to the sitting room.

Laurie caught her shoulder in alarm. "Has he hurt you?"

"No, no." She calmed down, seeing she was upsetting him. "I just don't know what to do for the best. I suppose I will have to tell Daddy, but he doesn't need it right now," she groaned.

"Tell me what he has done," Laurie insisted as Matthew peeled off her coat and manoeuvred her into an armchair.

"I bumped in to Marcia as soon as I got to the shops. She was very upset, and asked me who Alexander was; she couldn't believe he was Robert's younger brother – well there isn't much family likeness, is there? And she wouldn't have remembered him from school because he was only eleven when she left. I thought she wanted to see him again, to return his money, but then she told me how badly he behaved last night. I defended him at first because he told us she stole his money, when they went outside for a breath of air."

Laurie looked shocked. "I know the Williams family. That doesn't sound likely. They are good people. Carry on."

"Apparently, Alexander wanted to walk down to the shore, and within seconds he was all over her. When she objected, he ripped her dress right down the front then tossed the roll of money at her, telling her to buy a new one. She

111

came down to spend Christmas and New Year with her parents because her husband is posted abroad. She has been in the army herself since she was seventeen and they have quarters at Aldershot. Anyway, luckily she had put her coat on, before going outside and the car keys were in the pocket, so she drove home. Fortunately her parents were in bed, and didn't see the state she was in."

"Do you believe her?" Matthew asked.

Sophie nodded. "She took me to her parents' home; showed me the dress and the roll of money, which, by the way, is plain paper, with a one pound note wrapped around it. If she tells her parents they will go to the police and her commanding officer will find out. And she dreads what her husband would do to Alexander, because he would be put on a charge. It is all very embarrassing, but after seeing the dress and the money, there is *no* doubt who's telling the truth. She was so angry at Alexander's accusation, I thought she would tell her parents and blow the consequences. I persuaded her to let Daddy deal with him, and we would get in touch this evening. I hope she waits."

Laurie got up to put more coal on the fire and switch the light on. The room had darkened since the sun had gone down and it felt quite chill.

"Leave it with me. No need to worry your father," he said abruptly, adding softly, "Pop the kettle on Matthew; he will be here soon."

Sophie gave him a silent hug and he patted her shoulders.

"I have known the family for years. Marcia will trust me to deal with the matter. Say nothing to Alexander. Come now smile," he said as they heard the key in the front door.

*

The telephone rang and it was Laurie, wanting Alexander to go to his house urgently.

"What does he want?" Alexander grumbled, irritated at having his television disturbed.

"Laurie wouldn't send for you if it wasn't important. Get a taxi." Robert handed him a pound note.

He got up, anticipating one of Laurie's generous gestures. Probably feeling sentimental about Dad going to hospital – things couldn't be better as far as he was concerned.

An hour later he marched in to the library, where Robert was sitting and shut the door firmly behind him.

"What was it all about then?" Robert stretched lazily and put his book down.

"You may well ask."

Robert closed his book. "Go on then."

"Marcia spun him a story and he called me, to get my side of things. It won't go any further."

"So did you get your money back?"

"Uncle Laurie sorted everything."

Robert shook his head. "I don't understand why she went to him in the first place."

"Frightened by what she had done, I suppose. Let's forget it. It's freezing in here. I'm going to the sitting room."

Sophie and Matthew were curled up on the settee. It irritated Alexander beyond reason. Why couldn't they do that mushy stuff somewhere else? He turned the television on and sat down without a word. Robert sat on a stool, close to the fire. He looked frozen, in spite of the thick, Arran jumper that Abigail had knitted him.

"Why don't you use a sleeping bag, if you must sit in the library? Look how cold you are," Sophie scolded him.

"I would still be there if Alex hadn't mentioned how cold it was. I don't notice it when I'm reading."

"It won't do you any good," she tutted.

"Speaking of good. Uncle Laurie solved the problem of Marcia. Tell them, Alex."

Alexander gritted his teeth. What business was it of theirs? Sophie shouldn't have poked her nose in, in the first place.

"I saw Marcia earlier. She apologised for last night and returned the money, so there is no need to mention the subject again; she is embarrassed enough as it is," he said curtly.

Sophie looked at him and then at Matthew, who shook his head blankly. Robert, sensing the silence, turned from the fire and saw Sophie's expression.

"What?"

"That isn't true," Sophie said quietly.

"Yes it is. Uncle Laurie has sorted it out."

"It *isn't* true. I have seen the dress and the so-called money. Marcia told me the whole story, and I told Uncle Laurie. That is why he sent for Alexander."

Alexander had gone a dull red and his slate grey eyes were almost black with hate as he sprung to his feet, glaring at her.

"Oh, and you believe her instead of me, of course." He leant against the fireplace with one arm and looked into the flames, his mind racing, then, with one of his lightning changes, he grinned at Robert, who was standing beside him, looking dazed.

113

"It was only a bit of fun. You should have seen her face when I ripped the dress! It was so funny; just like the Dean Martin film." He laughed loudly at the memory.

"And the money roll? Which film did that come from?" Sophie asked scathingly.

"Oh, that was from an old James Cagney gangster film. *That* was really good." He giggled, as he mistook their amazement for amusement.

"Funny to you maybe, but as I'm sure Uncle Laurie pointed out, if Marcia's parents or husband find out, you will be in dire trouble and your parents will be told, no matter *how* ill your father is; so don't brag to your friends, these things have a way of circulating."

Matthew spoke with such sternness that Alexander's flippant mood disappeared.

"Will someone please tell me what all this talk of dresses and films and money is about?" Robert interrupted impatiently.

Sophie explained, while Alexander bluffed and blustered, "It was only meant to be a bit of fun, for God's sake."

"Marcia may tell her parents anyway," Robert insisted.

"She'd better not. She promised. *And* it cost me fifty pounds!" Alexander exploded, as Robert groaned, "Is there no end to this?"

"Where did you get fifty pounds from?" Sophie gasped.

"Uncle Laurie was going to give me a hundred for my seventeenth, now I shall only get fifty." Alexander gave the stone fireplace a sullen kick. "There was no *need* to pay her *anything*. She is worried to death about it coming out. That was my money and he gave it to her to make amends; what amends? All over a stupid dress." He kicked the fireplace again and scuffed out of the room, muttering about stupid women. They were left looking at each other, listening to him stomp upstairs to the top of the house.

"He *really* doesn't think he has done anything wrong," Robert said incredulously.

The rest of the week flew by. Robert haunted the sailing club hoping to see Celina. She was constantly in his thoughts and he dreamed of seeing her again. Sophie and Matthew joined him twice and she commented on his restlessness.

"He is looking for the girl. I thought you would realise," Matthew said eventually.

As they returned home the second night, Sophie said, out of the blue, "Celina has had to go to her mother, who is very ill in hospital. Colin doesn't know when she will be back, but she is living at the farm with his family." And as

Robert's face fell. "Oh and did I mention that Colin is her married cousin?" She added with wide-eyed innocence.

Robert gave her a resounding kiss on her cheek. "Have I ever told you how much I love you?"

"I shall never get tired of hearing it," she laughed, delighted that his world had been set to rights a little. She knew what it was costing him to forfeit his last year at Oxford.

*

The decorations were down, the piano had been restored to the east wing and the house was practically back to normal, but the light heartedness was missing. However, the news from Pamela was that Gerald was responding well to treatment, and hopefully his stay at the clinic might not be as long as anticipated. Even so, Felicity and Marie knew that, when the men went travelling, the house was going to be dreadfully empty with just them and Alexander. Felicity was glad now, that Charles had persuaded her to take driving lessons. Her test was the coming week and hopefully she would pass and be able to take Marie out shopping, because Pamela was a great miss in that department as well.

CHAPTER NINE

The weather was kind for Sophie and Matthew's last weekend, and on the Sunday morning they decided to walk along the cliff tops to the Point, then back along the beaches when the tide was out.

Robert was in his usual spot, making the most of his remaining day, before he and David set off the next morning. Their hotel was booked for three nights, which would give them Tuesday for the Board meeting and leave Wednesday free for Robert to explore the accounts department, where he would work later.

Alexander was keeping out of the way. He would be glad when they were all gone. Anyway, he thought life was far less demanding up here. He could watch what he wanted to on television, dress up and practise his imitations without interruption and Abigail was there to fetch and carry. For a fleeting moment a small knot of fear gripped him at the thought of not having this place... but no, just over a year and he would be free to do whatever he wanted; he wouldn't need any of this *or* them. He heard the telephone in the distance and disinterestedly guessed that it was Laurie. He always phoned when he was ready for Charles to fetch him. Well Laurie wasn't one of his favourite people either. He looked at the big nursery clock. It was two minutes past ten o'clock. Early! Laurie never rang until about twelve.

And that was exactly what Marie was thinking as she picked up the receiver and heard a woman's voice say, "I understand that Matthew Willard is staying there. Be good enough to tell him his Mother is calling."

There was a small silence as Marie got over her surprise, then she explained that he had gone walking and wouldn't be back for two or three hours. There was a loud 'tutt', and the voice told someone at that end, "The maid says he won't be back for hours. It really is very inconvenient. We must leave by five, at the latest."

Marie smiled to herself and spoke into the mouthpiece. "This is Mrs Anders speaking. I will give Matthew your message and he will telephone you as soon as he comes in."

"We have just arrived at the Trelawney Hotel, about five miles from you, and I really must insist on seeing him before we return to London tonight, ready for our flight to New York tomorrow."

"I can only ask him to ring you as soon as he comes in. They should be back by about two o'clock."

"This really is most inconsiderate of him." Her voice was plaintive.

"Was he expecting you, then?" Marie asked, puzzled that Matthew had not mentioned it.

"Well no, I haven't spoken to him since before Christmas, when he was staying at The Dorchester. Then, when I rang two days ago, the hotel said he had been invited to stay with a friend. No telephone number, no address; just a brief message to say he would be in touch when the term started. It has taken this long to trace him."

Marie began to feel sorry for her. She had obviously gone to a lot of trouble to see her son.

"Matthew will be back in London tomorrow lunchtime, if that helps," she said sympathetically.

"No help at all, our plane leaves at nine-thirty in the morning. If I don't see him today, it will be months before we see each other."

She sounded so woebegone that Marie's soft heart melted. It wasn't a good day for visitors and she hoped David wouldn't be too upset at being interrupted, so it was with some misgiving that she said, "Well, if you would care to join us, lunch will be at two o'clock; that way you will see him as soon as possible."

She waited, hoping the voice would refuse.

"Are you sure it won't put you to too much trouble?" the voice simpered.

"We are a big family anyway." Marie gave directions on how to find the house and replaced the receiver, feeling apprehensive.

Felicity echoed her uncertainty. "A bit soon to meet the parents. I'm not sure I'm ready for this yet. We've only just got used to the idea of Sophie having a boyfriend."

"Sorry, she sounded so desperate."

Felicity put her arm around her shoulders. "It sounds to me as if you did exactly what she intended you to," she said shrewdly.

They had intended to eat in the warm kitchen, as they always did on Lorna's day off, but now the table had to be laid and David was persuaded to light the fire in the dining room.

He gave a disapproving grunt. "Thought we were going to have a quiet day. Suppose I'll have to get changed now," he grumbled, looking down at his comfy old cardigan. Charles arrived with Laurie as he was carrying logs in.

"Here let me do that. Why aren't you getting one of the lads to help?" he chided.

"They are like buses, never one in sight when you want one." David's ill humour never lasted long and he was looking forward to his game of chess. Laurie was already sitting by the chessboard, waiting for him.

Charles was no better pleased at the interruption. He would also be going to Hampshire the next day, then on to Sheffield and after that, a visit to Gerald would take another day, so he would be gone the full week.

At a half-past-one, the doorbell rang and Charles went to open it. In view of the fact that he was to be away for the week, he had seen a client that morning and was wearing his business suit of dark jacket and pinstriped trousers. Clare Willard looked him up and down.

"Be so good as to inform Mrs Anders that Mr and Mrs Willard have arrived." Mr Willard had his back turned, and was looking around with interest at the driveway.

Charles hid a smile. He had never been taken for a butler before.

"Please come in. I'm Charles Hughes. Matthew is out with my daughter, Sophie. They won't be long."

She looked at him in horror. "Your daughter?" she said faintly. The thought that Matthew's friend was a girl had been bad enough, but that the girl was the daughter of the hired help didn't bear thinking about. Charles watched as her face stretched in horror and the man turned and put his hand under her elbow.

"Come, dear, we will sort things out when he arrives."

His accent was much broader than Matthew's. Charles summed him up as a successful businessman. He shot a glance at Charles, who was still holding the door open his face red with indignation. Their thoughts were obvious and he could have found the situation amusing, if the implications about Sophie weren't so insulting.

They walked past him and he shut the door, as Marie came out of the kitchen, smiling and holding out her hand. She had quickly slipped her pinafore off and smoothed her hair when she heard the doorbell, but her face was still rosy and flushed from the heat of the stove. Clare Willard regarded her uncertainly, until Marie introduced herself.

"Hello, we spoke on the telephone. I am Marie Anders."

"Clare and Joseph Willard. How do you do." The cream, gloved hand rested momentarily in Marie's. Then she winced as her hand was grasped in a vicelike grip and pumped up and down, before being released abruptly by the unsmiling Joseph, who was smoking one of the biggest cigars that Marie had ever seen.

He was a large man, in his late fifties, with large uneven features and sandy coloured hair. He wore an immaculate, cream suit, with the jacket unfastened, which accentuated his size and dwarfed his wife who, although not particularly short, was slim to the point of skinny Marie noticed, as their visitor removed her fur coat and handed it to Charles, with an air of dismissal. Marie was taken aback by the gesture and noticed that not only was Charles looking furious, but his natural good manners seemed to have deserted him, as he slung the coat carelessly over a nearby, open arm chair.

"Er, shall we go in and introduce you to everyone?" she suggested, darting Charles an anxious look, and he toying with the idea of escaping to the study, counted to ten and resisted, knowing that Felicity would be in need of his support. Instead he smothered his anger and went ahead to open the sitting room door. David and Laurie were engrossed in their game of chess, but rose immediately to greet the guests, as Felicity hurried in.

She had changed into a chocolate brown dress with shoes of the same colour and was wearing the smallest trace of make-up. Her shining gold hair was caught back with a large, brown velvet clip and she looked wonderful, Charles thought proudly, going to her before any more assumptions could be drawn. No way was his wife going to suffer the same indignity, but it wasn't to be.

"Darling, these are Matthew's parents Mr and Mrs Willard; this is my wife Felicity, and…"

The elegant figure gave Felicity a cursory glance then turned away, leaving Charles in mid sentence. Marie was embarrassed by the deliberate snub, and immediately explained that Felicity was Sophie's Mother.

"But you obviously haven't met Sophie yet, have you?"

"We weren't even aware of the *friend's* existence, until a week ago," came the high-pitched, rapier like reply, "and it has taken this long to trace our son's whereabouts. I am absolutely furious with him."

"Christmas isn't a good time to be left on your own," Charles said stiffly.

"And Matthew came for Sophie's birthday. He was invited to stay on, rather than be on his own," Robert said pointedly, entering at that moment and noting the strained look on Charles face. "Is there a problem *Uncle* Charles?" he asked with an enquiring frown, startling the Willards into realising their mistake.

"Thank you Robert. Not quite as big as it was, perhaps," Charles said with great dignity, giving the couple an offended stare and leaving everyone else to wonder helplessly at the reason for his unusual behaviour.

"Well, do sit down. I'm sure Matthew won't be long." David endeavoured to ease the awkward atmosphere. "No doubt they will be ravenous after their walk. Can I offer you a sherry, Mrs Willard? Mr Willard, perhaps you would prefer a beer?"

Charles said he would get the drinks and Robert offered to help. Marie went to check on dinner and Felicity said that she would help. David and Laurie were left to entertain the Willards. David made polite conversation but Laurie kept silent, wondering how Matthew was going to deal with, what he knew would be, the unwelcome arrival. He looked at the mother, sitting bolt upright, across the corner of the settee, from where she could survey the whole room. Matthew obviously got his looks from her, apart from the height. He could imagine her playing the piano in a long, black evening gown, even though at this moment she looked elegant in cream. A figure hugging, long sleeved dress, reaching just below her knees, revealed long, shapely calves and small feet, encased in sheer nylons and black suede court shoes, crossed neatly at the ankles. A triple row of pearls encircled her swanlike neck and large matching studs adorned her ears. Her black hair, drawn back in to an immaculate but simple twist, complimented dark, expressive eyes and olive skinned, narrow features. The only thing that stopped her from being really beautiful, in Laurie's eyes, was her mouth. It was thin lipped and at this moment, set in a straight line, boding no good for Matthew.

Joseph Willard chose to stand, with his back to the fire, inspecting the size of the room and asking himself how these people expected to keep warm without central heating. The house impressed him but the people lived without style. They appeared to have no staff and the lady of the house was actually cooking dinner herself. Very odd! Charles returned with a tray of drinks. Robert handed tall glasses of beer to Joseph, David and Laurie, left one on the side table for Charles and, excusing himself, was about to leave the room when Joseph said, "So you and my son are at the Conservatoire together. What instrument do you play?"

"No, Mr Willard. Sophie plays the piano; that is where they met. I was at Oxford University and met him through *their* friendship."

Charles had given him a quick run down of the situation while they were getting the drinks, so he added, with a defensive note, "When you meet Sophie you will understand Matthew's feelings for her."

"Feelings? What feelings? How far has this thing gone?" Clare demanded shrilly, looking first at Robert then at Charles. Laurie got up, excused himself and left the room, taking his beer with him. He couldn't sit there and listen to any more.

"That sounds like them now," Marie said passing him at the door. Charles handed her a glass of sherry as happy laughter crossed the hall, before Matthew and Sophie burst in.

"We're engaged, they cried together, before catching sight of Matthew's parents and stopping dead in their tracks, the light instantly fading from Matthew's eyes. For a moment there was complete silence, before Sophie, recovering first, asked Matthew shyly, "Aren't you going to introduce me?" But that was as far as she got.

Clare Willard said icily, "How dare you behave like this Matthew. What are you thinking of? And look at the state of you. No, don't come near me," she said, backing away as he made towards her. "Go and change immediately. You are filthy dirty and perspiring."

She looked at him with distaste, ignoring Sophie entirely, taking in the borrowed blue jeans that Robert had leant him, to save his designer trousers from getting sea-stained, and the thick, beautifully knitted, Aran jumper from Abigail.

"And take those dreadful clothes off!" she said, completely indifferent to the scene she was causing.

For a split second, it looked as if he was going to obey her. Instead he said quietly, "I must apologise to everyone for the disruption of your home; it is no way to repay your kindness to me."

Unaccountably, Joseph Willard didn't utter a word. He just stood with the big cigar hanging from his slackened jaw. He had never seen his son like this before. What had got in to him? The ill-kempt clothes were bad enough, but defying his mother? It was unheard of.

He listened as Matthew continued. "Is it possible for me to have a word, alone, with my parents?"

Charles nodded. "Use the music room, it's warm in there, Matthew."

"Thank you sir. This way, Mother. J.W.," he said, using his father's initials, as he always had. He ushered them out of the room and the rest of the party sank down, breathing a sigh of relief, as they heard the music room door close.

David held his hand up as Charles started to apologise. He went on to explain his anger. They smiled with him as he told them of being mistaken for the butler, but were equally annoyed at the Willard's attitude after that.

"I have never, ever, come up against such arrogance. Who do they think they are?" Charles started to get indignant again, just as Sophie let out a little giggle. They were surprised that she wasn't more upset, but then she told them of Matthew's life in America, which he had revealed to her during their walk, and his reasons for not telling them before.

"I have to be prepared for a lot of prejudice on their part, Matthew says, and he hopes that he is worth it." She smiled softly at such a ridiculous notion.

"I still won't have them saying that you aren't good enough, whether I am a butler, a dustman or a solicitor, just because *she* can play the piano," Charles ranted.

"They would be the same whoever it was Daddy. He is their protégée, *their future claim to fame*."

Laurie had taken himself outside, to the sheltered, sunny corner of the terrace. It was warm enough to sit in the small arbour, which David had created with conifer trees, planted at an angle to the large round bay of the east wing. He had only been sitting for a short time, enjoying the sea view with his beer on the table beside him, thinking about the scene he had left, when a woman's irate voice reached him.

"What on earth do you think you are doing, Matthew, mixing with people like this?"

The projected voice carried easily through the ill-fitting windows and with an exasperated sigh, Laurie made to get up and move, to avoid eavesdropping, but the voice, which was getting more strident as she paced the room with increasing agitation, came again, obviously in answer to something inaudible from Matthew, and stopped Laurie in his tracks.

"Maybe he isn't the butler, but it was an easy mistake to make and when all is said and done, he and his family are only lodgers here, they don't *own* even part of the house. They aren't even *distantly* related; *Uncle* Charles must only be a courtesy title."

This time Matthew's voice reached his ears, in heated defence of Charles. "I will have you know that Sophie's father is a very respected solicitor, and partner to Mr Harcott. Not that it matters, I would still marry Sophie even if she *was* a butler's daughter. You are a snob, Mother, of the worst kind. You forget that my *own* father was a dirt farmer, until he struck oil on the land his uncle left him."

"Don't speak to your mother like that," Joseph Willard thundered, finding his voice at last, as he realised the whole situation was out of hand, and subtlety was needed if their demand for Matthew to return to America with them, out of the clutches of this girl, was to succeed. But Clare was desperate and her tongue ran away with her. "At least we know our parents," she snapped.

"And what is that supposed to mean?" Matthew asked, in an ominous tone, which although lost on his mother, made Joseph despair, waiting for the next, obvious question.

"Both of your precious Sophie's parents were brought up in orphanages. God alone knows where *they* come from."

"You seem to know a lot about them." Matthew challenged quietly. "How come?" Laurie couldn't have walked away now, if he had wanted to. He was riveted to the spot, principles forgotten – waiting for the answer.

Realising too late her anger had given them away, she tried to cover up.

"We were worried when we couldn't contact you. I telephoned the school and spoke to the secretary."

It was a clumsy attempt, but she was used to Matthew accepting her word without question, so she put on a haughty expression, defying him to disbelieve her.

"That won't do, Mother. The school couldn't possibly know details like that. I want to know the truth." He tried to look her straight in the eyes but she turned her back on him.

"You mustn't upset your mother like this, she has a big performance in two days' time, and we have taken time to chase all the way down here, in the middle of nowhere, to rescue you from your own foolishness. What possesses people to bury themselves away from civilisation is beyond me." Joseph complained irritably, forgetting that given the chance, it was exactly what he would do.

"That doesn't tell me how you know so many personal details about this family," Matthew pursued the point. "Details I don't know and am not interested in."

"We made it our business to find out. We suspected gold digging and your mother is not convinced there is any other reason for them inviting you. It is well known that they never entertain. Why? What have they got to hide?" Although his father *spoke* the words, he knew the *thoughts* were his mother's. His father had oil wells and apart from them, his only other interest was to be with his wife and keep her happy, even if it meant accompanying her all over the world. He indulged her every whim; that was why he was here now, Matthew guessed, with a sudden rush of compassion. He was wealthy beyond most people's dreams and should have been married to a nice ordinary woman, of a similar age and intellect, but his acquired money had made it possible for Clare to follow her dream. She had married him at seventeen, when he was already in his mid-thirties and Matthew was born a year later.

"You have had someone prying, haven't you?" Matthew said in a shocked voice.

"Anything we have done has been to protect you. You know nothing about these people. Please, Matthew, come back with us, now," she pleaded tearfully.

He couldn't bear to see her cry, in spite of everything, but this time he was not going to back down, so he said gently, "Mother, they don't know who we are. Even Sophie didn't know until this morning, when we were out walking, and she had already agreed to marry me – I *had* to tell her then. You will love her when you get to know her, and I intend to marry her, whether you agree or not. Come now, you already have something in common." He pointed to the piano that she had automatically sat at, when she stopped pacing the room. Her attention was caught and she inspected the baby grand, allowing her fingers to arpeggio up and down before playing a few bars of Chopin.

Matthew plucked his violin from its open case, which was lying on a nearby occasional table, and in one easy movement placed it under his chin and picked up the lovely melody. They smiled at each other with real enjoyment, their differences instantly forgotten in the moment; he turned and nodded to his father, who gave a sigh of relief and left the room.

Out on the terrace, Laurie walked quietly away and back in to the house, wearing a look of resolve. The two men reached the sitting room door at the same time and Laurie stood aside to let the visitor go first, just as Sophie, with a look of wonderment, was making for the hall, in order to hear better.

Joseph looked apologetic. "What can I say, apart from offering my deepest apology for causing this upset in your home. We will be on our way – if we could just give them a few minutes."

"Why don't we go ahead with dinner and leave them to it?" Marie suggested. "It's all ready," she said looking around.

"That seems like a good idea," David agreed, looking at Joseph.

"I would have thought you would be glad to see the back of us."

"Let me get you another beer sir," Robert offered, as David drew up another chair at the chessboard, where he and Laurie had returned to resume their game.

"Just time for a few more moves," he said as Charles went off to carve the meat and Felicity and Marie followed to rescue the overdue meal.

Sophie was sitting at the end of the wide passage leading to the music room. Her face was rapt as she listened and little by little, moved closer, until she was right outside the door, which Joseph had left slightly ajar.

Neither Matthew nor Clare were aware of her as she crept in and curled up on the comfy old settee behind the door. They played in such perfect unison that she understood the bond that must exist between them. She didn't know the piece of music they were playing but recognised it as Chopin. In that moment she realised the difference between playing well and being a concert pianist; she would give anything to be that good but a seed of doubt was sown as she recalled Matthew inferring that there were other options. Even that couldn't spoil the moment though, as each note rang true and clear, filling the room with pure sound, echoed by the strings under Matthew's bow.

At the finish, there was silence. Clare had played herself into serenity and forgetting they were unaware of her, Sophie clapped and clapped, tears springing to her eyes.

"That was wonderful," she whispered, as they turned in surprise. Matthew held out his hand. "Come and meet Clare Windsor, world famous pianist and my mother. Mother meet Sophie, my fiancée," he said proudly. Clare nodded, eyeing her tentatively.

"Matthew tells me you play."

"I thought I did," Sophie blushed.

"I would like to hear you."

Matthew led her to the piano, "play that 'Golliwog's Cakewalk' by Debussy."

She was nervous and made a false start.

"Relax. Sit for a moment. Take three deep breaths – and begin," Clare said slowly and calmly, bringing her finger down on 'begin'. Sophie found herself playing well, as Clare walked up and down counting the beat with her long forefinger. As she reached the end, Clare walked briskly towards her, waving her away, starting to play the piece herself. The notes were clear and precise – sharp staccato, as Debussy had intended. She followed the music effortlessly, then, half way through stopped, rose from the stool and indicated to her to sit.

"That is how I want it to sound. Again!" Sophie played again, copying as well as she could, and this time earned a word of praise.

"Matthew was right. You play well, and with a lot of practice and dedication you could succeed, but is it what you want to do with your life? There are a lot of sacrifices to make, family life for instance. Matthew has to face that as well."

Matthew had never heard his mother speak in that way before, and for a moment, suspected she was trying to deter Sophie from marrying him, but if that was her aim, Sophie's next words dispelled any hopes.

"I thought it was the only thing I wanted in life, until I met Matthew; now I know I want both. Is it really impossible to combine the two?"

"Nothing is impossible; and at least you will have a sympathetic partner – as long as you don't outshine him, of course," Clare added with a glint of sardonic humour.

Sophie cast a wry look at him. "No danger of that."

"That dinner smells marvellous, and I'm starving." Matthew smiled down at her.

"That could be awkward," Clare said uncertainly.

"The last I heard, they were voting to eat and leave us to it. Mr Willard will have been introduced to Grandma's Yorkshire pudding by now, so we had better get a move on if you want some Matthew," Sophie teased.

Matthew looked down at their jeans and realised his mother had completely forgotten her shock at seeing him dressed so.

"Grandma won't mind, this once," Sophie assured him.

Once again Matthew marvelled at the graciousness of the family, as they took their seats and were handed the various dishes.

The Willard's departed at four-thirty, forced to accept that Matthew would return to London with Sophie, as planned, the following day. Everyone was relieved to see them go and the rest of the day was spent in preparations for the following week.

Robert's small suitcase mocked him, as he compared it with the trunk that was normally bursting at the seams for his return to Oxford, but there wasn't time to brood, his grandfather had a tight schedule planned.

Sophie filled her big trunk so full, her mother had to sit on the lid while she fastened it. Gales of laughter could be heard coming from the bedroom and Charles gave a sad little smile, as he and Matthew took the opportunity to play a last game of table tennis.

"They'll miss each other," he said simply, smashing the ball onto Matthew's backhand, anticipating that the excellent shot would be a winning one, but Matthew stonewalled it, and there followed one of their best rallies ever, leaving them exhilarated and eager to play on, laughing at their own prowess.

When it came time to take Laurie home, Sophie was washing her hair so Matthew went along for the ride.

Charles couldn't believe how much he had taken to the boy and Matthew said he felt as if he had known the family all his life.

On the way home, Laurie's mind was on the overheard conversation. Putting his silence down to tiredness, Charles went straight upstairs to put the electric fire on in his bedroom.

"You faced your demons then?" Laurie said to Matthew, with a wry smile.

"I didn't think Mother would give in like that; playing the Prima Donna usually gets her her own way, and neither J.W. nor I have ever stood up to her, in case we upset her performance. Artistic temperament they call it and if I ever show signs of developing one, you have my permission to wrap my violin around my ears."

"Not the Stradivarius?" Laurie said in mock horror, just as Charles came back to ask if he would like a hot milk drink or a whisky nightcap.

They stayed for an hour, making sure Laurie was settled. Charles was trying not to fuss too much, but he worried about leaving him for the week. It would be a relief when the Sheffield business was completed. The travelling could get too much for David as well. The worst of the winter was yet to come.

Aloud, he said, "Now if the weather is bad, or you don't feel up to going in, ring Jessica and cancel engagements until next week. I will be back on Friday."

"You're not to worry. I know you will get back as soon as possible." Laurie sounded more confident than he felt; he had got used to having Charles around. He enjoyed strolling to the office at ten-thirty, and leaving at three-thirty, these winter days.

In the car, Matthew said, "I could easily delay going back for a week, if you like."

"He would take it as lack of confidence in him, and that would never do. He will be fine. Felicity molly coddles him. Thanks for the offer though."

*

126

The house settled down after they had all departed. The kitchen had been a hive of activity and Lorna had come in very early to help. Marie lifted the coffee pot from the Aga and carried it to the table, where cups were laid ready.

"Hope we packed enough food."

"Only to reach John O'Groats and back." Abigail finished wiping the last few pieces of cutlery and placed them in the drawer, smiling at Marie, as Lorna chuckled, recalling the well-filled lunch baskets.

"Enough for the other passengers as well."

They sank down thankfully as Felicity came through to the laundry, carrying a huge pile of bed linen. It had been Pamela's idea to update the old fashioned washhouse. Electricity had been installed allowing two washing machines to be plumbed in. And a rotary iron now took pride of place on the big scrubbed table. The original enormous brick built copper in the corner and the old-fashioned mangle with huge wooden rollers remained – picturesque relics of a bygone age.

"Nothing to breakdown there and still capable of doing the job in another hundred years," David said sagely, viewing the changes, remembering his boyhood days when a woman from the village came early Monday morning and worked until late. The pulley lines overhead had been hung with snowy white bedding, tablecloths and towels. Everything had been white in those days he remembered. Not like today. And the lines still worked like clockwork, still in use, as was the huge butler sink.

"Best of both worlds," Marie said.

"I can't think how we managed before," Felicity said, returning from depositing her load and flopping on to a chair. Abigail passed her a cup of coffee.

"The best idea yet," Marie commented over the top of her cup. "Trust Pamela to make life easier. I wonder how she is coping; Gerald won't be an easy patient."

They chatted until Maisie arrived, then Lorna cleared the cups away while Abigail waited for Maisie to remove her outdoor clothes and collect her cleaning materials, before following her upstairs to help with the beds. There was always a slight antagonism between the two of them. Abigail was inclined to patronise the shy, young country girl, and secretly, Maisie thought Abigail gave herself airs above her station, but they tolerated each other on the few occasions they were required to work together, and the work was always completed quickly so that Abigail could get back to her own domain, where she reigned supreme.

Felicity retreated to her own rooms and paced restlessly. Tomorrow was the day of her test and she could have done with some practice, but with Charles away, she would have to be content with the lesson before the test. It suddenly seemed silly to keep it from Marie and she retraced her steps to the kitchen. Marie and Lorna were checking and making lists in the depleted store cupboard. Christmas had all but emptied the spacious pantry and a large shopping trip was high on their list of priorities.

"Sorry, Mum, I should be helping you."

"It's alright dear, you've got Sophie and Matthew's rooms to sort out. Lorna and I can manage." She looked up with an air of concern, pencil poised. "You sound harassed."

Felicity gave a sheepish grin. "We were keeping it as a surprise, but I shall burst if I don't tell you." She held up the Highway Code book. "My test is tomorrow and my nerves are in shreds."

"Oh! Of all the times for Charles to be away, but he wouldn't let you take it if you weren't ready. Positive thinking, deep breathing and that level head of yours, is all you need. You will pass."

Marie said it with such conviction that Felicity felt better, but she still needed to fill the day; housework gave her too much time to think.

"How about if we get the shopping in today?" she suggested hopefully.

"Right! Jed can drive us to town and we can get a taxi back. Won't it be wonderful when you drive? The list is just about complete, unless you can think of anything else, Lorna?"

Lorna added another couple of items and then got her baking bowls out, looking forward to time on her own. With an invalid mother to look after, she seldom had time alone and enjoyed the peace of the kitchen more than anything.

*

It had been the best day of Lorna's life, coming to work for Marie Anders, thirteen years ago. She was no longer at her mother's querulous beck and call all day, as she had been until her father died from silicosis. Their income died with him, so at the age of twenty she had to find her first job. Her only sister, Betsy, was already pregnant with her first baby when their father had become too ill to work so it had fallen to Lorna, at fifteen, to take care of him *and* her mother who had never fully recovered from the birth of a still born son, six years earlier. It was a sad case, which happened all too often, when through ignorance, lack of means, or both, women failed to seek proper medical care. Now unable to walk more than a few steps, or climb stairs, Jessie had her bed downstairs and found it impossible to even dress herself without Lorna's help. A neighbour popped in during the day and Betsy helped, but at thirty-four, she was six months pregnant with another child – her seventh.

Lorna couldn't help feeling exasperated. What if something went wrong, as it had with her own mother? Who would look after all those children? Maisie?

She was the eldest, at eighteen, then Ned, sixteen who worked on the farm; Dora next at fourteen; Mary, ten; Billy going on five and Derek, two-and-a-half. They were a large, happy brood and Betsy would just laugh when Lorna voiced her fears.

"Don't worry, I go for my regular check-ups. Everything will be fine." Lorna wished that she could be that carefree, but life had made her otherwise. Betsy's husband, Alf, was a happy-go-lucky man as well, who worked hard as a tenant farmer and had plans to buy their cottage and surrounding acres, when it came on to the market in a year's time. He saw *no* reason to deny themselves the large family that they both enjoyed to the full.

"Must 'ave my bit o' comfort after an 'ard days work," he would say with a twinkle in his eye, giving his wife a playful slap on her well rounded buttock and winking broadly at Lorna, who would throw her eyes heavenwards in despair.

"Can't be afraid of livin', girl," he would stress sympathetically. He was sincerely sorry for her plight. She was a good-looking woman and would have made some man a damn good wife. Could do with a bit more meat on her bones perhaps, but what chance did she have of catching a husband, with her mother so dependent on her. He was convinced Jessie had exaggerated her helplessness to prevent Lorna from going to work when the father became bedridden, but it wasn't for him to rock the boat, unless it interfered with him and Betsy.

It therefore came as quite a shock, on arriving home that Monday for his dinner, to find Betsy waiting for him in the lane, with the news that her mother was indoors. It was a damp, cold day and all he wanted was the warmth of Betsy's kitchen and the good hot meal she would have waiting for him, so, assuming she was just visiting for dinner he said, quite affably, "Well now, don't fret yerself, I expect dinner'll stretch to another mouth," and with that he put his arm round her expansive waist and pulled her towards the cottage.

"Ye don't understand she has to stay for eight weeks," Betsy said standing her ground and pulling him back.

"Whaat?" He jerked round with a look of shocked horror on his amiable face.

"Our Lorna has gone and broke her ankle and she'll be laid up for at least six weeks. There's nobody to look after Mother. The folks at the big house say they will take care of Lorna, thank goodness, otherwise I would be runnin' over every day, lookin' after them both. I just couldn't do it." Betsy looked close to tears, so with a resigned air, Alf spread his arms about her and held her. "There, there, me Duck, we'll get by."

On entering the cottage he wasn't so sure. His mother-in-law was not only in his home she was in his favourite chair, bristling with belligerence, obviously not relishing the situation any more than he did; in fact it was a great

129

inconvenience, being moved from the home where she was free to complain constantly.

"You would think at her age she would have enough sense to stand on her own two feet," his mother-in-law greeted him, as Alf eased his stocky, bluff form in to the sturdy carver chair at the head of the table.

"She didn't do it on purpose, Mam," Betsy defended Lorna tearfully.

"Nothing would surprise me about that girl," Jessie growled.

"One thing is fer sure. Ye don't deserve her," Alf snapped, his natural good humour deserting him at the sight of Betsy's woebegone face. "And another thing, the baby's due in three months; don't you go upsettin' my Betsy. D'ye hear?" He picked up his knife and fork and sat with them in his fists.

Jessie began to cry, she felt confused and lonely, away from her familiar surroundings, and she wasn't used to the noise of the two youngest children, who were making her head ache with their boisterous romping on the floor. And she was used to having her dinner later, when Lorna came home, and who would she call in the night when she needed a cup of tea, or her legs rubbed? She looked a picture of misery and kind-hearted Betsy suddenly felt sorry for her.

"Don't cry, Mam. Come to the table and have ye dinner." And in spite of declaring that she wouldn't be able to eat a thing, Jessie quickly made short work of a large helping of the excellent steak and kidney pudding and vegetables, followed by apple pie and custard.

"I'd best make up a bed for her in the front parlour," Betsy said, as Alf was getting ready to go back to work.

"Leave it until I get home. I'll give ye a hand. If yore worryin' about her afternoon nap, ye needn't," he grinned nodding towards his armchair, where Jessie was already snoring gently, in spite of the noise going on around her.

*

On arriving home, Marie and Felicity had been startled to see Doctor Davies' car standing in the driveway. Leaving the shopping in the taxi they had hurried into the house fearful of what they would find. Lorna was lying on a blanket on the kitchen floor and the doctor was examining her left leg. Her face was white and twisted with pain, but she nevertheless tried to rise and started to apologise, when Marie hurried towards her.

"Hush now, the main thing is you are alright," Marie soothed.

Dr Davies rose from his knees. "It seems to be a fairly clean break, but we will soon know; the ambulance is on its way."

"How did it happen?" Marie asked Lorna.

"I spilt some fat, went to get a cloth to clean it up and must have had some on the bottom of my shoe. Fortunately, I had just taken the last batch of baking out of the oven," she said with a look of relief.

The doctor gave a wry smile. "Typical! You break an ankle and all you can think about is rescuing pies. Dear Lord, give me patience: but hurry." He turned to Abigail, who was hovering nearby. "Strong, hot tea for the patient, young lady, and young Maisie as well I think."

Felicity put her arm round Maisie and led her to a chair. She was shaking and her eyes were as big as saucers. "I must tell me Mam. She's not gonna die is she? Can I go to the hospital with her?"

"Yes of course, and I will tell your mother. Drink your tea now before the ambulance gets here," Marie comforted.

The taxi man appeared in the doorway, laden with shopping bags.

"Oh! Just there please." Felicity, pointed to a bench, her arm still around Maisie.

"Need any help?" he asked looking concerned

"Lorna's broken her ankle and I need to let her sister know. Can you take me?" Marie asked.

He did more, he took Betsy over to fetch her mother, whilst Marie stayed with the two young children and then brought Marie home again, after it had been decided that under the circumstances, Lorna should stay at Anders Folly to recuperate.

CHAPTER TEN

Cheyne Walk, where Gerald and Pamela had been driven to earlier in the day turned out to be a pleasant, tree-lined area of Chelsea. The private clinic and sanatorium, a large, square, Victorian mansion set in its own grounds stood at the end of a row of other tall, Victorian houses, overlooking the south bank of the river Thames, just along from the Chelsea Pensioners' Hospital, where each year people flocked to visit the famous flower show. At high tide, gaily-painted houseboats, bobbed about on the water's edge, and across the river, Battersea Park, could be seen where trees already budding were waiting to burst in to verdant splendour. Bright lights and the faint sound of fairground music could be heard on still evenings, coming from the funfair, where the big wheel dominated the skyline. Pamela and Gerald strolled hand in hand along the water's edge, oblivious to London life going on around them, on that bleak, January evening. The hotel, a few minutes' walk away from the clinic, and aptly, if somewhat unimaginatively named Riverview, was nearby and as darkness fell they wended their way back, in plenty of time for a comforting bath and a drink in their room before dinner. The room, which Pamela would be occupying for the next few months, was comfortable, warm, dominated by a large Divan bed and boasted a well-equipped en-suite bathroom, complete with fluffy towels and luxurious, white towelling bath-robes hanging behind the door which they both slipped into gratefully, after the chilly walk along the river. Pamela lay on the big bed, stretching her long legs and arching her back, enjoying the unaccustomed laziness at that time of day, whilst Gerald poured wine from the carafe he had ordered from reception.

"Champagne when I come out," he promised, setting both glasses on the bedside table.

Pamela held out her arms, allowing her robe to fall open. He bent to kiss her, his tongue gently exploring her mouth and she closed her eyes, as he allowed his hand to wander slowly from her thigh to her breast. Nothing had changed over the years; the magic was still there; they still enjoyed arousing each other. Afterwards they lay back, her head in the crook of his arm. The room was warm and quiet, with only the dim light from the landing shining through a narrow skylight above the door relieving the darkness. Dismissing thoughts of this time tomorrow, he slid his arm away and reached for the glasses of wine. "Shall I bathe first or do you want to?"

"You go first. I don't want this to end yet." She took a glass, leaned up on her elbow and watched him, silhouetted naked in the bathroom doorway. He pulled the light switch, sending a shaft of light across the patterned carpet. Then she too diverted her thoughts by sliding off the bed and going to the window to investigate the merrymakers below – already celebrating. They would have been getting ready for the Yacht Club dance she thought wistfully, wandering back to the bathroom door. "I had forgotten it's New Year's Eve. Wonder what they are doing at home?"

"Mmm," was his only response, leaning back in the foaming water and sipping his wine, as she fetched the carafe for a top up, before slipping in the other end of the bath.

"You're missing all the fun," he frowned. "We would have been dancing tonight, having a good time, if it wasn't for me."

"Don't say that. I don't care where we are as long as we are together." She smiled, gently rubbing soap across his chest, with her toes, "And why does wine taste so good in the bath?"

"Because it makes you feel wanton," he said, leaning forward and caressing her nipple, through the foam. "Shall we miss dinner?"

She peered over the top of the glass, gasping in mock horror. "People will suspect we aren't married."

"Well *I* suspect you need more wine," he answered, retrieving the bottle from the floor.

They were a little late for dinner and the dining room was full, with a party on their way to the theatre. Gerald felt guilty again. "Wish you were going with them?" he asked.

"Not a bit," she lied easily. "I have a date with the most handsome man in the room and we have far better ways of seeing the New Year in."

"You're wonderful – but not a very good liar. I will make it up to you, I promise."

After dinner they telephoned home and regretted not ringing earlier as they had just missed the children, but Pamela promised to ring the following day when she had some news.

They breakfasted in their room, attending to last minute details until it was time to report to the clinic. Gerald, looking white and strained, gripped her arm on the short distance along Cheyne Walk. "Now you will be alright on your own, won't you?" he asked for the umpteenth time.

"I will be fine," she answered patiently, yet again.

Gerald felt as if he was entering prison as they walked into the sterile looking entrance hall, where a nurse greeted them and led them upstairs to a private room. Gerald was instructed to undress and get in to bed and Pamela stayed as long as she could, but eventually she was asked to leave, with the visiting times firmly impressed on her. On the dot of six o'clock, she returned to find Gerald decidedly subdued.

"I shall go mad in this place," he said desperately with a furtive look at the door. "That nurse is an absolute dragon."

Pamela gave a sympathetic smile. How many times had she heard that before? By the end of a week, *she* was desperate at his continued unhappiness. Apparently he sunk into depression between her visits, and wanted to know every single thing she had done while he was stuck in this prison.

The weekend visiting was a little more relaxed. The hours were increased and if he had wanted to, they could have sat in the large, airy day room overlooking the grounds at the rear of the property. The room boasted a television in one corner, cane chairs arranged in groups and several small card tables. Double doors opened out to a wide, covered balcony, and patients were encouraged to sit out as often as possible, but the windows were never closed, even on cold days and that applied to all rooms. Fresh air was the key to the cure. Other patients enjoyed the change from sitting in their rooms, but Gerald gave it a definite thumbs down.

The second week improved slightly. Sophie and Matthew visited him on the Tuesday, bringing news from home, and David and Robert arrived on the Thursday with the latest update from Southampton. On Friday Charles arrived and booked into Riverview in time for the six o'clock visiting hour, bearing the results of his negotiations in Sheffield. Everything was going according to plan; the partners were delighted at the opportunity to be sole owners again. The whole business would be wound up long before Gerald was discharged. This bolstered his spirits, and for the first time, Pamela returned to the hotel, ready to enjoy the evening meal before getting a good night's sleep, so it was a big disappointment the next morning, when she and Charles arrived, for a final visit before he returned home, to be told that the excitement of too many visitors had sent Gerald's blood pressure soaring and he had been given a sedative after a sleepless night, so no visitors were allowed until the evening, and then, only Pamela. Feeling abashed, they walked along the embankment and stopped for coffee in a small café. It was warm inside, but the smell of cooking made Pamela nauseous, so they drank up and went back out into the cold air.

"Sorry about that."

"Breakfasting alone should have reminded me that you can't face food before lunchtime," he apologised.

"I have coffee and orange juice sent up," she said absently, staring down at the water.

"I hate leaving you like this. You look terrible – well as terrible as anyone like you, could look," he added quickly, flustered by his ill chosen words. "What

I mean is, you don't look too good – no I don't mean that either," he blustered. "You look marvellous, as always."

Pamela patted his arm. "Quit while you are ahead, Charles. I know what you mean and I love you for it. I shall be all right. I knew what to expect when I came. It's just harder than I reckoned."

They drifted back to the hotel, where Charles retrieved his overnight bag and rang for a taxi.

"What shall I tell them at home?"

"That everything is fine and he is responding to treatment. That is true. Don't mention blood pressure, it will only worry them."

He left, giving her an uncertain wave as the taxi pulled away; she watched it out of sight, longing for the familiar faces of home.

The weekends were the longest she had ever spent. After visiting hour the evenings stretched interminably and by eight-thirty she would retire to bed and find herself, reading the same line over and over again of a story she couldn't remember.

On Monday morning, with forced cheerfulness, she made her way to Gerald's room to find it empty. She felt a slight shock, before chiding herself and sitting down to wait. He came within a few minutes, looking pleased with himself.

"I've just spoken to everyone at home. It was good to hear their voices." He gave a triumphant grin. "The Dragon has been off all morning and it would seem there is nobody on duty. The only telephone I could find was downstairs."

Pamela tutted, as she helped him back in to bed, automatically feeling for his pulse. It was racing.

"That wasn't wise," she remonstrated gently.

"How come we can make love without problems and yet here, the slightest exertion makes things go haywire?" he whispered breathlessly.

"Probably the medication. Now lie still and calm down."

"You sound like the Dragon," he gasped, as the door opened and a harassed looking, white coated man, with a stethoscope hanging on his neck, entered.

"Ah! Mrs Anders, your husband must keep to his bed and rest. His telephone was removed for reasons that have been explained to him. Perhaps you can have a word? Make him understand that it isn't for our benefit? Do that, will you? We have a small problem today. Nurse Bennet is off, but that doesn't mean that the patients can run riot," he snapped with an angry glance in Gerald's direction. He left before Pamela could answer, but thinking quickly she ran after him, caught up and half ran beside him as he walked with long, purposeful strides towards the stairs.

"I could help. I'm a nurse." He hesitated in his stride and scratched his chin. "Mm, that could be useful. Nurse Bennet will be back tomorrow, hopefully. Report to Matron, she is on the ground floor. Tell her I said to find you a uniform, and show you the duties. Oh, and thanks, I will catch you later."

Almost an hour later, Gerald heard the door open, saw a uniform out of the corner of his eye and sat up, about to demand the whereabouts of his wife until he saw Pamela and his mouth dropped open. "Why on earth are you wearing that?"

"You had better behave yourself; I am here for the day, so eat up," she warned, putting his lunch on the trolley and wheeling it over the bed. Without taking his eyes from her, he picked up the knife and fork and started to eat.

It was nine o'clock before she got back to the hotel, dinner had long since finished, but she had eaten anyway. Matron allowed her to eat with Gerald in his room. That night she fell into bed, even too tired to take a bath.

Early next morning there was a phone call from the clinic, asking her to go along as soon as possible. She dressed hurriedly and not even waiting for her coffee, walked quickly along the road, arriving out of breath at the main entrance, as a white Porsche pulled into the drive. The blonde haired doctor of yesterday climbed out and walked over to her.

"I didn't introduce myself, in the rush." He held out his hand and took hers in a firm grip. "William Jessop, or Bill. What are you doing here so early? I thought we had worn you out yesterday." He gave a lopsided grin.

"I got a message, asking me to come."

"Oh. Let's go and see why." He led the way through the glass swing doors, and into Matron's office, where she was sitting at her desk, with a worried frown. On seeing Pamela, her face cleared and she explained that Nurse Bennet had come in, but would have to leave by midday, because her husband had been rushed in to hospital. Pamela sat down abruptly on a nearby chair. "I thought it was my husband."

"Sorry, I didn't mean to worry you, just wondered if you are free to help out again, until the agency send someone. I'm presuming Nurse Bennet will be off for a few weeks."

It was eventually arranged that Pamela would work until Gerald was discharged, or Nurse Bennet returned. Later that morning, The Dragon, as Gerald insisted on calling her, gave Pamela a box of chocolates and thanked her for filling in, explaining that her husband was partly disabled, and stayed at home to look after their two school age children. The family depended on her wages, and working nearby meant she was on hand for them. She was a large, capable woman, with dark, darting eyes that missed nothing. She seldom smiled, but when she did, her face transformed. Pamela was touched by her situation.

"Not dragon-like at all, just a poor woman with too much on her plate to pander to spoilt patients," Pamela pointed out sternly. Gerald looked suitably contrite, and settled back on his pillows with a contented sigh, comfortable in the knowledge that Pamela would be there indefinitely.

It was raining hard as she started to walk back to the hotel on Saturday evening. After working the full week, the thought of sinking in to a hot bath, and having Sunday off, was bliss. She ached with tiredness, and the visiting hour from six o'clock till seven, which she normally looked forward to after finishing work at six, had seemed never ending but Gerald had been disappointed when she suggested leaving early. Collar turned up and shoulders hunched, she was unaware of a car pulling up, until a voice called, "Hop in, you will get soaked."

She turned, recognised Dr Jessop as he leaned over and opened the passenger door, and climbed in gratefully. "Thank you. I only have to go as far as Riverview."

"I'm going there myself. Ann is my sister. I often drop in for dinner; it's handy when I can't be bothered to cook for myself."

The car pulled on to the gravel drive and they made a dash for cover.

"Might see you later," he called as she made her way to the stairs and he headed for the bar.

"Maybe, if you are staying a while," she answered non-committally. At the moment, all she could think about was getting out of her soiled clothes and sinking in to a hot bath. She had hardly discarded her uniform, before there was a knock at the bedroom door and Mrs Murrey handed her a tray holding a large glass of white wine.

"With the compliments of Dr Jessop. He thought you could do with a pick-me-up, and would like to wait and have dinner with you, if that is alright?"

Pamela's heart sank but it would have been churlish to refuse, so forcing a smile, she took the tray, saying she would be down in half an hour. It was actually nearer to forty-five minutes, but he greeted her with, "Hope you didn't mind the liberty." The boyish smile reminded her of Alexander and suddenly she felt homesick. Was it really only three weeks? He sensed her unhappiness. "I've imposed."

"No, no," she said quickly. "I'm just homesick; it will be nice to have company, and thank you for the wine." Unconsciously, she gave what Gerald called her devastating smile as he placed a hand under her elbow.

"Our table *is* ready. Shall we go in?"

Over the meal they talked, both of them gradually unwinding. She learnt that he was born in this very house. It had belonged to his parents and when they died five years ago, they left it to Ann because he already had the clinic, which had been his grandparents' home.

"They moved out for the duration of the war and the ministry commandeered it. They were happy living in the country, so never returned. The place stood empty for years, which was a worry, but when I qualified, it was heaven sent."

"So the clinic is yours then?"

She was finding the story fascinating and told him of the similar situation with Anders Folly, which led them in to yet another long conversation. Before they realised, it was ten o'clock and everyone else had left; Ann had even reset the tables around them. Pamela rose hurriedly, apologising.

"Don't rush off. It's good to see Bill talking, instead of sitting on his own, pouring over some manual. He works far too hard," Ann clucked in a motherly fashion. "You are looking a bit peaky as well. Not working you too hard, is he?"

"Are we?" He looked concerned.

"Certainly not. It's better than waiting around for visiting hours, and my husband is well pleased," Pamela reassured them. "I must say I'm looking forward to laying in tomorrow though," she admitted. "Could I have my coffee at ten, instead of seven? Oh, and can you manage two extra for lunch? My niece and her fiancé are coming to visit Gerald. Sorry it's short notice."

Sophie and Matthew had rung earlier and she had suggested lunch.

"No problem." Ann made a note and said goodnight.

"Sorry if I kept you from an early night. The time has flown. Blame it on your fascinating company," Bill said, barely touching her shoulder. "Night. Sleep well." He went, leaving her feeling suddenly guilty.

She had been so engrossed she hadn't given Gerald a thought. Slowly she made her way upstairs, thinking of Gerald, but unable to dismiss the laughing brown eyes of her amusing dinner companion, and the light touch of his fingers on her shoulder, which somehow lingered.

*

She slept soundly, and woke looking forward to seeing Sophie and Matthew; however, their afternoon visit, after a pleasant lunch, was unaccountably strained. Gerald was morose; even Sophie's bright chatter failed to cheer him. He was using his oxygen mask frequently and pulled away as Pamela tried to make him comfortable.

"Don't," he said shortly. Automatically she looked at his chart.

"I wish you wouldn't do that," he rasped irritably.

"I don't understand, he was fine when I left, last evening," she said as they were leaving.

138

His pee.vish reaction, when she mentioned she might miss the evening visit, to wash her uniform for the morning and could do with an early night, startled her.

"I would have thought all your nights were early, but then, you would know best about that."

It was said with a cool stare and at six o'clock she was back at his bedside.

His relief was obvious in spite of his bad mood.

"Thought you weren't coming," he grunted.

"How could I not, when you behaved so badly?" she demanded, tiredness getting the better of her.

"Was it really necessary to get into Jessop's car, just to go that short distance?" he blazed back.

She gazed at him incredulously, and at that very moment, a white car halted at the gateway before swinging out on to the road. From the position of his bed, he not only had a wonderful view of the river but the whole of the driveway as well. If he got that upset about her accepting a lift home in the pouring rain – she decided not to mention having dinner together until he was feeling more himself.

"It was raining hard and I had just finished a long shift. The lift was very acceptable."

"It was just being stuck here and seeing you get in to the car," he mumbled.

She could see how dejected he felt and her heart ached to take him home. She lay down beside him and he held her until it was time for her to go.

*

When Pamela had left him the previous evening, the sound of her high heels fading along the corridor filled him with desolation. He remembered their last night together and pictured her alone in the room, then going down to dinner without him. He looked around. The well-equipped private room was bare and inhospitable in comparison but he hadn't noticed before; now with time hanging heavily, he allowed his gaze to travel. The bathroom, obviously a modern addition, was roomy and sterile, with white tiles from floor to ceiling; it had been built into a corner of the huge room but there was still ample space left for the few units of fitted furniture and the hospital bed. The pale grey linoleum covered floor was bare and spotless and the walls were a pleasant shade of turquoise, unrelieved except for a large print of Monet's 'The Water Lilies', hanging on the wall opposite, next to a television set, which could be operated from a panel beside the bed. Piped radio was also at the touch of a button. As hospital rooms went, it could be worse he supposed. His bored gaze travelled to the large bay window. Turquoise blinds, not yet closed, were the only relief to glossy white paint and in the mornings gave a blue tinge to the room.

"Like living in a blasted goldfish bowl," he muttered, looking out at the torrential rain, which was hitting the panes with some force. The drive glistened in the headlights of a car, and he sat forward eagerly as Pamela, huddled in to her navy blue coat and dodging the puddles came within sight. As he watched, a sleek, white car pulled up beside her and she disappeared into its interior, before it swung out of sight behind the high wall bordering the clinic. He found it hard to get his breath, recognising the car as the one Dr Jessop arrived in each morning. His stomach churned, and blind jealousy filled him with anger, as he visualised her sitting in the intimacy of the luxurious car with the attractive doctor. He was sure to ask her out for a drink, maybe even a meal. His imagination ran riot, picturing them, sitting opposite and smiling at one another, in a candle lit restaurant, to a background of soft music. He thumped the bed with both fists, just as a placid looking night nurse came in with his medication.

"Bored are we?" she said complacently.

"I don't know about we – I am," he snapped.

"Well, don't get yourself in such a tizz; you know what it does to your blood pressure," she said in the same complacent tone, little realising she was driving him to further fury. She took his pulse, staring at her watch, while he watched her, seething with frustration.

"Aha," was her quiet comment as she let go of his wrist and scrutinised his face, in the way that medical people do, leaving him to imagine that she had discovered some dire symptom.

"And what is that supposed to mean?" he frowned.

"It means, that if you don't calm down, you could be in here for a very long time." She left him with, "I will be back later and hopefully you will have taken my advice."

Out in the corridor, a young nurse was passing and she remarked to her. "Likes his own way too much, that one. Don't stand any nonsense."

He slept badly and woke very early; his first thought being it was Pamela's day off. If only his father or Charles would come and tell him how things were progressing, but after their last visit, strict instructions had kept them away. Didn't they understand he worried more when all he got was, "Everything is going fine. Don't worry. Concentrate on getting better." He would go mad if he heard another single platitude. And to make things worse, visiting hour wasn't until two o'clock; he was used to seeing Pamela first thing. He considered discharging himself, and immediately dismissed the thought. He was responding well to treatment. He would just have to sit it out, he decided truculently. Matron knocked and entered with a cheery, "Good morning, Mr Anders." She looked at his chart, clipped to the foot of the bed.

"Good morning, Matron," he said in a subdued tone.

Her practiced eye took in the heavy lids and the rumpled bedclothes – evidence of his restless night.

"Did the rain disturb you? It woke me, and nothing short of an earthquake usually does that!" She smiled, pulled the blinds, then went in to the bathroom and turned the taps on, wondering what had sent his blood pressure soaring again last evening. She would have to mention it to Dr Jessop.

The following Wednesday Matron called Pamela to her office to tell her that Nurse Bennet would be returning the following week. She received the news with mixed feelings. Her main worry was Gerald's reaction. He was so emotional and insecure; the complete opposite to his normal self and when she did tell him, she thought he was going to break down.

"Don't miss visiting, will you?" he begged.

"Have I ever?" she asked more sharply than she intended. The strain of the last six weeks was telling on her.

That evening, Bill dropped in on his way home. She was just finishing dinner and he joined her for coffee.

"I heard the news. We will miss you. Are you happy with the arrangement?" he asked.

"I have enjoyed my brief experience and yes, thank you, I am quite happy. Gerald has had time to settle in."

"He is used to being in charge; it can't have been easy for him, or you, for that matter," he stated directly.

She gave a rueful smile. "He is a pillar of strength in normal circumstances. We all rely on him. Now, suddenly his world consists of a hospital room and he is out of touch."

"You may find him a little lethargic over the next few days, we have given him something to calm him. His blood pressure is going up and down for no apparent reason. We will be doing more tests next week. Don't look so worried, he is responding really well to the treatment and if we can just keep his blood pressure stable, he will be able to have more visitors. That will help you as well, I imagine."

His solicitude brought her already strung up emotions to the surface, and to her embarrassment, tears filled her eyes. She brushed them away quickly. "Sorry, I'm not usually so silly."

"You need some relaxation. You can't have had time to go further than Cheyne Walk since you got here, with working *and* visiting. Tell you what, how about I get Ann to show you a bit of old London town? It would do you both good and she knows all the interesting places. Yes?"

His brown eyes smiled into hers and she nodded, finding his enthusiasm irresistible. He left the table before she had time to change her mind, went in search of his sister and was back within five minutes, looking pleased with himself.

"That's settled then. Ann will make arrangements with you later. Now I must go; see you in the morning."

At the doorway he turned and gave a cheery wave; suddenly feeling less lonely, she finished her coffee and made her way upstairs, finding it hard to dismiss how his laughing brown eyes had held hers.

*

There was a new lightness to her step as she hurried to work the next morning. In her pocket there were two letters. The weekly one from Marie and David and another from Robert, informing them: 'thanks to Granddad, I have been 'kitted out' by your tailor, Dad. Two new suits, six shirts, six ties, six pairs of plain socks and two pairs of shoes; one black, one brown. You would be proud of me, and Mother will be beside herself with gratitude to him. Gone are my lovely old sweaters and socks, the comfy Oxford bags and the duffle coat that caused you such despair Mother. I am now a well turned out business man – well I look the part anyway.'

She smiled to herself as she reported for duty. "You look happy," Matron commented.

"A letter from our son; alright if I just pop up and give it to my husband?"

"Of course. He could do with cheering up. Look in on room 10 afterwards, will you? And keep a close eye on Mrs Goldsmith today, she started a new course of treatment this morning."

Pamela ran lightly up the stairs, her thoughts momentarily distracted from the letters, in thanking God, Gerald's illness had been caught in its early stages, unlike poor Mrs Goldsmith. Rounding a corner of the landing, she saw Bill leaving room 10, looking serious; his face brightened as he saw her.

"Good morning, Doctor. Is there a chance that my husband's parents could visit him this Sunday? I had a letter from them this morning and they so want to see him."

"I think that will be good, but only the two of them for now. It is a long way for them to come," he said sympathetically.

"It is, but that won't worry *them*."

"You obviously like your in-laws?" His face relaxed in an enquiring grin.

"They are pure gold," she answered sincerely.

"Ann wishes hers would disappear into thin air," he said with feeling, "and they give *me* every reason to stay single."

They parted laughing outside Gerald's room and she went in to be greeted by a thunderous look. She quickly took the letters from her pocket and handed them to him.

"Robert's letter will make you smile, and I can tell Mother and Dad they can visit on Sunday. Won't they be pleased?"

She looked at him expectantly, but his only reaction was, "Is that what all the hilarity was about then? I could hear you from way down the corridor."

"Read Robert's letter, it will cheer you up."

"I am perfectly cheerful thank you, or I would be, if the good doctor would stop flirting with my wife."

"You are being ridiculous."

"So now I am ridiculous as well as spoilt and demanding."

She tutted, "Who said that?"

"The night nurse, but they all think it. Rich and spoilt I heard another one say."

She went to him and put her arms around him. He wasn't used to disapproval, but the staff did have good reason for their opinions. They didn't know the kind and caring Gerald, the Gerald who came from a working class background and worked so hard for his riches, had a title, but was reluctant to use it because he couldn't accept he had earned it. She held him at arms length and smiled mischievously.

"Perhaps you should use your title. That would make them sit up, and of course, if you really wanted to give them a leveller, you could let them know that Lady Anders has been emptying bed-pans and serving meals with the rest of them for the last six weeks. So much for the spoilt, idle rich. Eh?"

Normally he would have laughed at her humour, but instead he caught hold of her. "I'm sorry. I don't know what's happening to me. I'm confused and miserable. When we go home everything will return to normal. It will be lovely to see Mother and Dad. Thanks for arranging it."

He hugged her fiercely and they clung together for a moment before she pulled away.

"Try and get some rest," she said gently. "I have to look in on Mrs Goldsmith."

"Must you?" he pleaded and she replied with an airy wave, "not for very much longer," before leaving the room and allowing her brightness to vanish. It would be a relief when Saturday night came.

143

The thought of seeing Marie and David got her through the next few days. She had booked a room for them and they arrived in time for dinner on Saturday evening. Marie was shocked at how strained and thin Pamela looked and said so to David.

"She looks worn out, poor girl. She should never have taken on a job." They didn't know what to expect, so were nicely surprised to see Gerald sitting up in bed, eagerly awaiting their arrival, and he did indeed look bright eyed and cheerful; gone was the long face and the tetchiness. Thanks to the sedative, he was relaxed and calm, so they had no idea what Pamela and the staff had patiently dealt with over the past six weeks. During the hour they had waited so long for, they caught up on news from home that seemed to have escaped the regular letters. Felicity passed her driving test with flying colours and could now ferry them about. Alexander was studying hard for his 'A' levels, and Lorna was on the mend. Another two weeks and she should be well enough to return to work. Marie clapped her hand over her mouth as she saw Pamela and Gerald's surprised expressions and remembered that they had kept that unfortunate news from them, but looking after Lorna had been such a large part of her own and Felicity's life for the last few weeks, that she completely forgot in the excitement of the moment.

David looked at her fondly. "Everything is under control," he reassured them. "We are all a pretty good team, even if I do say so myself, and by the way, Robert wants to come to see you next week. He is doing a grand job assisting me, couldn't have done without him."

Pamela glowed happily and Gerald gave a contented nod. They couldn't wait to hear from Robert himself, on how he was coping.

David and Marie stayed over until the Monday morning then caught the train back to Southampton, where David put Marie on the train for Cornwall before going to the factory, where Robert would meet him later in the day.

CHAPTER ELEVEN

Now that she was no longer working, Pamela spent her time between visits by strolling along the embankment. On the second day, she got as far as the Tate Gallery and spent far longer than she had intended, viewing the wonderful paintings and works of art so consequently had to catch a bus back for the two o'clock visiting hour. She picked up every bit of literature she could find, to take in to Gerald, hoping it would stimulate him, but he showed little interest beyond flicking through the expensive catalogue of paintings. He had never been a great reader, unless it was the Financial Times newspaper, which he always read from cover to cover; he had no quiet hobbies, so time hung heavily for him, which meant she couldn't miss a single visit. Charles telephoned to ask if he could visit on Wednesday and Ann said she would be free, so it was the perfect opportunity for their half-planned trip on the river. Gerald would be more than happy to be alone with Charles; he would be able to talk business to his heart's content.

So far, the weather had been disappointingly grey with rain clouds scurrying across the sky, making the waters of the Thames look leaden, but on Wednesday it dawned bright and cold with a clear, blue sky. Ann would be able to get away by 11:30 and they would catch the ferry from Charing Cross, which would take them along the river to Greenwich. Rather than wait around for her all morning, Ann suggested Pamela should go sightseeing and meet her by the ferry terminal at midday. They would have lunch in a nice little Italian bistro nearby and board the ferry afterwards.

Pamela went off, happily clutching her A-Z. A full day seemed luxury indeed and there was so much to see, it was exciting. At Chelsea Bridge, she realised that weaving her way along the crowded pavements was going to take too long, so she hopped on a red double-decker bus with 'Westminster' blazoned in large letters on the front, and was soon bowling along beside the Thames. She watched, fascinated, from her front seat on top. People were going in every direction. The traffic was awesome; she had never seen so much traffic. Wherever she looked there was bustle: boats with their various cargoes, chugging along the river, high rise flats, for the most part ugly, but necessary to house London's teeming population, crowded buses spewing passengers out on to the pavement at each stop, then taking on the waiting queues – like a replay on film she thought, smiling to herself.

The Houses of Parliament, on her right, looking grand and imposing, told her she had reached her destination, so she made her way gingerly to the stairway at the rear of the bus. There was an art to walking on buses, she decided, watching a strikingly pretty West Indian girl, in high heels, nonchalantly swaying to its rhythm and gliding effortlessly down on to the pavement, just as the bus came to a jerking halt. Whilst she, on the other hand, clutched frantically at the rail to prevent herself from falling headlong down the same stairs, looked down at her sensible, fur-lined boots, and breathed, 'How do they do that?'

Westminster Abbey took her breath away. The size, the magnificent architecture the rich history, filled her with awe, and once again, she carefully folded a wad of leaflets and stowed them in her large shoulder bag, for Gerald. There was something about the whole atmosphere, even if you weren't religious, that made you want to kneel, and she chose The Battle of Britain Chapel in which to offer up a heartfelt little prayer. The plaque said it had been dedicated in 1947. She would have been twenty-two. Robert was born the following year. The years had gone by so quickly and she had hardly been out of Cornwall since the boys were born. They had been contented, fulfilling years with her boys and the love of the man she adored, a wonderful family life, which she had missed out on when her fighter pilot father was killed, and her mother had married a Canadian officer, and gone to Canada. At first, they had exchanged birthday and Christmas cards and the occasional letter, but even that stopped after two years, and in the last letter, her mother was so full of her new life, and the baby she was expecting, that Pamela felt left out and hadn't replied. Shortly after that she had met Gerald.

She left the abbey, by the massive, age-old doors, feeling a new sense of tranquillity after wandering slowly up and down, lost in thought, reading the inscriptions on the tombs, visiting Henry VIII's chapel and imagining the countless, famous feet that had trodden the hallowed floors, in centuries of pageantry.

Outside in the wintry sunshine, she found a seat and consulted her map. It was less than a mile to Charing Cross. She would walk. By twelve noon she was waiting on the Victoria Embankment, by twelve-thirty, when there was still no sign of Ann, doubt began to nag. If she left the spot to telephone, she might miss her, but how long should she wait? By one o'clock, she made up her mind to find the nearest telephone. Supposing Ann had had an accident on her way here? She started to walk away, but within a few steps, she heard pounding footsteps and a hand caught her shoulder.

"Phew! Just in time," Bill panted. She gave a startled smile and he went on to explain that as Ann was about to leave, the wife of Robbie, the resident chef, had gone into labour.

"Ann is so upset at letting you down, but they are worried because the baby is early, and it's their first. You will know how it is." He gave a sympathetic grin.

Pamela understood, but her crestfallen face told him how much she had been looking forward to the outing.

"Of all days! Poor you."

"Poor Ann, at least I am out on this beautiful day."

"Will you go on the river trip, by yourself?"

"Probably not. There will be another time."

"On a cheerful note, you could have less time than you think. The tests that we started on Monday show such a marked improvement on the X-rays, that your husband could go home quite a bit sooner than we thought." He waited for the news to sink in, and was rewarded by a dazzling smile. Gosh, she is a lovely woman, he thought wistfully, before reminding himself, yet again, that she had a husband. He missed her at work. He had enjoyed seeing her slim figure coming towards him, wearing the pale green and white uniform. She wore it with the same style and elegance as she wore her own designer clothes, and he was totally fascinated by the way a single lock of auburn hair always escaped the starched white cap. He had to stop himself from tucking it back. Today her hair hung loose, reaching her shoulders in such a glorious abundance of shining copper, that he wanted to sink his fingers into it, pull her towards him and kiss her. He suddenly realised she was looking at him enquiringly, having asked him a question he hadn't heard at all.

"Sorry?"

"I asked if you knew where the Italian Bistro was, where Ann booked a table? Would she have thought to cancel?"

"We could find out. I know it well."

He took her arm and guided her towards a small side street, where just inside, on the left, a gaily coloured awning covered a narrow entrance, made narrower by a potted bay tree on either side, which led to 'Toni's'. Inside it was warm and inviting and quite dark. Red furnishings gave an air of opulence, and the owner, a dark haired, olive skinned, stocky figure hurried forward smiling broadly, almost singing his greetings to 'Doctor Beel' and then when Bill introduced her, he began again, in soft, dulcet tones. "Bella. Bella, senorita," looking at her with admiring, large, brown, doe like eyes. "You sitta down. Plise." He gestured to an alcove. "I will fetcha you some wine. You musta have some wine." Bill tried to explain but he was left talking to thin air and they laughed good-humouredly as they slid behind the snowy white tablecloth.

"The table's booked and we have already kept them waiting nearly an hour." Bill debated. "I could make a phone call I suppose. How do you feel about eating?"

"Why not? If you have time," she said with enthusiasm, feeling good at the wonderful news about Gerald. "I need to celebrate and it isn't the same on your own."

Once again there was that brilliant smile and his mind was made up.

147

Toni returned, balancing two glasses and a bottle of red wine on a small, round tray, a snowy napkin draped over his arm.

Bill went off to make his telephone call. "That's settled then," he said on his return. "You have my undivided attention until six o'clock. You needn't miss your river trip after all." He smiled boyishly and her "Really?" was a little uncertain as she wondered what Gerald would say, but she smothered the thought. She was in London, sitting in a new and exciting place, with someone who made her feel – quite special. It was very exhilarating, after the last worrying few weeks; Gerald would be more than happy today, discussing business with Charles, she told herself.

She left the ordering to Bill, not having tasted Italian food before, and she wasn't disappointed. The starter was melon with Parma ham, followed by a main course of seafood lasagne, perfectly accompanied by a bottle of 'Soave Di Verona', one of Italy's best white wines; she had to refuse the scrumptious looking 'Zabaglione All Ameretto', which Bill tucked into with relish, waving her white napkin in surrender. The meal was a whole new experience for her, the piquancy was delicious, and used, as she was, to Marie's good, wholesome food, she realised the richness of the sauces and the liberal helpings of garlic, would probably not be acceptable to everyone at home. She imagined David throwing his hands up in horror and a little smile curved her lips.

"What?" Bill asked softly, looking at her in a way that made her catch her breath.

"I have never tasted anything so absolutely different and delicious. It makes me wonder what other dishes I should try," she said, holding her glass out.

He chinked it with his, saying, "Here's to new experiences then."

They were flirting mildly and enjoying it, when Toni arrived, bringing with him the wonderful aroma of freshly percolated coffee. He twinkled at them as he set the tray on the table, then went off singing 'Volare' softly. Bill grinned. "He is always telling me that I must 'finda a nicea girl, and havea many bambinos." He waved his hands in the air, gesturing as Toni did; she giggled uncontrollably at his accent.

"He and his wife are probably back there planning the wedding breakfast right now."

Pamela managed to stop laughing. "You mean he thinks – you and me?" She burst into more laughter as he nodded.

"They see romance everywhere and it is a long time since I lunched with a lady."

"Have you never thought of marrying?" she asked, more seriously.

"There was a girl once, but she said I was already married – to the clinic. Couldn't understand why I wouldn't agree to join her father, as junior partner in his very lucrative Harley Street practice, to keep her in the style to which she had become accustomed."

"So she left you, because you refused?"

"Not really. I left *her* because she said it didn't have to make any difference; Daddy would always increase her allowance for the time being, and Daddy would always find a place for me, when I got tired of playing hospitals and was ready to earn some real money. I was struggling at the time, you see."

"It must have made you more determined to succeed, I imagine," she said, indignant *for* him.

"You could say that, especially when she married a penniless friend of mine, six months later. He drives a Bentley and takes her on two foreign holidays a year now." He gave a rueful grin.

"Regrets?"

"None."

"Good." She looked at her wristwatch.

"Yes, it's time we were moving; I'll get the bill." He finished the last of his coffee and caught Toni's eye.

Stepping outside, they blinked in the strong sunlight, which seemed even brighter after the dimness and he took her arm to guide her across the road. "Just in time," he said, catching sight of the embarking ferry passengers as they neared the pier.

It was a perfect day to be chugging along the river, although as always, it was quite a bit colder on the water. She was glad of the fur-trimmed hood on her cashmere, camel coat. The coat was long and reached the top of her boots; beneath it she wore a mustard coloured dress. She looked stylish and completely at home in London, and Bill was surprised to learn she knew very little about the capital.

"How come?"

"Until I was sixteen, I was at boarding school in Surrey. From there I joined the nursing profession and spent the war years in Hampshire, working my way up to Sister. Promotion came quickly," she said modestly. "They were desperate for nurses. I met Gerald on my first appointment as Sister; we married just before the war ended in 1944. Robert was born two years later, I moved to Cornwall to be with his family and we have been there ever since."

Bill's jaw had dropped. "You aren't old enough to have done war work."

She blushed. "Thank you, kind sir."

They were standing by the rail. Bill had laughingly advised, 'the pointed end', and they had a clear view of everything. He gestured first to a towering obelisk, standing on the Victoria Embankment. "Cleopatra's Needle. It is sixty-eight and a half feet high and made of granite, and that is the dome of St. Paul's

Cathedral you can see in the distance. See? It's magnificent. Christopher Wren was the architect. No one can touch him in my opinion. You really should go and see it." Later he pointed to a ship, anchored at Tower Pier. "Look, there is HMS Belfast. She is a cruiser and she led the D Day landing at Normandy." Further on they passed Traitors Gate, through which prisoners awaiting execution were led to The Tower, long ago. There were numerous wharfs and piers; in fact the river was a hive of activity. Barges pulling as many as three tug boats chugged along, in a timeless way, piled high with cargo destined for one of the unloading bays, where cheery dock hands waited.

"There is Greenwich. The Cutty Sark is in dry dock here. She was the most famous of the tea clippers, bringing tea from China to Britain in the 19th century, and did you know that The Tall Ships Race commemorates her?" Bill said, thoroughly warmed to his subject.

Pamela watched his face, alive with enthusiasm, oblivious to everything except the history of the river. He sensed the silence and turned towards her with a self-conscious look. "Sorry, I get carried away."

"You've made it a fascinating trip and I've enjoyed every minute. You really love London, don't you?"

"Best place in the world."

"I'm beginning to understand that," she said softly.

They smiled together and he automatically moved nearer to share the intimate moment of discovering a mutual interest.

"There is so much I would like to show you," he said with a wistful smile. At journeys end they allowed everyone else to disembark before wandering to the gangplank, reluctant to end the afternoon. The winter sun was setting and the sky was darkening rapidly, even though it was only three-thirty.

"My car is parked five minutes away. I would rather drive you home safely, if you don't mind a small detour to pick up some notes I need for this evening."

She accepted, happy they didn't have to part company just yet. He quickly got them away from busy Westminster, driving unerringly through the side roads towards Chelsea and pulled in to a small cul-de-sac, where a row of four mews houses faced the black painted railings of a park. It constantly amazed her, how many small, well kept parks there were in the centre of London.

From the outside the houses were quaintly picturesque, and she gave a gasp of admiration. "What a wonderful place to live!"

"I fell for it the moment I saw it. Want to see inside?"

They stepped straight into the living area. It was surprisingly spacey, with an archway leading to a good sized kitchen, beyond which a sliding door led on to a walled patio; not big but completely private. A short staircase rose from the lounge up to one large room and a luxury bathroom. Pamela was full of admiration.

"I have never seen anything so compact."

"Not an inch of wasted space; rather clever, isn't it?" he said proudly as they returned downstairs. "Have we got time for a cuppa? It's only a ten minute drive to Cheyne Walk from here."

She looked at her watch. "Sounds good, shall I make it?"

"Ok, I'll get my papers together."

She leant against the archway, waiting for the kettle to boil, watching him deftly sort papers and stow them into a briefcase.

"Step into my office," he joked, waving his hand at the ingeniously fitted alcove, which held fitted shelving, a desk top, which pulled out, a typewriter and a direct telephone line to the clinic, all behind double pine doors.

"You are certainly organised. Do you have to bring much work home?" she asked, surprised.

"I find it easier. Too many interruptions at work."

She made the tea and poured two mugs, calling out to ask if he took sugar. It was all so casual, as if they had known each other for years and when she put the tray on the coffee table, he sat beside her on the settee.

She commented on the absence of a fireplace and it being so warm.

"Central heating," he explained. "Far less fuss."

"How sensible. We freeze in the winter, even with roaring fires." She made a mental note to mention the idea to Gerald and stopped short.

"What's the matter? You look like you've seen a ghost."

"Just feeling guilty."

He got up and put his jacket on. "C'mon, time to go." As he helped her on with her coat she reached up and kissed his cheek. "Thanks for a perfect day."

"For me too," he said huskily. His hands held her briefly before they drew apart and she gave one last look back before he turned off the lights and they stepped out in to the darkness.

"It's like a little haven," she said, not realising how wistful she sounded.

He kept the engine running when they arrived back at the hotel and reaching into the glove compartment, pressed a key in to her palm. "I'm home by seven-thirty most nights, but if you need a bolt-hole through the day, help yourself. Alright?" She nodded dumbly, too overcome to speak, as he went round to open the door for her.

Going straight to her room, she slipped her coat and shoes off and flopped on the bed, her mind in turmoil, but a knock on the door brought her upright again.

151

"Come in," she called expecting Ann but it was Charles bearing a tray with two glasses of sherry.

"Do you mind company?" he asked, setting it on the bedside table. She jumped up and threw her arms about him, making him laugh with embarrassment.

"I say, steady on old girl."

She burst into tears. "It's so good to see you."

"There, there, not really as tough as you make out, are you?" He sat her gently on the bed and held out a glass. "They allowed me to stay the whole afternoon. His mind is at rest about Sheffield and he seemed in fine form when I left. I'll come back with you at six o'clock. I was going home tonight but perhaps I had better stay." He gave her a concerned look, wishing Felicity or Marie, were there.

"Go home, Charles. Felicity will be expecting you. I'm alright." She wiped her eyes, smiled and took a sip of sherry. "There. See?"

"Another ten minutes," he said looking at his pocket watch – a habit of his when he was worried.

It was a fine, cold night and as they walked the short distance to the clinic; Charles must have been picturing her days, punctuated only by visiting hours.

"Your days are disjointed I imagine."

"I'm trying to see a bit of London; Ann and I have become good friends. There isn't time though, to go far between visiting hours. I *want* to visit of course, and it is *a lot* worse for Gerald," she added hastily, afraid that Charles would get the wrong impression.

"Mm, I see what you mean. I could come next Wednesday, would that help?"

"Could you?" she asked as they crunched up the drive, waving to Gerald's waiting figure. It reminded her of when Gerald had seen her getting in to Bill's car and she was glad she hadn't mentioned that Gerald might be released earlier than expected, she wouldn't have known yet if she and Bill had not met. Perhaps Gerald didn't know yet, either. As it happened, he couldn't wait to tell them and was so engrossed with future plans that *her* day out was forgotten. Charles went home happily, promising to visit the following Wednesday, when David would probably come as well.

In the meantime, Robbie's wife and baby were doing well, and Ann was planning a day round the shops for them. They chose Tuesday, the day when Bill's colleague was due to see Gerald.

They set off early and made straight for Harrods. One of London's most exclusive stores, where Pamela spotted a black dress that was hard to resist.

"Treat yourself. It will cheer you up," Ann urged, as she hesitated. She made other purchases, including some pure silk shirts for Alexander, and they arrived home tired but happy after a memorable day together.

Best of all though, Gerald's news was good. Depending on his continued progress, he should be allowed home in four weeks' time. Suddenly he was his old self again. The staff couldn't believe the change in him; Pamela was able to relax and miss the occasional visit, because he was up for a few hours a day and even went to the day room to play cards with another patient. The night nurse, instead of leaving his room as soon as possible, now stayed chatting and made sure he got his newspaper early; she was even heard to say, that although he liked his own way still, she didn't mind when he was so charming. Nurse Bennet had also succumbed when he sent them both a bouquet of flowers, with a small card thanking them for their patience in putting up with him. Pamela hid a smile and shook her head. He had them eating out of his hand – and he knew it.

With Gerald's improved mood, Pamela mentioned her desire to see more of London and go sightseeing together, when he was able to, and was completely dashed by his blunt refusal to even consider it.

"Definitely not. It won't worry me if I never see London again," he said shaking his head vehemently. She knew that look; he wouldn't change his mind, but she had set her heart on it and, come what may, she intended to see London.

The following Wednesday lunchtime, when Charles and David arrived, it was rainy and overcast, and she was at a loose end – no point in going with them, they would be talking business and she would be bored and in the way. The idea of hiding away in Bill's cosy house for a few hours beckoned. The key still burned a hole in her coat pocket and her heart thumped at the thought, but sitting around the hotel all afternoon would drive her mad she argued with herself and the decision was made.

The taxi, which she hailed at the end of Cheyne Walk, took her the short distance to Chelsea and at her request, dropped her beside a small parade of shops, one of which was a homemade bakery and delicatessen. She bought a crusty French stick and three different cheeses, picked up a bottle of wine from the off licence next door, and made her way to the cul-de-sac, telling herself all the time, "You aren't doing anything wrong." The warmth closed around her like a pair of welcoming arms, as she let herself into the cottage and shut the door behind her. Almost immediately the quietness fell about her seeming to create a vacuum, cutting her off from the outside world and the worries of the last weeks. She relaxed and gave a huge sigh of relief, took her purchases to the kitchen and slipped out of her coat and boots. She sat in one of the armchairs, glanced around then got up again, hugging herself with pure joy. A pile of women's magazines on the coffee table caught her eye and she wondered, curiously, to whom they belonged. There was a note attached to the top one: 'Dear Pamela, Welcome! If you are reading this, you must be here. Make yourself at home. Help yourself to food, drink and music. The magazines are for you. Bill.'

She gave a misty little smile, touched by his thoughtfulness and curled up on the settee with one of them. She didn't know how long she slept, but woke to the sound of a key in the lock and Bill's blond head peeping round the door; their eyes met in a smile.

"Hoped you would be here, Ann said you had gone out, and I couldn't imagine you walking around in this weather, so I took a chance." He came further in to the room. "I haven't come to disturb you; it's just that I have been given four tickets for the theatre tonight. They are for 'The Mousetrap'. Ann and Roy are coming; it doesn't start until eight o'clock. Plenty of time to fit visiting hour in first." His eyes twinkled at her. "You will love it, I promise. Say yes."

Her face lit up eagerly. A night at the theatre would be wonderful. Her face fell.

"What?" Bill asked.

"Gerald will get upset and send his blood pressure soaring."

He gave a soft: "Aah!" Then gently took her hands in his long fingers.

"What about the ferry ride? He didn't get upset about that, so why should he get upset if you go to the theatre with the three of us?"

She coloured and mumbled, "I didn't tell him. He made himself *ill* when he saw you give me a lift in the teeming rain." She gave a guilty shrug. "It seemed for the best."

"Is he always so jealous?" He frowned.

"He's never had cause before."

"Has he got cause now?" he asked softly, looking deep into her eyes, with a look that made her catch her breath. Senses reeling, heart thumping she averted her gaze, trying to stop the painful beating. He turned her hand over and kissed the palm, very gently.

"Don't answer that." He got up abruptly and went to the kitchen.

"Come on, I could do with a coffee." He let out a "Wow!" as he spotted the bread and cheeses. "Planning on a party while I was out, were you?" He wagged a finger at her as she followed him, laughing.

"I thought you would enjoy it with the wine tonight. Just a little thank you for lending me your home."

He fought the impulse to take her in his arms.

"Just got time for a quick coffee, then I'll have to fly."

After he had gone, she wondered who would take her place, overwhelmed with disappointment. The joy had gone from the day and after another cup of coffee, which she drank curled up on the settee, flicking aimlessly through one of the magazines, she put her boots and coat on, took a last lingering look and left. Sitting in the back of the taxi, which she picked up at the nearby taxi rank, she studied her feelings. Instead of looking forward to returning to Cornwall, her heart sank at the very thought of going back now. She was appalled at how deeply she felt about missing so much in her life. How could she not have realised that there was so much more to life than Anders Folly? But then she had two wonderful boys and a husband she adored, she argued with herself and after the war, it had seemed like heaven to get away from the constant reminders. The dreadful sights that she had seen in her nursing days had stayed with her for a long time. Not that she was the only one, she reminded herself, but where had the years gone? The last time she had seen London, so much of it had been bombed or boarded up; there were shelters, sandbags and debris everywhere you looked, but now it was throbbing with life: theatres, shops, museums, wonderful buildings to explore, and the river, a constant source of delight even on grey days. How could she possibly settle back into their old life, having had such a tantalisingly small taste of what London had to offer? She recalled Toni's restaurant and the memorable ferry ride afterwards, then riding through the crowded, darkening streets to the cul-de-sac and seeing Bill's home for the first time – but most of all, a pair of brown eyes laughing into hers. The thought that Gerald *might* be persuaded to change his mind brought little comfort. She knew now that it was Bill, with his zest and boundless enthusiasm for it, whom she wanted to see London with. This realisation both surprised and shocked her, but could not be denied.

Her thoughts were interrupted as the taxi stopped at the curb. It was still raining heavily, so she paid the driver through the glass partition, before alighting and running quickly into the hotel. Ann was beside the reception desk. "Guess what!" she beamed.

Pamela forced a smile. "You are going to the theatre."

"Correction. *We* are going to the theatre. All four of us."

Pamela looked dubious. "I went and fixed it up this afternoon. Your husband's father and brother were with him, obviously celebrating the success of some business deal. Champagne no less! Dinner has been ordered for the three of them – in the room – this evening. His father arranged everything while I was there. I was very impressed. What Mr Anders *senior* says, goes; and he says you should have a night out." She beamed again. "Bill said how disappointed you were; it was his idea for me to ask."

Pamela didn't know what to say, confused thoughts tumbled through her mind and she looked at Ann blankly, unable to take in the speedy change of events. Only a minute ago, she had been full of despair and now she was going to the theatre. She hugged Ann.

"I can't believe it," she whispered.

"Wear the black dress."

"It was supposed to be for Gerald's first night out."

"Buy another." Ann giggled delightedly.

"You sound like two school girls," Roy said with a disapproving tut, hurrying past on his way to the bar with a plate piled high with smoked salmon sandwiches.

"Bill is picking us up at seven. See you later." Ann hurried off.

Pamela flew upstairs, her spirits soaring at the prospect of not only going out, but being with Bill. She was quite certain something would happen to prevent their evening together, and lived on tenterhooks, until they were actually in the car on their way to the Haymarket.

The theatre was packed and the play every bit as good as reputed to be. In the interval, the four of them had drinks in the bar, where Pamela sat quietly drinking in the atmosphere. Bill and Ann exchanged smiles, enjoying her look of wonderment, as she took note of the clothes and hairstyles, eavesdropping unashamedly on snatches of conversation, until a bell signalled the performance was about to start again, and there was a general move towards the auditorium.

Bill took her arm and they followed Ann and Roy.

"You look absolutely beautiful," he whispered in her ear, as they inched their way back to their seats, and was rewarded with a dazzling smile as she fingered the orchid pinned to her dress.

"Thank you for my lovely flowers. You look pretty amazing, as well." She had only ever seen him in everyday clothes before, but tonight was an occasion, and he looked heart-stopping in his black evening suit and bow tie, so much so, that when he arrived to pick them up, bearing a corsage for Ann and herself, her hands had trembled so much she couldn't pin it to her new black dress, and he had done it for her, making her heart beat even harder with his nearness. Right now she was very aware of his hand on her arm and the way in which he was looking at her as they shuffled forward, but they reached their seats, at last, and the tension eased as she sat next to Ann and they opened their programmes. As the lights dimmed Bill eased across so that their shoulders touched, and remained so until the show ended.

On the way home in the car, Bill invited them back for a nightcap, but Roy refused. "Sorry Bill, we left Colin in charge of the bar, and he has to be up at the crack of dawn." Colin was their only son, and after studying Catering and Hotel

156

Management, had landed his first job in a big London hotel, where he started at some unearthly hour in the morning.

"Of course! I had forgotten."

"We also have to clear up before bedtime," Ann reminded him, "but come in and talk to Pam, while we get on, or *she* might even like to go back for a nightcap with you," she added as an afterthought. "It seems a shame to end *your* evening this early."

"Nice idea. It's only eleven o'clock and I could get you back by just after midnight. Would you like to?" Bill asked. Pamela made a show of hesitating, knowing full well she was going to accept.

"It would round the evening off nicely. Thank you, I would love to." She sounded cool and quite matter-of-fact, but it was far from how she was feeling. She knew she was playing with fire, but had to go; to be alone with Bill, was all she could think about at that moment; when might there be another opportunity? After dropping Ann and Roy at the hotel, they drove to Chelsea in silence. Once inside the cottage he slid her coat off and let it fall to the floor, then took her in his arms. She didn't resist. This was what she had been longing for and suddenly all doubts and feelings of guilt disappeared, almost as if she was another person, who only existed here and now. When he released her, she frowned, so he took her hand and led her to the kitchen, collected two glasses, put them in her free hand, then picked up a bottle of wine, before leading her to the foot of the stairs, where, in answer to an enquiring raise of his eyebrows, she gave a small nod. It felt so natural to be going upstairs with him; at that moment nothing else existed and her thoughts belonged to him, entirely.

His lovemaking was gentle and sensuous, making her moan softly with ecstasy, as he kissed and explored her naked body, before possessing her. Time stood still and she wanted it to go on forever. Here and now, this stolen moment was all that mattered.

Dawn was breaking when Bill took her back to the hotel. He kissed her and closed the door, leaving her rooted to the spot in the dimly lit hall, gazing in panic until a door creaked in the distance, galvanising her into action and she fled to her room. Ann must have known that she wasn't in her room when they locked up for the night. It began to dawn on her, just what was at risk, for her unforgettable night of passion, as she lay in bed, feeling so wide awake that sleep seemed out of the question. The repercussions if Gerald found out were unthinkable. His pride would never let him forgive her. What had she done? His face floated before her, as it always did when they were apart but then his face blurred strangely and a blond head appeared vividly on the pillow beside her, bringing a dreamy smile to her lips and a trance like feeling that lulled her in to a deep, satisfying sleep.

Ann woke her with coffee and fruit juice at ten o'clock, and she blushed furiously as memory returned.

"I expect you could have slept on. I wouldn't have woken you, but your husband phoned to say he needs his briefcase this morning. He sounds chirpy. I suppose that means you will be leaving soon. I shall miss you," she said sadly, perching on the side of the bed.

Pamela covered her embarrassment by sitting up and rubbing her eyes.

"Lovely evening, wasn't it?" Ann chattered on oblivious to Pamela's discomfort.

"Mmm, lovely." This was accompanied by a sleepy yawn.

"I see you aren't used to late nights. Comes from living in the country," she said cheerfully. "We often arrived home with the milk, before we started the business."

"We got talking. Hope I didn't disturb you, " she mumbled

"No, I knew it had to be you. Bill and Colin are the only ones with a key, and we have a buzzer in our bedroom: just a safety precaution. There is a different buzzer if someone opens the door from the inside. It has been known for one person to book in and later let someone else in, and two stay for the price of one, or even try to skip off without paying the bill."

Intrigued, Pamela gave up pretending. "Things like that really happen?"

"I could tell you a hundred stories. This is, after all, London in the sixties," Ann said with a philosophical shrug as she left.

"And anything goes," Pamela said softly, pursing her lips at the closed door, relieved that her behaviour hadn't caused comment.

Gerald was shaving and two nurses were changing his bed when she arrived with his briefcase, so she left quickly, promising to return for the two o'clock visiting hour. On her way out, she caught a glimpse of Bill, speaking on the telephone in Matron's office and raised her hand to him. He turned sharply away; she gulped and hurried on. It had been like a slap in the face. Why had he behaved like that? Her stomach churned. Had he lost interest now? Tears blinded her as she walked back to the hotel, all thought of sightseeing vanished from her mind. Hurrying up to her room, she threw herself on the freshly made bed. Filled with doubt, she berated herself. What a fool she had been. Nausea swept over her and she ran for the bathroom. After a while, she told herself that it didn't matter. What did she care? And what did she expect? He was a good-looking bachelor with his own home – a successful doctor. He must have women queuing up. Despairing tears ran down her face, and she yearned to go to the cottage, but the thought of further humiliation held her back.

Two pain-filled days went by without a sight or sound from him, days in which she struggled to behave as if nothing was wrong, but Gerald could see she wasn't herself, and suggested to Charles, perhaps Felicity would enjoy a week in London with her.

Felicity's arrival on the Saturday morning came as a complete surprise and Pamela was quite overcome to see her. Charles brought her, and the plan was for them to go sightseeing, while he took over the visiting until Sunday, when he would return home, and return to collect Felicity the following weekend.

By Sunday morning however, Felicity decided the plan to cheer Pamela up was not working. Pamela was obviously ill and needed to be at home with the family, so she asked Charles to take them both home on Sunday.

"You will be *fine* when you are *at home*, with the family. *Gerald* won't mind. He *knows* it's been an ordeal for you and in two weeks' time he will be home anyway. You need to rest before looking after him; *please* say you will come," Felicity begged.

Pamela was dismayed at the thought of leaving, but Bill was obviously keeping out of her way; Ann had received a very brief note saying: 'Gone to Scotland. Will explain later.'

"He does that sometimes. Says it recharges his batteries." She sighed airily. "Alright for some, isn't it?"

Depressed and distraught, Pamela kept asking herself why? She had been sure he felt the same way. He must have had second thoughts, couldn't face telling her, and run off to avoid embarrassment. What other explanation was there?

Her misery was misread. Fortunately the family were convinced she just needed to see the boys and home again; the whole thing had just been too much for her and in the end she gave way and agreed to leave. It would have been difficult not to, after such an issue was made of her health.

Ann was sad to see her leave. "You will come back soon, won't you? There is a spare room in our quarters and we could have another trip to the West End. Promise not to lose touch."

Pamela promised, hoping with all her heart she could keep the promise, as she waved goodbye.

She slept most of the way, from sheer nervous exhaustion, curled up in the back of the roomy Zephyr that Charles now drove, having passed his Morris Minor on to Felicity. The journey passed quickly, but driving through the trees that formed the entrance to Anders Folly, seeing David's impressive circular fish pond in the centre of the gravel drive and Marie standing in the doorway, just as she had been when they left, was like returning to another age, and her feelings were very mixed. Inside the house, everything would be exactly the same. Lorna would be cooking, Abigail would be helping, and David would have banked the log fire ready for the evening, which they would spend sitting round it. They were caught in a time warp of at least twenty years ago. Despondency swept over her and she wept.

An understanding look passed between Felicity and Charles. They were relieved to be back as well, after only a few days in London. She would be fine as soon as Gerald came home. Relief and exhaustion everyone decided, was the reason for her frequent tears. Everyone that is except David, who asked himself: what had happened since that night when he had seen her looking so radiant. The night she had gone to the theatre. It was by chance he had seen her. Gerald had changed his mind at the last minute, imploring him to fetch Pamela, insisting she should be celebrating with them, not gallivanting with strangers. David had laughingly tried to dissuade him, but Gerald was not to be thwarted, so he had reluctantly walked along to the hotel. Pamela was waiting in the foyer with the Mellors; a very different Pamela to the tired and worried one he had seen earlier. She looked wonderfully elegant and happy, but her radiant smile disappeared as she saw him walking towards her. She had obviously been expecting this. His fondness for her welled up inside him. It stemmed, not only from her devotion to his son, but also from a very real affection and understanding. If he had been blessed with a daughter, he would have liked her to be just like Pamela. It also occurred to him that she looked very much in keeping with her surroundings. He had never expected she would settle in Cornwall as she had, and he couldn't have been happier when she did, but *he* couldn't have settled for it at her age, that he knew. Marie's health had been his reason for going back to his old home, and it had been their best decision, as far as he was concerned. But then he had had the best of both worlds for the past twenty years. Pamela had yet to come to terms with Gerald staying at home. His travelling had made every weekend an occasion, for all of them, but most of all for Pamela. All these thoughts flitted through his mind as he approached her, watching her anticipated disappointment. He knew she would come if he asked. In that moment he knew he couldn't do it to her. She deserved a night out. She looked too beautiful to sit in a hospital room.

"All ready then?" He had greeted her, as they came level. "Just got to get something from my room. Have a nice evening, all of you," and he had carried on walking, but not before he had seen her smiling relief. He had no way of knowing how that evening had changed Pamela's life forever.

CHAPTER TWELVE

Alexander was bored. His parents should have been away for weeks yet, but not only had his mother come home already, but his father was due in less than two weeks and why was she walking around like a zombie? She didn't even hear half the things he said to her, let alone listen with interest, in her usual way. She didn't care. She was like all the others – except for Nanny, of course. He consoled himself with the thought of the silk shirts from Harrods. When he started work, he would wear silk shirts all the time, *and* silk pyjamas *and* underwear. Spurred on by imagination, the possibilities appeared endless and his eyes gleamed with excitement. He couldn't wait to get away from this place, he thought, gazing around as he climbed the main staircase.

As he reached the landing, his ear caught the muffled sound of a vacuum cleaner, coming from the room where Laurie had slept and with a further rush of excitement he realised the house was empty on this gloomy, Monday afternoon, except for Lorna in the kitchen – with the radio playing, and Abigail upstairs – with the radio playing. The others had all gone food shopping. Without further thought he sidled into the bedroom, the thick carpet and the hum of the cleaner deadening his footsteps. Maisie was unaware that he had shut the door and crept up on her, until he gave her a resounding slap on her well-rounded bottom.

She spun round, shocked and startled, eyes like saucers, cheeks bright red with both indignation and exertion from her efforts of vacuuming under the bed. His eyes took in the rise and fall of her creamy breasts, which swelled above the neck of her drawstring blouse. He made a grab for her and she stepped backwards, but she caught her foot in the flex and silence fell, as the plug was wrenched from the electric socket.

She would have fallen, had the bed not saved her and while she was trying to recover, he launched himself on top of her, pinning her arms to the bed with one hand and kissing her roughly, while his other hand tore at her blouse. She struggled and screamed as the drawstring slipped undone and the blouse fell away, revealing her full breasts.

Alexander gave an exultant cry and his eyes glittered lecherously; he raised himself on one knee to yank her skirt up, just as he had seen it done on the television, and in that moment, Maisie, galvanised into action, brought her knee up hard. He gave an agonised groan and doubled up clutching himself, just as the door opened and Abigail, wearing a look of utter disbelief, stood rooted to the spot whilst Maisie jumped up, adjusting her blouse and ran for the door.

But Abigail was barring her way and had recovered enough to demand, "What is going on? What have you done to him?"

It was Maisie's turn to stare in disbelief, but before she could defend herself, Alexander got in first.

"She was leading me on. It wasn't my fault," he gasped.

"That would be right. You haven't heard the last of this young woman. This could mean the sack."

Maisie found her voice. "We'll see about thaat; *anyone* could see what was goin' on. Anyone with a grain o' sense thaat is."

"Don't speak to Nanny, like that," Alexander groaned, still clutching himself.

Maisie realised there was no point in defending herself. "My Dad and brother'll be none to pleased at the way I bin treated today," and with that she brushed past Abigail, stormed down the stairs and marched in to the kitchen, where Lorna, in the act of putting a steak and kidney pie in to the oven, froze at the sight of her dishevelled niece.

"Whatever's the matter child?"

"That Master Alexander jus tried to 'ave 'is way wi' me and thaat Nanny o'his blames me; says I could get the sack. Supposin' they all believes 'im?" A sob caught in her throat and for an instant, Lorna thought that she was going to burst in to tears, but tossing her light brown hair, she said indignantly, "Why would I want thaat great lump when I got my Jake? Jake's gentle. I never been treated like thaat afore." This time she did burst in to tears.

"There, there, child, we know you better than that." Lorna went to her and put an arm about her shaking shoulders. She had obviously had a fright. Who would have thought that no good son would go this far? "Sit down, I'll make a cup of tea."

Inwardly she was fuming and ten minutes later, when Abigail strode in, obviously meaning business, Lorna was ready for her, saying with calm authority, "Before you say anything, this matter is too serious for a servant to deal with; I shall be speaking to his mother." Stony faced, she picked up her rolling pin and vigorously attacked the pastry, indicating that the subject was closed.

Abigail was taken aback. She had given Lorna time to remonstrate with the girl, and had expected a tearful apology. Suddenly she wasn't quite so sure of her ground. Alexander had obviously been feeling his weight, but all boys did at his age, surely. It was possible she had been too hasty in blaming Maisie, she admitted to herself, now she had had time to consider the scene she walked in on. This was all foreign to her and Alexander's pain had really frightened her, but he was as much embarrassed as hurt, she had to admit. Even so, the girl had no right – she stopped herself and mustered what dignity she could.

"Perhaps the whole thing is best forgotten. Mrs Anders isn't well. Do we need to worry her?"

"I think we do. My niece's reputation is at stake here."

Abigail could see Lorna's mind was made up. Maisie, however was just sitting there a picture of misery, afraid for her job no doubt, she thought and quickly tried again.

"I'm sure Alexander didn't mean to frighten you," she said more softly, while Maisie returned her look with narrowed eyes, wondering why the sudden change of heart.

"Come now, it was just a harmless bit of fun, between the two of you. He is after all a very attractive young man and who could blame you for flirting with him a wee bit? But you should keep your place," she couldn't help adding.

"Ye see ye do blame me. In thaat case, Aunt Lorna is right." Abigail realised that in her anxiety she had handled it badly and tried to backtrack.

"No, no. I don't. Perhaps if Alexander were to apologise?"

By this time, she didn't know what to believe, but she did know what trouble Alexander would be in, if his father got to hear of it. He always believed the worst of poor Alexander. Abigail had very little time for Gerald. He was too hard on her boy. Her love for Alexander transcended everything, and taking care of him for the last seventeen years had been all she could ever have wanted, and now she was nearly beside herself with anxiety so, burying her pride, she turned to Lorna.

"Please Lorna, I beg you. Maisie will listen to you. Say this won't go any further. Mrs Anders Senior has had so much to cope with lately, what with her son in hospital; his wife near to a break down – and don't forget, it isn't long since she was nursing you with your broken leg. Couldn't we spare her this added trouble?"

Put like that, they couldn't refuse and a silent look of agreement passed between them. Lorna nodded in Abigail's direction. "Very well. For Mrs Anders' sake, but I hold you responsible that nothing like this happens again."

Abigail gave a sigh of relief. "It won't. I promise you. I will fetch Alexander and he will apologise."

Maisie's head jerked and her words were shrill – staccato. "No. Keep 'im away from me; I never want to see 'im again."

"Very well." Abigail turned and left the kitchen with a last lingering look at Lorna, and a mumbled, "Sorry." Lorna remained silent, feeling almost sorry for the devoted woman. For the rest of the day Maisie helped out in the kitchen. The unfinished bedroom could wait until the morning, Lorna told her. They agreed it would be best not to tell the family. Knowing Alf and Ned, their tempers would flare, they would be up to the house and who could say what would happen then.

It seemed as if Alexander was to escape punishment, but one evening, a week later, he was returning from college. The bus stopped at the end of the private road and he started to walk the hundred yards leading to Anders Folly. He had only gone a few steps, when a figure stepped out in front of him. In the light mist and gathering darkness, it was impossible to recognise the heavily clad figure, menacingly barring his way.

"Get out of my way," Alexander demanded imperiously, as the bulky form took a step closer. Alexander turned, waving for help, as he heard a tractor slow down behind him. The next thing he knew, a sack was thrown over his head from behind and strong arms pinned his in a vice-like grip and forced him to the ground. He struggled, kicking and shouting until another pair of hands gagged him and tied his feet. Rendered helpless he was lifted bodily and thrown on to the tractor, where one of them sat on him. He was winded and shaking with fear and it seemed endless before the journey came to an end, but when it did, the silence was even more frightening. Rough hands dragged him off, ignoring his demands to be released and threats of dire punishment from his father, *Sir* Gerald Anders.

He had no idea where he was but there was a disgusting smell, then, without warning he was flying through the air, before landing in something soft that squelched and covered him with something evil smelling and he knew with dreadful certainty he had landed in a pigsty. Rough hands pulled at him and rolled him over, pressing his face down until he thought he would suffocate. The sack was clinging to his head and with his arms pinned to his sides he couldn't protect his face. Half dazed and incapable of movement, he felt himself lifted up and thrown on to the tractor again, cold and shivering with fright. He heard the engine start and paralysed with fear, wondered what was coming next, but their mission accomplished, his silent attackers took him to a small wooded area and dumped him unceremoniously on the ground. As he heard the tractor fade in the distance, he fought his way out of the sack, which they had loosened before leaving. It took him several minutes to accustom his eyes and realise, thankfully he was only half a mile from home.

The walk across the field was painful and took some time. His shoes squelched and his clothes stuck to him. It was dark and every now and then he stumbled in to a rabbit hole, twisting his ankles painfully. As he trudged, his fear was replaced by righteous indignation. How dare they? By this time he had no doubt who his assailants were. Their size told him it was Jake and Jed Edwards. They would be brought to justice for this outrage; Maisie was responsible. She would be sacked.

By the time he reached home though, the idea of telling the family didn't seem a very good one, so he cautiously opened the kitchen door and peered

164

round, hoping to see Nanny, but Lorna was alone, and let out a small scream, before she recognised him.

"Lord, have mercy! What has happened to you?" she asked, wrinkling her nose as she caught the smell.

"Stop asking damn fool questions and go and fetch Nanny," he growled.

"Don't you mean please?" Lorna said quietly, recovering from her initial shock.

"Please and hurry," he said through clenched teeth.

Within minutes Abigail appeared in a state of panic. Her horrified senses swam as she saw him, and for a moment Lorna thought she would faint, but his plea for help galvanised her in to action.

"Into the laundry," she ordered, leading the way and heading straight for a pile of laundry waiting to be washed.

"Get those things off and put this sheet around you."

She left, returning a minute later with a large plastic bag, to find him still struggling with his tie, which had contracted into a tight knot as he pulled. Back to the kitchen she went and returned seconds later with a carving knife. Without a word, she cut the tie then attacked his shoelaces and the belt on his trousers. The smell was horrendous but she helped him until every last bit of clothing was in the bag and he was wrapped in the sheet. The bag, she took straight to the dustbin outside, before beckoning him to follow her.

"Not a word to anyone, please," she begged. Lorna shrugged.

"Looks as if he's caused enough upset for one day, anyway. Didn't get away with it this time though, did you?" She gave an amused look as he glared at her.

The family were in the sitting room watching the news, so they reached the top floor without being seen. Safe in the comfort of the bathroom, he bathed in several lots of water, to which Abigail had added plenty of disinfectant, then he pleaded a heavy cold so that he could stay in his room for dinner. His body-bruises were hidden but the one on his face was going to be hard to explain.

By morning he didn't need to pretend. His head was banging and he ached all over, the bruise on the side of his face was black and his eye was closing fast. Abigail was distraught and Pamela had to be told.

"Who did this and why wasn't I told last night?"

"We didn't want to worry you, with you being so poorly," Abigail explained tearfully, which made Pamela even angrier.

"My children's needs come first," she exploded. "Why would anyone do this to you Alexander?"

He couldn't speak for the pain in his face, so she fixed Abigail with a piercing look, and the whole story about Maisie came out.

"She must have broken her promise and her family decided to punish Alexander." Abigail wept anew.

"Maisie should never have had to make the promise, poor child. I am ashamed of you Alexander. I will speak to her."

He managed a painful, "No. Don't say anything. Dad will be furious with me; it will make him ill again."

She looked undecided, realising how much trouble he would be in and salved her conscience by agreeing it would make Gerald ill but she *should* and *would* find the culprits.

The family were told he had a bad dose of flu and was confined to his room, to avoid spreading it amongst them. Much to his relief, after reassuring herself that no bones were broken, and there was no sign of concussion, Pamela left him in Abigail's care.

Four days later, Gerald came home and in the excitement, the incident was hushed up. There was only one bad moment, when Gerald insisted he must go and see him, but Pamela advised it was a particularly nasty flu going around at present and she didn't want him to risk catching it, so it was ten days later that Alexander finally faced his father and, of course, he did still look suitably under the weather, even though the bruises had all but disappeared.

CHAPTER THIRTEEN

Gerald's homecoming brought some relief to Pamela's depression, but waves of yearning still swept over her when she thought of Bill. One minute she would be hurt and angry, the next she would dash off to the bathroom to shed helpless tears, longing desperately to feel his arms about her, and his lips on hers.

David watched and worried, telling himself things would get better when Gerald was not so absorbed in what had gone on in his absence. He seemed unaware of her low spirits, apparently assuming she was just there for his needs.

Other than that, apart from Gerald being at home, and David and Robert travelling back and forth, life for the rest of the family carried on much as before.

The wind up of the Sheffield factory was being finalised and Charles looked forward to David settling down again, thinking that his worried look was because he was tired, but in actual fact, David was thriving on the activity. It was a long time since he had felt the rush of adrenalin that pulling off a good business deal gave him. The pride he felt in introducing his grandson, and seeing the admiration in Robert's serious brown eyes made him feel ten feet tall.

On one particular day, when they were travelling north with a first class compartment to themselves and a window seat each, David looked across at him, reading a book and wearing an absorbed expression, so like Philip's. How their minds would have matched and how they would have enjoyed each other's company. His eyes closed and as sorrow flooded over him an involuntary sob tore at his throat; his son was always with him, only more so these days. Perhaps it was spending so much time with Robert. From under his eyelids he saw Robert glance across the small space dividing them, checking he was alright, and having satisfied himself his grandfather was sleeping, hugged his book to his chest and gazed dreamily out of the window, a smile playing on his lips.

David shut his eyes tight, conscious of eavesdropping on Robert's privacy; that look could only mean he was thinking of Celina. They had been inseparable since she had first been introduced to the family, nearly three months ago. She was a lovely girl – and so incredibly like their Sophie. Robert had already made his intention of marrying her clear, much to Gerald's annoyance.

"Too young! Too young! Keep your mind on the business," he could be heard saying time and time again.

David had never regretted marrying young. He had left Cornwall and his home to find work as a boy of sixteen. Both he and Marie had been nearly nineteen and penniless when they married, but less than a year later the twins were born. It had given *him* incentive, and only now did he realise how fortunate he had been to be able to follow his dream, and how blessed that Gerald shared it. One thing was very certain: Celina had softened the blow for Robert over leaving university. His thoughts were centred on marriage now, and towards that end, he was eager to learn everything he could teach him. It was good to keep it in the family. And when this business was over, they would put Robert in a responsible position. Having spent this time with his grandson, he was confident Robert would make the best of the job that had, perhaps, been thrust upon him, as long as he had Celina by his side.

At the same time, he knew in his heart that Robert wasn't following his *own* dream, so as a grandfather, had regrets but bowed to his son's wishes. He half opened his eyes again. Robert was still gazing out of the window with that faraway look; there was still another two hours before they reached their destination.

He settled more comfortably in to the corner, and the rhythm of the train gradually lulled him into a troubled sleep, where his chickens were walking all over the long, boardroom table, while board members haggled the price of eggs, and drew up a plan to build a wall between Southampton and Sheffield, in his ridiculous dream.

Robert watched, concerned by his grandfather's restlessness. He felt very responsible for him. Charles had made him promise if there was any sign, whatsoever, of him overdoing things, the appointments were to be cancelled and they were to be on the next train home. He found himself watching David like a hawk. How would he know? This was a side of his grandfather he had never seen before, and he was deeply impressed. He vaguely remembered, as a small boy, seeing him and his father going off in their dark business suits; black Crombie overcoats and Homburg hats, but for years now, granddad's image had been one of comfortable cardigans, warm shirts and gardening shoes, so it was quite startling to see him dressed in his business clothes again, heading meetings and quoting figures that sounded like telephone numbers. Oh yes, David had soared in Robert's estimation, as it also dawned on him, to what extent his father had worked with, and taken the load from his grandfather – exactly what was expected of him, he supposed. In a perfect world, he would have been overjoyed at the prospect of being another 'chip off the old block', but he wasn't and nothing could alter that fact. He had always known about, and been half resigned to the plan, at the same time as hoping for a miracle. In time, he might feel more at home in this world that was governed by finance he told himself, his thoughts returning to Celina. She was the centre of his universe, the driving force in his life. She was the reason he was determined to make a success of the job; only then would he be able to ask her to marry him. His eyes glowed softly as he pictured her. She was everything he could ever want, and miraculously she felt the same.

It was early evening when they arrived at the hotel and went straight to their adjoining rooms on the second floor. The first thing David *always* did was to telephone Marie, who was always waiting for his call. On this occasion she sounded excited.

"You will never guess what arrived today," she said happily, "or did you know about it?"

"Er, no, my dear, I haven't any idea. What did arrive today?"

"This beautiful mahogany table. It is large enough to seat absolutely all of us, and apparently it is the boardroom table from Sheffield."

"How come?" David asked with genuine surprise.

"Well, apparently Gerald has always loved it, so he asked Brian to sell it to him, but Brian refused, and then today, it arrived with a lovely card, saying: 'Thanks for everything. Hope the family enjoy the parting gift.' Isn't it wonderfully kind of them? Say thank you from all of us, won't you, dear?"

David replaced the receiver with an indulgent smile, imagining Marie's smile as she pictured them all seated at Christmas. "Well done, son!" he said softly.

The next day at the board meeting, Brian announced a celebration lunch was being arranged for the following Tuesday and they hoped Gerald would be able to attend. Robert assumed he wasn't included but Gerald, on receiving the invitation telephoned to accept and Brian made it clear the four of them were expected. He had nothing but praise for Robert and Gerald swelled with pride. His dream was being fulfilled.

Alexander was highly indignant at being left out, and Gerald explained, patiently, that Robert had been invited because he had been working with them and knew the family, but when, against advice from both his mother and Abigail, Alexander continued to air his grievances, the situation ran its usual course, with Gerald losing his temper, which dampened all of their spirits, because his blood pressure shot up and there were serious doubts that *he* would be able to attend. Consequently, the weekend was spent very quietly and Alexander was warned to keep out of the way. Charles tried to console him, reminding him of his driving lessons and his job at Southampton, stressing it would be his turn shortly, just as it was Robert's now, but Alexander held obstinately to his claim that his father was purposely leaving him out, just as he always did. So, once again, Charles had to reluctantly leave him to Abigail in order to make all of the necessary arrangements for their brief absence.

A chauffeur driven car was hired and the Monday morning saw the four of them driving off in a very large and comfortable, midnight blue Bentley, which didn't help Alexander's frame of mind at all, as he waited in his mother's ancient Ford, to be driven to college.

"Time you had a new car," he pouted, as Pamela got in beside him.

"This does for our needs," she replied brightly. "It isn't as if we drive far, and even the school run will finish soon, won't it?" She glanced sideways at him, with a half regretful, half cajoling smile, but not even the thought of leaving college could cheer him, with the picture of Robert sitting in the back of the Bentley uppermost in his mind.

"You will be driving yourself before we know it," she persevered, hating to see him feeling so down.

"When is Robert starting at Southampton? I want to start first."

About to say that it might not be possible, she said instead, "I'll see if it can be arranged. As soon as you leave college, we will find you somewhere to live."

This won a glimmer of a smile and she added, "Perhaps we could do that for your birthday; you will need clothes, we could fit you out at the same time."

By the time she dropped him at the college, the humouring had worked, and he walked through the gates with a jaunty spring to his step.

With a satisfied sigh, she swung the car round, her thoughts drifting inevitably to Bill. On impulse she turned down a side road, leading to a quiet cove, left the car and wandered onto the sands. She very often felt the need to be on her own these days, away from the well-meaning glances. What would they say if they knew the real reason? Her heart ached at the unhappiness it would cause. If only she hadn't been unfaithful to Gerald. If only she could talk to Bill, just one more time. It might hurt but anything would be better than not knowing. Contradicting thoughts tumbled through her mind and tears rolled down her cheeks. She yanked a handkerchief from her pocket and something shiny dropped on to the sand beside her. The object glinted in the morning sun and she stood gazing at it for a full minute, before bending to pick it up. Her fingers closed round the forgotten key and she sank down resting her head on her clasped knees, rocking backwards and forwards in silent misery until she felt able to make her way back to the car and drive home.

The house was silent as she let herself in. Loneliness engulfed her as she thought of three whole days and nights of nothing but country, sea and domesticity. The house felt as if it was closing in on her; she had to do something or she would go out of her mind. She spied Marie and Felicity in the vegetable garden, taking their morning stroll and collecting vegetables from Jake for the evening meal. Jake came every day now; Jed came twice a week, or more if necessary. David was planning a walled garden for the coming year, in the hope of protecting the crops from rabbits and other abundant wildlife. He loved the idea of being self-sufficient, and was gradually working towards it. Pamela watched them fill a basket each, finding their simple contentment irksome; they apparently never wanted anything other than this simple lifestyle.

She needed to talk to Ann. Turning on her heel she half ran to the study. It always felt like treading on sacred ground when Gerald wasn't there – a kind of 'keep out' atmosphere. The loud, steady tick of the mantel clock accentuated the silence and she covered her ear with her free hand, then the ringing stopped and Ann's voice said, "Riverview Hotel, how may I help you?"

She tried to say, "Hello Ann," but emotion robbed her of speech and she replaced the receiver quickly, crying softly. If only she could stop this stupid crying. Five minutes passed and she just sat in the big swivel chair gazing at the telephone, tears streaming down her face, the sonorous tick of the clock getting louder and louder until the telephone rang, shattering her thoughts. She picked it up and immediately, Ann's voice questioned, "Pamela, what's the matter? Why didn't you speak?"

"How did you know it was me?" Pamela asked faintly.

"I phoned the operator. I just had a feeling it was you, but that isn't important. What is the matter?"

Ann listened then said, "You need to get away. Catch the next train; you could be here by teatime."

"I can't, there's Alexander. Heaven knows what he would do if I left as well."

"Bring him with you," Ann said simply.

There was a small silence, as Pamela wondered why such an obvious solution hadn't occurred to her. There was also the fact that Gerald wouldn't mind as much if she had Alexander with her.

"We will come," she said, making up her mind.

A quick telephone call to say she would be picking him up, and it was all arranged. Gerald would blow a fuse, but the exams were over, and she was past caring beyond her own need to get away.

Alexander was jubilant and Marie and Felicity were astounded, when she announced her intention of going to London. Any obstacles they raised, she quickly brushed aside, whilst busily packing the few things they would need, and when Pamela was in her present mood, they knew that nothing, less than an earthquake, would make her alter course.

"I'll run you to the station then," Felicity said, quietly wondering how Gerald would take the news. As it happened, a fault developed on the line, so he was unaware of Pamela's absence from Anders Folly, until he arrived home on Wednesday evening, shortly after Pamela herself.

CHAPTER FOURTEEN

Alexander looked about his room with interest. He had never stayed in a hotel before and it felt very worldly, to be bathing and changing into one's best suit, alone in a strange bedroom.

Mrs Mellors had shown them each to a double room and his mother had left, after unpacking his clothes, promising *herself* a long, hot soak in a deep bath, to wash away the dust of their journey and suggesting that he did the same

Left to his own devices, he luxuriated in the solitude, lingering over his bath, preening in front of the full-length mirror and finally fiddling with the intercom, until a voice answered, making him step back and switch it off hastily. The room palled after a while and he decided to explore, which inevitably drew him to where a young man with extremely short, almost *white* blond hair was shaking cocktails. He watched, sliding on to one of the high stools to get a better view. The barman gave an engaging grin, exposing a lot of even white teeth.

"Care to try one, sir? Guaranteed to please."

"Why not?" He gave an airy wave, caught sight of himself in the mirrored wall behind the well-filled shelves, and automatically flicked his hair, admiring his reflection. Yes, the pale mauve shirt and the purple kipper tie went well with the dark-grey suit.

A glass, complete with two cherries and a tiny umbrella appeared in front of him. "You must be Pamela's son." The barman wiped an invisible spot away as he spoke.

Alexander was offended by the use of his mother's first name – *far* too familiar, for a *barman*.

"As a matter of fact Mrs Anders *is* my mother."

Undaunted by his unsmiling reply, Colin grinned.

"The hair is the give away. My mother would kill for your mother's colouring."

"Really?"

A small group of guests arrived so the rebuke on Alexander's lips was checked, a fact which he was grateful for moments later, when Pamela joined him.

She and Colin greeted each other. "You two have met then," she said, surprised by Alexander's scowl.

Colin returned to mixing cocktails and he whispered fiercely, "Since when do barmen call you by your first name?"

She gave an enlightened smile and explained that Colin was Ann and Roy's son. Mollified, Alexander complimented Colin on his skilful display and they fell in to conversation, whilst Pamela sipped a cocktail and Ann came in to chat.

"This was a good idea," Pamela said gratefully, watching the boys chat easily, as Colin worked. Sitting at the bar Alexander looked more than his seventeen years. He shouldn't be drinking she thought nervously but he would never forgive her for revealing that he was under-age. At that moment he turned.

"Colin has suggested showing me London nightlife, tomorrow. As we haven't planned anything yet, would you mind?"

He looked at her intently, willing her to agree, relaxing visibly when after a moment's hesitation she nodded.

"That will be nice, where do you plan on going?"

"The West End. It will be new to him and I shall enjoy showing London to a newcomer," Colin enthused.

"Runs in the family," Ann chipped in, then catching a nervous look from Pamela, added, "Why don't we do Harrods again some time."

After dinner, when Roy had taken over in the bar and Colin was playing records to Alexander in his room, Ann invited her into her sitting room.

"Why are you so nervous?"

"If we can just not mention my outings with Bill. I didn't tell Gerald because he got so upset. Silly, I know." She gave Ann a sheepish look and saw enlightenment dawn.

"You and Bill? It would explain his mood lately, but what made you go home so suddenly then?"

"He went away with out a word; I thought he had regrets."

"Typical man," Ann sympathised, "but he had to go, it was – no, let him tell you himself."

Pamela panicked. "Don't tell him I'm here, I obviously took it too seriously, he must have a lot of women friends."

Ann shook her head slowly. "He isn't like that. I have wished he was at times, when he broke up with his fiancée, for instance."

Pamela gave a heartfelt, "Silly woman."

"I'm going to make you a cup of hot chocolate to take up to bed. A good night's sleep is what you need now." Ann rose abruptly, went to Colin's bedroom and reminded him of the time. It was only ten-thirty, but Colin appeared, explaining to Alexander about his early start.

"See you tomorrow night," he called casually over his shoulder. "Goodnight, all."

Pamela could never recall seeing Alexander look so happy; their trip had more than made up for not going to Sheffield, thank goodness.

"Colin's got the best room ever; it's piled high with records and posters. He says I can go to the next pop concert with him. I should be in Southampton by then."

Eyes shining, he was in a fantasy world of his own, reliving all that he and Colin had talked about. "Think I'll go to bed." He left the room humming a tune.

Pamela smiled indulgently. "Goodnight then," she said to the closed door.

Ann returned with two steaming mugs, passing Alexander in the hallway.

"He's happy; nice they hit it off."

"Hovering six inches above the ground, I would say. Thank you for everything, it's just what we both needed."

"We aim to please," Ann smiled fondly. "Off to bed with you now." She handed Pamela her drink and they touched cheeks. "Sleep well."

"And you."

Alexander woke her very early the next morning. He was already fully dressed and in high spirits. She squinted at him from her pillow, frowning at the hands on her small travelling clock that pointed to seven-twenty.

"Why are you up at this unearthly hour?"

"I don't want to miss a single moment of today. Breakfast starts in ten minutes and I'm starving, but I don't want to eat alone. Please get up."

"Breakfast? Ugh!" She pulled the clothes over her head.

"You promised we could go sight-seeing," Alexander pleaded.

Reluctantly, Pamela poked her head out. "Give me twenty minutes."

"Super! No longer mind, we have a lot to do."

She lay looking up at the ceiling, smiling. She knew that feeling, and it was wonderful.

Twenty minutes later she found Alexander tucking in to a huge breakfast. So much for not wanting to eat alone. She had her coffee and orange juice, listening to his plans for the day.

"I need a haircut and I want to buy a polo necked jumper for tonight. Colin says it is the 'in thing'. Grey I think, to go with my suit."

"We should be able to manage that. Did Colin say where to go for this haircut?"

"Definitely 'Ginos' of Kensington, in the High Street."

"Of course, where else?"

Alexander missed her whimsy and looked surprised. "You know it then?"

"Not really, but we will find it," she replied gently, leaning back and looking over her coffee to hide a smile, until she saw Bill and her smile froze. Their eyes met and he walked towards them – she just had time to glance swiftly at Alexander and note with relief that he was still preoccupied with his own thoughts, before Bill was beside their table.

"Good morning, Pamela, Ann told me you were here with your son. I've just dropped in for breakfast." He smiled at Alexander. "It's handy having a big sister."

Pamela nervously introduce him as Dr Jessop, who ran the clinic where his father had stayed – which held no interest, until she added he was also Colin's uncle – then he looked interested and they talked until Bill's breakfast was ready. His table was near the door and as Alexander hurried on, anxious to get prepared, Bill caught her attention.

"Can we talk this evening?" His eyes held hers and her heart gave the familiar little flip, before she glanced at Alexander's disappearing back, and gave a quick nod before following him.

The day went well. They found 'Ginos', where Alexander entered with his 'Beatles' hairstyle, and emerged an hour later with an exact copy of Colin's closely cropped one. She was taken aback and a little dismayed, because he looked so much older. What would Gerald and the family think? Then she realised that she actually liked it.

Alexander loved the shops and opted to give the sights a miss, in favour of Harrods, where Pamela spared no expense, to ensure his day was memorable.

By eight o'clock, Alexander and Colin, looking absolutely immaculate were waiting in the bar for Roy to take over. Of course, Alexander's appearance caused comment and he could hardly contain himself. Bill had arrived in time for dinner and was now sitting in one of the alcoves with Pamela and Ann. Pamela was laughing and Colin leaned over the bar with a sly glance in their direction and whispered, "Your Mother and Uncle Bill look cosy."

Alexander looked across, flushing angrily. "Don't be ridiculous, my mother is far too old for any nonsense and in any case, my father would never allow it."

Colin threw him a pitying look. He realised that Alexander was naïve and put it down to living in 'Lullaby Land' – his name for Cornwall, but just how naïve could you get?

Alexander watched his mother in the mirror, talking animatedly to Ann now. Colin was just trying to annoy him he assured himself. Well he wasn't in the mood to have his night spoilt. His good humour returned, and wisely Colin let the subject drop.

They left at nine o'clock. It seemed very late to Pamela but Colin assured her that London woke up then.

"I'm on late call tomorrow," Colin called over his shoulder, and they were gone, in a flurry of goodbyes.

Ann excused herself and Pamela found herself alone with Bill. For a moment they were both tongue tied, then they started to speak at once, then apologised together.

"We need to talk; let's go for a ride," Bill said abruptly.

Pamela went to fetch her coat and Bill followed a minute later. He waited in the foyer, undecided as she came towards him, how to handle the situation. Ann had said that she was feeling very fragile and he blamed himself. Her smile was guarded and when he took her arm she stiffened.

The night air was fresh and she wrapped her coat closer in a defensive action and in the car she kept her head averted. Treacherous tears brimmed but she was determined not to make a fool of herself again. The car drew to a halt and she blinked her tears away, wondering hazily where they were, realising in the same moment that they were at Bill's home. He held the door open and she followed him into the house, asking herself why she had come? It was stupid to humiliate herself like this but just seeing him again filled her with an overwhelming longing that was wonderful and, at the same time, hurt like nothing she had ever known. Emotion gripped her and she would have fled had he not caught her arm.

"I shouldn't have come. You don't need to explain." Her words were strained and she avoided looking at him. He let go of her arm.

"I think I do," he said softly. "I know now, you thought I had run away from us. I didn't, but when I returned I thought you had. I brought you here to show you something."

He moved to the coffee table and picked up an envelope.

"It was waiting for you on that dreadful day. I was so certain you would come, when there was no time to explain. My Goddaughter Laura is three and she was born with a lung condition. That morning, my cousin Rob, telephoned to say that a cold had turned to pneumonia. He and Carol were beside themselves so I had to go to them."

His face relaxed as he saw the question in her eyes.

"It *was* touch and go for a couple of days but she is doing well."

"That must have been when I saw you on the telephone that morning. If I had only known."

Bill was dismayed. "I didn't see you. I'm sorry. I left Ann a note, came straight back here, scribbled this note to you and caught the next flight to Edinburgh."

He held out his arms, enfolding her as she moved in to them and they clung together for a long time, softening the heartbreak of the past weeks before he held her away saying, "I can't believe you're here."

176

Too overwhelmed to speak, her eyes told him everything as she held her face up to be kissed – a long passionate kiss that drowned their senses, until he twirled her round with sheer joy, smothering her with kisses until she was breathless and laughing.

"That's better," he said, releasing her and taking her coat. "No more tears, no more doubts."

They spent the evening awash with happiness, their need for each other waking untold passion that transcended earthly feelings. Lying in the crook of his arm and feeling his heartbeat beneath her cheek, she thought her heart would burst with happiness. He stirred and brushed her upturned mouth with his, as if reading her thoughts.

"We must go," he murmured, bringing them reluctantly back to earth. It was strange how distant she felt from her other life, as if it had nothing to do with this one, but soon she must return to that life and this stolen night would be a memory. She had no idea when they would meet again, only that they would.

*

Alexander was very quiet on the way home. His feelings were mixed. Excitement and apprehension struggled for supremacy as he went over the previous evening in his mind. Colin had taken him to a number of bars, where he seemed to be immensely popular and kept saying, with a twinkle in his eye, "We must definitely end the night at 'Larrie's'," making Alexander agog with curiosity about 'Larrie's'.

At midnight, he hailed a taxi, asked the driver to take them to Soho and sat back grinning at Alexander, his face eerily outlined by the neon lights.

The taxi dropped them and he led the way down a very narrow side street to a dingy doorway lit by a flashing sign saying 'Larrie's'. He handed over a wad of notes in a dingy reception and gestured Alexander to follow him along a scruffy passage and just as Alexander was feeling doubtful about their surroundings, swing doors opened into a plush interior that took his breath away. Red upholstery, crystal chandeliers, gold-framed mirrors and Greek statues filled the spacious nightclub and Colin received many curious looks as to who his companion was.

Alexander stared and looked away in embarrassment as he saw two men holding hands. Colin gave him a sly glance. He was finding his innocence amusing, but there were no doubts in his mind. He could always tell.

The night was an amazing turning point in Alexander's life; so what, if the family didn't approve, he told himself, staring out of the train window as it hurtled through the countryside. He would be leaving home soon and be able to

177

see Colin as often as he liked. He looked across at his mother, the picture of respectability, and squirmed at the thought of her reaction. Colin was right – families wouldn't understand and no one need be any the wiser if he was careful.

*

A lot happened in the following week. Pamela received a surprising letter, requesting her to call at the London offices of Blake and Thurborn at her earliest convenience, and on the same day, Maisie's father and brother whilst chatting in the Smugglers Arms learnt that two army lads had thrown a boy in to a pigsty because he had attacked the wife of one of them, and although no names were mentioned, apparently he was a local rich kid and the husband was still murmuring about further reprisal.

"I know you suspected Jed and Jake, and I had my doubts, until Maisie told me she kept her word. All the same, I'm right glad it wasn't them. Two wrongs don't make a right," Lorna confided to Pamela.

"I think we can safely assume that it was a case of mistaken identity then," Pamela agreed, thankful to put the matter to rest.

"Ay." Lorna nodded sceptically. "That will be it."

Alexander went pale and commented that it was just his luck when Pamela told him. Inwardly, he thought it another good reason to leave Cornwall.

The following day, much to Robert's satisfaction, Gerald offered Celina part-time work as his secretary. He, like everyone else, admired her gentle, cheerful disposition and she quickly proved invaluable, especially when Marie went down with a really bad dose of flu that same week. Gerald, who had questioned Pamela endlessly about her spur of the moment trip to London, instantly forgot about it, and sat beside Marie's bed for two days, until the doctor insisted she needed to be left to convalesce, not woken at intervals to make sure she was still alive.

David suggested that Gerald should plan the walled garden, where his mother could tend her flowers, sheltered from the winds when she was better. As always he became obsessive and Celina's artistic talent for drawing helped tremendously.

Relieved of Gerald's attention, Pamela still had Alexander to deal with. He persistently confronted her. Insisting she should put her trip off for a week, until the end of term when he could go with her and sulked endlessly when she refused. And when the day came for her to go, he was practically beside himself with rage, but her desire to see Bill over-rode her need to please Alexander.

178

Bill had said he would meet her train and they could lunch together before her appointment.

She was intensely curious as to the reason for her appointment, but it still paled in to insignificance at the thought of being able to see Bill again so soon – until she learnt her mother had died two years ago, and the firm of Blake and Thorburn, having very little to go on, had been searching for her ever since.

It came home to her that *she* had actually been the one to cut the ties, because she had never told her mother of her marriage to Gerald. In fact she had torn up her mother's happy letter, telling her of a forthcoming baby, insisting to herself it was nothing to do with her, and never wanted to see her again. Hurt and angry, she had resented the luxurious pictures her mother drew of her life with the man who had taken the place of her adored father.

It had long since ceased to matter, because her own happiness had been complete all of these years and she had assumed, carelessly, that life for her mother had gone on in the same idyllic, spoilt fashion, but today she had learnt her mother had seen her baby boy killed at the age of four, by falling from his pony, and she had never recovered. Adored by her wealthy husband, she did indeed have everything money could buy, drifting in and out of a make believe world for fifteen years, where she still played with their small son.

Pamela wept as she heard how her stepfather had died six months ago and made her his main beneficiary in memory of her mother; and at last, allowed herself to remember the kindnesses she had scorned at the time.

It was a staggering sum, and at first she couldn't take in that the figure on the document read over half-a-million pounds. She left the office in a daze, clutching a small box, containing her mother's plain gold wedding ring, a half hoop diamond engagement ring and an eternity ring. She thought of ringing Gerald then decided she must see his face when she told him.

Bill pulled up to the kerb and pushed the car door open.

"Buck up, I'm on yellow lines," he grinned.

They drove and he outlined his plan for the evening. "Dinner at 'Toni's', I've booked a table for eight o'clock. A stroll around Piccadilly Circus to see the lights and then back home."

His eyes held hers and her heart leapt, in spite of her mixed thoughts. At last, they could spend a whole night together. Her elation changed to remorse. Bill saw her eyes cloud and raised his eyebrows questioningly.

"My mother died two years ago. The solicitors have been trying to trace me ever since, then my stepfather died six months ago. He left me some money," she shrugged.

"Wow! An heiress, eh? So why the sad face?"

Her eyes flashed.

"It's over half a million pounds and I don't deserve it."

"I thought you didn't care," he challenged softly.

"I convinced myself I didn't all of these years, but that was remembering her as beautiful and full of life. The picture I have now is very different and I've lost the chance to ask her forgiveness, or comfort her."

They completed the short journey in silence and it wasn't until they were in the house that Bill said solemnly, "From what you say, she was quite happy in her own little world, where all of the people she loved, lived on. I'm sure you were there too. Spare a thought for your stepfather; he was the one who suffered, watching her."

"I know," she said into his shoulder as he gave her a hug.

A few minutes later she could hear him moving about, getting changed and was surprised when he came downstairs, freshly showered and wearing a tracksuit.

"I can get something from the delicatessen, if you don't feel like going out."

He looked awkward and worried and stood uncertainly, flexing his fingers, waiting for her answer, obviously relieved when she said, "Let's stick to our plan."

He made no comment at her lightning mood changes as she went from being sad, to emotional, then loving and flirtatious as the rich, ruby wine took its effect. The ambience at Toni's was exciting and heady; all around them couples were engrossed in each other, oblivious to everything, except the romance that the restaurant created, with its soft music, candlelight, excellent fare and discreet service.

By the time they were ready to leave Pamela was quite tipsy so Bill suggested taking her straight home, but she insisted they must have their trip to Piccadilly Circus. Laughing at her suggestion she could walk that far, he hailed a passing taxi and requested a leisurely ride around the brightly lit streets. She was entranced by the crowds of mixed nationalities thronging the busy pavements and the tall buildings displaying neon lights, advertising the varied attractions of London nightlife, and he was relieved to see she had apparently forgotten her earlier sadness, even if it was only for a little while.

He drew her attention to well-known restaurants and theatres and the statue of Eros, with its winged figure of Cupid, surrounded by a fountain of water, splaying a myriad of reflected droplets into the air, and it was while pointing to this, he noticed a familiar blond headed figure among a small band of demonstrators. He leant back frowning, astounded by the sight of Colin carrying a Gay Rights placard. Impatience flared within him. Why did Colin have to join every protest? Would he never stop waving banners? It was 'Ban the Bomb' last month. At least that wasn't embarrassing. He dismissed the incident with a mental shrug, quickly drawing Pamela's attention in the opposite direction and telling the driver to take them back to where his car was parked in Westminster.

Unaware of anything amiss, Pamela leant her head on his shoulder, and in that moment Colin turned to speak to his companion, as the headlights of a passing bus lit up the inside of the taxi. He stared, then gave a delighted smirk. "Well, well, well. Very cosy," he murmured to himself.

CHAPTER FIFTEEN

On her return to Anders Folly the following evening, Pamela's astonishing news met with a mixed reception. David and Marie were sorry to hear about her mother, but thought it nice Pamela had been remembered. Charles and Felicity were awestruck, the boys gave a whoop of joy and Gerald, after the news sunk in, was gruff and terse, seeing changes ahead. Pamela already had a new radiance about her. While everyone else talked excitedly, Charles watched him sympathetically, guessing his thoughts.

Later, as they were getting ready for bed, Gerald broached the subject aggressively.

"It needs to be invested. You can't just spend and spend, you know."

He tugged roughly at his shoelace and it snapped. She saw the anxiety in his eyes, and wanted to comfort him.

"My brilliant adviser will see to it for me," she said gently, kneeling down in front of him and freeing the knotted lace.

"You have to learn control," he replied tersely, already regretting his attitude, as he looked down into her happy, upturned face, trying to convince himself everything would be alright, yet knowing in his heart, that another new phase in their life was about to begin.

Pamela took Alexander to Southampton several times before they found suitable accommodation for him, and they usually managed to go to London as well. Alexander disdainfully rejected the family tailor in favour of trendy fashions, which he chose for himself, while Pamela took the opportunity to see Bill. Robert had already moved into the cottage, where he would be able to surround himself with books, and drive himself to his job of trainee manager. Pamela was delighted. Everything was shaping up very nicely.

Alexander's accommodation was found, in the spotless, strictly run establishment, of one Mrs Dora O'Reilly. A widow with a genteel, motherly appearance, and a manner that said she would brook no nonsense from her eight single boarders. No visitors, or food in the rooms, and punctuality was expected at meal times. A list of the fortnightly menu, which never varied, was pinned to the back of each bedroom door and at the end of the two weeks, it started again. The food was plain but wholesome, and a young man on the same first floor landing assured Pamela it was plentiful. Alexander grimaced, but it would do until he passed his driving test, he vowed silently, nodding vehemently to his mother's enthusiastic assurances to Mrs O'Reilly, that her son would move in, in two weeks' time.

A family dinner was arranged for the last Saturday and Robert was coming home for the weekend. During the week however, Celina was ill and he drove down to be with her. Gerald was furious with him.

"You can't just walk out," he raged at Robert, who tried to explain that he had left everything in order, but Gerald stormed on, relentlessly. White faced and silent, Robert gave up and returned to the New Forest cottage, taking Celina with him.

"Wonderful! Now I haven't got a secretary." Gerald's voice could be heard complaining over the entire house, until Pamela, looking anxious and distraught told him that he was upsetting Marie and David. Only then did he calm down. Friday evening came and Robert was expected to bring Celina for the weekend but a quick telephone call to apologise was all they received.

Once again, Gerald exploded, and Pamela took a solitary walk along the sandy shore, longing to be in London, where no family problems existed.

Three weeks later, Robert and Celina returned. He looked serious, she white and drawn. Robert went to the study, stood in front of his father's desk and dropped his bombshell, very quietly.

"Father, I'm going to marry Celina."

"Nonsense. You are far too young and your place is helping to run the family business," Gerald said with finality, not looking up from the papers he was putting in order.

"In a week's time," Robert continued determinedly.

Gerald jumped up, his expression turning to anger, and sent the chair crashing back against the wall.

"Have you taken leave of your senses?" he demanded, his dark eyes boring into his son's.

"No. I have given the matter a great deal of thought, and it is what I am going to do."

"Out of the question."

The door opened behind Robert, and Pamela entered looking agitated, followed by Celina, looking white and frightened.

"Talk some sense into them for God's sake," Gerald snapped at Pamela.

"They want to get married. Celina is expecting a child," Pamela said, looking straight at Robert, and trying to sound calm.

Gerald sat down suddenly, his face aghast. "You little fool," he muttered through clenched teeth, as Celina looked up at Robert, her eyes brimming with tears. "You don't have to marry me," she whimpered.

"Of course he does. What kind of family do you think we are?" Gerald thundered, beside himself with helpless rage. Never before had either of the boys done anything so irrevocable, and just when he thought that Robert was under control again.

"I want to," Robert assured her, whilst Pamela nodded without saying a word.

"Just go. Get out of my sight, the pair of you," Gerald said despairingly and watched them leave, before turning accusing eyes on Pamela.

"You don't mind then, our eldest son tying himself down with a wife and child at twenty?"

"He loves her and doesn't see it like that," she pointed out patiently. He closed his eyes in speechless dismay and she added, "You are making too much of it."

She stood twisting the rings on her right hand, and he noticed, the thick wedding band, and the magnificent engagement and eternity rings left to her by her mother. He leapt to his feet, full of contrition.

"Darling, I'm sorry!" He raised her hand to his lips and kissed the rings. "What's done is done and there is no going back," he said, wanting to atone. "Let's go and talk to them again."

She breathed a sigh of relief, as he followed her through into the hall. "They will be in the Music Room I expect," she said over her shoulder; their footsteps made no sound on the thick carpet, as they approached the slightly open door. Lowered voices reached them. Pamela smiled and nodded, just as Robert's voice rose frantically.

"I will always treat the baby as mine. You must believe that."

"Why should you take the blame?" Celina protested tearfully.

"It doesn't matter. I love you. Please say you will marry me," they could hear him pleading. In that fraction of a second, Gerald, momentarily rooted to the spot, recovered and burst into the room. Robert and Celina jumped apart, startled by his sudden appearance and gazed dumbstruck at Gerald's furious face. For what seemed like an eternity nobody spoke, then Gerald roared, "What the hell is going on here? Not your baby? And you have the temerity to tell me that you are going to bring this wanton girl into our family."

Robert found his voice. "Don't speak of Celina in that way, Father. It isn't her fault."

"You're more of a fool than I thought, if you believe that." Gerald sneered, giving Celina a withering look.

She burst into tears and Pamela went to her. "Gerald you are upsetting her," she said; putting her arm round the girl's shaking shoulders.

"*I'm* upsetting *her*?" He fairly danced with rage, looking at his wife in disbelief. "You knew about this all the time, didn't you?"

"Yes," she admitted, after a moment's hesitation. "I'm sorry Gerald, but we thought it best if you thought Robert was the father, seeing he wants to marry Celina so much."

"Who *is* the father?" Gerald demanded, looking straight at Celina.

Avoiding his eyes she whispered, "I can't say."

"You can't say. You can't say?" Gerald repeated incredulously.

"Robert, do you know who the father of this child is?"

Robert hesitated and looked at his mother.

"He does know, but still wants to marry Celina. The father doesn't. So let that be an end to it." Her temper snapped, and she drew Celina towards the door. "Come dear, I will get Abigail to make you a cup of tea."

Gerald watched them leave, astonished by Pamela's attitude, convinced that everyone except himself had taken leave of their senses.

"I think it will be best if I go as well," Robert said quietly.

"Yes, go, and I don't want to see you again until you give up this ridiculous idea."

"Then it's goodbye, Father."

For one brief moment, he thought his father regretted his words, but with a stubborn lift of his chin, Gerald swung round and left the room, with the parting shot, "And don't think she is going to have her brat here."

Robert watched him go, desolate at the thought of how much he would miss the family, but giving in was not an option.

Pamela was comforting Celina when he found them in the kitchen. He had his outdoor clothes on, and the luggage was already back in the car.

"I can't stay on Dad's conditions," he said. "We will be at the cottage. Please explain to Grandma and Granddad." He could see David and Marie in the walled garden, but couldn't bring himself to say goodbye.

Pamela stood at the front door and waved them off, tears running down her cheeks, telling herself they would be back when the fuss had died down. Gerald needed Robert in the business. He wouldn't jeopardise that.

Two weeks later, Gerald called her into the study and asked if there had been any word from Robert, and her hopes lifted, only to be dashed by his next words, as she shook her head.

"They are to be out of the cottage in a week's time. See that they are informed."

185

"Gerald!" She gasped, "You can't do that. You will hurt him dreadfully."

"He has to be brought to his senses." Gerald's voice was cold and unrelenting. "Without a roof over their heads, she will soon go running home to her mother."

This was said with a satisfied grimace, and in that moment Pamela hated him but she made one last appeal.

"You are being too hard. Mother and Dad will be really upset. They would never have treated you like this."

"I would never have given them cause. And they know I'm doing this for his own good. He will thank me one day. Now that is an end to the subject. Just see he gets the message."

"Messages like *that* you can deliver yourself," Pamela stormed, marching out of the room and slamming the heavy door until the rafters echoed.

Gerald slumped in his chair, glowering at the slammed door. What on earth was happening to the family? Confident he was right and that Robert would see the error of his ways. He looked around proudly. This was his son's heritage; he wouldn't give up all of this for the sake of somebody else's child, he told himself grimly, reaching for pen and paper.

CHAPTER SIXTEEN

Pamela drove the silver blue sports car confidently. She had taken delivery the day before, and her first journey was to visit Robert and Celina. She tussled with the problem of her son and husband, as she drove through lush, green countryside, where New Forest ponies grazed with their newly born foals and families were taking advantage of the Easter spring sunshine to picnic in the softly undulating dunes.

By driving across country, she had made good time. She peeped the horn, smiling, picturing Robert's face, when he saw the gleaming sports car; then noticed his car was not in the narrow driveway. She should have telephoned. Perhaps they hadn't gone far though, she thought hopefully, rummaging for the key she always kept in her handbag.

As always, entering the cottage gave her a sense of coming home. Its low ceilings and casement windows, with views of the surrounding forest, gave a sensation of living in the forest itself, and it came as a surprise to find the curtains drawn, but she smiled, as it went through her mind Celina was saving the furnishings from the sun. Rather sweet really, when one considered the state of the faded carpets and curtains, and the chintz covers on the three-piece suite had definitely seen better days.

The place was spotless. Celina would make her son a good wife, she assured herself, heading for the kitchen.

Everything had a newly scrubbed look about it, and was so tidy; almost as if nobody lives here, she voiced her thoughts aloud. The slightly battered aluminium kettle stood on the ancient gas stove, and she took it to the tap, to find the water had been turned off. Frowning, she bent down and drew back the blue and white check curtain under the draining board, where the stopcock was and as a glimmer of suspicion dawned, crossed to the big old-fashioned fridge. The door was slightly ajar, propped open with a wooden spoon: it was empty. With long strides she ran up the winding staircase. Both bedrooms were empty of belongings, and the bedding neatly folded and stacked. Her legs gave way and she sat down abruptly on the foot of the bed. Where had they gone? Gerald's letter could only have arrived yesterday. Why hadn't they got in touch with her? How would they manage without somewhere to live? Questions flooded her mind as she reminded herself Robert still had his job; but for how long if he persisted in opposing Gerald? She made her way slowly downstairs, racking her mind as to where they could have gone. Celina's mother was in a hospice, terminally ill. Her house had been sold, and apart from the cousin in Cornwall, she had no other relatives.

Wandering from room to room, she debated what to do. Gerald expected her to stay at the cottage, and was waiting for her call saying she had offered Celina a large sum of money to disappear and never see Robert again. Pamela, of course, had no intention of doing any such thing, However, for her own peace of mind she did want to make sure they had adequate means, but she was at a complete loss as to what to do next. It was early evening and she hadn't eaten all day. She would find food and decide her next step.

The idea of staying at the cottage had lost its appeal since Robert and Celina weren't there. On her way to the front door she passed the telephone, and couldn't resist the temptation to ring Bill. She put her case down, and dialled the number with trembling fingers. The pleasure in his voice at her unexpected call warmed her, and the familiar ache for his touch tore at her heart. She explained her situation, and he listened in silence, before saying, "Could we meet in Guildford? I have to travel down tomorrow morning for an appointment but if we both left now?" He left the question in the air.

"We could be together in less than two hours," she finished softly.

Conscience smote her as she pulled the white painted door to by its wrought iron knocker and locked it behind her, but there was nothing she could do tonight, she comforted herself. Tomorrow morning she would go to Southampton and see Robert at work. With that thought, she drove off into the gathering dusk.

The Travel Lodge they had agreed to meet at was off the motorway, a short distance from Guildford. She drove in and saw him standing by his white Porsche. He gave a big, surprised grin as she drove alongside and parked.

"Hope you don't imagine you melt into the background in that," he said with dry humour, and her green eyes flashed merrily when he gave a murmur of appreciation, as she swung long, nylon clad legs out of the car. Her spirits soared. He made her feel desirable and she adored him. Nothing else mattered, for the moment. Cornwall and all the problems there seemed a million miles away. That once safe haven had turned into a suffocating prison she just had to escape from when she could.

Bill had already collected the key and they went straight to the room. The accommodation provided every need and food arrived promptly after they ordered. Replenished, they lounged back finishing the last of the wine, their delight growing with every caress. They slept as the first signs of dawn crept through the curtains; Pamela set her small alarm clock for eight o'clock, telling herself she could be in Southampton by mid-morning. They parted, with Bill promising to ring if there was a possibility of meeting again that evening. As she drove, she wondered if Robert and Celina left because of the letter or had they planned to anyway? And if so, why had they not told her? It had all happened so quickly, she felt they must have had something in mind and was hurt they hadn't confided in her.

Even more alarming, when she arrived at the office and asked to speak to Robert, the secretary showed her in to the manager's office, where Simon Hall told her Robert's resignation had arrived by post that morning. No forwarding address, just a box number for his cards to be sent on.

"Whatever's happened Mrs Anders? This isn't like him at all." Simon had worked for Anders since the war, and had known the boys since they were small. He wouldn't have been surprised at Alexander, but Robert was always so reliable. He scrutinised Pamela's lovely face that had suddenly lost its colour, and wondered why she had come, on *this* very morning, but her expression was closed, and he resisted asking questions. Instead, he said kindly, "You look as if you could do with a cup of coffee. This has obviously upset you. Perhaps I should fetch Alexander?" he suggested. She knew Robert wouldn't have confided in his brother, but she wanted to see Alexander so she thanked him. He left and almost immediately, his secretary entered with a cup of coffee; ten minutes later Simon returned with Alexander, murmured an excuse and left.

Alexander was genuinely concerned to see his mother upset, but when she explained why, his demeanour changed, and he said sulkily, "So what! He has got what he wants. He always does in the end, one way or another."

Pamela gave him a thunderous look, and he looked away as an idea struck him. In a conciliatory tone he made the observation that the cottage must be empty now. Pamela inclined her head. "Why?"

"I will move in. If it was alright for Robert, it's alright for me."

"You are better off at Mrs O'Reilly's. You couldn't look after yourself at the cottage. Anyway, how would you get to work? You haven't passed your driving test yet. It is out of the question."

Alexander flushed angrily. "Of course I can look after myself. Stop making me out to be a baby. I'm eighteen, and I can do what I like now – and my test is in two weeks' time."

His tone was confident, but Pamela looked at him with disbelief.

"You can't be ready yet."

"The instructor says I am. A friend has been taking me out every night. I'm a natural." He made the statement without boasting. In a few short weeks he had changed dramatically and become very sure of himself, she noted with surprise.

"Time to talk about the cottage when you have passed. In the meantime, I need to know where Robert is."

"You don't understand. I have to leave Mrs O'Reilly's at the end of this week."

This time he looked uncomfortable, and Pamela realised there was more to come.

"Why? What have you done?" she asked wearily.

"Nothing. That is the annoying part. This girl asked me to help her move a heavy chest of drawers, and while I was in her room, the old girl came up and created. Said I knew the rules about not going up to the girl's landing and gave me to the end of the week to get out. Wouldn't even let me explain, and the girl denied asking me, in case she got sent packing as well."

"I will go round and have a word with Mrs O'Reilly."

"Please don't Mum. I hate it there anyway. Please, please say I can live at the cottage. I can get a lift to and from work and I promise to look after myself. Please?" he implored, scissoring his hands together theatrically, seeing the well-known signs of capitulation.

"Very well then," she agreed, not without misgivings. "I will get in touch with Jenny Smith, the woman who keeps an eye on things. She will come in and clean for you."

Alexander started to object, but she held up her hand.

"Not negotiable, take it or leave it."

He spread his hands. "You win," he agreed, looking at his watch, and planting a kiss on her cheek. "Must get back to work. Bye, Mum."

Once outside the door, he punched the air. "Yesss," he hissed.

Unaware of this, Pamela was left wondering, why, when he said she had won, did she feel she was going to regret this latest decision.

Simon Hall returned and escorted her to the front entrance, promising to get in touch if he heard from Robert. She drove straight to Jenny's. Jenny was in her late fifties, full of bustling energy, and really pleased for the opportunity to earn extra income. Pamela handed over a key and a month's wages in advance, feeling slightly happier. With that settled, she returned to the cottage to await Bill's call, and search around for any clue leading to Robert's whereabouts but it was as if they had never been there. It occurred to her the telephone exchange might help if any calls had been made. At first she thought she had drawn another blank, and was about to replace the receiver, when the operator said an incoming call had been made from Oxford a few days ago. Pamela thanked her and sank down onto a nearby chair. Why hadn't she thought of that?

Bill telephoned to say he would have to return to London that evening. They were both disappointed and she promised to ring him at home, later. In that moment she decided to drive to Oxford. Should she call Gerald or not? It was his fault this had all happened, she thought crossly; she called anyway. His voice was precise and clipped, as he told her to come home and let Robert get on with it. He will soon miss his home comforts and come running back. She didn't mention Oxford, in case she was mistaken, but said she would return in a couple of days when Alexander was settled. Gerald's loud 'Tut' and 'Not again!' ended the conversation on an impatient note. She gave a resigned sigh. Their relationship seemed to go from one crisis to another these days.

Getting into the car, she edged carefully out of the concealed entrance, making a mental note to warn Alexander to be careful there. She realised now how easy it had been when the boys were young and had no say. Gerald wasn't used to having his authority flouted. He had always reigned supreme, and the fact that he couldn't control his own boys must be driving him mad. She felt a moment of sympathy, and shook her head sadly. Things would never be the same again – ever.

Three hours later, she drove into Oxford. It was teatime and the traffic was heavy. The deep throb of the sports engine gave her a sense of power. She could do anything and go anywhere she wanted to. She had money of her own, for the first time in her life and could actually spend without considering the cost. It was a great feeling.

Waiting for the lights to change to green, she wound the window down, and asked the driver next to her if she was heading in the right direction for the Oriel University, and was assured by a young man with a broad, Irish accent, who was openly admiring her car, that indeed she was, and he was heading there himself, if she would like to follow him. She thanked him and wound the window up, as the lights changed.

He led her along Abingdon Road, through St Aldates, passing the famous Bodleian Library on the left, and finally into the High Street, where Oriel University was on the right.

In the car park, he not only found her a space but got her a parking ticket, refusing the coins she held out, with, "And to be sure, you can be doing the same for me one fine day." His black eyes twinkled, and he gave a wide, infectious grin, exposing a set of the whitest teeth she had ever seen, and she found herself smiling back.

"Now, if there is nothing else I can be doing for ye, I have a lecture to attend, and I'll be in sore trouble if I'm late, yet again."

"Actually, I need to find Robert Anders. I'm his mother." Her words came out in a rush, and she apologised for taking up more of his time.

His face became serious. "Are ye now? He's a lucky fella, I'm thinking. I'll away and ask if the name is known. You wait here." He spoke slowly, as if giving himself, time to think, and Pamela watched him go, wondering if his manner had changed when she mentioned Robert's name, or had it been her imagination? With a slight shrug she turned, her attention arrested by the grandeur of the historic buildings surrounding her. There was a timeless aura of tranquillity about the towering, ancient spires and incredible architecture that held her spellbound, and she knew instantly why Robert had to return.

She was still gazing upwards when a quiet voice said from behind her, "Hello, Mum. Awe inspiring isn't it?"

Without turning, she replied softly, "It certainly is." They stood together in silence, soaking up the peace and tranquillity, until Pamela said, "Are you absolutely sure this is what you want? Your father will come round eventually, and things will return to normal."

There was a great sadness in her eyes, as she looked searchingly into her son's dark brown ones, so like his father's, but without the restlessness.

"I don't want normal, if it means being without Celina and going back to the firm. Can't you see how different my life is here? *This* is my world, Mother, and now Celina is with me," he spread his hands, "I have everything."

"You aren't just saying that to put my mind at rest?"

"You have my solemn word on it. I feel as if a great weight has been lifted from me. No more pressure to lead a life I'm not suited to, just because I'm the eldest son. Alexander will enjoy it far more – *and* make a better job of it. Just say you couldn't find me. Let me disappear, at least until I have got my degree. It will give the family time to settle down as well. Grandma and Granddad have been through enough lately. No falling out with Dad over me or badgering him to change his mind. I won't come home anyway – and I won't give Celina up. Don't worry Mum. Things couldn't be better. Be happy for me." He gave her a reassuring hug, and her eyes filled with tears.

"Where will you live?"

"We are in rooms, but Celina has already started looking for a small house. I will use the money you gave me." He grinned boyishly. "You told me not to spend it all at once; sorry."

"How do I get in touch with you?"

Robert retrieved a pen from his jacket pocket, wrote on a scrap of paper, and handed it to her.

"For your eyes only. We need time to work things out for ourselves. Promise?" She nodded, and he kissed her cheek. "Cheer up, Mum. It is all going to work out for the best. You will see. Where is your car?"

She had forgotten about showing him the new car, so now she pointed to the gleaming blue model. "What would you say if I said this one?"

"I'd say pull the other one."

192

She laughed, as she put the key in the lock, and watched his mouth drop open. He sat in the driving seat and played with the controls, saying over and over again, "What a beauty!"

"You could have one, if you came home," she said half teasingly.

"That's playing dirty," he accused, laughing loudly.

She felt torn as she drove away, watching him in the driving mirror waving both hands in the air. He looked so happy, anticipating his future with Celina, but there was an ever-widening gap between his and their lives.

Back on the motorway she followed signs pointing to the south, not having any clear idea of where she was. It suddenly occurred to her, no mention had been made of where she would stay, or the fact she had driven miles to see them. A sense of redundancy filled her, and at that moment a large signboard loomed into sight, indicating London was 52 miles, by way of the next exit, one mile further on. By her estimation, she could be there in under an hour. She pictured Bill's surprise, and put her foot down on the accelerator. Adrenalin surged as the powerful engine responded to her slightest touch and she realised that she was doing 90mph in a matter of seconds. Heart beating fast, she removed her foot, and the speedometer dropped as the exit loomed up. She could feel her eyes shining, and couldn't wait to get on another stretch of motorway to try again.

She reached Bill's home in record time, and let herself in, knowing he wouldn't be home for at least an hour. Just time to relax in a hot bath. She kicked her high-heeled shoes off at the foot of the stairs and bent to pick them up. Halfway up she changed her mind, retraced her steps, placed one shoe at the foot of the stairs and the other two treads up, followed by her skirt and then her blouse. Her under slip she hung over the newel post at the top, then stockings and underwear, led a trail to the bedroom door. She smiled impishly to herself, anticipating Bill's reaction, as she drew a bath and poured a lightly perfumed oil under the running tap. She hadn't realised how tired she was, until she sank beneath the water, and after several minutes her eyes began to droop. She roused herself reluctantly, and climbed out. Her own large cream towel hung where she had left it on her last visit and she wrapped herself in its, warm folds, shuffling dozily to the bedroom, where she sank into bed, telling herself, 'I'll be fine in five minutes.'

It was dark, and the sound of the front door opening and closing woke her, then Bill's surprised exclamation. "What the? – Pamela?"

He took the stairs three at a time, and had reached the top, when the doorbell rang. She heard him curse and walk heavily down again, then a familiar voice she couldn't quite place said, "Hi! Are you busy? Just thought I would pop in and say hello."

There was a slight pause before she heard Bill stuttering excuses about only just finishing work and it not being convenient right now, followed by, "Aah! Right! Sorry! Another time!" as Colin espied, shoes, skirt and blouse scattered up the stairs, while Bill unsuccessfully endeavoured to block his view. Colin turned and walked away, well pleased with himself.

The likelihood of there being two silver blue sports cars wasn't impossible, but the coincidence was enough to give rise to suspicions. Alexander had only mentioned his mother's new car that day, and there it was parked outside Uncle Bill's house. That would come in very useful, and to think, it was only by chance he had come this way home.

He whistled gaily as he climbed back into his car, leaving Bill to race back upstairs, and sweep her into his arms. "How long have you been here? I went to Ann's. I could have been here an hour ago."

"Never mind, you are here now," Pamela answered softly, settling back against the pillows, waiting impatiently for him to join her.

*

Driving back to Cornwall the following morning, Pamela reflected on her life. The evening with Bill had been wonderful, and they had cooked bacon and eggs at three o'clock in the morning. She and Gerald had never done that, although their relationship had been lively enough with their weekend honeymoons, as he called them. *Their* lovemaking was very unfulfilling these days, mainly because they always seemed to be at loggerheads over the boys, for one reason or another, but she had to admit that *some* of it was her fault as well. Gerald's very physical form of love making was the only kind she knew, until Bill showed her his slow and sensuous way; and now the romping set her nerves jangling. She thought sadly of when she had joined in wholeheartedly, and they had been as one, and knew those times could never be recaptured. Returning to her life at Anders Folly held no appeal anymore, and yet she adored everyone there. They had been her whole life, which she had loved, but suddenly knew that she had outgrown them, and without the boys, life would be an intolerable round of dull routine, which everyone else seemed so contented with. Her spirits sunk deeper as she caught sight of the ocean. The house would be in sight soon.

CHAPTER SEVENTEEN

Laurie stuck the last piece of sticky tape on the gold wrapping paper and drew the gift tag towards him. He sat, pen poised, before writing in his beautiful copperplate:

'To my dear friend Charles,

To celebrate the 21st anniversary of our wonderful partnership. God bless you, my boy, your friend Laurie.'

Having done that he slipped the parcel into his overnight bag.

Everyone thought they were just celebrating this special occasion, but no one realised how special it was to be – except Laurie.

With ten minutes to wait before Charles finished, Laurie lent back in his comfortable, leather swivel chair, which had taken on his shape over the years, clasped his hands over his round belly and surveyed the book-lined room over the top of his gold-rimmed spectacles. Seventy years. Where had the time gone? What if Charles hadn't come along when he did? No one else could possibly have fitted the bill, as he had. And who else could have given *him* that wonderful sense of belonging, but the incomparable family who had given him some of the best years of his life? His heart swelled as he thought of the warm welcome waiting for him. Marie's dear, smiling face, and David's cheerful nod from the window seat beside the chess board, where he would have two glasses of cold ale already poured – and the same old, 'Just time for a few more moves before dinner, eh Laurie?'

Deep in thought and smiling to himself, he missed the light tap on the door and Charles was actually standing in front of the desk, before Laurie became aware of him.

"Penny for them," Charles smiled gently, seeing the moisture in the old man's eyes.

"Time to go already?" Laurie blinked hard and cast another look around, before heaving himself out of the well-worn chair.

Charles gave a puzzled frown. Usually Laurie was ready and waiting in the hall for him.

"Alright, Laurie? We don't have to go until you are ready."

"Quite ready m' boy. I can smell that roast dinner from here," he said with a quick return to his normal lively self.

Charles held the door open for him, and they said goodnight to Jessica, who locked up after them.

The wonderful aroma of roast pork greeted them as they entered the house, and everything was comfortingly just as Laurie had anticipated. The excellent dinner, when it was served one hour later, would normally have been the highlight of the evening, but tonight, when the lemon meringue pie, had been cleared away, and Lorna had withdrawn after serving the coffee, Laurie cleared his throat rather noisily and she reappeared carrying a tray, holding seven glasses of sparkling Champagne, and placed one in front of each of them. Laurie stood up, and everyone waited, anticipating the toast; his first words brought a gasp of surprise.

"I have chosen this very special day to announce my retirement. Twenty-one years ago today, a young man walked into my office. That young man was to change the rest of my life completely, by introducing me to the people who I have come to look on as my family. Not only has he been the perfect partner; he has been a wonderful friend, and for many years now, I have had the privilege of being treated like a father by him and his lovely wife. I therefore take overwhelming pleasure in handing him this token of my esteem, affection, and gratitude. Charles, m' boy," he said holding the gold-wrapped parcel out to Charles, who just sat open-mouthed, then held out his hand as Pamela nudged him into action. His mouth moved but no words came, and then everyone was laughing, and David jumped up to shake Laurie's hand.

Marie remembered his cryptic words at Christmas.

"Is this what you were planning for April?"

"Nothing to stop you from coming to live with us now then," David said, pumping his hand vigorously.

Laurie beamed. "You hadn't forgotten, but first things first. Open your parcel, Charles."

He sat down and clasped his hands over his belly, with a satisfied look as Charles recovered enough to tear aside the wrapping. Inside, a long Manila envelope felt unaccountably heavy, until he withdrew a brass plate, with 'Charles H. Hughes' engraved in block capitals and underneath, 'Solicitor'. It gleamed in the light, and Charles sat transfixed for several seconds, before drawing out the stiff folded documents – the property deeds to the office. He sat looking from the documents to the brass plate, and back again.

"Say something," Pamela whispered nudging him again.

"I really don't know what *to* say." Charles spread his hands and looked across at Laurie. "If our partnership has been good for you, it has been marvellous for me. And now! Well! How can I thank you enough? – For both of us."

He caught Felicity's hand, his face red with emotion, and she got up and kissed Laurie on the cheek, adding her thanks for giving Charles such a wonderful opportunity.

"Not a dry eye in the place," Pamela said as the silence lengthened. Picking up her glass, she held it first to Gerald. "We must have a toast. Say something nice, darling."

Gerald's reaction was like someone coming out of a trance, as he quickly picked up his glass and responded with, "To two of the best people in our lives."

It was short, almost inadequately so Pamela considered, realising with a sense of shock that Gerald was resentful of Laurie, for being Charles and Felicity's benefactor. That was his role.

Over the next few weeks they all helped Laurie to move some of his belongings into the room on the main landing next to Marie and David, and shut his own house up securely. Isador objected loudly to being put into a basket, and it took three of them, Laurie, Felicity and Marie, to retrieve her from her hiding place under Laurie's bed, but at last they were all, in the car and heading back to Anders Folly. Once there, Issie made a dash for freedom when the basket was opened, and nearly frightened Lorna out of her wits by streaking across the kitchen floor, scattering a bag of rubbish in her wake. When the commotion died down, Issie attached herself to a warm spot by the Aga, and settled down very nicely, with a saucer of cream from Lorna – once she recovered and saw how frightened the poor cat was.

"I think you have just lost Issie to Lorna," Marie said returning to the sitting room, where David and Laurie were settling down to watch the six o'clock news.

"Issie always finds the best spot and claims it for her own," Laurie said, quite unperturbed by his cat's disloyalty.

"Knows where she will get spoilt rotten," David observed dryly, drawing contentedly on his pipe.

As April ended with its traditional showers, and May arrived in a sudden burst of warm sunshine, the lighter evenings brought a welcome change to the usual routine, and an after dinner stroll along the sandy cove became part of a nightly ritual, for Marie, David and Laurie. Gerald occasionally joined them, but preferred jogging along the sands, or sailing his small craft around the bays when someone could accompany him. Pamela had lost her taste for sailing because of the havoc it caused to her delicate skin. It was just another pastime they didn't share anymore.

Gerald found his enforced idleness irksome, and envied Charles his new challenges. Dealing with the factory business from this distance added to his feeling of inadequacy and he missed the cut and thrust of his old life. Very soon, he would get back into travelling he promised himself. The fresh air and exercise were restoring his un-toned muscles to their former fitness and every day he felt stronger. All would be as it should, once he was in the driving seat again. He had to admit things were going along smoothly without him, but that was because he had everything so well organised, he congratulated himself. And Alexander had turned out to be a nice surprise, after the first few weeks of throwing his weight about. Good reports came back from the manager each week praising his handling of the smaller accounts. At least one of the boys was making good. He determinedly put all thought of Robert behind him, telling himself it was his loss.

By the end of May, Gerald was certain he could return to work, but his local doctor, after consulting with Cheyne Walk Clinic, refused permission. Another two months was the decision.

"Rubbish!" Gerald stormed. "How can they say that, without even seeing me?"

"We could always make an appointment for you to have a check up with Dr Jessop himself," Pamela suggested, after his anger had subsided into gloom and despondency, and she was patiently despairing.

"If that is what it will take to convince them, I know what is best for me; make it soon," Gerald agreed impatiently.

The appointment was duly made for the following week, and a chauffeur-driven car was hired. Gerald grumbled about having to stay in London the night before, but there was no help for it. His appointment was for eleven o'clock in the morning. That same day, they would travel back to the cottage, stay with Alexander overnight, look in at the factory in the morning, then continue on their journey home.

Alexander sounded less than pleased when Pamela telephoned to announce their plans.

"You would be more comfortable in the hotel. Why don't I book you into the Appollo and join you for dinner?"

It did make sense. They would be on hand for the office in the morning, and spared any needless travelling. Gerald thought Alexander had shown caring and good sense.

The appointment went well. Bill agreed Gerald was making excellent progress, but persuaded him to wait another three weeks, to be on the safe side. Impatient, but in good spirits he reluctantly agreed and left the clinic, hardly able to wait to get out of London.

"Lunch will have to wait until we are well on the road to Southampton," he said to Pamela, before turning to speak to the chauffeur and she took the opportunity to glance quickly back at the ground-floor window. Bill raised his hand in farewell, before she stepped into the limousine. His face stayed with her, and she averted her head, feigning interest in the crowded streets. She knew them by heart, and ached to be staying longer.

In no time at all they were speeding along the motorway; Gerald commented on her quietness.

"I suppose you would have liked us to stay in London?" he said miserably.

She didn't answer straight away.

"You have discovered life at Anders Folly isn't enough, in the short time you have been recuperating." She said it without rancour, but he retorted defensively.

"Hardly short."

"Three months; and you can't wait to be on the move again."

"It's different for women. They have got the home and children."

She could have quoted the following argument, word for word, so she gave him a despairing look, and lapsed into silence again:

"Forest End has closed," he said abruptly. "I forgot about it, with going to London. A letter came last week saying the last four inmates were to be transferred. It doesn't warrant government funding anymore. Should we sell? The choice is yours." He sounded indifferent.

"You can't sell Forest End." Her voice and eyes were filled with dismay, as they met his dark gaze. Eye contact with him was something she found difficult of late. She blamed him for everything going wrong. Robert and Celina would still be around if he hadn't caused things to get out of hand, and now it was too late. Robert was jubilant to be free; with the years of pressure behind him he had never been happier. His only criteria was to make Celina happy. 'Please don't even try to reconcile Dad and me anymore; it would just rekindle the unhappiness again. Don't feel badly about our joint decision; but for you, I would still be tied to a dreadful office desk, instead of sitting in this wonderful library, writing this letter to you.' Those were the words indelibly printed on her mind, ending any hope she had of reconciling her family. Robert, not Gerald, would keep them apart now.

Sadness swamped her. It seemed she was losing everything she held dear. And now, Forest End, her first post as matron and where they had met. Gerald reached across and laid his hand on hers, as the memories replayed in her mind and tears filled her eyes.

"I was hoping you might feel like that, so I have arranged for us to make a detour," he said softly.

A look passed between them bridging the dissension; making them both keenly aware of how far they had drifted apart over the past few months. Her raw emotions longed to confess all; it would be so easy, she thought before the spell was broken and the moment passed. He put her hand to his lips, silently consoling *himself* that the problems between them would disappear once he was back working.

As the car swung into the long, tree-lined drive, Pamela sat forward, eager to catch a glimpse of the lovely old Manor House. At first she thought it was unchanged in the twenty years, and it was as if it were yesterday, but as they drew nearer, peeling paint on the wide mullioned windows and a general air of neglect became evident.

"It all became too much," Gerald said quietly, seeing her expression. "As numbers dwindled, government funding became less, and now it isn't up to standard with modern requirements." He shrugged despondently. "It will cost a fortune to refurbish, and it is likely the other two will go the same way, in the not too distant future."

"How about the children's homes?"

"There will always be a need for them. We have kept on top of repairs, with local tradespeople's help, so not too much to worry about there. Charles also makes a sizeable contribution every year and also donates his services free, when required."

"I didn't even know Charles took an interest."

"Not many do. He says it is his thank you, for his and Felicity's upbringing; she and Mother are always knitting for the youngsters."

Pamela was mortified. "It never occurred to me who they were knitting for, since the children grew up. It's just something they do."

"You had your nursing."

As they were speaking, Gerald put the key in the lock and the door swung inwards, revealing the high, glass domed hall. It was empty of furniture, and smelled musty. Gerald wandered into the room that had been the big ward, as she stood motionless at the foot of the bare staircase, gazing up to where sunlight filtering through the trees threw dancing shadows eerily around the upper landing. Voices from the past filled her head, and she felt herself swaying until Gerald's voice broke into her reverie, making her whirl round with wide startled eyes.

"You look as if you have seen a ghost," he laughed.

She gave a breathless little gasp. "Something like that."

"What do you mean? Are you all right? You look quite pale." He gave her a concerned look.

"Just for a moment, the moving sunlight appeared to be the flying souls of all the poor tormented boys who lived or died here. Look, can't you see?" She stared upwards again and the sob in her voice caught at Gerald's heart, as he followed her gaze. She had never spoken of her nursing experiences, not like this anyway. Suddenly he was frightened for her, she sounded so odd. What had been planned as a pleasant walk down memory lane had obviously revived memories better left in the past. He caught her shoulders and guided her towards the door.

"Perhaps this isn't such a good idea. In hindsight you have never shown any desire to come back, in all of these years. Perhaps we should seriously consider selling."

She gave a bewildered shake of her head, answering falteringly, "It just took me by surprise. I'm alright now."

He drew her to the nearest of the bench seats arranged round the edge of the wide lawn, and they sat, as Pamela remembered so many men, all in blue suits, had sat looking down the drive waiting for loved ones on visiting days. Some waited in vain, because loved ones couldn't face the mental torment of having their crippled husbands, sons or fiancés released and sent home to them. They were the saddest of all. They were the ones who remained in the homes, long after others were reunited with their families. A sob rose in her throat again and Gerald's arm went round her instantly. She hadn't been prepared for the memories the place could still invoke.

"I shouldn't have brought you. It was thoughtless. I had this crazy idea I would make the property over to you, and you could make it into a private nursing home. I thought it would give you an interest now the boys have left home. Apparently most women get empty nest syndrome."

She gave a weak smile. "Who told you that?"

"Dad. Mother told him."

"Very wise, coming from a couple whose son has never left them," Pamela observed dryly. "But they are right. And it is actually not a bad idea, except I don't want to go back to nursing, and this place has had its fill of sadness. How about turning it into a good hotel? Bring some life to it. Lay all of those ghosts to rest." She stood up, and tugged at his hand. "Let's go back in. I'm fine now."

"Are you sure?"

Her green eyes were shining, as he hadn't seen them shine in months.

He suddenly felt buoyant. They were planning together. His fear of losing her had been absurd. It was just a matter of finding the right solution, as he always had in the past.

By the time they were back on the road and heading for Southampton, several pages of his notepad were filled with Pamela's flamboyant handwriting. Her previous fantasies apparently forgotten, she chattered all through dinner about her plans, until Gerald waved his white napkin.

"Enough woman! You are making my head spin."

Alexander had sat quietly, listening but obviously deep in thought. Now he asked; "When do you intend to start?"

"As soon as possible," Pamela enthused, oblivious to the disquiet in his voice, but Gerald's eyes narrowed.

"Do you have a problem with that?"

"Only that I assume Mother will want to stay at the cottage, with it being closer than here, and I have told a friend, who is between jobs, he can move in with me until he gets settled, but it sounds as if the times will clash."

He shrugged, as if it was of little consequence. "It's just that he is a bit short of cash at the moment and I promised him, but of course I will put him off if you need to stay."

As he knew she would Pamela shook her head. "Can't break a promise. There is sure to be somewhere I can stay for the odd night or two. Don't give it another thought."

She was so engrossed she brushed the matter aside impatiently.

"Someone from around this way?" Gerald asked.

"No. You wouldn't know him, Dad, I haven't known him long, but we get on really well, and he is a hard worker," he nodded seriously.

"Oh well, if you are sure." Gerald did his best to sound unconcerned. This was a new side to Alexander: one that he liked. He sounded responsible and mature. So he must show him trust in his judgement.

The next morning, his confidence in Alexander increased as he watched him moving amongst the staff, making comments and generally working side by side with them. He suspected some of it was arranged to impress him, but nevertheless, when they left for Cornwall, it was with a great sense of relief and anticipation that his young son was actually going to make the grade.

Pamela kept very busy over the following weeks, hiring decorators, selecting wallpaper, and watching as the house was stripped from top to bottom. The smell of fresh paint, paste, plaster and sawdust replaced the heavy, age-old, nose wrinkling odours, as the workmen plied their trades. Her inheritance was being put to good use she prided herself, and it was her job to make a success of The Vintage, as she had decided to rename the house. In her view the change of name was crucial, to avoid any link with a previous image and surprisingly, so far at least, Gerald had agreed with all of her decisions. In fact he had made a point of leaving her to it, and only dealt with the financial side of things when she asked him to. In fact everything was going swimmingly, until she decided to call in on Alexander.

She had hardly seen him since work started on the house and she wanted to make sure he was looking after himself, without appearing to check up. Popping in for a coffee on her way home for the weekend could hardly be considered interfering, she assured herself, edging her car into the narrow driveway. It was mid-morning; he was sure to be home, probably still in his dressing gown if she knew her son.

She walked to the front door, her steps crunching on the gravel, and noted with mild surprise, fresh plants under the bay windows either side of the front door. There was no answer to her knock but she could hear a radio playing, and followed the sound to the back garden. A lone figure was standing by the table, adjusting a large green sunshade, over a table set with a yellow and white checked tablecloth, knives, forks, yellow paper napkins, and a tall glass jug of fresh orange juice.

The attractive scene aroused her curiosity towards its creator – a slim-hipped, headless figure, with its back to her. Spotless white jeans topped by a white T-shirt were all that was visible from under the umbrella.

"Excuse me; is Alexander about?" she called.

The figure froze visibly before ducking from under the fringe.

"Good morning, Pamela. He has just popped out to get fresh milk."

She recoiled as Colin emerged, greeting her with an arrogant stance and hard, ice blue stare. She walked quickly to a garden bench, beside the open kitchen door, to overcome her surprise.

"He obviously won't be long then." She spoke calmly, straightening her pleated skirt with exaggerated care, feeling peculiarly at odds with the attitude of the young man, who had frequently and charmingly served her drinks at his parents' hotel.

He had got over his initial surprise and was smirking in an over familiar way, which disturbed her.

"Of course, you didn't know I was here." He tossed his blond head and following her with quick short strides. She caught the smell of bacon cooking and stood up again, wrinkling her nose.

He curled his lip. "Of course, you don't do breakfast, do you?"

"It is of no importance and I'm sure Alexander has many visitors."

She spoke nonchalantly looking at her small gold wristwatch, taking a deep breath to stem a sharp remark. Perhaps she was being too sensitive, but premonition stayed with her, as she wandered across the lawn, and gazed unseeingly into the forest beyond.

Without a sound he appeared beside her and her head jerked nervously. He was studying her and standing unnecessarily close, causing her to step back.

"I'm not visiting. We live together. As in a couple?" His voice was low and his words were measured so she could not fail to understand his meaning.

Her senses reeled, and she heard herself from a long way off, saying, "Don't be so ridiculous!! Alexander would be furious if he heard you say such things. Why are you behaving in this objectionable manner?"

His smile slipped and he said urgently, glancing frequently towards the house, "I knew *you* would find out, sooner or later, so I will come straight to the point. Alexander knows his father won't understand about us, and will disown him, so for all…"

Pamela interrupted him. "If you think you can corrupt my son, and enlist my help to keep it from his father, then –" This time he interrupted her.

"Ah, but I think you will, as I was about to say, for *all* of our sakes. Alex will never forgive you, you know. He thinks you are such a paragon of virtue, but he doesn't need to find out if you co-operate."

His narrowed eyes quelled the angry retort that rose to her lips, and she remained very still, knowing in that dreadful moment what was coming, closing her eyes in dismay as he whispered in a barely audible voice.

"We both have a secret. So you *will* do as I say and not a word to Uncle Bill. Understand?"

He was smiling affably now, and pointing to a squirrel leaping through the branches of a huge old oak tree, as Alexander walked round the corner of the cottage carrying a pint of milk. She had missed the car, but Colin hadn't. Alexander looked relaxed and happy and apart from self-consciousness she had never seen him looking happier.

"Hello, Mother." He smiled, walked towards her and kissed her cheek, unaware of any tension.

"Now you're here, I'll rescue breakfast. Are you sure you won't stay and share it, Pamela?" Colin asked with a challenging smile.

"I have to be on my way." She was desperately trying to gather her wits and mistaking her bewildered look, Alexander put an arm round her shoulders.

"You know, don't you? Please don't be upset. For the first time I know who I am."

His eyes pleaded with her, and her heart softened, even as a million questions filled her mind.

In the following two weeks, Colin demanded two thousand pounds; unaware of this, Alexander gave glowing reports over the telephone of the wonderful changes they were making to the cottage. She listened angrily as he told her Colin had spent a thousand pounds of his own hard earned savings, and was it fair as it was dad's property? Burning with resentment, she sent him a cheque for a thousand pounds and received an unwelcome visit to thank her.

She was selecting carpets from a huge pile of samples and her heart lurched as she saw them approaching.

Colin was loud in his admiration of the blue and gold Regency striped wallpaper, and the matching plain blue velvet curtains, with thick, gold tassels for tiebacks.

"Your mother has exquisite taste."

Alexander raised his eyebrows at her. "Praise indeed, coming from the expert himself. You won't recognise the cottage."

He and Colin exchanged smug looks as Colin insisted loudly he just had to see the kitchen. Pamela followed them with growing suspicion that there was another purpose behind the casual visit.

The gleaming stainless steel kitchen was all but finished and he ran an approving eye over the layout. "I could work in this kitchen. What say you, Pamela?"

"There you are, Mother. A London chef, right on your doorstep and ready to start *anytime*."

"I already have an excellent applicant, thank you."

Alexander frowned heavily, as she turned away considering the matter closed.

"It's funny, I just have this odd feeling I am meant to work here," Colin said looking at his wristwatch. "We must be going, Pamela. See you soon," he called to her retreating figure.

She continued walking, at that moment incapable of even saying goodbye to Alexander, knowing when the hotel opened, Colin would be in the kitchen.

That evening, she sat at a corner table in the hotel bar picking at her meal. It was quiet at this time and she kept an opened book beside her, to deter friendly chat from the landlord. From time to time she would turn a page, to all intents and purposes engrossed in reading, but her mind was battling with the threat taking over her every waking moment.

Several times when she and Bill had been able to snatch a precious evening together, she had thought to end their relationship, but when they met and he held her in his arms so tenderly, and made love to her, she escaped to that wonderful world where nothing else existed. She had always been able to convince herself they were separate – another life, to enjoy without hurting her family. Sadly though it had come home to roost with a vengeance, but so much she valued was at risk and even if she ended it now, the blackmail would still go on.

Her thoughts went off at a tangent. The trips down river, meals at Toni's and only last month Bill had taken her to Drury Lane Theatre. She had been fascinated by the beautiful old theatre, built in Charles II's time, three-and-a-quarter centuries ago. She had watched and listened, enraptured by the music of 'The Great Waltz', and in the interval he had told her about the ghost of a young man, complete with 17th century powdered wig and tricorn hat, referred to as 'The Man in Grey' who was rumoured to haunt the upper circle. She remembered looking nervously up at the balcony, as Bill laughed at her, and now worryingly she recalled again the visions that still appeared at The Vintage in quiet moments, when the waving trees made shadows on the walls. That was why she decided to rent a room here during the week, and made sure she was never on her own in the old convalescent home.

Conflicting thoughts tumbled through her troubled mind, and she felt faint. She helped herself to a glass of water from the jug and gave up any pretence of eating the omelette, which had gone cold by now.

"Are you alright, Mrs Anders?" the landlord called from behind the bar.

"Yes. Yes, I'm fine, thank you." She started to rise, and sat down again quickly just as a tall figure entered and made for the bar. For a moment she was too dizzy to move, and watched in a haze as the landlord pointed to her giving a concerned shake of his head. With four long strides Bill was by her side.

"Let me help you to your room," he said taking her arm.

"What are you doing here?" she asked vaguely, giving him a vacant stare.

"Let's talk in your room," he said quietly, adding in a louder voice, "I think my friend is a little faint. Don't worry, I'm a doctor. Send coffee to her room would you, please?"

She was glad of his steadying hand, as they climbed the narrow staircase leading to her bedroom. He sat her down on the bed, gently pushing her head between her knees and after a few moments she felt well enough to rest back against the pillows. The coffee arrived, brought by the busy landlady, who was only too happy to leave her guest in the capable looking hands of her doctor friend.

"Could cause gossip." Bill grinned, hoping the little joke would raise a smile, and was horrified to see tears spring to her eyes.

"You haven't phoned for over a week. It must be something serious. Tell me."

At first she wouldn't say, but he gradually coaxed the full story.

"That little – I'll kill him!"

Alarmed she cried, "Don't tell him I've told you. He will tell Alexander about us."

He paced up and down.

"I can't believe he would do such a thing. I'm responsible and I will put it right, I promise. I love you and know we could be happy together, but you need your family."

He settled against the pillows with her, drawing her into the circle of his arm.

"The thought of ending our wonderful times together doesn't bear thinking about; but we must. I will always be there for you, our friendship doesn't have to end."

She nodded dumbly, tears streaming down her cheeks. The landlady tapped the door and asked if she could get Mrs Anders anything before the bar closed, looking pointedly at her watch. Bill ordered a hot milk drink and asked if there was another room available, to which she nodded and became less disapproving.

"I will make sure Mrs Anders is alright before I leave, but I do need a six o'clock call, please," he said following her to a room further along the landing. The landlady made several pleasantries he barely heard, because he was already planning what he was going to say to Colin very early the next morning.

Five days went by, while Pamela tried to believe she would hear no more from Colin, during which time Alexander called in once, on his way home from work, to see if she had reconsidered Colin's generous offer, and when she asked, "What generous offer would that be?" he had flushed angrily.

"I thought you had accepted our relationship."

"My decision has nothing to do with you and Colin. I have already made it clear; the position is filled. We have provided him with free accommodation. Stop trying to buy his friendship, Alexander."

Without another word, he turned on his heel and seconds later his car screeched out of the drive.

She didn't see him again until the Friday, when she was packing to go home for the weekend. Colin was with him, and his smirk and Alexander's stony expression told her the worst. Her stomach churned.

Without greeting her, he said in a voice that shook with anger, "Colin has explained to me why you won't employ him but if he is prepared to overlook your behaviour; the least you can do is to give him the job, so I suggest you have the contract drawn up immediately."

She looked at him with astonishment. "How dare you speak to me like that?"

"I dare because I have just discovered that my sanctimonious mother is an adulteress."

His look of disgust made her colour violently and she glanced at Colin who was regarding her discomfort with a triumphant gleam in his icy blue eyes.

In one swift angry movement, she turned on her heel and walked the full length of the hall before turning.

"I will speak to you alone, Alexander. Now."

Her voice shook and tears scalded her eyelids as she walked into the office. Some of her fighting spirit came to the rescue as she heard Alexander's even tread approaching on the bare floorboards, and anger, born of humiliation, filled her.

Cheeks still burning, she stood behind her desk and waited for him, furious with herself for being so stupid. She should have realised *he* had nothing to lose by telling her son but they would both lose if he told Gerald.

Alexander stood in the doorway. "Well?" he demanded with a look of disdain.

"Close the door please. This is a private conversation between my son and I," she added as Colin sidled up behind him.

"We have no secrets from each other," Alexander said with cold insinuation.

She looked him straight in the eyes.

"Now listen carefully. I don't want to hurt your father, but if you continue to follow Colin's lead I will make a clean breast of everything – and I mean everything. I will not be dictated to. You have as much to lose as I do."

Colin realised he had overplayed his hand. This was the second time he had underestimated her. "Forget the job. It can stop here and nobody will get hurt." Pamela gave a derisive, huh! "You mean *you* won't get hurt. *We* already are."

Alexander ignored her and turned to Colin. "No, you have set your heart on this job; it's perfect for you. No travelling, no bosses. And I intend you to have it." Alexander stood stiff-backed, as he had as a child.

"Give me a chance, Pamela. You won't be sorry."

"I am already sorry I ever met you," she answered scornfully, "and I am Mrs Anders to you."

Colin shrugged and looked at Alexander. "I tried."

"He won't have told you he has been blackmailing me?" Outraged by Colin's calm indifference she gave a last try.

"He told me you offered him money to keep quiet; as I said we have no secrets." His look of disgust hurt her more than anything, and it was obvious he wasn't going to believe anything she said now.

She gathered her coat and handbag and without another word made to brush past them but Alexander caught her arm. For a moment she thought he was going to strike her, and she recoiled at the fury on his face.

"You are so selfish. I thought I mattered to you, but you don't care about anybody but yourself."

He let her go and her shoulders slumped. Slowly, she returned to the desk, took an application form from the drawer and threw it at Colin, then with all the fight knocked out of her she left the office went to her car and drove off.

CHAPTER EIGHTEEN

Sophie and Matthew arrived with news of going to America in September, and wanting to get married before they went. There was much talk of when, and eventually August 10th was decided on, and although Pamela offered to provide the reception at The Vintage, they shyly requested it should be held at Anders Folly. Charles and Felicity were overjoyed when Gerald claimed, "Where else should a girl get married, but the place where she was born?

Charles sat with a bewildered grin, listening to the plans being bounced back and forth.

"Just have your cheque book ready," Laurie advised with one of his hearty chuckles.

It was a happy weekend and Pamela's preoccupation if noticed, was put down to her latest project. On Sunday morning, David found her wandering along the sandy cove alone.

"Good heavens, what are you doing up at this hour?"

"Couldn't sleep," she said simply as he fell into step beside her.

"We don't want you overdoing things you know. You look a bit peaky," and then after a short pause. "How's Robert?"

"Happy and well – they both are."

He noticed her face lifted and ventured to say, "Where are they living?"

"They have a nice, three bedroom house, near to a park where Celina will be able walk the baby. It's perfect and Robert assures me he has everything his heart desires." She slipped her arm through his. "He sends love to you both, and says you aren't to worry about them."

He patted her hand, "Even so, I'm sure he could do with some help to buy that house."

"It's all been taken care of," she said with a soft smile.

"I should have known."

She squeezed his arm, and they walked in silence until he blurted out, "I would like to see him. Can it be arranged, without upsetting Gerald?"

"You could come back with me. I could book a room for you where I'm staying, then we could travel to Oxford, and return the next day."

"Best if we don't say anything to anyone," David said brusquely straightening his shoulders with an abrupt little gesture.

"That would be best," she replied sympathetically and the matter wasn't referred to again.

But later, when they were all sitting round the big table, eating Sunday lunch, David said casually, "How is the house going, Pamela? It must be nearly finished by now?"

"Yes, we open next month. Why don't you come and see it for yourself?"

Gerald looked up sharply. "It's a long way for Dad to travel. He could see it just as well next month. I assume we will all come for the opening."

"I would hope so." Pamela threw a dazzling smile round the table.

"If Dad feels up to it though, I would love the company."

"Then it's settled. I'll travel with you tomorrow morning," David said quickly looking uncomfortable.

Marie patted his hand. "It will do you good, dear. You have been working far too hard in the garden lately."

"What will you do when Pamela is working?"

Gerald looked perplexed and would have pursued the matter, but Marie diverted the conversation by offering more food to everyone – then it dawned on Pamela it was her idea. Not that she would ever admit to it, but 'Needs must when the devil drives' she could hear Marie saying. And although Robert was very special, it must be costing them dearly to go against Gerald's wishes.

In the morning, as Pamela was pulling away, Laurie leant into the car. "Would you post this for me, please?" and slipped an envelope into David's hand.

They drove off with everyone waving from the broad stone steps and at the first post box Pamela asked where the letter was going, as it might get to its destination quicker if it was posted further on. David turned it over and stared at the name written in Laurie's familiar copperplate, then held it up for her to read, saying wryly, "Nothing much gets past Laurie, does it?"

Pamela smiled and shook her head as with a quick sideways glance she read 'Robert'.

By late afternoon, they had booked into their rooms, had a snack in the bar and were on their way to The Vintage. They were inspecting the newly laid bedroom carpets when Alexander and Colin appeared. Alexander was alarmed at seeing his grandfather and shot his mother a sharp look, until David greeted him fondly, whereupon he introduced Colin as a friend lodging with him, and Colin shook hands respectfully. Gone was the insolent attitude, they were just two smartly dressed, polite young men, taking an interest in the progress.

"Mother may have told you, Colin is to be chef," Alexander said chattily.

"How nice."

Pamela suddenly felt driven to retaliate.

"You mustn't let Alexander pressure you. You should concentrate on your career.

"It's been agreed, Mother," Alexander glared.

Pamela gave a dismissive wave of her hand, feeling ridiculously reckless with David there, knowing at the same time how fleeting her victory was, but it was worth it just to wipe the smile off Colin's face.

"We must be going," he interrupted quickly, seeing Alexander getting ready to make a scene.

"Will we see you again, Mr Anders? How long will you be staying?" He smiled affably again, while Pamela looked on with rising apprehension, wondering what that smile hid.

"Until Friday, but I have business to attend to, so we may not be around all of the time. However I'm sure we will see something of you both."

"I could drive you," Alexander chipped in. "I'll tell the manager you need me. I'm sure they will cope."

David stifled a smile. "Thank you, but everything is arranged. Your mother will drive me."

"But I would be better." Alexander spoke as if it was decided, and this time David replied very firmly that he preferred to stay with their arrangements. Alexander's face suffused with colour, and once again Colin stepped in by offering his hand to David.

"Goodbye, sir. Sorry to rush away, but we have an appointment. Hope to see you before you leave." He shot Pamela a look.

"You will." David shook the proffered hand then turned to Alexander.

"Don't worry about your mother. I intend to make her rest."

He watched speculatively as they walked away, deep in conversation. Colin briskly, looking straight ahead, Alexander spreading his hands defensively.

The next morning they awoke to grey skies and heavy drizzle. The trees dripped with monotonous rhythm and the forest had taken on an altogether different mood to the sun dappled, leafy green haven of the day before. David was glad to be spending the day at the office. A car was laid on to drive him there, and take him back to The Vintage at four o'clock.

Everything went according to plan, except that Alexander cancelled the car and insisted on driving his grandfather back. He danced attendance on David all day, saying at every opportunity, "I would be far more help to you than Mum."

Colin had told him he was behaving like a spoiled brat and he was desperate to show him he was more than a junior employee.

Back at The Vintage they found Pamela looking harassed. Her day had not gone well. Six rolls of ground floor carpet were discovered to have a flaw and had to be returned, which meant a delay of over a week. They would be cutting things fine for the opening.

211

"Really, Mother! What are you playing about at? You must accept Colin's help or you will *never* get this place off the ground. You need his experience and help. Stop being so obstinate." He looked at David and tossed his eyes.

Alexander's patronising was the least of her worries and she chose to ignore it, but at that moment Colin walked in and her nerves snapped.

"Don't you two *boys* have anything better to do!" she demanded icily, collecting her things together.

David stood silently, taking it all in and wondering why Pamela was not her usual doting self towards her youngest son; especially when the suggestion appeared to be helpful. He considered intervening, thought better of it and followed her out to the car.

They drove in silence and he could see she was struggling to hold back the tears so, at a suitable spot, he asked her to pull over.

"Are you alright?" she asked in a shrill voice braking sharply.

"I'm alright, but you aren't. You are so jumpy and the air could be cut with a knife between you and Alexander. You obviously don't want Colin working for you, and yet Alexander really wants him to – which would normally be enough for you. Tell me what's wrong."

David had always been the one she could turn to, but it was asking too much to expect him to understand *this* situation. She had no answer to give him but the tears couldn't be held back any longer and she sobbed.

"Come now, you are making yourself ill. What does it matter if the opening has to be postponed? A bit of bruised pride, that's all."

If only that was all, she thought. He put a finger under her chin and turned her face towards him, puzzled by the absolute misery he saw. There had to be something more. He recalled the scenes with Alexander and Colin, his mind flying back to when Alexander was intimidating Marie – surely not his mother? They had a special bond, and yet a similarity struck him – and perhaps Colin was a little too smooth. He looked her straight in the eyes, and this time she didn't look away. She wanted to tell him.

"What's going on?" he asked gently. "Why are you putting up with this nonsense? I know he can twist you round his little finger, but something is making you ill. It must stop."

She stared, her mind going blank; all she was aware of was rain hitting the car, turning into a roaring sound. The next, David was patting her hand and holding a hip flask of brandy to her lips. She knew she had to fight the giddiness and get them home. They were a mile from anywhere. After a while she felt a little better and made to start the engine, but David caught her hand, saying firmly, "We aren't going anywhere until you tell me what this is all about."

She shook her head vehemently. "I can't. You could never forgive me."

"So I'm a complete ogre, am I?"

"You don't know what I have done."

"Something to do with London? And how much you enjoyed the life?"

She stared at him again.

"Don't look so tragic my dear. You have made Gerald very happy over the years but I knew when I saw you going to the theatre you had realised what you had been missing. I also know you would never purposely hurt Gerald, but it hasn't been easy lately, has it?"

Suddenly she was telling him everything and his face grew sterner and sterner until she finished lamely, "Can you ever forgive me? I am so sorry. I won't even pretend I don't still feel for this man, but it is over. You have my word on that."

He nodded, his face unreadable. "Start the car. I need to call on Master Alexander and his friend."

Pamela looked startled. "They *will* tell Gerald."

"No he won't, because not only will his father cut him off, but his grandparents will as well, and then let him find himself a job and salary to match the one he has. There is also a very serious penalty for blackmail. Colin may think he has the upper hand, but at the end of the day, greed will make him toe the line."

He leant back with a grim expression as she pulled away, and they drove in silence to the cottage where she waited in the car, whilst David strode up to the door and disappeared inside for just ten minutes, before letting himself out and returning to the car wearing a grimly satisfied expression.

"Let's go home, I'm starving," was all he said.

They made an early start the next morning and were on the road by nine, in good spirits at the thought of seeing Robert and Celina. They had telephoned and arranged to take them to a small restaurant by the river, but first David had to be given a guided tour of their new home. The nursery was already decorated in lemon, with balloons and clowns on the wallpaper and curtains, and Celina proudly pointed out how Robert had done the painting and papering himself. They were so obviously happy, David knew he could at least put Marie's mind at rest, even though it wouldn't make up for not seeing Robert for herself. He also missed the boy dreadfully, especially after spending all that time with him. His heart hardened as he thought of Alexander. All of his worst fears had been realised, but he would keep silent for the sake of the family, providing he and his friend caused Pamela no more grief.

Shopping for the baby took up most of the following day and the visit went all too quickly. Pamela bought a beautiful carriage built pram, with all of the trimmings and Celina chose a cream painted drop side cot, with nursery rhyme transfers, from David and Marie.

Robert goggled at the cheque his grandfather handed him as they were leaving, along with the envelope in his inside pocket. Robert opened it to find a warm letter from Laurie, wishing them both well, and another cheque that took their breath away.

"Make sure they don't go without anything. You are always in our thoughts," David said with brimming eyes, as he hugged them both.

"I will be back soon," was Pamela's, parting promise.

And that was the last time they ever saw them. A heavy drizzle had started to fall, and two miles along the motorway, a transport lorry pulled in front of them, causing Pamela to brake on the slippery road. They went into the lorry and the car behind went into them.

Robert heard about the crash almost immediately, because Sean, the Irish student Pamela had asked directions from, happened to be passing the scene shortly after the crash, and recognised the distinctive silver blue sports car from the mangled mess. He conveyed the heartbreaking news to Robert that they had both died instantly. Beside himself with shock, Robert telephoned home, where Abigail answered and told him they had just received the news. Marie had collapsed and they were waiting for the doctor to arrive. She gave a loud sob, and Robert realised she would be feeling as grief-stricken as any of them. He rang off, debating whether Celina would be all right travelling all the way to Cornwall and decided they must try.

Supporting her back and legs on cushions in the back seat, he travelled all night and arrived at Anders Folly very early the next morning.

Felicity met them at the door, her eyes red and swollen, and for a moment Robert feared he was too late, but she motioned him to go straight up and took Celina's arm.

"Your father is with her. She keeps asking for *you*."

He took the stairs two at a time, and opened his grandmother's door. For an instant it could have been his grandfather sitting beside the bed with his head bowed on his hands, such was the likeness. His father didn't look up, didn't even appear to be aware of his presence, but Robert's main concern was his grandmother and he went to the other side of the bed and kissed her forehead.

"Hello, Grandma, it's me." Marie opened her eyes slightly and he took her hand in his, as Gerald raised his head and relief flooded over his face. He looked exhausted and Robert's heart went out to him.

"Get some rest, Dad; I will stay with Grandma."

"No, no, I must be here whenever she wakes."

214

The door opened and Felicity crept in carrying two cups of tea. Her relief at seeing Marie's eyes open brought tears of emotion, and clasping Robert to her she said, "She will rest happier now you are here. She has asked for you ever since we heard, and your father hasn't left her side."

They looked across and saw he had sunk into an exhausted sleep, with his head resting on his arms.

"Let's make him more comfortable, he won't leave her," Felicity suggested.

Marie watched without expression while they settled him comfortably on the big Chesterfield settee at the foot of the bed then closed her eyes as a single solitary tear trickled down her cheek. Robert sat with her and an hour later she woke again. He was beside her instantly. She gave a tiny smile of recognition, her lips moved soundlessly and she drifted off to sleep again. It lasted for three days; seemingly she woke to make sure he was still there. In the meantime, Gerald was under sedation and they took it in turns to sit with them both. On the fourth day, Marie showed signs of improvement and in another two days, was propped up in bed being spoon fed with some of Lorna's chicken broth. Gerald refused to take any more medication, and never left her bedside. It was therefore well over a week before he became aware that Celina was in the house. In fact, it wasn't until Robert and Charles carried Marie downstairs for the first time and sat her on the long settee. Gerald gave Celina one long hard stare then ignored her completely.

When Marie was settled, Laurie put a rug over her lap with great tenderness, fighting back the tears of relief at having her with them again. Never in his life had he suffered like it. Grieving for his dear friend David and fearing they might lose her, had tormented him beyond endurance and his ravaged features bore evidence. Charles had dreadful visions of him dying as well.

Marie sat dry-eyed, staring into space and Gerald, when not with her, hid himself in the study. Life became automatic, with an unreal stillness pervading the house, affecting them all. No one said much and when they did it was as if their minds were elsewhere. Marie sat motionless, her eyes now fixed dully on David's empty chair, her knitting lay untouched, in spite of Felicity's comments that they should be knitting for the new baby. Laurie tried placing the chessboard beside her, but her eyes just filled with tears and he quickly removed it. Robert just sat with her and read his book, which seemed to bring her a little comfort, but after everyone had tried something, they were helpless to ease her pain, until Gerald, unable to bear it any longer, eased her out of her seat on the settee and gently lowered her into the maroon wing chair. For a moment she cringed.

"Just try it," was all he said, sitting beside her, and gradually a faraway smile crossed her face, and she lent back and relaxed.

Charles and Laurie gave each other a look that said 'He's done it again'.

215

From then on the empty chair was not a problem, and Felicity had the idea of lighting a candle each, for David and Pamela, every evening, which brought a certain comfort to all of them. And slowly they made the painful journey back, learning to live without two much needed loved ones.

Alexander had arrived on the day of the funeral, on edge in case anything had been said before the accident. His biggest fear had been Robert, him being the last one to see them alive; had they told him? The huge relief when it became obvious they hadn't, and the fact that things could never have been the same between them ever again, helped to console him for the death of his mother. She had let him down badly even up to the last, because now he knew why he had been left out again and he was filled with hatred for Robert.

Consequently, when Robert and Celina left he wasted no time in pointing out to his father, that if his mother and grandfather had not been going to see Robert they would both still be alive today, and was smugly satisfied to see Gerald's jaw harden as the bolt went home.

Marie had implored Robert to make things right with his father, and he had promised to do his best, little knowing what the future held.

Driven to distraction by his mother's health and the loneliness of life without Pamela and his father, Gerald brooded over Alexander's words until in his own mind, Robert was responsible. Had it not been for him, they would never have been near Oxford. And the visit to see The Vintage was just a cover-up. And even after he had made his views so very clear, Robert still had the effrontery to bring that woman into the house. Well he needn't think it was going to happen again.

Frowning deeply, he reached for his writing paper and wrote furiously, all his pent up anger spilling out onto the sheet of headed cream vellum.

Robert visited his grandmother just once more after receiving that letter, cruelly holding him responsible for the deaths of his mother and grandfather. He travelled overnight and arrived very early, spent the whole day with Marie, explained to Charles and Laurie why he wouldn't be coming home again and left without even glancing in Gerald's direction, as he stood in the study doorway.

They were shocked to the core by the accusation, but loyalty made them assure Robert his father was obviously under a great deal of strain and would apologise when he had had time to reconsider his words, to which Robert replied, "Nothing he could say could ever make up for that letter, and I'm glad he doesn't know how wrong he is, because from this day on Celina and I can live our own lives."

Charles and Laurie watched helplessly as he climbed into his car and drove off, giving a wave and a long lingering look at his grandmother and Felicity, who were waving from Marie's bedroom window, unaware of the hurt he was suffering.

In the meantime, Alexander and Colin took advantage of the situation to gain control of The Vintage. Alexander presented the application form to Gerald and convinced him it was Pamela's dearest wish for Colin to manage the hotel. It was a plausible story and Gerald signed the contract without question, glad to have the whole thing taken off his hands, knowing absolutely nothing about the catering business.

"There will of course be a monthly report required but providing it pays its way he has carté blanche to run it as he sees fit. Your mother obviously had faith in him."

He closed his eyes in weary resignation as Alexander picked up the signed contract, *his* eyes gleaming with triumph.

CHAPTER NINETEEN

Summer passed; Sophie and Matthew's wedding was a quiet affair with only the immediate family present and afterwards they reluctantly left for America where great plans for a post-wedding reception had been made by Joseph and Clare Willard. Long letters describing the magnificence of it all arrived from Sophie who, although homesick, was deliriously happy. Charles and Felicity read and re-read the pages, picturing their girl in her new surroundings and wishing they could be with her but to leave Marie and Gerald was unthinkable.

Christmas came and went. Marie, a shadow of her former self, was a constant reminder to Gerald of the loss of his father and he yearned for the old days, with Marie bustling around and David at the helm. Life had changed so dramatically and it was hard to accept that those times were gone forever. Marie quietly joined David ten months later. She was sitting in David's chair and Laurie was opposite with the chessboard between them. Marie made her move, leant back with a small triumphant smile and Laurie exclaimed, "By gad! I think you have beaten me." He looked up, his face wreathed in a big smile and it looked for all the world as if she had dropped off to sleep, as she did quite often of late, until her stillness told him otherwise. His smile faded and the tears ran unchecked.

Gerald appeared from nowhere as if he had been summoned and knelt down, taking her hand in his, pressing it to his lips with a resigned look at Laurie. Yet again Laurie was stunned by his profound awareness. The smile still hovered around Marie's lips and Gerald said gently, "She will be happy again now; she is with Dad."

Once more the house was plunged in to mourning. At the last minute Sophie and Matthew were unable to attend the funeral, so Felicity decided they had to go and see Sophie for themselves, imagining all kind of terrible reasons it would take to keep her away from Marie's funeral.

Sophie and Matthew were delighted about the visit and invited Gerald and Laurie too. Gerald refused saying he didn't feel well enough to travel, but Laurie accepted gratefully. With David and Marie gone, he had already made up his mind to move back to his own home. The loneliness he felt at their loss was constantly with him. Never for a moment had he anticipated outliving them, and to be here without Charles and Felicity as well was unthinkable. Robert didn't attend the funeral service either but Gerald knew his son had been nearby. A wreath in the shape of an open book, made of white roses with a single red rose laid across it had been placed on the grave with a card saying: 'To my beloved

Grandmother – a wonderful friend. With heartfelt thanks and deeply devoted love – R.'

Gerald could hardly contain his impatience to be left alone. He wanted solitude to find a way to deal with the absence of his cherished parents and wife. Charles offered to stay, even though he desperately wanted to see Sophie so Gerald had to be quite forthright in his refusal.

"Lorna won't let me starve and Abigail will see I have a clean shirt – and I am not completely useless myself, you know. For God's sake just leave me in peace." His voice softened. "Go and see our girl is alright."

In actual fact after they had gone he felt desolate and three weeks stretched interminably as he wandered aimlessly about, unable to decide what to do. He could see Pamela and his parents everywhere. There was no escape. He walked for miles and sat on the cliff top, gazing out to sea for hours, anything to be out of the house. After breakfast he would set off alone and be gone for the whole day armed with a map and a packed lunch. Lorna always gave a sigh of relief when he returned – he looked so downtrodden her heart ached for him. In a small way it alleviated her own sorrow; for now that Marie was no longer there, Lorna also knew a kind of loneliness she had never experienced before. Even the death of her mother had brought a certain sense of freedom mixed with the grief. She also wondered whether she would be required to live in now. After the accident, when Marie had needed constant care, Lorna had moved in to the old servants' quarters. "I'd like to be on hand," she said simply.

The room had not been used in decades, but Jake and Jed had painted, papered and finally piled all of Lorna's bits and pieces, (her mother's before her) into their van. There was a high single bed with a plump feather mattress; a round table with four chairs; a small sideboard; one armchair and her treadle sewing machine. All her worldly goods were contained within the one room and in ten months, the cosy low-beamed room had been more of a home to her than the cottage ever was. The thought of leaving weighed miserably on her mind and she reluctantly broached the subject when Gerald paid her monthly wage.

"When would you be wanting me to move out, sir?" she asked anxiously.

"What ever gave you the idea I would?" Gerald frowned, as she fumbled agitatedly with the small brown envelope he had just handed her.

"Just that I'm not needed now, sir."

"You are! Every bit as much, my dear! Your home is here for as long as you wish to stay. The comfort you gave my mother during those nights didn't go unnoticed. You have my eternal gratitude for that alone."

He spoke kindly and sincerely making Lorna blush with confusion and delight.

"No need for thanks, sir. It were a privilege. She were a fine lady."

"Yes," he said simply. It was the only time he ever spoke to her in that way, but she never forgot. From that day she felt a new sense of belonging. Her cup ran over with pride to be told by Sir Gerald, of all people, that she was needed. She returned to her precious room and looked about with a happy, possessive air of satisfaction.

Abigail, on the other hand, was feeling less than appreciated. Her position now seemed to fall in to the category of general housemaid. Gone was the status of 'nanny' and taking meals with the family. Even her little world at the top of the house, which she always thought of as privileged, just felt cut off now Alexander had gone and Pamela wasn't there to pop up to discuss personal details concerning the boys. Her weight plummeted, but this went unnoticed because she isolated herself by taking a tray to her room rather than sit alone with Gerald or share the kitchen with Lorna and Maisie, where things were still strained. In fact, she hadn't a soul to talk to. Everyone she cared for had gone and she felt very scared. She couldn't imagine living anywhere but Anders Folly. She told herself she was obsolete as she cried herself to sleep every night and in this frame of mind, she wrote to Alexander. Resulting in Alexander storming down and accusing his father of neglecting her. Gerald was totally astonished and after speaking to Abigail, decided she should see a doctor, who diagnosed depression and recommended a holiday. Gerald was flustered and rang Alexander, anticipating she could go and stay with him, at the cottage, for a few weeks, but Alexander was travelling to Europe to study export methods. Of course Gerald was delighted to hear of the trip, but it brought home to him that he should have known about his plans. He had been neglectful of late, but nothing seemed to matter anymore.

Felicity telephoned that same evening and after listening to his problem, suggested Jessica Lewis would probably be more than happy with an all expenses paid holiday. She was, and even attended to booking Abigail and herself into a small hotel on the Scilly Isles for two weeks.

Gerald gratefully returned to his solitude, deciding two days later that work was the answer. It was time he put in an appearance at Southampton – he thought of all the sympathetic faces and changed his mind. He would check on the The Vintage. Emotion filled him; Pamela would be there. He had never suffered from indecision and it was driving him insane. He should have gone to America. They wouldn't be back for another two weeks. With only Lorna and himself, the house felt enormous and deserted. On impulse he decided to go to the yacht club. It would be quiet at this time of day.

220

Although it was mid-June, the steadily falling rain was cold and the clubhouse was full. Once again he shied away from well meaning sympathy, drove home and went straight to his bedroom, where he gripped the slender bedpost of the huge four-poster bed, leaning his face against its smooth surface, gazing at the neatly smoothed covers and picturing a mass of red hair sprawled across the snowy pillowcases. His heart ached with longing as his eyes were drawn to the bedside table where a silver framed picture of Pamela stood. She was smiling intimately; just the way she used to smile at him and in spite of the pain he smiled back, reminiscing. Her small antique bureau they had chosen together stood beside the window on her side of the bed and he went slowly to it, running his fingers over the smooth rosewood surface. Her presence was everywhere – filling his whole being. He could smell her, feel her, hear her light, slightly husky laugh as she teased him with those wonderful green eyes.

He awoke to find himself on the bed, with no idea how he got there or how long he had slept, but he felt refreshed and strangely at peace. Sunlight was filtering through the curtains – the rain had stopped. A glance at the clock told him he had slept for three hours. He was suddenly ravenous. The house was silent as he went towards the kitchen and poked his head round the door. Lorna had drawn a chair up to the Aga and was gazing into space, her thoughts on Gerald. With motherly concern she had watched him depart and return, going dejectedly to his room. Still waiting to serve him lunch, she jumped when he spoke, her features lifting at his happy face.

"Sorry I'm late. Has lunch ruined?"

She rose quickly. "Chicken salad, don't spoil, sir."

She hummed softly to herself, carving thick, succulent slices of chicken.

The next day, he tried to mesmerise himself again but disappointingly nothing happened. It seemed she had come to him in a dark hour. Unwilling to give up he moved to the huge mahogany wardrobe. Pamela's clothes hung as she had left them.

He fingered the fine wool dresses and suits he remembered her in and tears welled. Shoes stood neatly in pairs. Cashmere and silk scarves hung with precision over the brass rail on the door. He didn't recall her being that orderly – but then he wasn't aware that Abigail worshipped her things. His hands lingered over the soft, cashmere coat, halting as he touched something small and hard in the pocket.

Mildly curious he retrieved a door key, similar to a Yale but larger. Probably belonging to, The Vintage. He tossed it in his hand before slipping it on his key ring.

Recapturing the experience became an obsession and he spent hours in his room, but Lorna was content to see him so much happier.

Charles and Felicity returned with sad news. Sophie had miscarried on hearing about Marie, and was really glad they went. Clare was still irate because Matthew cancelled his engagements to look after Sophie.

"And her music?"

"Apparently, Clare was over-optimistic."

"Or was she?" Laurie put in sceptically

"What do you mean?" Gerald asked

"Laurie thinks it was a clever ploy to get Matthew back home," Felicity explained.

"Don't like the sound of that," Gerald frowned.

"They are happy; that is all that matters."

Abigail returned looking well and surprised everyone by announcing she was going to look after two small children, for a couple who ran their own flower nursery in the Scilly Isles.

"All that remains is to hand you my notice in a proper manner," she told Gerald solemnly.

Gerald gave her a generous cheque, glowing references and, feeling that it was expected, permission to leave when she felt ready.

"Never forget that you saved my sanity, twenty years ago," he added warmly.

They were sad to see her go. The top of the house wasn't the same without her.

"Our household is getting smaller," Felicity commented sadly at dinner that evening, when yet another chair was empty, regretting her words as an unhappy silence fell.

His voice husky, Laurie said, "Speaking of which, we three were to become old codgers together and I need to go home."

They all understood but didn't trust themselves to speak.

*

Gerald became convinced a curse had befallen Anders Folly and hated the emptiness. Memories held him in a vice and he would visualise Pamela sitting at the dressing table in her floaty, soft green negligee, with the lamp-light falling on her red hair and he could be heard talking to her or his parents late into the night.

The doctor assured Charles that grief took many forms, so as the wind howled and rain lashed the house, they waited for that dreadful winter to pass.

222

In March, Gerald received an appointment for Cheynne Walk Clinic. He reacted violently.

"I'm alright," he shouted at the empty study, as Felicity was passing.

"Are you?"

"Perfectly, and I'm not going all the way to London to be told so." He glared shaking the letter at her.

"Pamela wouldn't be pleased."

Gerald's jaw dropped; his look was comical and she knew he would go.

CHAPTER TWENTY

Gerald sat facing the desk, with its neatly arranged leather blotting pad, marble penholder, two well-filled 'in' and 'out' trays and two bunches of keys. His gaze was transfixed on the smaller one – antiseptic assailed his nostrils as visions of Pamela in the white Porsche filled his mind.

"See you in a year's time." Bill smiled, and Gerald escaped gladly. He waited in the car, fingering the key from Pamela's pocket. There must be hundreds like it, but he had to be sure. The sun shone warmly through the windows making him drowsy; the five a.m. start was catching up. The flask still held coffee. It would keep him awake. Fiddling with the radio he almost missed the white Porsche swinging out. Craning his neck he pulled away; the white car had turned right and he raced to the corner in time to see it disappear left. A car pulled in front of him and he braked sharply, but the white car was still in sight. He followed until they reached a cul-de-sac. Dr Jessop leapt out and hurried inside a small, terraced house. Gerald parked and walked back in time to see him jump back into the Porsche. There was nowhere to hide as the car passed.

He reached the door, praying the key wouldn't fit but it swung inwards and he entered, driven on by his need of proof. His wildly searching eyes found it in the bedroom: a photograph of a couple looking lovingly into each other's eyes. Pamela's expression devastated him. This man had kept everything as she left it as well. He felt something akin to pity before rage took over and he stormed out, leaving the key in the lock and the door wide open.

*

After his flying visit, Bill returned home an hour later to find the door wide open. He suspected a break in, until he spied the key in the lock; his heart lurched as he felt the tell-tale notch; it *was* Pamela's. His eyes hadn't played tricks then – Gerald Anders *was* standing on the corner of the Mews. Colin had broken his word. Why? He had paid willingly to buy Colin's silence and protect Pamela's memory. He had been a fool to trust him.

Two days later he drove to the cottage. It was Sunday morning, every chance Colin and Alexander would be at home. His heart was heavy as he knocked and waited. Colin came to the door in his dressing gown, apprehension, replacing surprise, when he noted Bill's grim face as he brushed past him.

Alexander poked his head round the kitchen door and scowled. "Bit early for visiting isn't it?"

Bill strode past him and stood facing them. Feet astride, fists dug deep into his anorak pockets.

"I gather the money wasn't enough; or perhaps you thought I wouldn't find out?"

Colin glanced furtively at Alexander.

Alexander yawned. "Anyone care to enlighten me?"

"That would seem a good idea." Colin gave a nervous hunch and also yawned.

"I see." Bill gave them a disgusted look. "Well, end of game; end of two hundred pounds a month. I was a fool to trust you."

After he had gone Alexander asked, "What two hundred pounds?"

"Monthly allowance. His idea." He poured water in the teapot. "Must have upset him somehow. Let's eat."

"I'm starving."

Two miles down the road Bill changed his mind. Pamela had said they were in it together but he was sure Alexander hadn't been faking. He turned the car round and went back.

*

Gerald drove home without stopping. Late as it was, he went straight to his room tore Pamela's clothes from the wardrobe and threw them on the bed before yanking out draws and adding the contents to the heap. Every last thing was bundled together in the bedspread, dragged roughly down the wide staircase, through the sleeping house and out to the vegetable garden, where with a can of petrol, he set light to them and stood back to watch the blaze.

For the few hours left of the night he sat in the chair, his thoughts sullen and bitter; then as dawn crept over the horizon he bathed, dressed, packed a large suitcase and startled Lorna by requesting breakfast. His rock hard expression forbade any comment. When she carried in scrambled eggs, bacon and mushrooms, he was staring morosely at the full-length portrait of Pamela hanging over the high mantelpiece. She was wearing a cream off-the-shoulder dress, with her auburn hair caught back softly, showing her lovely shoulders off to perfection.

"She was a real beauty," Lorna ventured timidly.

"Beauty is as beauty does," he answered coldly picking up his knife and fork.

Lorna withdrew, startled.

Within ten minutes Gerald came to the kitchen, obviously ready to leave.

"While I am away, please see my things are transferred to my parents' room. I shall be sleeping there from now on, and tell Mr Charles I will telephone later."

Lorna watched the maroon Daimler drive away, her thoughts in turmoil.

An hour later Jake came to the kitchen. "What's bin goin' on?"

"What do you mean?"

"You best come see."

Lorna followed him to the kitchen garden and gasped at the easily recognisable charred remains. "We must tell Mr Charles," she whispered.

Wearing dressing gowns hastily thrown over their nightwear, Charles and Felicity gazed in speechless dismay at the remains of Pamela's wind scattered, charred belongings, searching for a reason. She voiced his worst fear in a tearful whisper. "He's lost his mind."

*

After calling at the office to see Alexander, Gerald drove straight to The Vintage. Eyes smouldering he strode to the reception desk and thumped the brass bell.

Colin emerged, senses sharpening, as he recognised him. When Alexander had thrown him out of the cottage, he had desperately wanted to keep the job and had decided to wait for events. Perhaps this was the end.

"I wish to speak with the manager."

"We haven't met, Sir Anders." He smiled disarmingly offering his hand. "Colin Mellors. What can I do for you?"

Gerald ran a hand across his brow, suddenly exhausted. Discovering that Alexander had been trying to contact him before leaving for Europe had been the last straw. He knew nothing anymore.

"You look done in, sir. There is a bedroom prepared. We could talk after you have rested perhaps?"

Gerald reluctantly agreed, feeling he was losing control. The sleepless night, the long drives, the anger were all taking their toll. Colin showed him to a first floor room, poured a stiff brandy from a tray of drinks and left.

He awoke to daylight and assumed it was evening, but a look at his watch told him it was ten o'clock and he had slept since two the day before. Someone had put his suitcase just inside the door, with his car keys on top. He washed and changed then made his way downstairs.

Three brogue-and-tweed-clad couples with maps were on their way out. Genteel opulence he thought, with visions of Pamela floating before him. In that moment he decided he never wanted to see the place again.

A cacophony of sound from behind the baize door, where chefs in snowy white overalls were preparing lunch, briefly broke the silence as Colin appeared.

Noticing Gerald's expression he motioned him to the office behind reception and ordered coffee on the intercom.

"You are very at home here. How would you like to buy the place?"

It came out of the blue and Colin stared in disbelief. There he was expecting the sack. Speed was of the essence though. One word from Alex and …

In a stunned voice he said, "It would be like all my birthdays rolled in one."

"I will get Mr Hughes to draw up the papers." He mentioned a low sum making Colin gasp.

"It is the current price for the property as a house. That is all I want. Good luck, boy."

He went to the door, as Colin sat open mouthed. "Won't you even stay for lunch, sir?" he asked in a daze.

"No thanks."

Colin listened to the Daimler crunching out of the drive, asking himself: had it really happened?

Gerald motored to the cottage and let himself in. He was impressed by the changes. Alexander was doing well. A half-made decision was finalised. He would make it his. Charles would attend to the legalities. He suddenly remembered he hadn't telephoned home, and went to the hall to dial Charles's office number.

Charles was relieved until he heard Gerald's instructions. It all sounded so impetuous. "Don't you even want to think about it?"

"Nothing to think about. I will be in the company suite, catching up with things."

His sentences were clipped, and recognising the futility of reasoning, Charles said goodbye.

"We will just have to wait until he is ready to tell us," Felicity said when he told her.

.   *

For six months Gerald threw himself frenziedly into new ideas for export, where Alexander was showing great promise. Now, driving home, he thought of

227

sailing and walking along the cove. A daily workout had restored his natural fitness and after a few days, he would start work again.

He put his foot down. Charles and Felicity would be there and Lorna would cook his favourite meals. That was what he liked about Anders Folly, nothing changed; life continued, surely as night follows day.

A warmth encompassed him as he saw Lorna; warmth instantly dismissed by her greeting.

"Mr and Mrs Charles apologise, but Mr Laurie is ill and they are with him."

The dream crashed. They were all supposed to be there – Laurie included – sitting around the table, hearing about the changes he had made. He felt cheated.

With an impatient 'tut', he strode to the telephone. Felicity answered, sounding worried.

"Laurie is in a lot of pain and we are waiting for the ambulance."

Voices in the background saying the ambulance had arrived, brought the conversation to an abrupt end.

"Shall I come?" he asked.

"Only if you want to. Nothing you can do. Must go."

Gerald replaced the receiver, inventing excuses. It could be hours before they knew anything. No point in them all sitting about.

The need to be active grew stronger as he strolled out on to the terrace. The calm water beckoned invitingly and the next minute he was hurrying upstairs to change, telling himself he would check the boat, in case Charles could sail with him tomorrow.

Driving beside a sparkling sea, the warm sun relaxing him, he felt good. His life was back together. He was on top form and there was no stopping him now.

The clubhouse was quiet. He ordered a gin and tonic and watched the small craft bobbing offshore. The urge to join them was irresistible.

He glanced at his watch, wondering with a slight sense of guilt whether Felicity had telephoned, but there was no message when he reached home. It was five-thirty and he hadn't eaten since breakfast but Charles and Felicity were sure to come home for dinner. A piece of Lorna's cake would fill the gap he thought, heading for the kitchen. Lorna was filling the teapot.

"Must have smelt the pot," he said, using his mother's old saying and they smiled reminiscently at each other.

An hour later when there was still no message, Gerald began to fidget. They must know *something*. He rang the hospital and was told to 'hold' while they located Mr Hughes. He drummed his fingers, imagining the smell of disinfectant; then Charles, sounding distraught said, "Hello Gerald, they are operating – suspected burst ulcer. It's bad."

"Are you going to stay?"

228

"At least until he comes out of surgery, which hopefully won't be too much longer. I'll ring with any news. Need to get back now."

Gerald turned to Lorna who was waiting anxiously.

"He is still in surgery. I think I will have dinner, they could be very late."

He missed her surprised stare.

It was another hour before the call came to say Laurie was out of surgery.

Charles sounded exhausted.

"Are you coming home now?"

"Yes."

Five minutes later Felicity called. They had decided to stay at Laurie's house, to be nearer to the hospital "You could stay if you like, Gerald."

"I'll probably get an early night. I'm pretty tired after the drive."

"Of course. See you tomorrow then. Sorry we weren't there to welcome you."

*

The hands of the grandfather clock pointed to eight o'clock. He had forgotten how silent the house could be. A wave of loneliness caught him. There was no one to care, except Charles and Felicity, and even they had chosen not to come home.

He went into the sitting room, flicked through the television channels then turned it off. He wandered out into the walled garden. David and Marie still haunted the pathways that David had so painstakingly laid. It was looking wonderful and the only sounds were those of the countryside. The chickens clucked contentedly in the hen house and somewhere a nightingale filled the gathering dusk with enchanting song but the serenity was lost on Gerald. He retraced his steps, fretting disconsolately about his ruined plans. A slight breeze through the open French doors taunted him and walking onto the terrace he leant against the balustrade, breathing deeply. Whispering waves lapped the shore, stirring an overwhelming desire to feel the deck beneath his feet. With every deep breath he could feel his depression slipping away; this weather was just not to be missed.

Striding purposefully, he hurried upstairs, found white shorts, T-shirt and deck shoes, set a sailing cap on his head at a jaunty angle and struck a pose, surveying his image in the mirror. He set the alarm for dawn refusing to dwell on the fact that he was in his parents' old room.

Showered and dressed by four-thirty, he stowed food into a canvas bag and, as an afterthought, left a hastily scribbled note for Lorna. Gone sailing. Back for dinner.

The sea beckoned as he sped along the deserted coast road, spirits soaring. What a morning to be sailing! Other enthusiasts were already on board their vessels and mouth-watering aromas greeted him as he went down the worn steps.

The morning sky threw a rosy glow over the calm water, creating countless prisms. It was magical. Charles would have loved it – and with luck the breeze would oblige later. Having breakfasted on bacon, eggs and freshly baked bread, he carried a large mug of strong tea up to the small deck and prepared to set sail.

The harbour master hailed, "Ahoy there. Good to see you back. Watch the weather."

Gerald saluted and gave a reassuring thumbs-up, sailing between the two jutting headlands, which formed a natural mouth to the sheltered harbour. On the open sea there was a deceptive swell and a gentle wind sent the boat whipping across the water. Hugging the shore, confidently steering away from the rock-strewn coastline, he took great breaths of salt-laden air, feeling his adrenalin race as the deck beneath him rose and fell. He grappled with all his might as the wheel spun, laughing with sheer jubilation at his own dexterity as he controlled the small craft. The sun was scorching and by mid-morning a hot wind had risen, enough to send the boat skimming across the choppy water. In his element, he fought the sea and by midday ravenously hungry, he dropped anchor. Lorna's Cornish pasties could wait no longer. He ate two of the well-filled delicacies and washed them down with beer, which he found in one of the lockers. What a stroke of luck! He grinned, settling comfortably in the sheltered stern. Replenished, he closed his eyes, deciding to turn for home in ten minutes, but the early start, the alcohol and the warm sun took their toll.

An hour later he awoke shivering. The sun had gone, rain clouds scudded across a leaden sky and the small craft was rocking violently. Lurching towards the mast, it took all his strength to lower the sails, but once the motor started he raised the anchor. It was exhilarating battling with the sea and he laughed out loud, enjoying the challenge as he decided to make his way along the coast and go ashore at Anders Bay. It was closer than the harbour.

Anders Bay was actually in sight when the heavens opened and driving rain tore into him. The wheel was wrenched from his grasp as the boat tossed about like a cork and it was some time before he was able to regain control. By then he was close to rocks and being dragged towards the neighbouring bay, only to be caught on a huge wave, dragged out to sea and along to Anders Bay again. This happened several times and Gerald became desperate. His strength was as nothing, pitted against the mighty Atlantic rollers.

Lorna and Maisie watched terrified from an upstairs window. There was only time to close some of the windows when the squall blew up so quickly before catching sight of Gerald's struggle. Lorna immediately called the coast guard and they continued to watch mesmerised. One minute it seemed the boat would be swept to safety and the next it was swept out to sea again. Then disaster struck. One huge wave dashed the boat on the rocks and Gerald was flung amongst the wreckage like a rag doll, just as the lifeboat men arrived, then as quickly as it started the squall passed. It took time to recover Gerald's body so Lorna was convinced he must be dead, but miraculously he still had a pulse and was rushed to hospital. Lorna shook so much that Maisie had to dial the number and ask the nurse to inform Charles and Felicity. They were at Laurie's bedside, shedding tears of relief.

CHAPTER TWENTY-ONE

After endless examinations, and physiotherapy, consultants came to the reluctant conclusion that Gerald would never walk again, so after four, never-ending months he lay in his own room and demanded of Charles, "Why didn't you just let me die, instead of condemning me to this living death?"

A day nurse came and was replaced at five o'clock by a night nurse, strictly on doctor's orders, he was not to be left alone.

"It must be driving him mad," Charles sympathised.

"We could dispense with the day nurse, if he would cooperate," Felicity said wearily "He refuses to even look at the wheelchair and won't hear of installing a lift."

"You know how proud he is. I'll try talking to him again," Charles said without much hope.

Their one bright note was that Sophie was pregnant again and the baby was due in four weeks' time – but there was also Laurie. It had come as a shock when he was ill, to learn that he was actually ninety-seven, and it was out of the question to take him with them.

Gerald finally stopped talking suicide when both nurses left with exasperation and Felicity burst into tears.

That was when Marcia Roberts, small, round, olive skinned, dark eyes topped by a mass of shining dark hair, was engaged. The hospital sent her as a resident nurse; her references were excellent and when Gerald tersely agreed to a trial they held their breath.

After a week, Lorna reported he was asking for his favourite foods and a week later Felicity saw Marcia pushing the wheelchair into his room. She followed to find him sitting beside the window, with a small radio playing and an altogether serene air. The bed had been made up with clean sheets and Marcia was speaking from the bathroom.

"A shower would be good."

To Felicity's surprise Gerald looked interested.

Marcia poked her dark head round the door, saying, "What do you think?" and saw Felicity. "Sorry, Mrs Hughes, I didn't realise you were there."

Felicity gave a delighted smile. "Carry on, that sounds a wonderful idea, doesn't it, Gerald?"

It was hard to take in the transformation. He was looking almost eager.

"I'll get Charles on to it."

He turned to Felicity. "Marcia has so many good ideas. A pulley over the bed, a lift from the hall to the landing, an electrically driven chair."

Felicity recalled these things being vetoed, but said nothing. How the woman had managed it wasn't clear, but she went to tell Charles, who hurried upstairs before Gerald could change his mind and found him eager to discuss alterations. Like Felicity he was mystified, until he saw Marcia give a flirtatious little smile.

Smiling broadly, he went downstairs, where Felicity was setting the table for lunch.

"What's the magic formula then?"

"Surprising what a pretty face can do."

Felicity gasped. "You're not serious?"

"Believe it." Still smiling, he went to the sideboard, poured three glasses of sherry and set them on a tray. "Let's tell Laurie."

Laurie looked up from the Sunday paper, Charles put a glass in his hand and Felicity said, "Gerald is much better."

"Here's to better days," Charles toasted with a catch in his voice.

*

The following week holiday brochures appeared, and Gerald said Marcia had booked them a cruise.

"I shouldn't stay with the dust of the alterations, it will be bad for my chest. I need sunshine and a change of scenery, she says. We go 3rd November for six weeks."

Marcia was organised to the last detail, to ensure Gerald's welfare and Felicity was full of praise.

"It is a big responsibility, even *with* first class accommodation. And you will *never* be off duty with an adjoining cabin."

"Well it *is* a *working* holiday for me," she said.

It was comforting to know Gerald was in safe hands and not alone anymore. Now Charles felt free to plan their visit to America.

Even Alexander had only visited his father once in hospital, and that had been disastrous.

After listening to Alexander's rapturous report on his success in the export department, Gerald had closed his eyes in dismay, forced to accept his own big plans would be handled by someone else.

Thinking he had fallen asleep Alexander cursed. "Try to cheer him up and he's not even interested enough to listen. Well he's all washed up anyway – no use to anyone now."

He met Charles at the door.

"Going already?"

"Well I didn't come all this way to watch him sleep."

"A little compassion wouldn't go amiss."

"Compassion won't make him walk again. Face it. He's had it. I've got to get back and keep an eye on things. Why did you let him give mother's hotel away?"

Charles had watched him go, wanting to say many things, but it wasn't the time.

Gerald opened his eyes; he had heard everything.

"He didn't mean it. He's upset," Charles had said miserably. Gerald had looked scornful, but not before Charles had seen his pain.

They had heard nothing from Alexander himself, since. Simon Hall passed on any news concerning him.

Five weeks passed and Gerald telephoned from Italy to say they had found this wonderful villa and would be staying another month. The waiting was over; Felicity decided to book their tickets. Laurie was her only concern, but Lorna offered to stay in his house and look after him.

They sat sharing a cup of coffee, Felicity making a list of things to do.

"Don't forget the keys," Lorna reminded her; neither could remember the house being shut up before.

Lorna went back to preparing lunch and Felicity drifted into the hall, still dwelling on the house being empty for the first time since 1946. She touched the polished surface of the big round table, seeing in her mind's eye Pamela's brass urn filled with chrysanthemums and hearing Marie's voice calling from the kitchen. The dreadful ache and impromptu tears were never more than a breath away. If only those halcyon days could return. A crunch of wheels reminded her that Charles was coming home early, and they were going Christmas shopping.

It was a blustery December afternoon and it quickly became obvious that Felicity's heart was not in shopping.

"How about ' The Sound of Music'?"

She looked at him vacantly.

"The film. You said you would like to see it. Leave the shopping. You can go with Sophie in America."

She looked relieved and nodded. How many times had he seen that stricken look and shared her grief since Marie and David had died?

Charles's request for the back row raised a smile from the usherette. "I expect she thinks we are too old," Charles whispered as they settled into the double seat. Felicity was just grateful to rest on his shoulder and allow her tears to fall in the friendly darkness.

Gerald's accident and Laurie's operation had caused terrible grief, but Marie, David and Pamela's deaths had left an irreplaceable void. A whole way of life had gone.

*

After their long journey from Heathrow, following the seven hour flight from America, sleep took over, so it was some time before Lorna, relieved to be back in her own domain, got to fuss around them, bringing tea and hot buttered crumpets in front of the roaring log fire. They showed her snapshots of the baby and proud parents, and when the tea-tray had been cleared, they settled down to open the accumulated mail. They sorted through the separate piles, with Felicity making the odd comment or putting aside a letter for Charles to read. She had nearly reached the end of her pile when she recognised Gerald's handwriting.

"How nice, one from Gerald."

Charles was engrossed and grunted, until a loud gasp made him look up. Felicity was staring at the letter in utter dismay.

"What's he done now? Bought the villa?" Charles joked.

Wordlessly she handed it to him.

"Married?" Charles whispered, before exploding. "He hardly knows the woman."

Worrying thoughts ran through Felicity's mind. "Why would she marry him? She is young enough to be his daughter."

"Money is the obvious answer." A small silence followed his statement.

"Gerald is nobody's fool," she said hopefully.

"Not normally, but he is probably trying to prove to Alexander he isn't all washed up." Then he had to explain the incident at the hospital.

"That would destroy him," she said pityingly.

He scanned the single page again. "Married on Christmas Eve, home on the 14th," he read aloud.

"That's next Tuesday."

They sat digesting the news until Lorna came to ask if they would like a bedtime drink.

"Two hot chocolates, please."

"Make that one; I think I need a whisky," Charles corrected.

Lorna gave a shrewd look as she left. Nothing escaped her when it came to the family.

"Do we tell Lorna?"

235

"You obviously didn't finish the letter."

"I only got to where it said they were married," Felicity confessed.

Charles invited Lorna to sit when she returned with the hot chocolate. He, in the mean time, had fetched himself a whisky. Lorna braced herself. Their serious faces warned that something had happened. She had to fight for composure as they broke the staggering news.

"Mr Gerald, married to *that* woman!" she gasped, before she could stop herself and then apologised. "Sorry sir, Ma'am, not my place to comment. Oh, but ..." she cupped her chin in her hands, distress bringing tears to her eyes.

"We must pray it will be alright," said Felicity. They had shared so much sorrow that Lorna was more like one of the family and there was no doubt she had Gerald's best interest at heart.

Tuesday arrived all too quickly. Charles and Felicity dreaded the changes to come. The hired car pulled in to the drive at four o'clock. Marcia was driving. She waved Charles aside and operated the chair lift, lowering Gerald to the ground. Then pushing him towards the front door she said over her shoulder, "Get the suitcases, Gerald needs to be out of this cold wind."

"Of course." Charles went forward willingly, calling to Jed for help, when he saw the number of cases. Marcia's one battered suitcase had been replaced with four large brand-new ones plus Gerald's three.

"I suppose you can't blame her, but she hasn't wasted any time, has she," Charles murmured.

They were all happy to see each other and Gerald, relieved to be home would have settled in the sitting room but Marcia whisked him away for a rest, via the new lift that had been installed in their absence. On the way up she could be heard briskly giving instructions and saying, "You will be taking yourself up and down in no time."

"Anyone would think he had never worked a lift before," Charles commented irritably, disappointed that their homecoming chat had been delayed.

"Perhaps she was right, it was a long journey home and there will be time to talk in the morning."

"I have to work in the morning," he scowled. "Shall I bring Laurie to dinner?"

"Why don't you do that?"

It was after ten when Marcia, using the new intercom, ordered breakfast. Felicity offered to take the food up, marvelling at how much easier it was with the lift. She thought of the times they had struggled upstairs with loaded trays for Marie and then Laurie. "Got to give her full marks for organisation," she murmured to herself, tapping the bedroom door. Marcia opened it but stood in the way, preventing Felicity from pushing the trolley in. "I will take it from here. I expected one of the staff; it certainly isn't your place."

"Well I wasn't busy, I thought it would be nice to say 'Good morning' and see how Gerald slept." She looked past Marcia (still barring her way) to Gerald, who was sitting up in bed. "Morning, Gerald, how are you?"

"He's fine. Why wouldn't he be?" Marcia answered.

"Everything is perfect thank you." Gerald raised a hand in salute. "See you downstairs."

Feeling dismissed, Felicity turned away as the door closed. Perhaps she was being too sensitive she told herself as she returned to the kitchen. Lorna had just made elevenses. She and Maisie stopped talking and they all chatted companionably. Lorna asked how Mr Gerald was.

"He was well. We didn't talk much, he will be down soon."

She didn't look up, just concentrated on stirring her coffee. Lorna gave Maisie an: 'I told you so' look. She had been warning her, "She's not what we've been used to, so mind yourself girl."

Charles came home for lunch, went straight upstairs and tapped on Gerald's door. "What is it?" Marcia's voice demanded.

"Just came to say 'hello' Gerald, alright to come in?"

Through the door he heard a loud tut, before the door opened revealing Marcia in her white overall.

"Gerald needs peace and quiet," she said sternly.

"Let him in, my dear," an exuberant voice called.

Charles strode to the bed. "How are you old boy? Recovered from the journey? Good to see you looking so well." They clasped hands firmly.

Gerald smiled, his eyes going to Marcia. "All down to the excellent care I'm getting." His eyes glowed with affection, never leaving his wife.

"Coming down to lunch?"

"We had breakfast late," Marcia said quickly.

"See you at dinner," Gerald assured him.

"That's good, Laurie is coming, knew you would want to see him."

"Dinner has to be at six, seven is too late for Gerald."

"Right you are, I'll tell Lorna."

"I already have. I have also changed the menu. Chicken is better than beef for Gerald." She was still holding the open door.

"She thinks of everything, doesn't she," said Gerald proudly.

"Doesn't she though?" Charles said faintly. "Must go."

On joining Felicity he sat down, laid his napkin across his lap with precision and said, "I think I've just been put in my place."

Felicity had been watching him from the corner of her eye, "Yes," she said simply, placing a bowl of soup in front of him.

"You too, eh?"

"We should really have expected this, she *is* the lady of the house now."

Charles tore his roll angrily. "Start as you mean to go on, I suppose. Why don't I take you to Laurie's for the afternoon and we will all come home together. Did you know, by the way, that dinner is at six?"

"Lorna did say."

Having finished lunch, Felicity poked her head round the kitchen door explaining she would be out for the afternoon. Lorna nodded, giving a worried shake of her head as she heard the front door close. Already the atmosphere of the whole house had changed. What was to follow?

It was hardly a relaxed dinner party. Marcia fussed over Gerald and interrupted any conversation Charles and Laurie tried to have with him and Felicity hid her feelings by avoiding all eye contact. Only Gerald appeared to be obliviously happy.

After dessert, Maisie came to clear the plates and Felicity automatically started to help.

"That is not necessary." Marcia's dark eyes flashed. "You may serve coffee in the drawing room, Maisie." She leant across to release the brake on Gerald's chair, allowing her long hair to sweep across his face.

"The staff really must be allowed to work without interference," she whispered loudly, manoeuvring him to the door.

"Of course, dear." He smiled dotingly.

"We are being treated like strangers in our own home," Charles said through clenched teeth, as they followed.

"The lady of the house is asserting herself," Laurie observed dryly.

As they sipped their coffee, Gerald seemed indifferent to Marcia's criticisms.

"Gerald says I can choose new wallpaper, and these curtains must certainly go," she sniggered patting his hand.

He smiled indulgently. "Whatever makes you happy, sweetheart."

Laurie suddenly declared he needed to go home and Charles and Felicity jumped up.

Gerald shook hands warmly. "Come again soon, old chap."

And Marcia added, "Yes Laurie. I will send you an invitation."

Felicity couldn't help herself. "Laurie doesn't need an invitation."

"Part of the family." Gerald agreed.

Marcia's eyes flashed.

"We must be off," Charles intervened quickly.

Sitting at the kitchen table while Felicity made Laurie's bedtime cocoa, Charles looked forlorn.

"I'm not sure how we fit into the scheme of things anymore."

"As far as Lady Anders is concerned – I'm afraid you don't." Laurie said gravely.

"Why didn't I see this coming?" He covered his face with his hands, as the extent of their situation dawned.

Laurie looked devastated for him. "The relationship *was* unique; none of us could have anticipated such changes. Don't blame yourself too much m' boy." His head drooped.

"Let's get you to bed," Felicity said gently.

For the first time ever they didn't want go home and talking long into the night, they decided to leave, before the situation got worse. Gerald's happiness was important but not at the expense of *their* self-respect.

In the morning Charles waited until Marcia left the bedroom and approached Gerald.

"This is your home. I won't hear of you leaving," he said loudly, just as Marcia returned. She was furious and cornered Felicity afterwards.

"Gerald obviously feels indebted to you for some reason but I am in charge. So s*tay out of the kitchen* – it encourages disrespect."

"Mr and Mrs Anders' way was excellent," Felicity defended quickly.

"Well I am Lady Anders now and things *will* be done *my* way."

Felicity walked away not trusting herself to answer.

Lorna and Maisie watched miserably as everything changed. Grey cotton uniforms with white aprons were provided for them, along with instructions to address her as Ma'am and him as Sir Gerald. On the odd occasion when Felicity did visit the kitchen, she refused coffee, knowing it would cause trouble. Unhappy and lonely, she went out continually, and Marcia told Gerald she was jealous of their refurbishments.

Rich swathes of silver grey curtains reached the floor, complimenting heavily embossed wallpaper of the palest blue. And the settees had been recovered in pink damask, all cleverly picking out the muted colours in the carpets. The overall effect was elegant.

"Very delicate," Felicity said admiringly.

Marcia curled her lip. "*Anything* had to be better than *her* taste."

There wasn't the choice, or money at the time," Felicity said defensively, giving Gerald a reproachful look.

Knowing they intended visiting Laurie after dinner, Marcia waylaid them to show off a beautiful pale gold wallpaper, intended for his room and made it clear she no longer considered the room his, adding smugly, "It will be for my guests – when the place is presentable, Gerald says I can have anything I want. He hated his first wife, but what can you expect when she had an affair with his doctor." Her voice was shrill, knowing Gerald had made her promise not to tell a soul. She had her moment of triumph as their faces stretched, deciding quickly she would have to say they drove her to it, as Charles strode into the study.

"Why did we have to learn from *that woman* that Pamela was unfaithful to you?" He demanded

"*That woman* happens to be my wife."

"And we, as friends for much longer, needed to understand your hatred."

"Well now you do." Gerald said unable to look him in the eyes.

"We don't belong here anymore."

"Please don't start that again."

"I need to think." He turned on his heel, too hurt to care how Gerald felt.

*

Laurie was feeling low. His dinner was untouched and he had taken to his bed.

"Would you like some warm milk?" Felicity asked anxiously.

He smiled. "Sweet girl. Let me sleep for a while."

She kissed his brow. "Alright dear. Turning the bedside lamp off she left the door open, allowing the landing light to throw a comforting oblong of light; noticing with a last look that his eyes were already closed. She went sadly downstairs, where Charles was sitting staring into the fire.

"I'm not happy leaving him; we should stay."

He nodded and her heart went out to him. He took everything on board with such patience and loyalty.

Emotionally exhausted, they fell asleep in the armchairs and woke to dying embers; the room had gone cold. Charles rose stiffly, stretching. "I'll check on Laurie."

He was gone a long time and she called up to him quietly.

He came to the head of the stairs and just looked. She went up and they stood and held each other – too upset to cry.

The funeral was arranged for the following week. Sophie, Matthew and baby Laurie were due to arrive on the weekend, but there had been no word from Robert.

"He will be there," Charles said confidently

Felicity began to prepare Sophie's old room and in a stomach churning moment, realised Marcia would expect to be consulted. She mentioned it to Charles, who, with the event of Laurie's death, had been too upset to give their situation anymore thought.

"This is ridiculous. No way are you asking permission from *that woman*. I will speak to Gerald."

Gerald was indignant. "Where else would Sophie and her family stay?" adding hastily, "*I* will deal with it."

When they arrived, echoes of old times came with them.

*

As Laurie's executer, Charles contacted Olive Harcott when he found a will tucked away at the back of the office safe. It was dated 1939 and left everything to his younger brother who died in 1952. She was therefore the beneficiary. Felicity helped Mrs Reynolds put things in order, hating the idea of anyone else living there. And while she was stripping the bed, it occurred to her that the woman might be prepared to sell to them.

Charles's eyes glowed when she mentioned the idea. "Laurie's house would be wonderful."

It gave them fresh hope. Living at Anders Folly had become intolerable and with Laurie gone it was like being orphaned again. He had been a father and grandfather to the family.

Disappointingly, Olive Harcott was not interested in selling. "I won't have to rely on my sister's charity anymore," she said with relish, sitting with her feet up and looking around possessively. They were devastated.

The church was packed. Laurie would be sorely missed for his wisdom and humour. The funeral was conducted by a boyhood friend, who at ninety-four made it a very moving occasion. Expensive wreaths and single bunches of violets sat side by side on a sunny windless day – the kind that Laurie liked best. Charles was well pleased.

"Very fitting for such a grand old gentleman," he said to Gerald. Marcia had tried to elbow him away, but he had stood his ground and now walked slowly behind his friend; his once dynamic friend who had been reduced to living in a chair, and but for his young wife, would probably still be stubbornly bedridden. Mindful of that, he wheeled the chair to the waiting car and thanked a surprised Marcia as she took over.

At Laurie's house, Betty Reynolds had laid on an admirable spread and Olive received the mourners with possessive confidence, speaking fondly of 'dear Laurie'.

Amongst them was a scholarly looking, grey haired man, who asked, for Charles Hughes. She pointed to a man holding a baby and he made his way across, offering his hand.

"Geoffrey Gammons, of Gammons and Pritchard. Could we have a word in private?"

Felicity was nearby.

"Would you like a boy," Charles asked quizzically handing baby Laurie over, before leading the way to the study.

When they emerged, Charles told her that they and others were required to attend the reading of the will, at five o'clock.

When the time came those required were gathered in the sitting room, with the exception of Robert, Celina and Alexander. Olive looked ready to faint.

The new will was drawn up a year ago and revoked all other wills. There were small bequests to Betty, Jessica and Lorna for their kindness. Robert and Celina, and Sophie and Matthew received twenty-five-thousand pounds each; another five thousand to be put in trust for little Laurie, and the Stubbs original painting went to Gerald, 'wishing him joy. To my brother's wife I leave ten thousand'.

Geoffrey Gammons cleared his throat.

"The rest of my estate I leave to my dearest Charles and Felicity who I love as son and daughter. God bless you both."

Quite overcome Charles held Felicity as everyone cheered, except Olive. Shocked and angry she struggled up.

"These people have inveigled themselves into his affections for this purpose. I will be contesting the will."

Geoffrey Gammons looked directly at her and read on: "In the event my brother's wife contests my will, her share will be forfeit."

Returning the papers to his briefcase, he said, "You will all be hearing from me in due course and you, Mr and Mrs Hughes, according to my instructions, are free to move into the house whenever you wish."

He gave them a benign smile, replaced the chair and bid them all good day.

Olive left without saying goodbye and Charles opened a bottle of Champagne, left by Laurie for the occasion.

*

242

Dinner was late, in spite of Lorna's preparations before leaving for the funeral, but Charles assured her she would be forgiven this once, to which Marcia added sternly, "As long as it is this once."

Matthew eyed her balefully, saying to Charles in an aside, "We will help you move before we leave."

"Gerald is not going to like it."

"Time you thought of yourselves. It's what Laurie wanted for you."

Sophie was all for the idea; Felicity sat shedding tears of relief, when they talked later.

*

Marcia opened the door in her white uniform. The radio was playing and Charles could see Gerald sitting up in bed eating breakfast.

"A word, Gerald?" he called.

"Come in." He looked bright eyed and relaxed and Charles felt momentarily grateful to her, until, "Are we to have no privacy even in our own room?" she complained in a low voice.

Ignoring her, he walked into the room, nerves jangling. He and Gerald had always talked everything over. The same could not be said of Gerald's decisions lately though, he admitted to himself. He missed their solidarity.

"We thought while we have help, it would be a good time for us to move in."

He received a look of reproachful resign. "Marcia *said* this would happen, even *before* Laurie left you the house. She said Felicity would never put up with her being in charge."

"Did she now?" Charles transferred his gaze to her, standing silently behind Gerald's pillow, only a satisfied gleam giving her thoughts away.

*

Matthew struggled with a heavy box, while Felicity came to the decision that something would have to go to make room for the piano.

"I say," Matthew's eyes shone, "would you consider letting that wonderful old radiogram go? I love it."

"How do we get it home?" Sophie laughed.

"Ship it."

"He is actually serious," Charles said in astonishment, adding softly "Laurie would like that."

Edward's van had hardly disappeared before Marcia ran joyfully upstairs to Charles and Felicity's vacated bedroom and twirled around arms outstretched. At last they had gone! Heaven knows how long it would have taken if they hadn't inherited that house.

What did Gerald see in the country bumpkin hangers-on? She gave another twirl and flopped onto the big striped mattress, her eyes dwelling on the ornate ceiling. This one was to be shell pink, with Victoria plum wallpaper. Tamara would like that.

She leant up on her elbows, her mood changing. She had lacked the courage to tell him while they were here; now she would find a way to tell Gerald about her daughter. She hadn't anticipated marriage when she applied for the job, but when it became obvious that Gerald could easily be persuaded to make her Lady Anders – well!

Now she had to choose the right moment to tell him about her nine-year-old daughter, at boarding school in Surrey. The fees had been crippling her, but with full control of the housekeeping, her problem had been solved. She shuffled forward on her bottom and stood up. Hardly able to contain her high spirits, she practically ran along the landing; slowing down when she saw Maisie watching her from the corner of her eye, as she dusted the banisters.

Maisie waited for her to disappear then hurried down to tell Lorna, who was still crying from the tearful goodbyes – she was also afraid for her job, although with Mr Laurie's thousand pounds in her very own post office book she was rich beyond her dreams. She loved her job though and her room; and Mr Gerald was *still* her first concern, even though he had done such a dreadful thing in marrying *her*.

The following day, decorators started on Charles and Felicity's old room, and a week later, when Marcia was out shopping, Lorna and Maisie stared at the wallpaper and curtains in amazement.

"Mauve fairies everywhere," Lorna told Felicity when she telephoned to ask if there was any mail for them.

"Very strange," Charles agreed later. "But nothing to do with us."

He was determined to put Anders Folly behind them, but the hurt would take a long time to ease.

*

Gerald's routine relaxed as Marcia's plans progressed and in spite of misgivings, he enjoyed her enthusiasm.

She eventually told him about Tamara by bursting into uncontrollable tears. Amid sobs she managed, "I thought you would despise me. I was in love – he left me – hard to find work – I miss her so." She sobbed afresh.

"Of course you do; she should be with you," Gerald consoled. And by this time the tears were real enough.

It was decided Tamara should remain a boarder and come home for the holidays.

She was a striking child: dark haired like Marcia, but her eyes were disconcertingly like Pamela's; unable to take to her for that reason, he compensated by spoiling her and so she became precocious, whilst Marcia looked on with indulgent gratitude.

*

When Alexander finally did decide to come home, he was beside himself with rage at what he considered to be his father's senile behaviour. To marry at his age was bad enough but a fortune hunter, thirty years younger was lunacy. He asked Charles about having his father declared incompetent, and he would take over. Charles personally felt that could be an even worse disaster but sympathised, and gravely pointed out he could take no part in such an action, which he seriously doubted there were sufficient grounds for anyway.

"You can't think he is in his right mind?" Alexander's slate grey eyes bored into him across his desk.

"I do."

He stomped out shouting, "Then you must be as mad as he is."

Charles sighed and returned to his work. Later that morning a well-known firm of solicitors, knowing his connection, telephoned, asking his opinion of Alexander's claim and Charles advised, "Don't touch it. Gerald Anders is perfectly sane and not a man to cross swords with."

"Thanks," was the brief reply.

He wasn't approached again but hearing rumours decided to warn Gerald.

Looking very neat in a black and white uniform, Maisie shyly ushered him into the sitting room, where he found Gerald and Marcia with four strangers.

"Perhaps another time. We need to talk privately," Charles said making to leave.

"Join us for cocktails. Introduce my friends, Gerald," Marcia gushed.

He declined the drink and shook hands with Stella, Bob, Babs and Jason.

They were all Marcia's age and both women had worked with her at the hospice. As he told Felicity, they were painted and wore embarrassingly short skirts and low tops.

The men were estate agents and hardly endeared themselves with remarks about 'the old pile being worth a fortune', while looking about with eyes clocking-up pound signs. They looked totally out of place Charles thought, fighting down his repulsion.

Gerald read his expression and when he could, suggested they went to the study.

Smothered laughter followed them, and once the study door was closed he said gruffly, "They are young. Their ways are sure to be different."

"Of course."

He hated Gerald's embarrassment, but that feeling quickly vanished as he imparted his news.

"Put yourself in his shoes. Anders Folly has been held as the 'be all and end all' and he is putting his heart into the firm. Now he sees his inheritance going to a new young wife. Share your hopes; don't shut him out."

"You heard him," Gerald growled. "I'm all washed up. No use to anyone. Well I showed him. Marcia is my hope."

His sentences were clipped and defensive, confirming their fears.

"Marcia has pulled me through."

Charles just stood there, weeping inside for him.

"Go now. Just go."

He waved him away and turned his chair about.

CHAPTER TWENTY-TWO

After a severe warning, Alexander cut short his visit and returned to the cottage, where his frustration grew to such an extent that he made plans to get his own back. If the old fool was determined to spend *his* inheritance on that woman and her brat, then he had to get back to Europe.

He went into the hallway, dialled the number, and stood doodling on the telephone pad. Marcia's voice answered, and gritting his teeth he managed to say civilly, "Good morning, Stepmum. A word with Father, if you please."

There was a moment's silence, when he thought she was going to refuse, but he heard her say, "Don't let him upset you again," before his father's voice asked curtly, "What is it, Alexander?"

"Just to apologise, Dad. I was shocked and upset but I see now I was wrong. Can we make up?"

Gerald was gratified. Alexander had never apologised before; he had also given a lot of thought to what Charles had said, but he still asked cautiously, "Why the change of heart?"

"The important thing is, Marcia is making you happy." He bared his teeth silently.

"Thank you, son. Now keep me in touch with what you are doing."

"Not much to report lately. Britain isn't anywhere near as interesting. I would love to get back to Europe, I was learning such a lot."

He waited with bated breath.

"Leave it with me, I will speak with Simon."

"That would be great. Thanks, Dad."

"I'm not promising, you understand."

"'Course not. 'Bye, Dad."

He replaced the receiver and punched the air. He was as good as on his way.

Simon would agree; his father was 'one who must be obeyed'. Irritating – but useful in this case – he punched the air again.

Ten days later, he was on a plane heading for Paris. The salary, which they considered generous, wouldn't cover his needs, and the flexible expense account wasn't flexible enough, but he had become an expert juggler, he grinned to himself. He was a good salesman and his French was excellent, which went down well with French customers.

By the time they landed he was keyed up to start looking for a property, where goods could be delivered without raising suspicion. Within three weeks he found a derelict farmhouse for rent, off the beaten track. The living quarters left a lot to be desired, but with basic improvements, he was able to spend odd nights there. When necessary he slept and lived in the big square kitchen, where an ancient wood-burning stove gave him warmth and somewhere to heat food. An equally ancient telephone line miraculously still worked, and several barns gave shelter where work could be carried out.

Over a few weeks he employed two mechanics, established a regular trade in stolen cars and filtered numerous expensive parts into his operation. Some of the large orders he sent home for, simply disappeared without trace, and deliveries to the farmhouse were explained away by scaffolding and half-finished projects.

The scheme worked well for three years, before Alexander tired of the constant pressure to cover his tracks and, moreover, the insurance investigator, was demanding double his backhander. Also something far more lucrative had cropped up; a lot more risk involved, but a new lifestyle beckoned with untold profits.

*

For a long time Simon had vaguely suspected Alexander of somehow cheating the firm. His order book tallied and it appeared goods went missing in transit, but he still couldn't rid himself of his suspicion. Even though the insurance company covered the cost and in spite of thorough investigation they were still unable to catch the thieves. And as far as they were concerned no suspicion fell on Alexander, because the investigator was reporting it as the work of an elusive hijacking gang operating in the area, but the insurance premiums had rocketed.

Very recently Simon had heard that new evidence had opened up a new line of enquiry. It was causing him sleepless nights and he decided he had to speak to Alexander.

He telephoned Alexander's hotel for three days running, leaving messages to contact the office and finally came to the conclusion he would have to go to Paris himself. He travelled by ferry to Le Havre, arriving at five o'clock on the Saturday and took a taxi to Alexander's hotel.

Having booked a room for the night he settled in the lobby to wait. The desk clerk, who spoke a little English, had assured him Alexander always arrived around seven o'clock and ate in the restaurant. At five-to-seven, he arrived looking very pleased with himself – until he saw Simon.

"Mr Hall, what are you doing here?"

"We need to speak on a delicate matter, Alexander."

Eyeing him speculatively, he said curtly, "I'm hungry, let's eat."

Simon followed him, hurrying to keep up, as he strode to his usual table.

Two waiters appeared and Alexander ordered his usual wine and studied the menu. Simon looked at the menu and turned a dull red. Seeing his discomfort, Alexander ordered a dish and explained he had ordered chicken for him. Simon nodded, feeling his confidence ebb. Alexander had changed, he was no longer 'the junior'; he was very much a 'man of the world' and completely at home ordering food from French menus and speaking knowledgeably about the dishes to the waiters. In spite of himself, Simon was impressed. Alexander glanced about with a slightly bored expression.

"Well now, what *is* this delicate matter which we *must* discuss Mr Hall?"

Simon put two fingers in his collar and stretched his neck.

"You seem uneasy," Alexander observed.

"It's about the merchandise that's been going astray."

Alexander twisted the slender stem of his wine glass and regarded him coolly.

"The insurance company are confident they have evidence that *will* lead to early arrests."

"That's excellent news." Alexander responded, noting how he kept his gaze fixed on his coffee cup and dabbed at the beads of sweat on his upper lip with the linen napkin, realising he suspected him, and had come all this way to protect the firm. What loyalty from a mere manager! Pity and disdain made him wonder how his father commanded such loyalty? Money, he decided; something *he* intended to have a great deal of soon.

"In fact that calls for celebration. Brandy?" Without waiting for an answer he summoned the waiter and ordered two large brandies.

Simon looked relieved. Alexander's reaction had reassured him; his suspicions were unfounded. He relaxed, sitting comfortably with his drink, admiring their surroundings whilst Alexander's mind raced and conversation became stilted. Simon yawned and looked at his pocket-watch.

"Goodness gracious, look at the time. Ten o'clock – past my bedtime. Thank you for a pleasant evening," he said courteously as Alexander ordered another brandy for himself.

Simon fell into a deep sleep as soon as his head touched the pillow, and woke three hours later with a raging thirst and a pounding headache. The unaccustomed wine and brandy, plus the stifling central heating of the hotel were suffocating him. He tried to open the windows, but found them securely locked, then looked at the air conditioning, to discover the only directions were in French. As a last resort after going to the bathroom for a glass of water he decided to go downstairs to the foyer. Dressing clumsily he left the room and took the stairs, knowing the movement of the lift would cause him to be violently ill.

249

In the cool of the night, he took great gulps of air and leaned against one of the marble pillars supporting the entrance, telling himself he would ask the night porter to adjust the air conditioning. With cool air fanning his face, he became aware of the surprising number of passers-by there were at that time in the morning. Animated French speaking voices reached him; amongst them a familiar voice caught his attention.

"Speak in English; it's safer."

"What about the rest of the stuff?"

He could see them now walking towards him, and drew back behind the pillar.

"Make sure absolutely everything is cleared tonight; nothing must remain at the farmhouse. You understand?"

"Remettez-vous. It will be done." The Frenchman gave an indolent shrug. "When will I see you? Where shall I send everything?"

"It's yours. I have no further use for it."

There was a delighted guffaw, as they shook hands. Simon waited for Alexander to enter an elevator, before scurrying back to his room, all thought of sleep and getting the night porter to see to the air conditioning completely gone; his only desire was to prevent him from being thrown into a French prison and embarrassing his father – and the firm.

On his return to Southampton, late morning, he telephoned Gerald advising him to bring Alexander back immediately, promising to put a letter in the post that very day explaining why. Trusting his judgment implicitly, Gerald tried to contact Alexander, but as usual he was unobtainable. He left a message at the hotel desk asking him to telephone home, but no call came, and he rang again only to be told that Mr Anders had checked out two hours earlier. By this time Gerald was *really* worried, having received Simon's letter by express delivery explaining his fears.

Alexander finally contacted his father, three weeks later, a short note saying he was in Belgium, moving about a lot trying to get new orders. There was no mention of the unreturned phone calls.

"He wouldn't get away with this if I wasn't in this accursed wheelchair," Gerald ranted to no avail.

Whilst Marcia assured him, "He obviously doesn't want to be found – therefore he won't be. Stop his allowances: that will bring him to heel," she said with airy conviction, but Gerald had already considered that and shrunk from the consequences of unpaid hotel bills, imagining big headlines in all of the papers. He might be helpless now but woe betide Alexander when he did put in an appearance, he vowed.

CHAPTER TWENTY-THREE

Life changed dramatically for Gerald in the seven years he and Marcia were together. She had refurbished all of the rooms and even claimed for *herself*, the locked bedroom he and Pamela had shared – after much cajoling. The dusky pink silk drapes and bed hangings were edged with Brussels lace, and Queen Anne furniture stood against ivory wallpaper. An exquisitely feminine and costly refurbishment, it was also a triumph to her. Gerald was always unstintingly generous to compensate for his physical disabilities and his was a necessarily functional bedroom.

He yearned to share fully in the delights she teased him with, but was tantalisingly limited to sitting in the beautiful room, watching her model the lace and silk lingerie, from her numerous shopping trips, and enjoying the seductive massages she would indulge him with, when she was in the mood. She wasn't beautiful, in the sense that Pamela had been, but there was something very appealing about her small, well-rounded body, and the huge dark eyes, that could turn from laughter to tears so readily, prompting his protection.

Tamara also recognised and exploited his disability: playing him off against her mother to satisfy her whims. One such whim came on her fifteenth birthday, when she informed Gerald she just had to have a pony, because the other girls at school had one, and therefore thought she was deprived.

Stung into action as Tamara knew she would be, Marcia promptly suggested that Jake could fix up the old stables, beyond the walled garden.

Gerald hummed and hawed, but eventually consulted Edward, who suggested contacting the local livery stable, run by Janet Forbes.

So it was arranged that on Tamara's birthday they would go along to look at the pony Mrs Forbes thought could be suitable.

The dapple-grey mare whinnied softly as Tamara went towards her, before galloping off to the far corner of the field. Tamara pouted.

"I want this one," she said, reaching over the fence to stroke a huge, black mare that had trotted over at the sound of her owner's voice. It was a beautiful animal, with a coat that shone like satin and a soft muzzle she nudged Tamara's hand with.

Mrs Forbes smiled. "Midnight isn't for sale, and in any case she is much too big for you yet. How about the bay, over there?" She pointed to a small sleek pony grazing a little distance away. "We call him Storm, because he was born in a thunderstorm; he is a spirited little character."

Tamara shook her head. "I must have the black; I just can't bear not to."

Her face crumpled, and Mrs Forbes turned to them apologetically. "I'm sorry, she is just *not* for sale."

By now, Tamara was in floods of tears, much to Gerald's embarrassment, so he suggested to Marcia she should take her back to the car. Both Tamara and her mother looked sulky, but once they were out of earshot, Gerald turned to Mrs Forbes persuasively.

"You could name your price for the animal."

"It isn't just money, Sir Gerald; Midnight has a month old foal, and they can't be parted. She is also a thoroughbred mare and not suitable for a learner. However, before I sell you *any* one of my ponies, I would have to inspect the stabling you have in mind. I always insist on good homes, and I don't mean it rudely, when I say you obviously know nothing about horses, if you would even *consider* Midnight for your daughter."

He was perplexed having assumed it was a simple matter of buying a pony and providing a stable.

Through long experience, Mrs Forbes guessed his thoughts.

"More complicated than you thought? I know you don't want to disappoint your daughter, but she has to be made to realise that one of the other ponies is the only option – from me anyway."

Gerald gave her a long, worried look.

"I think I would like you to explain to my wife and daughter, just what keeping a pony involves. Tomorrow, perhaps?"

"Tomorrow," she agreed.

He returned to the car, and waited for George to wheel him onto the ramp, irritated by the sight of Tamara weeping into her mother's shoulder. The weeping got louder as Bob switched on the electric lift, and she remained inconsolable until Gerald told her Mrs Forbes would be coming the next day to take a look at the stables, then she stopped crying to dart a triumphant look at Marcia.

"I knew he would get her for me."

Gerald was not amused. "The black is not for sale, and certainly not suitable for you; now let that be an end to it."

"I do *know* how to ride," Tamara said indignantly.

"She does," Marcia confirmed.

Gerald shot them a warning look.

Janet Forbes arrived early, and declared the stabling suitable, but pointed out that the large field alongside must be fenced off to form a paddock. And then there was the matter of who would tend the pony. Gerald was amazed at what this was turning into.

"I think we will have to employ a groom, darling, for the mucky jobs."

Janet looked relieved. "That would make good sense, Mrs Anders. I happen to know Bob Johnson is looking for a position. He is an excellent man with horses. I could give you his telephone number."

Marcia looked at Gerald and nodded. "I think so. Yes, darling?"

"What about the pony, first?" Gerald said firmly. "Will you be content with the light brown one?"

Tamara pouted.

"You could have Storm before you go back to school, I expect," Marcia encouraged.

Tamara's face lit up and Gerald gave a sigh of relief. Dealing with Tamara was like dealing with a female version of Alexander, he decided wearily.

Bob Johnson was duly hired. In his mid-forties he had rugged good looks and a muscular build, which greatly appealed to Tamara. She turned up in her best clothes and leant on the paddock gate trying to flirt with him, until on the third morning he told her to go and get into something suitable and help to scrub the stall in readiness for Storm. She gave her usual pout, but finding it didn't cut any ice with him, knuckled down to learning a pony's needs. She worked hard to win his approval, quickly discovering he was a hard taskmaster and gave little praise, but she was keen and Marcia was impressed, watching Tamara's riding improve under Bob's skilful tuition. She was even tempted into mounting Storm herself. Bob gave her modest encouragement and said she should learn to ride.

"I would be earning my keep, with two horses to look after," he said with a rare, lopsided grin.

Marcia told Gerald, but instead he approached Bob with the idea of driving him to Southampton sometimes, because Marcia found it boring. Bob jumped at the chance to extend his duties; used to working in a busy stables, he had taken this job short-term to fill in while he was recovering from a riding accident, but he had quickly come to love the peace of Anders Folly. He opted to live in the spacious hayloft over the stables, instead of the room over the garage.

"I'm comfy being close to the horses," he said with an engaging grin.

As Gerald's life broadened beyond Anders Folly again, it whetted his appetite for the old life, but he had been away too long, he was just a figurehead now; a new direction was what he needed, he told himself restlessly, sitting in his study one morning, and in a way Laurie was responsible for his next venture.

The Stubbs painting hung over the big, stone fireplace, and as his attention drifted from opening the mail, his eye caught the graceful lines of the black mare and her foal against a rural background. It could almost have been painted *here* he mused, an exciting idea forming in his mind, and without further ado he steered his chair through the hall, and out onto the terrace.

The path had been continued down to the stables recently and he took himself in search of Bob. It was the first time he had been able to venture to this area, and Bob greeted him with a cheery, "Today the stables – tomorrow the world." Gerald found Bob's easy-going manner relaxing.

"I want to buy the black and her foal from Janet Forbes. Will she sell do you think?"

Bob's face lit up. "Midnight? For Mrs Anders?"

Gerald shook his head. "I fancy breeding thoroughbreds. Would you be interested?"

"It would be a dream come true; next best thing to owning my own stud farm, which is my big ambition one day."

"You would have carte blanche of course." Gerald nodded vigorously and spoke quickly, as always when he was fired up, and Bob responded with equal enthusiasm.

It was all very quickly and satisfactorily negotiated with Bob's help – much to Gerald's approval, even though he was staggered by the asking price, but Bob assured him as they turned them into the paddock, that the mare and foal were worth every penny.

Marcia stared in disbelief as Bob paraded the two of them around the paddock. She had been woken by the crunch of the horsebox being driven onto the gravel drive, and now she stood watching, in her dark red velvet housecoat, astounded at seeing Gerald in the stable yard at six o'clock. It was a beautiful morning and the sun was already high in the sky. The huge, vividly coloured flower heads of the horse chestnut trees against their deep green leaves made a wonderful backdrop for the two black animals, and both Gerald's and Bob's eyes shone with excited pride as Bob ran a practiced hand over Midnight's withers.

"Aren't they a pair of beauties?" So rapt were they in their appraisal, Marcia's arrival went unnoticed and they even failed to look up when she spoke.

"What on earth is going on at this ungodly hour? And what is that horse doing here? Have you bought her for me?"

Gerald turned round, his face alight with anticipation. "You are looking, my dear, at my latest investment. Bob and I are going to breed thoroughbreds."

Marcia coloured hotly as Gerald outlined their plans.

"Why wasn't I told?"

"I wanted to get things organised and surprise you." He seemed oblivious to her displeasure, and kept looking over at Midnight and the foal.

"Well you have certainly done that. So you *haven't* bought her for me then?"

"We will get you a horse of your own; when the right one comes along. Midnight is far too big for you." He lost interest and guided his chair nearer to the fence, watching Bob with the foal.

"It will be a long time before that one earns his keep," Marcia commented disparagingly.

"All in good time, he will more than earn his keep," Bob replied confidently.

It had been his dream for so long, to be in sole charge of a wonderful string of horses that her dampening attitude made him more brusque than was wise. He and Gerald fell into deep conversation again about two more mares and Marcia's eyes flashed. Good groom or not he would have to go if he was going to behave disrespectfully towards *her*.

"I'm going back to the house. I will help with your chair Gerald."

He turned his head briefly saying, "You go ahead, dear, I can manage on the new path," before suggesting to Bob, "We could go this weekend. It's only an hour away."

"I'll make arrangements," Bob replied enthusiastically.

"We have guests coming for the weekend," Marcia reminded him.

Gerald looked annoyed. "Since when? They were only here two weeks ago."

"It's been arranged for weeks; it's Barbara's birthday."

Bob walked a discreet distance away.

"We will be back by lunchtime, if we start off early."

"That is very rude. What will they think?"

"That they can have you all to themselves," Gerald smiled, not to be put off.

"Well you have obviously made up your mind, although I can't imagine what is so important that it won't wait for another week."

She walked away bristling with anger, feeling threatened by this new pastime, and the strong minded man who could hold her husband's attention so completely.

"They won't even know I've gone. They don't go to bed until four o'clock, and get up just in time for lunch." They exchanged conspiratorial looks and Bob touched his cap.

Marcia's house parties had become more frequent – in fact, far too frequent for Gerald. It seemed it was always someone's birthday or anniversary. He had asked why it always had to be at Anders Folly and she explained.

"Because although it would be nice to have a change; other homes are not geared to a wheelchair, so please be nice," she begged sweetly.

It seemed a valid reason, because he *was* sympathetic to her need for company and *did* appreciate, as she pointed out, that she had given up a lot to look after him.

This weekend, however, proved to be the last straw. Extra staff had to be hired to help and no expense was spared. *It was Babs' fortieth birthday.*

On the Saturday morning, banners and balloons appeared everywhere and there wasn't a quiet corner to be found anywhere. Gerald made straight for the study when he returned home, to find four men, all strangers to him, helping themselves to his whisky. All made a hasty exit when Gerald glared.

Marcia's friends, and friends of friends, had driven from far and wide to spend another luxurious weekend at her husband's expense.

The music was loud, the drinks flowed, and the more drinks flowed, the louder the music became. No one went to bed, and at five o'clock in the morning, Marcia organised breakfast. The staff were exhausted and Lorna had long since retired to her bed, but once they had eaten, a blissful hush fell over the house and everyone slept until late afternoon.

Going down in the lift in the morning, Gerald surveyed the debris of the night's festivities and knew with certainty he had to put a stop to the continual round of parties that were ruining his home life. In search of peace, he made for the stables, where Bob was contentedly tending the two horses they had brought home the day before. He watched for some while, before Bob became aware of him and nodded happily. "Morning, sir. Wonderful stock!"

"It doesn't take an expert to see you know your horses," Gerald praised him.

"Mrs Anders will be able to manage Starlight." He brought the smaller of the two horses over and handed Gerald a carrot, showing him how to hold it on the flat of his hand. Gerald felt an unexpected rush of warmth and wonderment, as the soft muzzle groped his outstretched hand, understanding to a small degree Bob's love of them, then embarrassed by his emotions, he coughed and said, "Perfect! That will please her."

They talked of adding new stables to the existing ones, and fencing off a second paddock, and time passed so swiftly that Gerald was surprised when Lorna came to say lunch was ready.

The house was still quiet, and at least the downstairs was orderly once more, but it was late afternoon before the visitors drifted down, in a half-hearted attempt to leave. A buffet was laid in the dining room and afterwards, with many subdued goodbyes, Marcia waved goodbye to the last guests at six o'clock. It had been the longest weekend Gerald could ever remember, and he heaved a heartfelt sigh of relief as the last car pulled away. Marcia closed the heavy, oak doors, her air of gaiety falling away like a cloak. She knew by his face that Gerald had something disagreeable to say and quickly declared her intention of having a long hot bath before dinner.

"I have sent the girls home and told Lorna to go and rest; they are all exhausted. Everything can wait until morning; the downstairs rooms are littered again, with crockery from 'The Snack'," he said with heavy sarcasm, referring to the mountain of food that had been devoured at teatime.

"What about dinner?" Marcia complained.

Gerald raised a quizzical eyebrow. "There is plenty of cold food in the kitchen. We will prepare ourselves a tray – and then we must talk."

She gazed indignantly at him, about to speak, thought better of it and marched to the lift. He watched her glide out of sight, before turning his chair towards the study. On the table between the wing chairs there were two trays set with cold chicken, new potatoes and salad.

Marcia took her time; it was seven-thirty before she returned. When she saw the trays, her only comment was, "Thank God. I'm exhausted."

"I don't think *He* had much to do with it, Lorna more like."

Marcia's dark eyes flashed. "She's well paid."

"Not to cater for constant parties she isn't – and while we are on the subject, at the risk of being accused of begrudging you your fun, I must insist you curb your desire for these frequent and expensive parties. Even you must admit three out of four weekends this last month is excessive?"

"Weekends are so boring without company and what is the point of having money if you don't know how to spend it?" she pouted contemptuously.

"Buying friends and knowing how to spend money aren't necessarily the same thing," Gerald flung back with equal contempt.

Marcia jumped to her feet, face flaming with indignation. "How dare you? They were my friends long before I met you *and* could entertain them."

There was silence as they faced each other. She glaring reproachfully, ready to burst into tears, his expression softening slightly, remembering how she had helped him in his hour of need. He had realised for a long time, that regardless of all of the material things he was able to give her, she wasn't happy and it had been a mistake on his part to marry at such an emotionally unstable time. Reminding himself again of how much he owed her, he caught her hand persuasively. "Sit down, my dear – I shouldn't have said that."

Slightly mollified but still wearing a hurt expression she sat down.

"I think we should come to some agreement, don't you? It isn't the cost as much as the disruption. There were forty people. It is unreasonable to think that you can entertain so often, especially when the parties go on so late that none of us can sleep."

Marcia pouted. "I thought you wanted me to be happy."

Gerald watched her disinterestedly pushing food around the plate with her fork.

"Of course I want you to be happy."

"Then you don't really mind, as long as I look after *you* nicely?" she coaxed.

Gerald had to harden his heart, knowing if he gave way things would just go on as before.

"I'm afraid I do. One house party every two months is all I'm prepared to agree to, and even that is more than most people have."

Laying down her fork, Marcia regarded him icily. "Then there is nothing more to say. I will have to make other arrangements until you are prepared to be reasonable." She rose and walked to the door, waiting for him to call her back as he always did – but he didn't, and with a toss of her head she hastened her step.

Gerald slumped. What now? He knew she wouldn't leave it there and true to his expectations, she wasted no time.

The following morning, she walked into his bedroom very early, greeted him cheerfully and announced she would be spending the next weekend with friends, and would arrange for a nurse to come in. She chatted as if nothing was amiss, laying out his clothes and turning the shower on for him as usual, taking satisfaction from his crestfallen face, convinced he would give way very soon.

Weekends on his own became a regular occurrence and at first he missed her desperately and resented her absence, but the relief of not having hoards of people around strengthened his resolve. He spent more and more time with Bob and the horses, and the idea to hire a manservant actually came from Bob.

And so, after numerous interviews, George Watts was engaged, and Marcia, – much to her chagrin – arrived home one Sunday evening to find him already installed.

She had always been confident it was only a matter of time before Gerald gave in, but she could only stand by and watch as George dealt expertly with Gerald's needs. The irony of it was, instead of making herself *more* needed she had made Gerald independent of her and she was no longer the kingpin. Gerald was in charge again.

There was an immediate rapport between Gerald and the ex-army batman. In his late forties, bull necked and stocky, George Watts was respectful, methodical, and cheerful, achieving everything with a minimum of fuss. In fact, after a very short while, Gerald became so glad of waking up to the burly,

Cockney's good-humour, he told him one day what a comfort it was to have him around.

Pleased and embarrassed, George replied, "Thank you, sir. *I'm* lucky to be doing a job I enjoy, in beautiful surroundings. I daresay I'd find it hard to be cheerful, stuck in a wheelchair all day – especially after the life you obviously led before your accident."

That conversation led to many talks when George sensed it gave Gerald comfort to reminisce. A faraway look would come into his eyes until a certain memory brought pain, then a shutter would come down and he would check himself mid-sentence.

Lorna had warned George not to mention the eldest son Robert, but hadn't said why, and George also noticed the first Mrs Anders was never mentioned either. He spoke frequently of his parents and the good times they had spent with people called Charles, Felicity, Sophie and Laurie, and he spoke guardedly of the younger son, who seemed to worry him a lot, but all things considered, it was a good arrangement. George had a room in the old servants' quarters, where Lorna's was, and Bob had taken him to see his room over the stables. He had been surprised at how simple, comfortable, and orderly, Bob had made it and even more surprised to find how companionable even *he* found the movements of the horses below. Work was in progress on one of the big barns, apparently being converted into living accommodation for Maisie and Jake when they got married in the spring. It was all very close knit, some might even say insular, but George knew he was glad to be a part of it.

"I think my father would like everything I'm doing here," Gerald confided, one pouring-wet day when they were confined to the house.

"You both obviously loved this old house, but tell me sir – why Anders Folly? An odd name for such a beautiful house."

He watched Gerald brighten, thinking, as a humorous smile spread across his employer's thin features, that in spite of everything he didn't look his years. He was still a dynamic-looking man, with expressive eyes prematurely dulled by the cruel blow fate had dealt him, but as he related the age-old tale, George listened to the humour in his voice and pictured him as the proud, self-reliant figure he must have been.

"My great, great grandfather built this house around 1750. Apparently he was a 'bit of a lad' and loved the local women. He was a seafarer and made his money from smuggling – rum, brandy, silks – and anything else you can name. The story goes he built this house for his mistress to live in, and one night after he had been drinking, enraged by his behaviour with the local girls and knowing his weakness for gambling, she challenged him, in the local ale house, to a single turn of the cards. If she won, the house and its surrounding land was hers, but if he won she would leave him to his orgies. In his drunken state, he gambled and lost and went to live in the lodge on the top of the cliffs. The mistress lived here until she died, some thirty years later. During that time, my great, great grandfather married and had one son, who became the new owner of the house under the will of the mistress. In her will she admitted to cheating by having an ace of spades in her fur muff. When the will was read – the story goes my great, great grandfather, by then a very old man, laughed raucously for a solid ten minutes and kept saying, "What a girl!" The house was *given* its name by the locals – I'm told. How true the story is I don't know, but it is an amusing little Cornish tale passed on down through the years, is it not? It took us a long time to piece it together, with the help of local people."

George gave a deep chuckle, shaking his head as he put another log on the fire. "It could well be true – it *could* well be. Cornwall, from what I hear, is most certainly a place of unusual happenings."

That conversation had taken place a year ago, when George first joined the household, and since then, with his help Gerald had regained a dignity of life he never expected to enjoy again. He *felt* in charge. He would be the first one to give Marcia credit for all she had done for him, and the only way he could explain it was he didn't feel obligated to George, because he was paying him a wage. With this had come an easing of the mind, enabling him to view more tolerantly Marcia's need for a busy social life, which eventually led to him suggesting she should move into the lodge, where, Gerald pointed out, she could entertain to her hearts content and leave him and his household in peace. He made her a generous allowance, and she was free to do as she wished, on condition that the name of Anders was never brought into disrepute. Divorce was not an option; he didn't believe in it.

It wasn't exactly the solution Marcia had envisaged for herself, she *had* hoped Gerald would tuck himself away in a corner of Anders Folly and leave her to occupy the rest of the house, but she had her freedom without the luxuries being curtailed, and after all, she *was* still Lady Anders.

When the day came for Marcia to actually move into the lodge, George packed her extensive luggage into the boot of the car, and Gerald, equipped with a bottle of Champagne, accompanied her to her new home. The derelict cottage had been extravagantly refurbished to Marcia's exacting standards, and was like something out of an American magazine, where most of the ideas had come from, but Gerald was happy in the thought that he had done the right thing by her, and he could settle back into a life where he was master in his own house.

*

260

Peace reigned for a blissful ten months, until it was rudely shattered by the appearance of Alexander. He arrived very early one morning, looking thin and haggard and had obviously been travelling for some time, according to his dishevelled and dirty appearance.

After a brief, incoherent talk with his father, he ate ravenously and went upstairs to his old bedroom, which Lorna and Maisie had hurriedly prepared for him, and fell into an exhausted sleep. He slept for two days, during which time Gerald sent George to look in on him constantly. Unable to account for the state Alexander had arrived home in, Gerald telephoned Simon, only to learn there had been no contact from him for months.

"He arrived home early this morning. Don't concern yourself. I will contact you soon." Gerald rang-off still none the wiser.

George reported on the third day that Alexander was awake and asking for food to be sent up; only then did it occur to Gerald that he had asked for his old room, instead of one of those already prepared, knowing his father couldn't reach him. The more he thought, the more convinced he became, something was dreadfully wrong, and the next morning he demanded that Alexander was to see him in his study. Unwashed and unshaved, wearing an old silk dressing gown he had long since grown out of, he faced his father across the desk, as he had as a child.

Gerald was shocked by his appearance and asked brusquely, "Are you ill?"

"Just tired." Alexander spoke without any of the old arrogance Gerald had been expecting, and some of his anger changed to concern. He jabbed at a chair.

"Sit down. How do you come to be so exhausted?"

"It was all a horrible mistake. I was arrested in Turkey and accused of smuggling drugs. I bribed a policeman, escaped and got on board a cargo boat headed for Spain. From there I found a boat that brought me all the way here. They dropped me off further down the coast. I walked from there."

Gerald gaped in horror; he had heard dreadful stories of Turkish prisons.

"I lost my papers and luggage. There are clothes at the cottage, but I just wanted to come home." His voice broke. "Sorry, Dad."

Gerald was too overcome to speak. He guided his chair round the desk and put his hand on Alexander's shoulder, eventually managing to say, "Go back to bed, son. I will ring the outfitters at Southampton and have them send you everything you need."

Alexander closed his eyes in genuine gratitude. "Thanks, Dad."

The doctor was sent for and declared he was suffering from shock and dehydration, so for the next week he was pampered and allowed to lay in bed, undisturbed. Tucked away at the top of the house he relived his narrow escape and shook violently, remembering the filthy conditions of the prison, and the rough handling he had suffered from the police. Never again would he go abroad. He had the all-important contacts now.

Most of the story he had told his father was true, but he had missed out the fact that he had been fully aware of what the parcel contained when he agreed to carry it through customs, foolishly thinking that as an Anders' representative he would be exempt from being searched, after all he had never been searched before. He broke into a sweat, recalling the moment when the police had arrested him and the contact had sped away in a fast car.

Hiding away in his room he waited for some form of repercussion, listening in fear every time the telephone rang, but nothing happened; obviously the two thousand pound bribe, to allow him to escape, had been enough. All he wanted now was to get to the cottage and see if a safety deposit key was waiting for him. He had, after all, kept his side of the bargain.

He gazed up at the sloping ceiling, listening to the sound of the sea dashing against the rocks, his mind going back to crossing the Bay of Biscay in the hold of a stinking fishing boat, as the sea tossed it about like a cork. He had been seasick all the way back to Cornwall. He buried his head under the bedclothes in an effort to shut the sea out, and in spite of his thirty-six years, shed tears for Nanny.

Gerald was greatly surprised and relieved when he appeared at breakfast the next morning looking more or less like his old self; clean-shaven and immaculate in the extremely conservative clothes Gerald had ordered for him, but he couldn't be choosey at the moment, he reminded himself. His father was being more understanding than he could ever have expected. They talked companionably about the changes that had been made in Alexander's absence – mainly about the horses, which Alexander found very exciting. He would love to learn to ride he said, and hid his glee when Gerald told him about Marcia moving in to the lodge. That woman and her brat were out. That alone made him feel a whole lot better, but he turned sympathetic eyes on his father.

"How are you coping?"

"Better than ever! George is the best thing that could have happened. I'm not *obliged* to anyone. He likes the job, and I pay him." Gerald buttered a piece of toast and spread it with Lorna's homemade marmalade, while Alexander digested this piece of philosophy.

"Lesson for the day," he said seriously.

"And a good one. Hope you never have to put it to the test. Now," he said abruptly. "We shall need to let Simon Hall know what is happening. When do you think you will feel up to returning to work?"

Alexander had his answer ready. "I thought I might give next week a try, but not back to Europe."

"Very well," Gerald answered slowly. There were a lot of unanswered questions but *this* was not the right moment.

"If your man George could drive me to the cottage tomorrow, I could start on Monday."

"I'll have a word with him after breakfast."

"Thanks."

Alexander breathed a sigh of relief as he returned to his room, thankful the barrage of questions hadn't come.

*

George watched Alexander in the driving mirror as the Daimler sped through the Devon countryside. At seven o'clock the roads were deserted and the sun was still low in the sky. It was a fine morning with a nip in the October air, and the heater was lending a welcome warmth to the interior of the car. The trees turning to their autumnal colours, made vivid splashes against the rolling, lush, green hills creating a wonderful sense of well-being in George; a morning when it was just good to be alive. Not so Master Alexander, George guessed, watching his unseeing eyes dart restlessly from side to side. He was obviously on edge and his sudden decision to return to work had surprised George. He had seen enough malingerers in the army to recognise one, and he could easily have got another two weeks out of his father without trying too hard. His stress was real enough though. He had obviously had a bad shock, and yet there was something about him he couldn't put his finger on.

He became aware of George watching him and their eyes met in the driving mirror. George returned his attention to the road, saying easily, "Would you like the radio on, sir? It might help you to doze and pass the journey. We have a fair way to go yet."

"Good idea." He leant back and closed his eyes, all he could think of was the key that should be waiting for him. He was beside himself with worry. If it didn't arrive, the risks would have been for nothing and years of scheming gone down the drain, back to square one; the contacts lost forever, because not for all the money in the world would he go back to Europe and risk being arrested again.

They reached the cottage mid-morning. George retrieved the two suitcases from the boot, dropped them in the hallway then went back to get the large box of groceries Lorna had packed, before asking Alexander if he should take the cases upstairs.

"What? Oh yes," he replied in a distracted voice, frantically sorting through a huge pile of mail heaped on the hall table and tearing open a small, padded envelope.

"Yes, yes," he muttered, closing his eyes ecstatically.

In spite of the bright morning, the interior of the cottage was quite dark, due to the thick, cherry red velvet curtains being closed and George watched as Alexander went around throwing them back exuberantly, his previous mood disappearing like quicksilver. George was also taken aback by the flamboyant style throughout the cottage, and stared in open amazement at the crystal chandeliers, ornate gold framed mirrors in every room and sumptuous settees. It was opulent and over-the-top, but there was a quality to everything that said no expense had been spared. He went into the kitchen to unpack the food and marvelled at the cleanliness of the extensive range of high quality fittings and appliances, seeing Alexander in a very different light to the rather pathetic figure he had cut at Anders Folly.

"Will that be all, sir? Or shall I prepare breakfast before I leave?"

"I can manage, George. Shut the front door as you leave, will you?"

"Very well, sir." George turned on his heel and left without receiving a single word of thanks, or even goodbye from Alexander, who had collapsed into an armchair and was staring at the ceiling, pressing his fingertips together with a triumphant smirk on his face.

George got back into the car, with a grim expression. "Thank you, George, for getting' up at five-thirty and drivin' me all this way. You must have a cuppa tea and somethin' te eat, before the long journey 'ome."

He gave a snort of disgust, hunger robbing him of his usual good humour and reached under the dashboard for a map of the area. The New Forest was completely unknown territory to him. He spotted what he was looking for, looked at his watch, and started the car.

Within ten minutes he turned into a tree-lined drive and glimpsed an old manor house, with mullioned windows and high chimney stacks. From his office Colin saw the maroon Daimler purr to a halt, and walked into reception. One didn't forget a car like that, especially when its owner dropped the opportunity of a lifetime in one's lap, but what was Sir Gerald Anders doing here? Then he saw George get out of the driver's side and leave his chauffeur's cap on the seat before locking the door.

Colin greeted him at the reception desk. "Good morning sir, am I right in thinking that is Sir Anders' car?"

"It most certainly is. Sir Anders is not travellin' terday, but I saw your 'otel on the map and wondered if I could get breakfast."

"Certainly. Are you staying in the area?" Colin asked chattily as he led the way to an empty table in the dining room, which at ten-fifteen was quiet except for a few late stragglers.

"No, I shall be returnin' to Cornwall, directly. I drove Sir Anders' son up this mornin'."

"You must mean Alexander. I know him well. I thought he was still abroad though."

Colin was anxious to make it known how well he knew the family, hoping he could glean some information about Alexander.

"Tragedy about Lady Anders, wasn't it? She actually refurbished this place and died before she could open it. I was going to be her head chef. The family were terribly cut up, especially Alexander. How is he? I haven't seen him for some time."

George felt uncomfortable discussing his employer's family, and picking up the menu ordered the full English breakfast. Colin raised his hand and a waiter came to take the order, but it became obvious Colin was reluctant to leave.

"What a wonderful old 'ouse this is," George said steering away from the subject of Alexander.

"Yes, isn't it? It was a bit of a wreck before Pamela refurbished, because it was a convalescent home during the war. Forest End – as it was known then – has quite a history."

"Forest End, did ya say?" George asked, his ears pricking up.

"That is what it was called until Pamela changed it to The Vintage. Alexander would be able to tell you more. Is he staying at the cottage?"

George was staring about with avid interest. "This is where my father was sent, when 'e lost an eye during the Normandy landin's. It was in the New Forest. It's gotta be."

"So is Alexander staying at the cottage?" Colin repeated, trying to sound casual.

"Oh – er – I suppose so."

"And is he alone?"

"'e was when I left 'im." George saw his breakfast arriving and tucked his napkin into his collar; he didn't like the questioning, so he ate hungrily giving noncommittal answers to several probing questions and Colin finally had to take the hint.

Before leaving he wandered around the extensive gardens, telling himself his father had probably stood on this very spot, or leant against this very tree, as he was doing now. He left with a smile on his face and drove home, realising with a rush of affection, that that was how he thought of Anders Folly. It was a long time since he had felt he belonged anywhere. Constantly on the move with the army, he had looked forward to finishing his time and settling down, but then his mother and father had split up, selling the only home he had ever known. His father had lost the sight in his other eye and he had taken care of him until he died, five years later – then he applied for the live-in position at Anders Folly.

He hummed softly to himself anticipating the evening ahead, sharing supper with Lorna at the big kitchen table. Ah, she was a grand lass – but not to be trifled with he reminded himself, his eyes alight with amusement as he recalled her indignant remark and scarlet cheeks when he had given her a playful pat.

"Mr Watts, behave yourself." Even so, he had caught her smiling to herself later.

On reaching home, he found Gerald in the stables with Bob and reported all was well, then went in search of a much needed cup of tea. Lorna was baking and the warm aroma of rabbit pie wafted towards him as he entered the kitchen.

"You'll never know 'ow good it feels to be 'ome," he said with feeling as he poured boiling water into the teapot.

"I assure you I do, and the feeling never leaves you at Anders Folly," Lorna said with simple sincerity.

They sat in comfortable silence until George told her about the coincidence of finding Forest End. She was intrigued but reluctant to offer an opinion about mentioning it to Sir Anders.

"All I know is we never talk about Mrs Gerald, but it's up to you. Thankfully, he has been much happier lately."

Changing the subject she asked how his Lordship was and knew by her tone who she was referring to. It was the only time he knew her to be sarcastic.

"'ard to say really; 'e suddenly came alive when we got to the cottage; somethin' in the post as far as I could make out. I wasn't there ten minutes – didn't even offer me a cuppa tea."

"That would be right," Lorna said with a sniff.

"Incredible kitchen. Does 'e cook? The 'ole place is posh 'n' and over-the-top – not to my taste or yours."

George paused and hid an enlightened smile, as he put two and two together, realising what had been escaping him. Alexander was gay! It wasn't immediately obvious, not like the fellow in the hotel, who asked so many questions about him, but he knew he was right and suddenly a lot of things fell into place. He looked at Lorna, but she was intent on her baking again, and his guess was she wouldn't know what he was talking about anyway. That was what he liked about her.

*

Colin sat at his desk watching George drive away, debating whether to telephone Alexander. Was he still furious with him or would time have healed the rift? He decided to arrive unannounced with a good bottle of wine and some caviar – a luxury he had become very partial to in the intervening years. He had spent time with two other partners, but he found the Anders' wealth a hard act to follow. It was the air of prosperity he craved to be part of. At the time he thought power over Alexander would get him everything he needed, and in a way it had but losing him had never been part of the plan.

At midday he packed the wine and caviar into a basket, adding strawberries and cream, and profiteroles as an after thought – Alexander had always liked profiteroles. Well pleased with himself, he got into his white sports car and drove to the cottage. There was no reply to his knock and after several irritating minutes he got back into the car, turned the key viciously and rammed the engine into gear, just as a taxi drew up behind him. In his rear view mirror, he saw Alexander alight, carrying a small suitcase. He watched him pay the driver and hurry indoors, then retraced his steps to knock again; several minutes passed before the door opened. He was minus the suitcase and seemed flustered.

Colin held the basket up. "Heard you were back. Brought lunch. Can we talk?"

Without smiling, Alexander held the door wider. It was good timing. He badly needed company and time *had* dulled his anger.

"Go through, I'll be with you in a mo." He disappeared upstairs, and hearing his movements, Colin knew the cottage well enough to recognize the two loose floorboards being lifted.

He unpacked the basket and laid the food out on a tray, then opened the bottle of wine and fetched two glasses from the glass fronted cupboard over the worktop.

They sat opposite each other on the plump settees, with the long coffee table between them and covertly weighed each other up.

Both of them had changed from young twenties to mid-thirties, and Alexander now looked the older of the two. He had lost his boyish looks and it was evident he was no longer an easily led youngster. Colin trod warily.

"What's been happening in your life then? Anything exciting?"

"Too much," Alexander answered with a lopsided grin, going on to tell a much exaggerated and erroneous version of his arrest.

"You were cool; I would have been terrified," Colin said, knowing flattery always won the day with Alexander.

"The name of Anders doesn't carry any weight out there, I had to rely on my wits. They knew they weren't dealing with a *nobody* though. I've made a lot of money and it talks the same language anywhere in the world."

His confidence now, and his earlier agitation made Colin intensely curious about the suitcase. "So what do you do with all of this money, invest it?"

"No, I intend to strike out on my own; I've got big things in mind."

"Anything we can do together? I've got a bit put by."

"I am talking serious money, not a bit put by." He gave a supercilious sneer and Colin, realising the wine was loosening his tongue, refilled his glass.

"My associates are–," he checked himself. "That reminds me, I have things to do. Sorry old boy, we will have to continue this some other time."

He rose and gulped his wine, leaving Colin frustrated and red-faced at his dismissal, but he recovered quickly.

"Come to dinner tonight – on the house of course."

"Thanks. About seven?"

"Perfect! I'm glad we've talked."

Alexander watched him walk to his car and turn to wave, thinking how unsophisticated he had become – or had he always been like that? He had seemed so worldly when they were younger, now he still seemed like a boy, compared to the company he had kept in Europe. He would miss that life and perhaps it would be amusing to pick up with Colin again, but if things went according to plan it would only be for a short time. His thoughts raced excitedly at the endless possibilities, now he had money.

He spent the afternoon buying a racing green, MG sports car and arrived at The Vintage, just before seven. Well-placed lighting in the shrubs surrounding the house, lent a prosperous air and he particularly liked the entrance. A model of a *Vintage* Rolls Royce stood on one side of the revolving glass doors, and waxen figures of a couple, dressed in 1920s style, holding champagne glasses, and cigarettes in long holders, adorned the softly lit interior. It gave the feeling of stepping back in time to a more gracious era, and Colin rose in his estimation. With imagination like that perhaps he could fit into future plans. His mother would have liked it as well, he decided – little dreaming the idea was one of many left amongst her personal papers.

Colin emerged from his office to greet him, immaculate in black tie and dinner jacket and led the way to the small lounge bar. It brought back memories of Riverside, where they had first met and for a time they reminisced, then Colin offered him a menu. It was ornately decorated with an embossed vintage car on the leather cover. Alexander commented on his mother's choice of name, which leant itself so easily to an attractive business theme.

"It's our logo. It looks very good on stationary, brochures etc."

"I might be in need of a few inventive ideas, with the project I have in mind."

About to give Pamela credit, Colin changed his mind and murmured modestly, "Just say the word."

They dined together in the blue and gold dining room. The food was excellent and when Alexander was obviously feeling thoroughly relaxed, with the well-laden dessert trolley to choose from, Colin excused himself saying, "I always pass on the sweet stuff, and duty calls for a few minutes. Have whatever pleases you and I will be back in time for coffee and brandy."

Alexander enjoyed two large portions of liqueur drenched delicacies and sat back. Music played softly in the background, and he gazed at the opulent furnishings, considering once again whether Colin could be of use to him. He certainly knew his business. Colin rejoined him, wearing a resigned look. Caught up in his own thoughts Alexander hadn't realised he had been absent for half-an-hour.

"Sorry about that – minor upset in the kitchen." He beckoned imperiously to a waiter who hurried over with coffee, followed by another bearing two large brandies, then appeared to quickly forget his problems. Their coffee cups were refilled and brandy glasses replenished, as Alexander got more and more talkative somehow without giving anything away.

"Are you going to be alright to drive?" Colin eventually asked him. "You could always stay the night."

He raised his eyebrows suggestively and Alexander smiled. "Another time perhaps. I need to go home tonight."

Colin returned his smile affably having partially satisfied his curiosity in the half-an-hour he had been missing, by using his old key to let himself into the cottage.

There must have been half-a-million pounds under the floorboards – no wonder he didn't want to leave the cottage unattended overnight.

Alexander drove home feeling rather pleased; his former idolisation of Colin was something he could laugh about now and he looked forward to resuming their friendship, to show him how worldly he had become, he thought gloatingly. He drove on, fiddling with the radio and investigating what each knob was for on the new dashboard, congratulating himself on his choice of car.

On reaching the cottage he parked and gave the bonnet an affectionate pat. He felt jubilant. "Night old girl." An owl hooted and he mimicked, "Goodnight to you too," giving a small sideways hop and clicking his heels together in the frosty night air.

The cottage was warm and bright and the radio he had left on was playing dance music. He threw his dinner jacket off, poured a brandy and slumped onto the settee laughing out loud with sheer joy, then rose again, deciding to go and take another look at his riches. He made his way upstairs, carrying the brandy and undoing his bow tie and the buttons on his shirt with his free hand.

Concealed lighting threw a glow over the cream curtains and bedding and lent elegance to the gold patterned wallpaper and cream fitted furniture. It reminded him of Colin, whose choice it had been and smiled, imagining his amazement if he could see his wealth. The loose floorboard was in one of the wardrobes. He slid the mirrored door along and lifted the deep pile gold carpet back, noticing the board wasn't quite flush. He must be more careful. The bank notes just fitted between the joists – it was a perfect hiding place. Excitement made his heart pound as he removed the board, exposing the money before trying to replace the floorboard; it resisted and he tried again; it usually slotted back easily. Repositioning it he found it still resisted and moving the bedside lamp to shine in to the space he saw something dark caught on a splinter of wood. On investigation it proved to be a tiny fragment of cloth with a small button attached. For a moment he was transfixed before frantically ripping the board up again. The money was all there. He knelt back on his heels studying the button, then slowly getting to his feet he wended his way downstairs, hardly able to credit the suspicion dawning on him. A mental flash back to the restaurant, as he inspected the cuffs of his own jacket, confirmed where the button had come from. In his mind's eye he saw Colin smiling at him, and beckoning the waiter for refills of coffee and brandy – saw again the frayed cuff as Colin held his hand up. Fury filled him as he realised Colin had planned all along to nip back here and pry. Even after all these years he would remember the sound of the floorboards being removed. Sleep was out of the question. It was all he could do to stop himself from rushing back and confronting him. He could so easily have taken the money. Why hadn't he? His mind began to work calmly. At least he knew Colin was still as cunning as ever, and once again, much to his own chagrin, had outfoxed him. To think he had considered taking him into partnership, but he would say nothing until the time was right. Somehow or another he would find a way to get even. Colin Murry had made his last sharp move on the Anders family.

Sleep overtook him at last and he slept heavily until noon, when a loud hammering on the front door woke him. Rolling out of bed he ambled downstairs grumbling about disturbing people at this time in the morning.

Colin pulled a face at the sight of his pyjamas as he walked past him into the kitchen. "Thought you must have died, I've been knocking for ages. Thought you would be up and starting on these great plans of yours," he teased cheerily, holding a basket aloft. "Brunch?"

Alexander scowled as the previous night's happenings flooded back and for a moment his temper almost flared.

"That's what kept me awake half the night," he growled.

Colin started to unpack hot croissants, Parma ham and fruit, then filled the coffee pot. Alexander squirmed at his easy familiarity, realising if it hadn't been for the button, he would have been unaware of Colin's duplicity, and responded to his overtures.

They ate in silence until, "I'm selling the cottage and giving up my job; it won't please Papa but I'll get round that."

"Is it wise to upset your father," Colin asked, upset at the thought of the cottage being sold. He had used it regularly while Alexander was safely out of the way.

"I want to be my own boss. You should understand that."

"But to leave the family firm *and* sell the cottage. Cutting yourself off a bit, aren't you?"

"Not with the plan I've got in mind; I'll be closer to home than ever, although the old man doesn't know about that yet."

He smiled briefly, before saying seriously, "I need money to make my plan work."

"How much?" Colin asked thinking of the stash under the floorboards.

"More than you could raise."

Colin bridled. "I'm not exactly without connections, at least give me first option on the cottage."

"I've already had an offer. Cash deal." The lie slipped out glibly.

"You don't hang about, do you?" he reproached.

"You've got the hotel, why would you want the cottage?"

"It's nice to get away from the job sometimes, and the cottage feels like part of me anyway."

Alexander raised an eyebrow, ignoring the sentimental inference. "You would have to come up with at least two hundred thousand."

His expression changed. "Bit over-the-top, isn't it?"

"Take it or leave it." Alexander seemed to lose interest. "I'm going to get dressed; I knew you couldn't put your hands on that sort of money, that is why I didn't give you first refusal."

"Give me twenty-four hours."

He heard a derisive laugh as Alexander disappeared upstairs calling. "In your dreams."

Colin cleared away the remains of the meal and left the house, walking jauntily down the drive, eyes alight with anticipation. Alexander watched from the bedroom window, knowing the price he had quoted was outrageous; he also knew Colin would put himself in debt to get the cottage.

As he expected, Colin arrived late in the afternoon on the following day carrying a suitcase, which he opened with a flourish to display the banknotes inside. With another flourish he produced a legal document.

"And there is my contract, signed and ready to exchange." It was his turn to grin, as Alexander looked suspicious.

"You're in a mighty big rush, all of a sudden."

For a nervous moment he wondered if Colin was ahead of him again.

"You gave me twenty-four hours. Remember?"

"Yes of course. I'll get my solicitor onto it straight away." He still had this nagging doubt about how Colin had been able to raise the money so quickly, but now he had to keep his end of the bargain and find a solicitor quickly. Charles was out, if he wanted to keep it from his father until it was all signed and sealed.

Strings were pulled and contracts signed within three weeks. Only then did Alexander telephone Gerald to say he was resigning and returning to Cornwall.

Gerald didn't know whether to be angry or relieved. Reports of the chaos his son was causing in the department by disappearing without explanation, missing appointments and leaving others to explain to irate customers, all forced him to believe it was for the best if Alexander came home where he could keep an eye on him. For a while, he actually thought he had learnt a lesson and was going to settle down; he should have known better. Even the much coveted, *Seat on the Board* had proved to be another nine-day wonder.

Gerald viewed the homecoming with something less than enthusiasm and it therefore came as a pleasant surprise when Alexander asked to move in to Charles and Felicity's old apartment. He had anticipated him hiding away at the top of the house again and agreed readily to the new arrangement.

Alexander of course had his reasons for relinquishing his safe haven. He could come and go by the French doors, any time of the day or night, without question – perfect for nocturnal meetings. Everything was going to plan, he told himself rubbing his hands together. All he had to do now was convince his father the yacht was a legitimate business plan.

CHAPTER TWENTY-FOUR

1992

Gerald woke with a start to find Charles sitting quietly in one of the wing chairs.

"Must have dropped off."

"You look better for it." Charles looked at his wristwatch and smiled. "Lorna has been in and invited me to lunch: roast beef and Yorkshire pudding. I said yes, of course."

Gerald gave a good-humoured tut. "You've made her day."

George who had been listening for any sound, entered to say lunch was ready and Gerald steered his chair to the door.

"That sleep did 'im the world o' good," George cheerfully informed Lorna on his return to the kitchen.

"More like Mr Charles did. Those two did everything together until her ladyship came along." Lorna gave a loud puff of disgust and George looked sympathetic, knowing how fond she was of them. He realised no love was lost between Lorna and Lady Anders, but it was the first time she had made a comment like that. It must be a sign she trusted him. They had worked closely for a long time now and George had great hopes that she returned his feelings. He was pretty certain the signs were there and very soon he would present her with the ring he kept in his tallboy.

"Take the tray of vegetables in, George, and look smart, you know Mr Gerald don't like to be kept waiting and Mr Charles will be starving, if my memory serves me right."

She puffed out her chest and smiled happily, picking up the other tray, anticipating the pleasure on Charles's face – she wasn't disappointed.

"Ah! Roast Beef a la Marie. Thank you, Lorna." Charles beamed at her, and Gerald looked on indulgently, remembering the banter over Marie's dinners.

"What did I tell you?" Lorna said on their way back to the kitchen. "Mr Charles will put things right; you mark my words."

"You could well be right," George agreed, noticing how she had slipped back into calling Sir Anders Mr Gerald. Her Ladyship would not be pleased he mused happily but Lorna certainly was. He would propose *tonight*.

Having done justice to the roast beef and two helpings of Lorna's treacle sponge pudding, they settled themselves on the terrace. There was a cool breeze coming off the sea but in the shelter of the fir trees it was warm enough to sit and watch the calm water: where only the movement made by the sleek, white yacht told of the huge swell underneath. Gerald's life was like that, Charles thought – apparently peaceful and tranquil on top but underneath there was always this undercurrent keeping him in turmoil. Watching Gerald's frown he asked, "Apart from finding Robert, what else is troubling you, old friend?"

"That!" He pointed, as three horses came into view, their hooves sending up great sprays as they galloped through the shallow waters, with three scantily clad figures riding bareback and whooping with delight.

Charles frowned. "You don't like them riding on the beach?"

Gerald snorted. "If only that was all. Alexander's entire life is spent pleasure seeking. He is a degenerate hedonist. You have no idea how wild the parties are, and they go on for days. I thought when Marcia moved into the lodge I would be free from a never-ending round of parties but compared to these—" he spread his hands. "I thought he would tire of it but he shows no sign at all of settling down and producing heirs. I'm thoroughly disgusted."

Charles looked blankly at him as he continued following the riders, was he actually unaware his son was gay or was he denying it in the hope it would go away? He shied from bringing the subject up, promising himself he would another day, when Gerald was feeling stronger, asking instead who the other riders were.

"Tamara is riding Midnight, the big black one. She is Marcia's daughter and Fabian is on the brown. He is the chef and right-hand man I'm given to understand. That enormous white monster is a holy terror, which seems to amuse Alexander. He calls him Bucephalus after Alexander the Great's horse and he has already wrecked two stalls. *Everything has to be so theatrical*. I wish to God I had let him take up acting when he wanted to; at least he could have taken a stage name and I could have disowned him. It seems I am never to be free from this demon child," he said with feeling. "Perhaps it is my punishment for not being able to love him as I did Robert, but Pamela doted on him so much and..." His words trailed off and hung in the air between them. He had never spoken her name aloud in all these years, and it was like a door from the past being opened.

"Would you like me to have a word with Alexander?"

"For all the good it would do. I have told him the yacht must be moved but he says it isn't seaworthy now." He sighed deeply. "And at the end of the day he is all I have, without Robert."

"Sophie keeps in touch with Robert. She wouldn't give us his address – said it would divide our loyalty, but I will explain the circumstances. Sophie and Matthew have two boys and a girl now, Laurie, David and Ellie Marie," he said proudly, introducing a lighter note.

"Mother and Dad would have liked that."

Charles swallowed hard. "I must be getting back."

He stood up and Gerald caught a picture of him on that first day in his father's office, wearing the dreadful suit and shirt, with curled up collars and the shock of unruly brown hair that David had regarded with such dismay. He had hardly changed over the years except the hair was now grey and neatly groomed and the suit was well tailored – and it had to be said he looked every inch the successful and respected solicitor he was.

"Prosperity suits you," Gerald said, emotionally grasping his hand.

"You aren't to worry anymore, I shall give the matter my immediate attention and we will find Robert very soon."

He held Gerald's hand in both of his for a long moment then walked quickly to the door, where he turned to look back at Gerald's lonely figure; his heart ached as he hurried out, passing George, he gripped his shoulder. "Look after him."

After a brief call at the office he went home early and surprised Felicity by taking her in his arms, hugging her really tightly and whispering into her hair, "I'm such a lucky man."

She asked no questions; Charles secretary had told her where he had gone. They seldom talked about Gerald these days; they had both been very hurt, even though they understood his need for a partner, and they had both worried for him when he asked Charles to draw up a new will to ensure Marcia was well provided for, at the same time as ensuring Anders Folly stayed in the family. She had telephoned Lorna several times since Marcia had left and was assured each time, he was happier than he had been for a long time and keeping well. They hoped Gerald would get in touch with them but he didn't and they assumed he wanted to lick his wounds in private. They had heard rumours about the high life Alexander was leading, but as he was anchored in Anders Bay, obviously with Gerald's consent, they took the view it was not their place to interfere. Several days later, when Charles finally talked to her about his visit, they both wished they had buried their pride and gone to him.

"He has got himself in a real state over Alexander. I telephoned Sophie, but she says Robert hasn't been in touch for a long time and her letters have been returned unopened. Apparently it was a box number. She can't explain; they were all four very good friends. Incidentally, did you know Marcia had a daughter?"

"Can't say I did. Nothing was ever mentioned. How old is she?"

"I only saw her in the distance, on horseback. Not a child though, and from the sound of things she has joined forces with Alexander in making life intolerable for Gerald."

It brought home to them how much they had lost touch with Anders Folly and Felicity said Charles should tell Marcia to speak to her daughter – especially now they no longer lived there. He said he would, but as fate would have it,

Alexander was suddenly confined to bed with a suspected virus. He retreated to his room at the top of the house, and refused to come down, indeed, George doubted he had the strength to. On hearing the doctor had been sent for he locked his door, saying he would decide if he needed a doctor. Tamara visited him every day and left crying, running from the house before she could be questioned. Gerald became so alarmed that he sent for Charles.

"Try and talk some sense into him, will you? I can't get up those damned stairs. I should have had those rooms boarded up years ago," he ranted helplessly.

Charles went to the bedroom ready to do battle, suspecting Alexander was just being his usual difficult self. Tamara was beside the bed dabbing his forehead with a damp towel, and they didn't hear him enter.

"Hello, I hear you aren't too…" He caught his breath in horror as she swung round, towel in hand. Alexander was deathly pale, sweating profusely and covered in great spots; his eyes were listless and he seemed to be having difficulty breathing.

"How long has he been like this?" Charles asked urgently.

"Until yesterday we thought it was the flu virus, but suddenly…" She burst into tears begging Alexander to see a doctor.

"Of course he must see a doctor." Charles strode from the room and returned within minutes. "An ambulance is on its way."

Alexander was contrarily relieved the decision had been made for him.

He never returned to Anders Folly. When he was released from hospital he went straight to the yacht to live out the remaining short time left to him, with Tamara and Fabian to look after him. His own worst fear had been confirmed and the good times were over for him. The good times, that had cost him his life.

CHAPTER TWENTY-FIVE

Gerald glanced over the top of his morning paper as Lorna entered the dining room.

"Good morning, Mr Gerald."

Lowering his paper he said, "Good morning, Lorna. Guests will be arriving sometime this afternoon; two very young children – and a woman," he added impatiently. "See that suitable rooms are prepared for them, will you?"

Without a flicker, Lorna placed his breakfast of grilled bacon, kidneys and tomatoes in front of him and poured coffee from the heavy, silver pot.

"Yes, sir, will that be all, sir?"

She hovered about the long sideboard in the hope that he would enlarge on the situation, but no explanation was forthcoming and she had learned long ago not to question when Mr Gerald was wearing his 'all in good time' expression.

*

Fran's first glimpse of their destination came as the chauffeur-driven car sped along the narrow Cornish road, from where the land dropped gently away, and she saw a rambling, stone-built house sprawling comfortably in its grounds, with the sea glistening in the background. The road had climbed steeply for the last mile between high hedges, leaving her totally unprepared for the breathtaking panoramic view and as they topped the rise. Adam said, "We're nearly there. That is Anders Folly."

Fran caught her breath, wondering what the owner of such a place could want with her and the children. Eyes wide, she voiced her thoughts to Adam, who was sitting in the front passenger seat. He turned and gave a sympathetic smile.

"It won't be long now," he assured her. "It might be as well to wake the children though."

It had been a long drive and the twins had fallen asleep, lulled by the smooth hum of the engine and plush comfort of the big Daimler, but they woke and were instantly agog with excitement that the journey was at an end, as the car swept up the drive and drew to a halt in front of the wide entrance, to the accompaniment of, "Are we going to stay here for a holiday? Can we paddle? Can we make a sandcastle? Who lives here?"

"Hush now," Fran warned as she met the searching gaze of a woman dressed in a severe grey dress, through the car window.

"That is Lorna Pennington, the housekeeper," Adam said. "You will love her."

"You think so?" Fran said, for the moment unconvinced.

Lorna greeted her and the children with a polite smile and informed Adam that Mr Gerald was waiting in the study.

He stood aside allowing them to go first and she saw a large square hall with a round table in the middle, a huge grandfather clock, ticking sonorously in one corner and highly polished floorboards glowing between softly coloured rugs. The smell of wax polish filled the air, mingling with the scent of roses and lavender drifting in from the closely packed borders, edging the sweeping drive. Fran was overwhelmed by a feeling that to speak above a whisper would be almost sacrilege – a feeling obviously shared by the children, judging by the fearful look they were giving the long flight of shallow stairs, rising gracefully to a horseshoe shaped landing above. Fran was mesmerised; Adam had to touch her arm, as he knocked on one of the doors and a voice bade them come in.

As he ushered them in, her first impression was of dim, dark panelling and dark red chairs, a big flat-topped desk and one of the biggest fireplaces she had ever seen.

Her roving gaze was lastly drawn to the owner of the voice as he and Adam greeted one another.

Adam introduced her first, then the children. She saw a strong featured, silver-haired man whose face was inexplicably familiar and it came as a slight shock to see he was sitting in a wheelchair. For a full thirty seconds he said nothing to Adam's introduction and didn't even appear to notice Fran's outstretched hand, which she hastily withdrew. His searching gaze never left Tim's small, sturdy frame, and Fran found herself moving towards him protectively.

"Come here, boy," he said at last, in a strange voice. Tim looked at her nervously and she walked with him, keeping her arm around his shoulders.

The old man's eyes seemed to bore into him then come to a decision; he held out his hand. "You don't know me, but I would like us to become good friends."

Tim shyly put his small hand into the outstretched fingers, as the old man turned to Adam and said, "Yes, he is an Anders."

Adam gave an enlightened gasp and said, "I think Miss Anderson is entitled to an explanation." Gerald glanced disinterestedly at Fran.

"All in good time – all in good time," he muttered, his eyes returning to Tim, whose hand he still held.

Fran was decidedly entitled to a long overdue explanation, she told herself and drew Sam forward saying firmly, "This is Samantha, Timothy's twin sister, and I need to know the reason we were invited."

Once again Gerald ignored her and reached out to Sam, who slipped her hand into his, saying with an offended air.

"I'm only twenty minutes younger than my brother."

"Are you indeed? Well I hope we can also be friends," Gerald said twinkling at her. "Now if you would both like to go along to the kitchen, Miss Pennington will find you some milk and biscuits while I have a chat with your aunt."

Adam smiled at them and opened the door. "Come along, I will show you where the kitchen is."

Left alone, Gerald turned to her, abruptly dropping his affable manner. She waited uncertainly and was flabbergasted at his first words.

"I will take them off your hands now. You will of course be reimbursed for any expense that has been incurred and it would be advisable if you remain temporarily until they settle in, during which time a suitable nanny will be found. You will naturally be paid for your services."

His haughty, unwavering gaze and his obvious assumption that he only had to speak and wave money about to be obeyed, astounded her, but it was his hostility she found insulting and seeing he was about to speak again she said quietly, "I think you are forgetting something."

He eyed her coldly. "I don't think so."

"Firstly you haven't explained why we were invited and secondly why you imagine for one minute, I would just leave my brother's children with a perfect stranger and lastly, when I leave – so do the children."

She delivered her speech with quiet dignity, two red spots on her cheeks being the only sign of how angry she felt.

"If you force me to, I will apply for legal guardianship," Gerald retaliated, adding in a matter of a fact tone. "There is no doubt whatsoever who would be regarded as the most suitable guardian. *You* are only their father's illegitimate half-sister, whereas I am blood related."

With a disdainful look he turned his wheelchair to face the French doors, making it clear he considered the conversation at an end. In truth he was exhausted and just wanted this woman out of his sight. He had sent for the children, not her, but Adam had assured him, it would be all three or none, as Miss Anderson would never allow the children out of her sight, even supposing they would come, without an almighty fuss.

A small sound made Fran turn and realise Adam had heard their exchange and was approaching the desk.

"Sir Gerald, it would appear to me, Miss Anderson is totally unaware of any connection you have with the children – indeed I am drawing conclusions myself. Mr Hughes instructed me to contact Darren Anderson and beyond that I am as much in the dark as Miss Anderson herself."

"More to the point," Fran interrupted hotly, "how dare he call me illegitimate. That is slander. And now I should like to return home – *with* the children; as their only living relative there is no question that I am their legal guardian."

"Let's not be hasty, Miss Anderson, there are matters to discuss."

Adam put a placating hand on her arm and tried to guide her to a nearby chair but she resisted, too angry to sit. She was also shaking and apprehensive. What had she got them into? She should never have agreed to come. The situation in London was worrying but it was nothing compared to this. She wouldn't let him see she was afraid though, she determined as the wheelchair turned slowly back and the old man regarded her through narrowed eyes.

"Are you trying to pretend you don't know who I am?"

"I understand your name is Sir Gerald Anders; beyond that I neither know nor care."

She turned to Adam. "And now Mr Wesley will you *please* take us home."

The word home conjured up the familiarity of the flat and suddenly she knew she could cope with all of her old problems, if only she could get them safely back there.

"Pretending, young woman, will get you nowhere; you may as well accept that I will have the children living here with me, whether you like it or not. It is *my* right and *theirs*," Gerald snapped.

Adam returned Fran's bewildered look and decided it wasn't feigned.

"I think I should hand the case back to Mr Hughes, sir. I understood it was just a simple case of finding Darren Anderson, but there are obviously other issues at stake I feel you don't want to confide to me, and in all fairness to Miss Anderson, cards should be laid on the table."

Gerald held his hand up and shot Fran a withering look.

"As Miss Anderson very well knows, her stepfather was my son, therefore the children are my great grandchildren."

Fran's face cleared with relief. "It's obviously a case of mistaken identity; I didn't have a stepfather. Well I'm really glad that's settled, I was getting worried there for a bit."

She smiled at Adam. "So now we really *can* go home."

"Don't talk such nonsense, Girl. I know an Anders when I see one. That boy is the living image of my son at that age."

"A lot of children look alike when they are young. I *know* Sam and Tim and we haven't any living relatives; my parents told my brother and me from when we were young, that we had no other family."

It was Gerald's turn to look taken aback, before saying slowly, "I disowned him when he married your mother; that will be why he changed his name."

Seeing she was still unconvinced he reached into the drawer of a small side table, drew out a silver framed photograph and handed it to her. Fran's eyes clouded at the sudden reminder of the man whose face was so dear to her.

"Was that your father?" Adam asked gently and she nodded unable to speak.

"And he never, ever mentioned the name Anders, or told you about his father's home?"

"Never!" she answered in a stricken voice.

"Then you have misjudged your granddaughter," he said turning to Gerald.

"She is nothing to do with me. *My son was not her father,*" Gerald roared.

White faced, Fran demanded, "What are you saying?"

There was a hard, embittered look on Gerald's face as he answered.

"Your Mother was my secretary for a short time, and during that time she got herself pregnant – wouldn't say, who the father was. Fool that he was, my son took pity on her – insisted on marrying her – ruined his life."

"I think not," Fran interrupted defensively, remembering the closeness her parents shared.

"What would you know?" Gerald asked bitterly, sinking into his chair dejectedly.

"Because they were happy," Fran answered simply.

"Happy? Impossible! He couldn't be happy without his background – his heritage – his loving family around him."

"Loving?" Fran cried, unable to hold back any longer. "You call that love? Believing he couldn't be happy and yet disowning him anyway, just because he didn't fall in with your wishes. If you ask me, you didn't disown my father – he disowned you and that is why he and my mother never spoke of you. I'm glad we weren't brought up here. You may have a lovely house, but we had a happy home and childhood. We had real beliefs, and nothing you can say will persuade me to let Sam and Tim grow up here with your so-called love."

She hadn't meant to be quite so forthright and tears were streaming down her face, at the heart breaking, undeniable truth she had to accept, as she waited for this old man's reaction, but without another word he pulled the bell cord beside his chair and turned to Adam.

"We will discuss this further in the morning – shall we say ten o'clock?"

Adam agreed as the door opened and Lorna entered.

"Kindly see the children and their aunt are made comfortable and send George in."

He was obviously under considerable stress and catching a warning glance from Adam, Fran bit back words of protest and brushed her eyes with the back of her hand, but as soon as they were out of earshot she said firmly, "I want to return home with the children immediately – you said I could if I didn't like it, and I don't."

"It is a very long journey for the children to do again today. Please just stay and discuss the situation more calmly in the morning. Sir Gerald isn't a well man and you won't be seeing him again today. He isn't used to being spoken back to," he added wryly.

"I'm sorry, but he can't trample my feelings just because I'm not an Anders."

Adam held up both hands in mock surrender and gave a lopsided grin.

"Alright – alright. I give in. Strictly off the record you did have provocation but he isn't always like that – in fact he is usually very caring. Unfortunately you hit a nerve."

"Well he hit a few himself," she said indignantly, lowering her voice as she saw Lorna waiting for them at the foot of the stairs.

"Look after them, Lorna. I will be back in the morning." He touched Fran's shoulder by way of goodbye and she watched unhappily as he left, suddenly feeling dreadfully alone, only remembering how awful he must be feeling when she saw how badly he was walking.

The children were already in their room and greeted Fran excitedly, showing her the view of the sea from their window. It was much larger than anything they had been used to, but to Fran's relief the housekeeper pointed out that it adjoined Fran's own room by way of a connecting bathroom. The thought of wandering about the winding landing when Sam cried out in the night was nothing if not daunting. At the door, the housekeeper paused.

"Dinner is at seven o'clock, Ma'am. The beach isn't far if you need a walk after the long journey and I daresay you could do with a cup of tea?"

She smiled and Fran thanked her, grateful for the kindness after the dreadful greeting from her host.

"I'll send Maisie up with a tray straight away. Oh, and if you do go for a walk, don't venture round the headland, the tide comes in very fast and can cut you off," she warned as Sam and Tim gave delighted squeals.

Having refreshed herself with the tea and homemade scones, some of which the twins had already sampled in the kitchen, they left the house by way of a rear door and descended a shallow flight of steps onto a sandy track, which led down to the beach. Sam dashed ahead with her make believe spaniel, but Tim clutched her hand.

"Something bothering you, Tim?" she asked gently. "I know it is all strange but there is nothing for you to worry about."

"Who is the old man, sitting in the chair with wheels on?" Tim blurted out.

Fran hesitated before deciding the truth was the only way. "It would seem he is your great grandfather."

"Are we going to stay here then?" he asked solemnly, looking up at her with wide, brown eyes, so much like Darren's it hurt.

"Would you like to? You don't have to unless you want to."

Tim looked thoughtful. "I might. Miss Pennington said she would show us the big rocking horse if we have time. Will we have time?"

Fran smiled in spite of the ache in her throat. "I'm sure you will," she assured him, as he scampered off to tell Sam.

Seated on a rock, alone with her thoughts, she looked out over a perfectly calm sea and turned the day's events over in her mind. That dreadful old man who assumed his word was law and left her in no doubt as to how unwelcome she was. A lump rose in her throat as she pictured the man she had accepted as her father since childhood and asked herself the inevitable question. If he wasn't her father – then who was?

The next morning they had breakfast alone and then Fran went to wait on the broad, stone terrace with its view of the sea, a sea that had changed its mood overnight to restless; a mood she thought more in keeping with her own. Lorna had taken the twins to see the rocking horse, which was apparently in the nursery at the top of the house. She thought about London and the flat and compared it with the freedom they were experiencing here. Was she right to deny them all of this? But how could she part with all she had left of Darren? She looked up; Adam was standing in the doorway regarding her questioningly, and she had to remind herself he had coerced her in to this situation, as her heart somersaulted.

She was wearing the one smart dress she had packed; the occasion seemed to call for it, and remembering it was Mike's favourite gave her confidence. The cool green linen complimented her and the button-through, straight skirt suited her slim figure. She had tied her hair back and only an escaping lock stopped it from being severe. Entering the study, ready to do battle again, she was disconcerted by Adam's first words.

"Sir Gerald regrets you are upset. You obviously care a great deal and he suggests you consider very carefully before *attempting* to deny the children their rightful advantages, which as *his* family they are entitled to. If on the other hand

283

you agree to them staying, Sir Gerald will adopt them legally, you will receive fifty thousand pounds immediately and be free to lead your own life."

He pointed to a paper on the desk in front of her and held out a pen.

"All you have to do is sign this paper saying you will not, at any time, try to claim them."

During Adam's speech, Gerald had remained looking out of the window with his back to them and now – as pre-arranged – he pulled the bell rope and George ushered the children in. He turned and greeted them, holding out a hand to each one; they went shyly and stood either side of his chair. Fran felt a stab of jealousy that he, who held her in such disdain, could win their confidence so quickly, but right now the only look he gave her was questioning.

Seeing her resentment, Adam intervened again saying gently, "You have already had to face how confined your lives will be, and their care when you are working."

Fran realised he was referring to the conversation he had taped and shot him a reproachful look. She had been tricked. He understood her thoughts and returned the look with a straight gaze, which denied any complicity on his part. She sought desperately for a reason to justify taking the twins home with her, but knew everything he said was true. Stern faced, Gerald waited for her answer. It had been Adam's suggestion to appeal to Fran, but he was even prepared to risk publicity.

Sam started to fidget and he told them they could play just outside until he had finished talking to their aunt. Fran saw his determined expression; and realising it was only a matter of time before he got his own way, she said, "I would be prepared to move to the area, so the children could be near you."

Gerald gave an impatient tut. "It is not my intention, young woman, to be a doting grandfather with treats now and then. I can give them a lifestyle befitting their inheritance."

She stared at him, her mind grasping at last why such an issue was being made of this whole affair; why had he not just come out with it? And why had he waited so long to look for them, if it was that important?

Gerald had the grace to flush as she put the question to him and explained haughtily, "I wasn't aware of my son's death until a few months ago and I was unaware of the children's existence until yesterday."

Fran felt a moment of pity, which was instantly dispelled by his next words.

"My other son is terminally ill and will not be able to succeed me."

"It would appear you are a victim of your own pride," Fran couldn't help pointing out. "But tell me, would you have traced my father's family otherwise?"

Adam's eyes closed in dismay, as he allowed, "Touché."

Gerald glared at her, resenting her frankness. "Yes I would, but my reasons need not concern *you*," he stormed, and in that moment he considered her to be the most infuriating woman he had ever met, forgetting that Pamela had frequently had the same effect.

"I disagree," Fran retorted. "My father obviously went to a lot of trouble to distance himself from his family and I'm beginning to understand *his* reasons. This obsession you have apparently takes priority."

She ended her tirade, speaking to the back of his chair; he had no answers to her undeniable accusations.

She turned to Adam, standing silently by and held out her hand.

"You can keep your money. The children are not for sale. The price is that I can see them regularly."

"I'm sure that will be honoured. Yes, sir?"

Gerald gave a short, "Yes" and remained looking out of the window.

She signed the paper and left with Adam. Charles emerged from the adjoining room, where Gerald had asked him to witness everything that took place.

"A very spirited young lady." He stopped himself from commenting on her extraordinary likeness to Pamela – even to the lock of hair that strayed.

"She is obviously telling the truth. She turned down the money and only asks to stay in contact with the only family she has now. I would say she is standing up pretty well to the rigorous time you are giving her."

Adam had told him the whole story and Charles felt a deep compassion for the girl – being alone was something he knew all about.

Gerald grunted. He had also noticed the lock of hair, whilst catching the sharp edge of her tongue.

*

Adam kicked sand from the toe of his well-polished shoe and replied earnestly to Fran's reproach.

"I promise you I knew nothing of the children's relationship to Sir Gerald – I was as surprised as you, when he said Tim was an Anders."

"Why did you tape our conversation?"

"Purely for my own notes; it was remiss of me and I should have asked your permission but I'm sure you found it easier to talk, not knowing."

"Oh I did that alright," she answered embarrassed.

"No one else was supposed to hear it – not even Sir Gerald. All I was supposed to do was ascertain Darren Anderson's address and ask him to contact Mr Hughes, then I learnt he had been killed and you were trying to cope on your own and I actually thought I might get you some help." He shrugged. "You know the rest."

"What have you done with the tape?" Fran asked suspiciously, remembering with embarrassment how she had confided all of her thoughts to him, including how devastated she felt about Mike's lack of response.

It was Adam's turn to look embarrassed. "I'm afraid it was stolen on the night I was attacked, along with my briefcase. That is what precipitated the invitation. We thought you might all be in some danger."

Fran looked at him blankly. "This is all so incredibly unbelievable."

"Please trust me. I really thought nothing but good could come from your visit, and to a point I was right. It has to be better for the children to have security and for you to have peace of mind. I'm sure you made the right decision."

Fran snorted. "You see it as *my* decision? I was coerced – as well you know. That awful old man would have taken the children from me anyway – with all his wealth and power. At least this way, I shall be able to keep in touch with them – unless he goes back on his word," she said bitterly.

They both glanced to where the twins were paddling in the sea then taking her by her slim shoulders Adam turned her to face him. With one finger he tilted her chin until she was looking straight into his eyes.

"Believe it or not, Sir Gerald never goes back on his word, but I will personally make sure you see them as often as possible, even if I have to bring them to London myself," he promised in that same earnest tone.

"Thank you," Fran whispered unable to drag her eyes away from his mesmerising gaze. She felt as if she was floating, unaware of anything but Adam's hands burning her arms through the fine material of her dress. A stillness existed between them – where there was only the cry of the circling seagulls coming from a long, long way off; for a moment she was sure he was going to kiss her and she leaned ever so slightly forward, until with shattering swiftness the spell was broken by a low, melodious voice.

"Adam, darling, what are you doing here at this time of day?"

Adam's hands dropped to his sides as they both started visibly and turned. Standing back against the rocks engrossed in conversation, they had not seen the bikini clad figure jogging around the headland and approaching them from the shore. She was tall and statuesque with long dark hair that hung straight to her tiny waist and with big, dark sloe shaped eyes and a deeply tanned skin she could have been mistaken for an Italian, although her English was without accent.

She made straight for Adam, her luminous gaze never leaving him to even flicker in Fran's direction. Only as she drew near did her expression change, registering surprised dismay at the sight of his bruised face.

"Darling, what have you done to yourself?" she gushed allowing her cheek to brush his undamaged one while lightly kissing the air.

"It's nothing." Adam seemed impatient and sounded reluctant as he introduced them.

"This is Tamara, Sir Gerald's stepdaughter," he managed to say before Tamara interrupted him.

"And, your fiancée, darling," she pouted prettily. "Don't forget that," she teased, linking her arm through his.

He disentangled his arm. "It is of no consequence to Miss Anderson."

"Why?" she demanded childlike.

"I am here on business, Tamara."

"Doesn't look like it," she pouted, turning away abruptly. Wearing an unreadable expression he watched her go.

"I must go. I'll be back tomorrow at the same time, and don't worry." He smiled adding sternly, "And that's an order."

She gave a wan smile, trying to deny, as she returned his backward wave, that her renewed feeling of dejection had anything to do with him being engaged to the lovely Tamara. Then, strolling towards the children still playing at the water's edge, she glanced along the beach to where the lissom, suntanned figure was jogging back along the sands and almost as if she felt herself being watched, Tamara stopped and turned. Even from that distance, Fran could sense the animosity in her body language as they exchanged stares, before Tamara turned away again.

Curiosity, made her follow the girl's progress, wondering where she was heading for; at first glance there appeared to be no other way out of the neighbouring cove, but as she watched, the girl vanished from sight to appear again a minute or two later, higher up the sheer cliff face. By shading her eyes Fran could just make out a flight of roughly hewn steps leading to the top and allowing her gaze to travel on up she saw chimneys etched against the clear, blue sky. Was that where she and Adam spent time together? She had a sudden, terrible longing to see Mike – dear comfortable Mike who didn't make her restless and unsure. If only it hadn't been Adam she had poured out her troubles to in that moment of loneliness, but he had been so easy to talk to and now it was all on tape and heaven knows where that was. She tried to recall her exact words, mortified at the thought of a stranger listening to what must sound like a woeful little tale of martyrdom. How could she have been so indiscreet? She should have known better than to put herself at such a disadvantage. And now, Adam, the only one within several hundred miles she could turn to for advice, owed first loyalty to his client – so where did that leave her?

As they returned to the house for lunch she was aware of Gerald Anders watching from one of the upstairs windows. He drew back as she glanced up. Seething inwardly she lifted her chin, calling to the children to hurry.

The hallway was dim after the glare of the sun and at first she didn't see George who was hovering waiting to give her a message.

"Afternoon tea is at four o'clock in the sittin' room Miss Anderson. Sir Gerald is expectin' you and the children."

She bridled. "Thank you—er?"

"Just George, Miss."

"Well, Just George, you may tell his Lordship I have other plans but I will ask the children if they would care to and let you know."

George raised his eyebrows, taken-a-back by her spirited reply and checked an impulse to smile as he saw her satisfied expression.

"Very well, Miss."

Fran felt better. It was a petty triumph but at least the servants needn't think she was at their Lord and Master's beck and call – why couldn't he simply ask, why was it always an order?

On his return to the kitchen, Lorna noted George's pre-occupied amusement.

"Anything the matter?" she asked.

"Well at the risk of understatement, the young lady would appear to be an unwillin' guest."

He related what had happened, with a mixture of admiration and disapproval.

Lorna pursed her lips. The arrival of the unusual house guests and the frequent visits of the solicitor, plus Gerald's suppressed excitement and moodiness, and now Fran's obvious reluctance to stay, had given rise to a lot of speculation on her part. Out of loyalty to Gerald, she had refrained from gossiping; now she couldn't help imparting some of her knowledge of the family history.

"So if my guess is right, he will keep that boy here – come hell or high water," she said, enjoying George's reaction.

"Stone the flippin' crows," he exploded gently, giving a long drawn out whistle.

"You mark my words," she emphasised with a knowing nod. "That boy is here to stay, if he is who I think he is – with or without his aunt's approval."

George recalled snippets of conversation he had overheard and put two and two together. "I reckon yer could be right yer know," he said thoughtfully. "And that will be what the young lady isn't 'appy about, but have you thought who else won't be too 'appy either?"

Lorna nodded knowingly. "You're on about her Ladyship," she said with a satisfied grimace.

"Sir Gerald is gonna need a lot of support," George predicted. "That was a nasty upset 'e 'ad yesterday, and today don't promise to be much better by all accounts," he said recalling the raised voices in the study that morning.

A sound made them turn to see Bob Johnson standing in the doorway of the partly opened kitchen door, and they exchanged looks wondering how long he had been there, but he showed no sign of having overheard their remarks, as rubbing his hands together he enquired cheerfully if lunch was ready.

Once a week, Bob had lunch with Gerald to discuss the day to day running of the stables. Under his supervision the stud farm had prospered. For Gerald it was an absorbing interest but to Bob it was his life. He worshipped the magnificent creatures in his care and nursed a burning ambition to own such a stable himself one day.

Now as he waited in his good clothes, George was reminded and apologised for not telling him of the change.

"Sir Gerald regrets he is unable to 'ave lunch with you today. 'e 'as 'ouse guests."

Lorna started to dish a plateful of cold ham and new potatoes. "Sit down and eat, Bob."

He sat down and helped himself to salad and pickles.

"Thought I heard unfamiliar voices around. Children aren't they? I expect they would like to see the new foal that was born last week; he's a right little cracker!"

He started to eat with relish, apparently oblivious to their exchanged glances.

"How long are they staying? Will he be free for the county fair?"

"'e won't wanna miss that," George said.

*

Marcia replaced the handset on the ornate Victorian telephone beside her bed and threw back the lace duvet cover. What could be so urgent at six o'clock, she wondered, looking at the small, gold carriage clock? She hurried into the cream and gold adjoining bathroom, showered quickly before wrapping herself in a large, fluffy towel and returned to select cream jodhpurs and matching silk blouse from behind the mirrored doors of the fitted closet filling one wall of the sumptuous dusky pink and cream lace bedroom – the delicate furnishings from her bedroom at Anders Folly, and if anything, she considered they looked even better in the cottage.

Within twenty minutes, she was driving into the stable yard. Bob touched his cap and picked up a bale of hay, following her to where Starlight was stabled. They embraced briefly, mindful of discovery. They had begun an affair two years ago and knew even a breath of scandal would mean instant dismissal for him and severe cut backs for her; therefore they were very discreet, until such time, they promised each other, she was free to be with him, with the unspoken promise it would be in Anders Folly. In the meantime they made opportunities to ride together and whenever possible Bob would visit her in the evenings, confident that discovery at the isolated cottage was unlikely.

Tamara was the biggest danger, but Marcia encouraged her to spend as much time out as she could.

She was free to do pretty much as she pleased but if Gerald got wind it was with one of his trusted staff – that would be a *very* different matter. In the beginning it had lent added excitement to luring him into her bed and she had pursued him relentlessly, jealous of his comradeship with Gerald – but it quickly became much more as she had become obsessed. Even as they stood together talking, she could feel her desire mounting, but Bob's thoughts were elsewhere.

"Something is going on at the house, and from what I overheard it's to do with an Anders heir. Sir Gerald *was* pretty pre-occupied when I spoke to him briefly last evening and I saw two children on the stairs. I tried to ring you, but Tamara answered and I put the phone down."

Marcia frowned as Bob said, "What do you make of it?"

"I don't know," she answered slowly, her mind fully concentrated now. "But I will soon find out. Now I'm here I had better take a ride, then drop in casually afterwards."

An hour later she strolled into the dining room, which at this time in the morning was always set for breakfast, even when Gerald was alone. Her timing was good. He was alone, seated in his usual place and as she dropped a light kiss on his forehead she said brightly, "Good morning, how are you this morning?" Then without waiting for a reply, "I've been for a ride – heavenly morning! Thought I would just drop in and see how you are, don't mind if I join you for breakfast, do you?" she asked casually, noting three extra place settings.

"Please do, I will get Lorna to set another place," Gerald said, affably waving her to a chair.

"Sure I'm not intruding?" she asked as if seeing the table for the first time. "It looks as if you are expecting company. That's not like you, darling."

She laughed lightly and he ignored the jibe, not fooled for a moment by her spur of the moment visit. She hadn't 'dropped in' for months. Veiling his eyes he studied her as she helped herself from the well-laden sideboard, wondering if she could possibly have had anything to do with the attack on Adam and dismissed the idea immediately.

I'm glad you called in, there are things I need to discuss."

"Oh yes?" Marcia paused in the act of removing a lid from one of the silver dishes.

"After breakfast when the company has gone," he said hearing voices on the stairs.

"Hungry company by the look of things – anyone I know?" she asked, hiding her impatience with difficulty.

"You are about to meet them by the sound of things," Gerald answered almost gaily as running feet were heard crossing the hall, pre-announcing the twins who rushed in and ran to him, as Fran's voice warned, "Gently now."

There was no doubting the genuine pleasure in his eyes as he greeted them and in spite herself, Fran was thinking it would be nice to be part of a family again.

After the introductions, Marcia's silence went unnoticed in the excitement of the visit to see the new foal after breakfast, and they ate so quickly, Fran had to check them several times while Gerald looked on indulgently.

"Can we get down now?" they choroused looking at Fran even before the last mouthful had disappeared.

"If it's alright with your grandfather."

He nodded appreciation and said, "Run along then."

Excusing herself Fran followed them, glad to get away from Marcia's sharp scrutiny; as she left she heard her say, "I didn't know you had grandchildren let alone great grandchildren. How long are they staying?"

There was an edge to her voice and he looked at her sharply.

"That is what I need to talk to you about. They will be living here permanently, which will mean changes – but," he added quickly as he saw her face harden, "your life will not change." She relaxed slightly until Gerald said with great emphasis, "*They* are my heirs, now Alexander is ill. You of course will be well provided for and the cottage will be yours for your lifetime. However," he paused. "If any harm should befall them, my entire estate will go to my children's homes. I also wish you to sign a statement swearing you will not contest the will or create any undue publicity for my family."

Marcia made a derisive sound. "You must think I'm simple. Why would I sign such an agreement?"

"Because you recognise a good offer when you hear one, but if it doesn't satisfy you then by all means see a solicitor and we will commence divorce proceedings; I understand the law won't raise any objections, because we have, after all, been living apart for a good many years. Yes, I'm even prepared for that now, if you force me to," he said, as she looked startled. "In fact I will do anything I have to – to ensure the children's safety."

Marcia could have wept. Her dreams of inheriting everything crashed around her, as all hope of sharing her life with Bob disappeared.

"It just isn't fair," she accused him.

"I was hoping we could settle this amicably, as we have done our other differences in the past. You can't say I haven't been *more* than fair, and you still won't want for *anything.*"

"But I am your wife; it's insulting to pension me off like some servant."

Gerald's look spoke volumes and she coloured furiously.

"Think carefully before refusing and let me know within the week," Gerald warned, manoeuvring his chair to the door.

Marcia watched him go, her pulses racing with anger, then with a set look she stormed out of the house, climbed into her car and drove off, leaving Bob to wonder as she scuffed the drive, sending gravel flying in all directions.

CHAPTER TWENTY-SIX

"Do you ride?" Adam asked, joining Fran as she stood with her arms resting on the paddock fence, watching the children with the foal.

"At one time, but not since my parents died."

She looked up at him and her heart leapt in the way it had a habit of doing.

"I'm sure Sir Gerald wouldn't mind. Shall I ask?" he offered, wanting to bring a smile to her face.

Fran shook her head. "I won't be here long; thanks all the same."

"Do you wish you *were* staying?"

She shot him a reproachful look. "I feel about as welcome as snow in June."

"Could you stand the slow pace of life, after London? Or would you yearn for the bright lights?" Adam persisted, almost as if the answers mattered, she thought irritably.

"What difference does it make, how or what *I* feel? I'm absolutely 'de trop'." She turned impatiently and started walking quickly back to the house; he caught up and fell into step.

"I really came out to say Sir Gerald has asked me to open up accounts for you to buy whatever the children need in the way of clothes. He also suggested you should come with me to choose suitable shops. If you are free we could go this afternoon."

"I must look in my diary," Fran said dryly, then regretting her churlishness added, "that would seem very sensible – and thank you, I would enjoy looking around."

"I'll treat you to a Cornish cream tea afterwards – a treat not to be missed I promise you – if you don't mind being seen with someone who looks like a prizefighter, that is," he teased.

"As long as no one thinks I did it," Fran rejoined, walking on as he stopped at his car.

"I'll pick you up at two o'clock," he called cheerily.

After opening the accounts and purchasing essentials like swimming costumes, shorts, sandshoes and extra underwear, she chose three pretty dresses for Sam and smart trousers and shirts for Tim, because they had nothing suitable to wear for dinner in the evening, which their grandfather expected them to attend.

Adam carried the parcels back to the car and then insisted on taking her to one of the numerous quaint little tearooms lining the narrow, cobbled streets. The cream tea was delicious, as he had assured her it would be, and flatteringly he was still reluctant to end their afternoon together.

It had seemed the most natural thing in the world when he had taken her hand in his to guide her through the steep, winding streets, pointing out interesting pieces of local colour, and leaning on the harbour wall with his hand resting on her waist as they watched the activity where he pointed to a squirming mass of freshly caught lobsters, in a big, round basket on the deck of a boat drawn up to the quayside below. Time seemed to stand still and Fran gave herself up to imagining how life must have been centuries ago. He laughed at her fantasies.

"I can see you would believe every Cornish tale and superstition ever quoted," he mocked gently, his eyes smiling down into hers, making her feel quite breathless. The air had brought a rose-coloured flush to her creamy cheeks and made her green eyes dance. His arm pulled her closer as he teased her and she reminded herself hazily that he was engaged.

When at last they were driving home, he said quietly, "Nothing to stop you from going ahead with your wedding plans now I suppose?"

His words brought her sharply back to earth and she answered almost vaguely, "No, I suppose not."

"Will you?" He shot the words at her.

Flustered, she replied shrilly, "I don't know, I don't know what I will do now I have given up the twins, and anyway I can't answer for Mike."

Adam frowned deeply but made no comment, then after a small silence, Fran asked tentatively, "What about you and Tamara, when do you plan on getting married?"

"That is something I intend to settle at the earliest possible moment," he answered in a determined voice. "Our *engagement* has gone on long enough."

They pulled into the drive and there was no time for further talk as he retrieved the parcels from the car boot, before saying goodbye almost impatiently. She went into the house, feeling suddenly and unaccountably depressed after the wonderful afternoon. George was in the hall and she enquired where the children were.

"They went off to the beach with Miss Tamara – some while ago now, Miss."

She glanced at her wristwatch; it was five-thirty – just time to walk down and spend a few minutes with them before getting changed for dinner. On reaching the beach there was no sign of them or Tamara and she retraced her steps to the house. George suggested that Tamara could have taken them to her house.

"It's only a few minutes walk along the cliff top path, Miss. Would you like me to fetch them?"

Fran declined his kind offer and fifteen minutes later, after climbing the steep track she walked up the neat garden path and found the front door open. She rang the doorbell, looking back over her shoulder as a car pulled into the driveway. It was Adam, and he gave a surprised 'hello' as he got out of the car.

"I've come to collect the children; George says they are with Tamara," Fran explained coolly.

Adam gave a puzzled frown. "You'd better come in," he said walking through the open door and into a sitting room. "Tamara, Fran is under the impression the children are with you. Are they?"

Tamara rose unsteadily and slunk forward, clad in a scanty black bikini and balancing a partially filled glass in one hand; she put the other possessively through Adam's arm and stared at Fran.

Adam was watching her with a look of fear, before demanding urgently, "Tamara where are the children?"

"They are here aren't they?" Fran asked, alarmed by his manner.

"I sent them home ages ago," Tamara reeled and gave Adam a blank stare, as he demanded sharply, "Which way did they go? Which way did they go?" he shouted gripping her by the arms and shaking her.

"She wrenched herself away and fell into a chair, spilling the remains of her drink down her as Adam bounded out of the house and raced for the cliff steps. Fran followed; he was already out of sight, racing down the uneven steps. One frenzied look told her the water was over the lower rocks as with trembling legs she stumbled after him dreading what she might see. He suddenly appeared, carrying a small, drenched figure.

"Sam," the name came weakly from Fran's lips.

"Take her," he ordered and was gone.

Sam clung, sobbing and shivering as Fran struggled back up to the cliff top with her just as Adam appeared again, carrying Tim.

"Into the car," he rapped.

Back at the house, pandemonium broke out as the children were quickly stripped of their sodden clothes and tucked up in bed with hot water bottles and warm drinks.

The doctor came and Gerald ranted and raved until, so distressed, he had to retire to his room. When the fuss had eventually died down, the doctor joined them in the sitting room where George had served a tray of tea.

"That was a close thing. What were they doing in *that* cove at this time of day? Everyone knows it's a death trap."

Looking grey and shaken, Adam said he assumed the heavy latch on the iron gate must have snapped shut behind them and the children weren't strong or tall enough to lift it up again.

"How they managed to climb on that rocky shelf and hang on was nothing short of a miracle, another ten minutes…" Adam left the sentence unfinished and took a gulp of tea just as Fran's cup started to rattle in its saucer. Both men turned to see that she was shivering uncontrollably and Adam leapt up to take the cup and saucer from her, his face full of concern.

"It's reaction," the doctor said calmly, reaching for his bag. "Hardly surprising. Call Miss Pennington and we will get the young lady into bed. I will give her a sedative and she will be as right as rain in the morning."

As soon as she was settled, Adam popped his head round the door. "Can I come in?"

Fran smiled sleepily. "Of course! Sorry to create another flap. Are you all right?"

He nodded and advanced towards the bed self-consciously.

"Just had to make sure *you* were, before I pop off home." He bent swiftly, kissed her lightly on the forehead and was gone before she had time to recover. She touched the spot where he had kissed her and her lips parted in a slow smile as she drifted off to sleep.

*

Fran opened her eyes to see Maisie, peering closely.

"'Scuse me, Miss, Sir Gerald sent me to see if you was awake."

"Thank you. What's the time?"

"It be twelve o'clock, Miss."

Fran's eyes flew open. "Twelve?"

"You're not to worrit, Miss. The children are right as rain this mornin'. I'll get a nice cuppa tea for ye." As she spoke she was drawing the curtains. "Such goin's on theres bin and no mistake." She was agog with news. "Sir Gerald sent for Miss Tamara – right dressin' down she 'ad I can tell ye; then there was Aunt Lorna, she 'ad no right to let them children go anywhere without 'is permission, Sir Gerald says. Then Aunt Lorna says that Miss Tamara said they got 'is permission, but 'e says 'e knew nothing about it. Aunt Lorna don't offen cry – and that's the truth. Up come of it all is that Miss Tamara is to 'ave nowt to do with litluns ever." Maisie's eyes were as big as saucers as she finished her garbled story but Fran got the gist of it and quickly swung her legs over the side of the bed.

"Don't bother with the tea; I had better get downstairs by the sound of things."

Sir Gerald said you wasn't to be disturbed Miss – doctors orders like – but 'e sent me up a dozen times or more t' see if you was awake."

Impatient to get dressed, Fran ushered her to the door, wondering what kind of reception she was likely to get from the irate master of the house. All was quiet as squaring her shoulders, she knocked and waited for his 'come in' then entered the study and faced him boldly.

"You wished to see me." It was a statement more than a question.

"I just wanted to say that until a suitable nanny is found, would you not let the children out of your sight. Nothing like yesterday must ever be allowed to happen again." He looked haggard, toying with a pencil.

Fran flushed and retaliated. "If you are inferring I am in any way to blame, it is another instance of how bigoted you are towards me and you would do well to remember I left the children at your request and – as I thought – safe for the afternoon. *I* can't believe it was allowed to happen."

Gerald held up his hand. "Yes, yes I know you are not responsible in any way, and I know they are safer with you than anybody. My staff are all excellent at their jobs, but not used to being in charge of small children and I should have realised that."

To Fran's surprise he gave a repentant smile and held out his hand. "Can you forgive me? I have been wrong about you."

The unexpected kindness brought tears; she took his hand.

"Sit down," he said kindly. "I can't talk to you standing up. Confounded wheelchair!"

"What happened? When?" Fran asked blinking back the tears.

He talked about his accident for a while with Fran perching on a low, tapestry-covered stool beside his chair, and then, "And what about you? Adam tells me you gave up wedding plans to look after the children."

Her face crumpled and she could only nod.

"The children could have been fostered – or adopted," he suggested, watching her closely and giving a satisfied smile as she shook her head fiercely, long needed tears streaming unchecked down her face. He gave her a moment to compose herself and then asked, "Do you still want to go ahead with your plans, now the children are safely taken care of?"

"I don't know what I want anymore. I know I want to see him again but I'm confused and I need time to think. Suddenly I'm not sure of anything because I don't know who I am any more. I have no identity."

He looked into her tear-stained face, nodding slowly. "I understand. So instead of returning to London and unhappy memories, why don't you stay here and sort your thoughts out?"

She looked at him questioningly, just as George entered to announce lunch was ready.

"Take as long as you need and be sure the decision is the right one for *you*."

297

For the first time since her arrival she felt comfortable, in the knowledge that she was not totally unwelcome.

Disappointingly she saw nothing of Adam for the next three days, but Gerald had taken to inviting her into his study, after dinner, and she found herself looking forward to their chats. At first he avoided talking about her past but gradually got round to asking where they had lived.

"We lived in the centre of Oxford. My parents owned a huge bookshop and we lived in the flat above. It was very successful; Dad had an affinity with books. He became a regular supplier to the universities, colleges and schools, and also lectured at the university. I was sixteen when mother and dad were killed in a car accident in Switzerland; it was the first holiday they had ever taken without us."

She saw his expression fall but sensed he didn't want her to stop.

"The shop had to be sold. Darren went to boarding school and I went to live with an old friend of my mothers – my godmother in fact. She was very elderly and has since died, but she was a lovely lady and very kind to us. Darren went straight to Officer Training College, and was only nineteen when he married Zara. The twins were born a year later. He was—" Her voice broke – "He was only twenty-four at the beginning of the year and the twins will be four, in two months' time. I suppose if mother and dad had lived I would have run the bookshop. Darren only ever wanted to become a pilot – and he did," she said proudly.

By the time she had filled in the missing years, Gerald was actually smiling reminiscently.

"Robert always said he wanted to be a bookseller, from the time he was a small boy – it drove me mad. I remember…"

A knock at the door interrupted him and Adam entered. Her heart gave a happy lurch and she waited while he greeted Gerald and handed him a bulky, brown envelope, for him to greet her. When he did he was off-handed and her smile froze as she wondered what could have changed so, since he kissed her on the forehead.

"Sit down, m' boy. I'll ring for some more coffee. Francesca and I were just reminiscing."

She warmed to Gerald's use of her full name and smiled but there was no answering smile from Adam, instead, "Don't let me disturb you; I can come back in the morning."

She rose, glad of the excuse to escape. "I have got things to do anyway. Goodnight." She kissed Gerald's cheek and nodded to Adam.

As the door closed behind her the conversation became serious. Gerald opened the envelope. "Any problems?"

298

"They were not happy about handing it over at first, but your letter convinced them."

Gerald drew out the stiffly folded papers, while Adam sat quietly, watching him read his eldest son's will, wondering if it was just curiosity or if there was a deeper reason for his latest assignment. His thoughts were soon answered.

"There is no reference to Francesca being his *step*daughter, or her *real* father, as I hoped there might be. Robert left her a half share of everything. It isn't a fortune, but it does mean she isn't entirely dependant on her salary."

Adam shifted restlessly; he wasn't comfortable with prying into Fran's affairs again, and he wanted to get home. He had been away three days – two of which were spent travelling – first to Oxford, for the will and then London; added to which, the reason for his errand to London had irritated him beyond endurance. He referred to it now.

"There was the other matter, sir. I called on the newspaper, as you instructed, gave them a general idea of the situation and left your address and telephone number. The ball is in his court now."

Listening to the inflection in his voice Gerald sensed disapproval. "You think I was wrong to interfere, but anything must be preferable to this state of limbo she is living in; better to *know* surely if he doesn't want her?"

"Oh he will want her, now it can be on his terms. I just don't think he deserves her, running off like that when things got tough. Goodnight, sir. I will see myself out."

As he approached his car, Fran stepped forward from the shadows and sounding uncertain said, "I wanted to speak to you."

He walked slowly towards her and when they were face to face he asked stiffly, "What's the matter?"

"That's what I wanted to ask you," she said softly.

"I just want to get home. It has been a long three days." His tone was dispirited, almost accusing. "This was purely a call to confirm I had carried out my instructions, to relieve me from having to call tomorrow."

Bewildered by his curtness, she stepped back and started to move away.

"I'm sorry I didn't understand."

Adam caught her arm. "It's very simple. Your fiancé will come running soon – that's what you told Sir Gerald you wanted, wasn't it?"

"What makes you think Mike will come here? Puzzled, she peered up at him in the gloom trying to make out the expression on his face; they were very close and suddenly Adam caught her to him, his lips coming down hard and firm on hers. Just for a second she resisted and then she was returning his kiss with every fibre of her being and their embrace became lingering, gentle and demanding, lulling them into a state of euphoria which both were unable to resist.

At last he released her, saying unhappily, "I've wanted you since we first met, but all *you* want, is to know what *he* wants – and I'm the fool who has told him where to find you. You will be happy now."

Her senses still reeling, from the amazing emotion his kiss had stirred in her, she couldn't speak, and taking her silence as confirmation he turned away. Thoughts in turmoil she watched as he got into his car and drove away leaving her asking herself: *Is that what I want any more?*

CHAPTER TWENTY-SEVEN

Tamara glared angrily at Marcia. "Surely you aren't going to just take things lying down, are you?"

"If I don't sign the paper I could end up with a great deal less; plus a lot of aggro and unpleasantness. It would be foolish to make a court case of this."

Marcia paced the room clasping and unclasping her hands. It was six days since her talk with Gerald. She had gone straight to a solicitor, who advised her, with no hesitation at all, to sign the paper, pointing out that as she hadn't lived in the marital home or performed any wifely duties for the past nine years, he doubted if any court would award her more. There were also other benefits. *Tamara's* generous allowance for instance, which Gerald wasn't legally obliged to provide, and the feeding, stabling, blacksmiths and vet bills of their two horses. All of these things would be taken into account if she took it to court.

At first she had considered seeking the advice of another solicitor, but on reflection had reluctantly come to the conclusion it would be better to sign and get it over with. Bob would be wondering why she hadn't contacted him since their meeting in the stables and why her answering service had been on permanently. She couldn't pluck up courage to tell him that the stables and thoroughbred stock he adored would never be hers after all, because she was certain she would lose him.

Unaware of her mother's thoughts, Tamara ranted on. "And what about me? Where do I come in your great scheme of things?"

"I'm sure you will get something," she answered absently.

"Something?" Tamara screamed. "I expected the lot. Not just the pitiful allowance I get now. Why else do you think I stay in this godforsaken hole?"

Marcia stared, having always assumed that providing her luxurious lifestyle was maintained her daughter would give little thought as to *how* it was. She had certainly shown no inclination to put her expensive education to good use, and had accepted everything without a hint of gratitude.

"Your pitiful allowance, as you so lightly call it, is treble what I got for working forty hours a week," she said peevishly.

"More fool you," Tamara snapped sulkily.

Marcia's eyes flashed furiously. "Fool or not, it led to a pretty nice lifestyle for you young lady, and don't you forget it. See if you can catch *yourself* a rich old husband before you call me a fool."

"You should never have moved out of the house. You would be in a really strong position now if you hadn't," Tamara accused.

301

"It's all very well for you to talk. You weren't the one incarcerated with an invalid," Marcia flung back. "The only chance I had was when Alexander got ill, and that changed when he found his grandchildren," she ended miserably, her anger turning to despair.

"Gerald would never have gone looking for the brats, and Alexander would have inherited everything and I would have been the lady of the house. It's just not fair. Why did he have to go and get sick *before* Gerald died?" Tamara wailed childishly.

Marcia looked at her beautiful, spoilt daughter suspiciously. "I didn't know you were on such good terms with Alexander."

She stopped wailing and flushed. "He likes me – that's all."

Marcia stopped pacing, a look of horror dawning. "Is that all?" she asked quietly.

She returned her mother's stare; angry tears welling. "Yes, of course."

Ashen-faced Marcia asked faintly, "Are you telling me the truth?"

"What is it, Mother? Why are you looking like that? We were partners, and he said you would spoil everything, if you knew, and that his father couldn't last much longer and then we could do as we liked, but then he got so ill and now he doesn't even recognise me sometimes. I really love him, Mother. He is the only person who has ever understood me," she sobbed.

"You don't know what you are saying," Marcia shrieked.

The sobbing ceased abruptly as her distraught mother shrieked louder.

"He's cruel, wicked. He deserves every bit of pain and unhappiness he's got." She was beside herself with fear and rage.

"What do you mean?" Tamara pleaded. "Alexander loved life – and for that, and trying to give everybody a good time, he was labelled corrupt, in stuffy circles – but you had a taste of that yourself; look how Gerald objected to *your* friends."

Drawing a deep, calming breath Marcia fought the desire to blurt out the truth. Instead, she asked scathingly, "Don't you realise how old he is?"

Tamara gave an indifferent shrug. "What has age got to do with anything?"

"You can't honestly be in love with him?"

"Don't be ridiculous, Mother. That *isn't* what I said. You must know he is gay."

Marcia stared in disbelief. That couldn't be.

"You must be mistaken – it's not possible. Are you sure?" She ended weakly, forced to accept the truth in Tamara's eyes.

"Well it isn't something you shout from the roof tops, but you do know what he is dying from – don't you?"

Marcia shrugged. "I wasn't interested and Gerald has kept it all very hush-hush. I had no idea you kept company with that crowd though. I would never have allowed it. I thought the sailing club was your scene."

Tamara sniggered. "That is what you were supposed to think."

Too late she realised she hadn't asked questions when Tamara stayed out all night, because it meant Bob could stay. She ignored the comment and said, in a more gentle tone, "Adam is far more suitable."

Tamara gave a derisive laugh. "How long do you think that will last? He is no more in love with me than I am with him. He has tried to break it off twice, but I'm not ready yet. Poor fool doesn't realise I tricked him into believing he proposed, when they spiked his drinks for a laugh. He didn't remember a thing and I needed someone. I had found out that day that Alexander was really ill." Her eyes closed in pain.

Marcia listened feeling more and more perplexed. She had set her heart on Tamara marrying Adam.

"If you have any sense at all, you will stop this nonsense and marry Adam as soon as possible."

She gave her mother a despairing look and sighed. "Mother, you haven't been listening. I don't *want* to marry Adam, and he doesn't *want* to marry me. I could never settle down to his pipe and slippers life and he isn't capable of giving me the life I want. Alexander was excitement. Every weekend was party time." Her eyes lit up then faded again. "Now the yacht is lifeless and we sit there on our own, with only Fabian for company."

"If only you had told me all this before."

"You were always too busy," Tamara answered in a brittle voice, "with your weekend house parties and trips to London; I was in the way when I left boarding school. That was when he was there for me. I haven't got *anybody* now." Tears swamped her huge brown eyes.

"You still have me," Marcia said in a choked voice.

Tamara hesitated, not completely trusting the moment of remorse, but there was a caring look in her mother's eyes she hadn't seen for a very long time and badly needed right now. Slowly she took the outstretched hand and drew closer to her. Too late Marcia realised what a terrible lie she had allowed her only child to live all of these years and how near to disaster it had led her. Supposing Alexander hadn't got sick? She would never have known about all of this until Gerald died. Pictures flitted across her mind as a thought struck her.

"So you were on board for those notorious 'yacht set' weekends?"

Tamara gave a gleeful little laugh. "On board? I *organised* them. It was exhilarating."

Marcia felt sick, as old bitter memories surfaced. She and Alexander had first met when she was a student nurse and he had just started working in Southampton. They both roomed at Mrs O'Reilly's. She was on the top floor and he was on the first one. He had said daring things to her and taken her to good restaurants. It had been exciting to be with someone who splashed money about like he did, but she had become nervous when after only a matter of weeks he suggested coming to her room at night. She had made the excuse they would get thrown out if Mrs O'Reilly caught them, but a few days later, after working a night shift she was awoken by him creeping in to her bed. She had tried to resist but he put his hand over her mouth.

"It's alright, the old girl's out shopping. I watched her go then slipped back in and borrowed her spare key to your room."

He had given a daredevil grin, waiting for her to laugh at his daring, but she was too frightened; she had never been with a boy before. Her protests had made him impatient so he forced himself on her. She had struggled, but he was strong and filled with his own sense of power. When it was over she laid in bed crying while he got dressed, grinning down at her with amusement.

"Why are you crying? You know you led me on. You can't play with fire and not get burnt." He had heard that line in a film.

She had protested she hadn't led him on, but he left, laughing loudly. The following evening, she overheard him boasting to his colleagues about how desperate she was for him. Rumour soon got around and she had applied for a transfer to another hospital. There had certainly been no suggestion of his being gay then.

That was the last she saw of him until after she had married his father. She had kept her pregnancy from him, because, in spite of the hardship it caused her, she never wanted to see or hear from him again. If at the time, she had realised he came from such a wealthy family, it might have been a different story, but as it was, after the birth she posed as a widow and took a position as live-in housekeeper, come nursing companion to a wealthy elderly lady, who allowed her to keep the baby with her. That lasted until the old lady died. She left Marcia five thousand pounds in her will and with it she enrolled Tamara, who was six years old by then, in to a good boarding school. A year later, she married Gerald.

It was unbelievable when Alexander turned up out of the blue, and even more unbelievable, that he didn't remember her, at all. It occurred to her now, his illness was probably the only thing that had ever touched Tamara, or prevented her from having her own way. With that in mind she said, soothingly, "You will miss him but someone will take his place. You'll see."

"Nobody can ever take his place. Nobody else knows how to deal with life the way he does."

Marcia was curious. "What do you mean, dear?"

"Well *he* wouldn't let two kids stand in his way. *He* would get round it somehow," she said vehemently, thumping her knee.

"How do you think he would do that?" Marcia asked, even more curious.

"I've tried to think. If that stupid aunt hadn't come when she did…"

"As I understand it the children would have drowned," Marcia said, aghast.

"I didn't know they had gone that way. I just told them to go home; I was fed up with their whinging." Tamara shrugged. "As it was, I got it in the neck from Gerald for something that wasn't my fault."

Marcia couldn't believe what she was hearing.

"Tell me exactly what happened."

"The kids came to the stables when I was saddling Storm and wanted a ride. Bob said not without their aunt's permission. They said she had gone out with Adam, then the girl started crying, so Bob told them to go and ask their grandfather if they could have a ride. They ran off and came back saying it was all right with Granddad, so I sat them on Storm and walked along the coves with them. They wanted to see the steps, so I showed them where they were, then sent them back to the house. Then, I went to see Alexander. He was having a bad day and I wanted to give one last party to cheer him up. Fabian said I was mad and we had words. Alexander told us both to get out. I didn't mean to upset him and I felt really bad, especially when there was no one I could talk to. I came back here and opened a bottle of wine. You know the rest but Gerald wouldn't even let me explain," she ended sulkily.

Marcia gave a huge sigh of relief, her worst fear put to rest… She had arrived home to find Tamara terribly drunk and being sick in the bathroom. Then Gerald bellowed down the telephone at her, babbling something about the children could have been killed, but with her recent treatment from him still festering, she had offhandedly accused him of over-reacting to what was probably an unfortunate accident. It was then he threatened serious action if either one of them ever came near the children again. She had been so agitated, thinking about Bob and her own spoiled plans, she carelessly put it down to him being paranoid again – but what had made him suspicious in the first place?

Rocking Tamara back and forth, she asked warily, "Did Alexander tell you to do anything about the children?"

"No. He didn't know about them. He said his brother's son was the last of them." She gave a great sob. "Alex always says if you want something badly enough, go for it – don't let anything or anybody stand in your way. But I don't know what to do. He doesn't remember what I tell him anymore. He's no help at all. I found out about the kids myself, but now I don't know what to do anymore," she repeated, as Marcia grappled with the disjointed sentences.

"Perhaps I can help. Tell me how you found out about the children?"

Tamara stopped crying and sat up straight, her eyes suddenly very bright.

"Alex would have been really proud of me. I was on the terrace and I overheard Gerald talking on the phone to that Charles. He repeated the address of the grandson as he wrote it down. I found the place in London but the girl got suspicious, so I followed Adam when he was sent up to find Darren. I listened at the letterbox and later I took the tape he made. Everything was on the tape. Alex would have been so proud of me." Her eyes bright with excitement, she described how she had disguised herself. Even Adam didn't recognise me. Pity about the bruises." She grinned. "I got carried away."

Marcia was suddenly concerned about her mental state. Why hadn't she seen it before? But Tamara had always been up one minute and down the next, energetically pursuing every whim that took her fancy. In hindsight it must have been building up for some time and Alexander's illness had tipped the balance. He was to blame. Hate filled her at the thought of him and she listened numbly as Tamara babbled on.

"It all went so smoothly; he would have been proud of me." Her face fell. "Then he was too sick for me to tell him; it was so disappointing."

"Don't you think it was a very wrong thing to do?" Marcia asked, hoping for some sign of remorse.

She jumped up snapping, "Don't moralise, Mother. I knew you wouldn't understand. Alex is the only one that ever understands anything."

She sat down again and buried her face in her hands. "What am I going to do without him? My life is nothing without him," she sobbed again.

Marcia put her arm across her shaking shoulders. "Why don't we go and see Alexander? He may be having a good day and you can talk to him," she suggested, consolingly.

Tamara jumped up. "Do you really think so? I'll get ready. Do you really think so?" She was out of the door before she had finished speaking and a frenzied opening of doors and drawers followed.

*

"You are exaggerating as usual, Stepmum," Alexander sneered with slightly less confidence, as she stood facing him. She hadn't kept anything from him.

"Exaggerating, am I? Well apparently, although it would be sad if the children had drowned, *you* would have remained your Father's heir, *she* would have got everything her little heart desired, and you would have been proud of her. *Now* tell me I'm exaggerating." Marcia shouted, not caring that his eyes were wide with shock.

"You weren't there for her. That's why she turned to me," he rasped.

"And *you* taught her to live a lie, to get back at me, for marrying your father, I suspect."

"No, no. Well not for long. I really love her. It was just big talk. I didn't mean…" his voice faded at the look of disgust she gave him.

"You *really* don't remember me *at all*, do you?" She laughed horribly. "Well, the joke's on you because she is *your* daughter."

His reaction was sneering disbelief.

"Mrs O'Reilly's boarding house? *You* were eighteen, and a naïve little nurse made the mistake of falling in love with you, and you forced yourself on her."

Alexander had gone very still and she realised this was the moment she had waited a long time for. He opened his mouth but nothing came out. At last there was remorse.

On hearing raised voices, Tamara and Fabian rushed in and stopped in their tracks at his shocked expression.

"What have you done?" Tamara cried accusingly, running to kneel beside him, while Fabian wiped his sweating face with a damp towel.

Alexander clung to Tamara. "I never meant to hurt you, baby. I love you."

"I know," she soothed. "No regrets. I would sooner have had a few years with you than a lifetime with anyone else."

Marcia went to wait in the speedboat, her thoughts drifting. She also knew what it was to have loved Alexander. He would be gone soon, and she would have to get treatment for her beautiful, unstable daughter. And what about Gerald? Would he cope with this latest news, or would it be the last straw? Suddenly she knew how much she would miss him.

Fabian dropped lightly into the boat and started the engine as Tamara looked over the side of the yacht.

"I'm staying with Alex, Mother." She spoke calmly, blowing her a kiss. "Don't cry. Remember there is only pain left."

Marcia nodded in dumb misery, telling herself she would do what must be done, when Tamara had said her goodbyes.

Tamara telephoned during the evening to say how happy she was to know that Alexander was her father. Her only regret was not knowing before. She repeated that there was only pain left, and urged her not to be sad. She sounded happy – as if she had come to terms with his impending death.

She hardly slept for thinking about Tamara and when the doorbell rang, very early, she hurriedly threw on a robe, assuming she had forgotten her key, and was therefore startled, descending the stairs, to see the outline of a wheelchair through the frosted glass door. Illogically her thoughts flew to Alexander but, on opening the door, Gerald, looking very serious indeed said, "May we come in?"

She held the door wide for George to push the chair through to the sitting room.

"Make some tea will you, George?" Gerald inclined his head, then said very gently, "Sit down, my dear."

She sat, wondering why he was being so solicitous – but nothing could have prepared her.

"Tamara has taken her own life. There is a note saying they wanted to die together, but according to Fabian, she received news after you left, that she was HIV positive. Apparently they waited for him to go to bed and took an overdose of drugs. I'm so terribly sorry, dear."

Marcia closed her eyes in silent agony and vaguely heard him instructing George to help her into the car and take them home.

CHAPTER TWENTY-EIGHT

Talk of funeral arrangements seemed to fill every waking moment of the following week and, much to her relief, Fran was not expected to attend. Adam came and went without attempting to speak to her and after waylaying him to offer condolences; she avoided him.

On the day *before* the funeral, she took Sam and Tim to be fitted for riding hats. Bob was to give them lessons, ready for Gerald's surprise birthday present. It was a relief to get home and she left the engine running while she tipped the front seat forward, to allow them to clamber out and run indoors; they were hot and cross from the shopping trip, and had chattered endlessly all the way home.

"Get your swimsuits on and wait in the hall while I put the car away," she called to them. Gerald had put the red Austin at her disposal for the remainder of her stay and after driving into the old carriage house, where all family cars were garaged, she walked the short distance back to the house.

The familiar scent of lavender and beeswax polish, greeted her as she entered the cool entrance hall and made her way to the kitchen to collect cool drinks and fruit to take to the cove; she welcomed the warm sense of home. As usual, Lorna was preparing dinner and George was cleaning silver, but today, there was an air of excitement about them and George kept nodding at Lorna who went bright red and eventually said shyly, "Me and George are getting wed next Saturday. We've fixed it with Sir Gerald and we would like you and the children to come. Two o'clock at the village church, then afterwards at Alf and Betsy's big barn. It's to be a barn dance," she said proudly.

George grinned widely as she congratulated them; their happiness was so touchingly simple, it made her smile to herself as she went back into the hall. Typically, Sam was jumping off the two bottom stairs while Tim sat and waited patiently. They ran ahead, eager to get down to the water. There was a welcome sea breeze and she sat on a rug with her back against the rocks, from where she could watch the children playing in a nearby rock pool. The sun was warm on her bare skin and she closed her eyes, listening drowsily to the far off cries of the gulls perched high up on the cliff face. London was a whole world away and it was hard to believe they had only been here for two weeks. She had never felt so completely at one with a place – spellbound in fact – the thought of leaving made her desolate. She thought of Adam, and drew a long, deep breath reliving their kiss, just as a shadow fell across her, blotting out the sun. She looked up, shading her eyes.

"Hello, Half-pint."

Mike grinned down at her and she jumped up laughing as they hugged each other. For the next hour, they exchanged news. A lot had happened to both of them. Mike had been in hospital, with a bout of malaria picked up on his last assignment.

"I can't tell you how sorry I am about Darren. By the time I was able to read your letter, you'd vanished without trace, until this fellow called at the office last week – and here I am. I phoned and spoke to Sir? Anders." As he questioned the 'sir' he looked askance and gave a mocking little bow.

Fran nodded, her eyes twinkling. "You don't have to bow – just tug your forelock."

"He said I would find you here so, I booked into the local pub and came straight over; I couldn't wait to see you." He looked at her steadily and asked quietly, "Ready to pick up where we left off?"

A short while ago she would have given anything to hear those words. He noted her hesitation and raised questioning eyebrows.

"I'm really glad to see you, but so much has happened that I need to come to terms with." She told him briefly of the situation.

Mike nodded. "Don't spoil the rest of your life over a man who didn't care. Your real father was the man who brought you up and loved you enough to make no difference between you and Darren: he was your real father."

Fran smiled through her tears. "You always did say the right things."

At that moment the twins came racing up the beach demanding a drink, and the conversation was put on hold, while Mike marvelled at their change – not only their little brown bodies and faces glowing with health, but at the new contentment already replacing the lost look he remembered.

"You have obviously made the right decision for them. Oh, and by the way, I've been invited to dinner tonight."

Fran looked questioningly and he gave a nonchalant grin.

"None other than Sir Gerald himself."

She had a moment's disquiet, wondering why Gerald had gone to so much trouble to reunite her with Mike.

"Is that alright with her ladyship?" Mike asked, seeing her expression.

"I shall wear my best tiara," she assured him with a brilliant smile.

Dinner, understandably, proved to be less than a jolly occasion. Adam arrived unaware of Mike's invitation and was very quiet. Mike was restrained – aware that he was being scrutinised, and Marcia, having opted to stay in her room all week, had joined them at her husband's request and was sitting silent and pre-occupied with her own thoughts. Charles and Felicity had come and she cried when she met Tim and Sam. She told Fran about David and Marie, and Robert and painted vivid pictures of how the house used to be, then asked how long she was staying.

"Until a suitable nanny is found."

"We aren't in any hurry to lose her." Gerald said smiling down the table. The twins, as always sat either side of him and he spoke to them frequently whilst they hung on his words.

So different to his relationship with Robert and Alexander, Felicity commented quietly to Charles.

"Different times, my dear – different times," Charles murmured.

In an effort to make conversation and include Marcia, Mike referred to a hit musical that was currently showing in London and asked, "Do you like the theatre Lady Anders?"

An awkward silence followed.

"You will have to forgive my wife; I'm afraid she isn't feeling herself," Gerald intervened, wishing he had not persuaded Marcia to join them. She looked so unhappy.

"Sorry, thoughtless of me," Mike apologised looking across at Marcia who, engrossed with her own thoughts, continued looking down at her food, which she was making very little pretence of eating.

She had spoken to Bob and said she would be returning home after the funeral. His manner had been sympathetic about Tamara, but she badly wanted to explain things and have the comfort of his arms about her again. The evening for her seemed never ending.

Fran was in good spirits, which didn't help Adam, who put it down to Mike being there, but she knew she was looking her best, in a long, black evening skirt and a pale blue, sleeveless lace blouse, with delicate frills down the front which looked particularly becoming with her newly acquired suntan. The skirt and several blouses had been purchased shortly after her arrival, on discovering she was expected to dress for dinner; even though Adam *had* assured her Sir Gerald would excuse her, under the circumstances; the truth being she really enjoyed the sense of occasion it gave and Mike commented he had never seen her looking so well.

"Cornwall suits her," Adam said shortly.

"He's mighty interested isn't he? Could he be the reason you are turning me down?" Mike whispered, only half joking.

"Now don't put that newshound nose of yours into action," Fran whispered back, laughing.

"Ah, so there *is* something to nose out?" He was still whispering and enjoying Adam's reaction to their intimacy.

"Don't be silly, Mike; I hardly know him," she fibbed, but as she brushed his remark aside she caught Adam's reproachful glance across the table and flushed.

Adam left first; his curt 'good night' dampening her spirits considerably – a fact that didn't go unnoticed by Mike. Then as *he* was leaving, Gerald asked him how long he intended staying?

"It depends on Fran, sir. I was hoping she would return to London with me in the next few days or so – but—" he shrugged doubtfully, "I don't know."

Gerald understood. "She needs time; these last few weeks have brought about a number of changes." Reaching out he caught Fran's hand.

"Whatever she decides, it won't be lightly – she is a girl in a million."

Fran coloured at the unexpected compliment. "I had a very good teacher in your son," she murmured in embarrassment.

"I never met your son, but come what may, he will always be Fran's father. Goodnight, sir. I'll call in the morning, if I may?"

Fran shot him a grateful look and Gerald suddenly found it necessary to blow his nose.

Charles and Felicity stayed on and she helped to get the children to bed, commenting on the way upstairs that Gerald's own children would never have been allowed to stay up so late.

Fran pulled a face. "Neither would these ordinarily, but their grandfather seems to need them around and I feel better when they are with me. This house is bigger than we have been used to."

"I remember finding it daunting at first; you soon get used to it though."

"I won't be here long enough for that." She spoke without realising how wistful she sounded.

The children fell asleep immediately and they returned downstairs to find Gerald and Charles arranging when to deal with Alexander's affairs.

"How about Lorna and George's wedding?" Felicity said, wanting to lighten the conversation. "Will we see you there?"

Fran had time to nod before Gerald said, "That reminds me, could you and Charles come and stay? I would like to give them their honeymoon as a wedding present."

"What a lovely idea. Is that alright, Charles?"

He gave a complacent nod.

"We need a cook and a butler," Gerald joked.

"Wouldn't be the first time I've been taken for the butler."

The three of them laughed and Fran looked puzzled. By the time they had explained, it was time for Charles and Felicity to leave.

"Nearly like old times," Charles said softly on their way home, reaching for her hand. Felicity squeezed his hand in both of hers.

*

On his return to The Smugglers Arms, where he had booked in that morning, Mike found the bar empty except for the landlord and two locals, who immediately stopped talking and stared at him inquisitively. Mike grinned to himself, ordered a whisky and invited the three men to join him in a drink; it was always a good way to learn local gossip. Fran chided him about his incorrigible nosiness, but it was what made him one of the best newshounds in the business, as he always pointed out to her.

It only took a few minutes to establish that he had dined at the big house in the cove.

"Anders Folly, you mean? Where the grand funeral is tomorrow?" one of the men asked. "What you be doin' up there then?" the other one asked.

"Yes, that's the name and there was talk of a funeral. I'm not well acquainted with the family. It's a friend of mine who knows them. Did you know the deceased?"

"Knew of 'em more like; their kind don't mix with the likes of us," the first one volunteered.

"Rum do that," the landlord commented, dourly.

"How come?" Mike pushed his glass across the counter motioning to the landlord to fill the other three glasses as well, then waited, patiently while he handed him his change and relit his pipe.

"Folks about 'ere do say 'twas a love pact an that there girl killed 'erself 'cos 'ee was dyin'. Beats me; lovely young girl like that, engaged to that nice solicitor an' all."

The landlord warmed to his subject. "If you ask me, it all started when the old man cut his eldest off wi'out a shillin'." He waited for his remark to have its effect and grunted in answer to Mike's "Really?" Satisfied of his listeners' full attention he continued.

"Nice young gent 'ee was; not like this un, wonder what ever 'appened to 'im? This un was a wild kid. Grew into an arrogant young buck; an' 'ee didn't calm down none as 'ee got older – by all accounts. Always throwin' wild parties and such like, with that misbegotten bunch 'ee mixed with from the City. Made sure to keep 'is goin's on from is father though, I'll be bound, or 'ee'd have got the same treatment as the olden."

313

"Why did he cut the eldest son off?" Mike asked, engrossed in what promised to be a good story; already conjuring up in his mind, an eye-catching headline, but he had to wait until the landlord had relit his pipe again.

"Married beneath 'im – proper upset the old man was; 'is own secretary – and pregnant, by all accounts. I reckon that old 'ousekeeper could tell 'ee a thing or two – if she 'ad a mind to. Close as the pages of a book she be."

Making a mental note to have a word, Mike drank up. The landlord looked at the clock. Well past closing time!

"Aint you lads got no 'ome to go to?" He chided the two locals.

"Goodnight. Thanks for the interesting chat," Mike said casually and went off to his room feeling rather pleased with himself.

Early next morning he called at the house and suggested to Fran they should take the children out for the day.

Fran agreed readily and suggested a picnic on the headland. "You really must see the view from up there: it's breathtaking," she enthused.

"Sounds great, but it was supposed to be my treat," he demurred.

"Miss Pennington won't mind if I pack a picnic. She would normally insist on doing it herself, but I know she is preparing mountains of food for after the funeral."

"In that case I will come and help," Mike offered eagerly, recognising a possible opportunity to follow up his intention of pumping the housekeeper.

The twins were already in the kitchen. Lorna, looking flustered gave a relieved look, when they appeared.

"I thought I told you to play outside," Fran said sternly.

"Soon have them out of your way Miss Penny." Mike took over sending the children off to collect their things then turning to Lorna he guided her to a chair.

"You need a cup of tea. Children and kitchens don't mix, in my estimation," as if for all the world he had experience of both.

Fran packed a picnic and listened in amusement as he turned on the charm and completely overwhelmed a surprised Lorna, by saying he couldn't wait to sample her Cornish pasties, he had heard so much about, even in London, until she was red with embarrassment

Once outside, Fran turned to him accusingly. "What are you up to?"

"Don't know what you mean." He pretended to look hurt.

"You're up to something; what is it? Come clean."

He grinned. "You want to know who your father is, don't you?"

She stopped in her tracks. "What makes you think Miss Pennington knows?"

"Perhaps she does – perhaps she doesn't – or perhaps she knows and doesn't realise she knows; then again perhaps she knows, and isn't saying – just leave it to Uncle Mike." He tapped the side of his aquiline nose with his index finger

The rest of the day passed pleasantly. The Headland, as the local beauty spot was called, was a vantage point, from where it was possible to see for miles around. Gerald had suggested the place as an excellent spot for the children to try out their new binoculars: a present which gave them endless amusement. At that particular moment, Tim could be heard explaining to Sam in a lofty voice why they couldn't touch the birds that seemed to be within arms reach on the beach far below.

Mike was good company and his amusing stories had Fran laughing helplessly as they sat on the cliff top with his arm resting casually along her shoulders.

Quite spontaneously, he kissed the tip of her nose. "It's good to see you laughing." She returned his gaze fondly.

"We would have been on honeymoon now," he reminded her.

"So we would," she said softly, looking out to sea.

"My New York appointment starts in three weeks. They gave me a new date. If we got married straight away, we could still go together."

She agonised with herself. Mike was such a wonderful companion; why couldn't she feel the same as she had before?

Her silence led him to ask, "Aren't you in love with me anymore?"

"I shall always love you dearly; I'm just not sure it's the marrying kind of love anymore," she answered miserably.

"But you're not sure it isn't either," he encouraged.

She returned his optimistic grin with a non-committal smile. It was impossible to stay unhappy for long with Mike; he had such enthusiasm for life.

Tim gave a sudden shout, making her jump. He had tired of watching the terns diving for fish and had trained his binoculars inland.

"I can see Mr Wesley," he crowed delightedly. "Look Sam. There he is just getting into his car."

They all turned sharply, staring to where Tim was pointing and saw a cottage standing in splendid isolation. From this distance it was impossible to see with the naked eye, but the sound of a car engine echoing across the water seemed to confirm Tim's claim.

"Is that where he lives?" Mike asked in a subdued voice.

Fran pulled her gaze away and found Mike's searching look disconcerting.

315

"I don't know. I didn't even realise there was a house there." She purposely sounded off-hand and called to the children to come and eat.

They delayed their return home for as long as possible and were relieved to find that all of the cars had gone except for Adam's.

"I want you to go in very quietly and straight to your bedroom," Fran warned Tim and Sam. "Your grandfather won't want any noise today. I will be up shortly."

Waiting for Mike to collect the picnic basket from the boot of his car she said, "Come on, I'll see if I can rustle up a cup of tea," leading the way to the kitchen.

"My dear young lady," Mike whispered in a perfect imitation of Gerald's voice. "One doesn't *rustle up* a cup of tea in a joint like this. One has a pot served."

She tried to give him a reproving look but ended up stifling helpless fit of laughter.

"Shush now. I want you to be quiet," he said, reminding her of her own instructions, but as she put her hand to her mouth Adam spoke in a stiff voice from the sitting room doorway.

"When it is convenient, there is someone Sir Gerald would like you to meet, Miss Anderson."

Her laughter faded and she flushed.

"I'll just tidy myself up and be there straight away."

"You look fine as you are," he said more gently, taking in her windswept hair, flushed cheeks and dancing green eyes.

For a fleeting moment their eyes met, before Mike said, "I'll cut along, when I've delivered the picnic basket to the kitchen and pick you up at half seven, Fran."

Five minutes later, she presented herself in the sitting room, after changing her flat walking shoes for sandals and applying a trace of lipstick. The sun had lightened her hair to a corn colour and she had clipped it back softly.

On her way through the hall she noticed Mike's car still in the drive. He was obviously following up this morning's effort. Hope filled her.

The visitor proved to be a sprightly sixty-year-old and was introduced as the boys' old nanny; the 'boys' being Robert and Alexander of course, Gerald explained.

"Nanny Spence has offered to step in and take care of the twins, my dear. It will relieve you considerably if you decide to stay on – as we hope you will, or leave you with an easy mind if you want to join your young man."

Fran took an immediate liking to the capable looking little woman, who sat alert and upright, regarding her with undisguised curiosity. Her bright, humour filled eyes, Fran felt sure, still missed nothing.

"Perhaps you would like to introduce the children to Nanny when she moves in tomorrow; it's been rather a long day for all of us today."

"So soon?" Fran said without thinking.

"It's as well to be prepared; your young man is obviously intent on resuming your plans. The decision is yours now."

Adam, who had been standing silently behind her, suddenly excused himself.

"If you don't need me anymore, sir, I'll be off." As he said goodbye, he took her hand in both of his and looked down at her sadly. "I'm glad everything has turned out the way you wanted it to. It's been really nice knowing you."

Her heart cried out to him but all she could say was, "And you." If only she could be alone with him, but what for, if he was feeling so wretched about Tamara?

After he had gone, Gerald said: "Poor boy is taking this whole rotten business hard."

Abigail, always one to speak her mind, now claimed the privilege of age to do so with some asperity and greater insight than even she realised:

"One would wonder why she became engaged to him, when her feelings for Alexander and his way of life ran so deep. It makes me wonder if she ever intended to marry him, or if she was just using him; it's for sure he must be asking himself the same question."

Fran held her breath, wondering what Gerald's reaction would be to such forthrightness, but she was obviously a privileged employee, because all he said was, "We will never know. Her suicide must have come as a nasty shock, whatever her reason."

Abigail seemed to feel the need to press the point. "Well perhaps it isn't in very good taste to say so, and maybe he wouldn't agree right now, but in my opinion, he has had a very lucky escape."

Fran suddenly felt she could take no more of that particular conversation. "I must see to the children."

"Of course, my dear, I'll see you tomorrow morning. Ten o'clock sharp, in the nursery."

Fran felt like jumping to attention and saluting, but hid a smile, as she caught the twinkle in Gerald's eye.

Mike's car was still in the drive, so she put her head round the kitchen door. He jumped to his feet, guiltily wiping crumbs from his mouth.

317

"That Cornish pasty was the best thing I have ever tasted," he said to a beaming Lorna, darting a fearful look at Fran, who was standing – hands on hips and lips pursed.

"I must go," he whispered loudly and sidled past Fran who followed him with her eyes until she couldn't hold back the smile any longer. Lorna wiped away tears with the corner of her apron.

"He should be on the stage, Miss."

"I hope you mean sweeping it." Fran returned the age-old joke.

Mike popped his head back round the door. "Hey, I heard that!"

"I can't ever remember laughing so much." Lorna's face suddenly went grave. "I don't think Sir Gerald would approve – not today of all days – it don't seem fittin' somehow."

Mike pulled a long face and withdrew with Fran on his heels, shaking her head and tutting.

*

The theme of The Three Tuns, like a good many Cornish pubs, was based on the old smuggling days. The restaurant furniture consisted of large oak barrels, which had been cleverly turned into comfortable armchairs and oak tables, set out in alcoves and corners to give intimate dining areas. Brass bric-a-brac hung on white painted walls and an imitation log fire gave a glow, which, even on a warm evening was pleasing to the eye.

Mike placed a glass of wine in front of her and settled himself on the seat opposite, retrieving two menus from under his arm and handing her one.

"So what did you find out?" she asked, unable to contain her curiosity any longer.

"Do you know that poor woman has never been more than ten miles from that house? Just imagine – in this day and age. Anders is the only job she has ever had. She's absolutely devoted to the old man and I couldn't get much out of her except that the youngest was his mother's favourite and she was always getting him out of scrapes. Your father was the old man's blue-eyed boy and he never forgave him for going against his wishes. Robert wanted to be left alone with his books but his father wouldn't have it. He wanted him to take over the family business. Until recently, when he had a change of heart. He sounds as if he has been a complete martinet – not that she sees it that way."

"Is that all?"

"Afraid so, and I don't suppose I will get the chance to speak to her on her own again. I was lucky today, George was out chauffeuring for the funeral."

Their meal arrived and, as usual, Mike soon had them laughing again; it wasn't until they were saying goodnight in the driveway of Anders Folly that he took her hand and became serious.

"Does all of this really matter, Fran? Why not come to America with me and forget about it – it's only a passing phase and these people are only half living. It's certainly not for me, or you either I would have thought. Don't shut yourself away from life, down here."

"But I love it. I can't explain – somehow I feel as if I have come home."

"I think you are kidding yourself – it's a certain person that's making you want to stay, isn't it?"

Fran was glad of the darkness; she should have known, with his uncanny knack for searching out the truth, Mike would not be fooled.

"I knew the first evening," he reflected sadly. "Does he know how you feel?"

She shook her head whispering, "No."

"Have you considered he will be on the rebound? He's obviously cut up about his fiancée."

Reluctantly, she admitted to herself he could be right. "You wouldn't want me to marry you, feeling the way I do, surely?"

For an answer, he moved closer and took her in his arms and she wished, with all her heart things could be the same as before. His kiss was lovely as always, and she relaxed, but her thoughts were with Adam and she drew away with a sharp intake of breath, as she realised it was Adam she was responding to, in her reverie.

"Don't fight it, darling; it will be wonderful again," Mike whispered, misunderstanding.

"Please, Mike, you deserve better. You are very special to me, but..." She broke off unable to say the hurtful words.

"Anything my lady desires," he teased, easing into his car seat, adding placidly, "We will just wait and see what tomorrow brings."

Although it was late, George was waiting up to let her in and there was a light under the study door. Surprised, she asked, "Is Sir Gerald still up, George?"

"Yes, Miss. You will be saying goodnight to him, won't you?" It was a request more than a question; accompanied by a whimsical smile.

With a warm rush of understanding, she nodded. "It's a long time since anyone waited up for me," she whispered, deeply touched.

"Goodnight, Miss."

Gerald laid his book down as she popped her head around the door.

"Ah Francesca! Come in," he greeted her. "I've been reading and didn't realise the time," he lied, as she settled herself on the footstool beside his chair.

319

They talked for a while about her evening, then, as she was preparing to leave, he said, "Adam telephoned to say he won't be available for the next ten days. He has gone to tour Scotland – needs to get away – he says."

Fran's heart leapt painfully. "The funeral must have upset him," she said, trying to keep her voice steady.

"Mm," Gerald grunted watching her carefully.

CHAPTER TWENTY-NINE

Charles gave a low whistle. He was reading Alexander's will.

"Have you *any* idea how much Alexander was worth?"

"No." Gerald replied absently, craning his neck to watch the twins being led around on two Shetland ponies.

"Would one and a half million surprise you?"

Gerald spun round.

"Are you sure? How did he make that sort of money in a few years?"

"It isn't very clear. *And* that doesn't include The Vintage."

"I sold that place to his friend."

"I know – I did the conveyance. But it belongs – belonged to Alexander for the last three years."

"How very odd!"

"There is a newspaper cutting attached to the deeds, referring to drugs being found on the premises and another about alcohol in the cellars not coinciding with the receipts. He was closed down by customs and went bankrupt. It would appear Alexander bought the place for less than Colin Murrey gave you. There is also a big 'Yes', and a drawing of a clenched fist on the cutting. Wonder what that means?"

"So is it standing empty then?"

"It would seem so. No wait – there's a reference to it being booked for weekends quite frequently. Conferences by the look of things, filling the whole place."

"Sell it. I don't want any part of it."

As it was the day after George and Lorna's wedding, Charles and Felicity had come to stay.

"He must have had a finger in a good many pies to amass such a fortune in so few years," Charles said taking another folder out of the strong box.

"Above board do you think?" Gerald asked, sounding doubtful.

"Well his declared income was from the weekly parties. He charged for giving them but it's a bit of a mystery how he bailed Colin Murrey out with ready cash."

"His inheritance from his grandparents and mother?"

"That would certainly account for some of it, but there is the yacht – also paid for with cash." Charles's voice took on a conciliatory note. "I'm sure there is an explanation. It isn't your worry in any case."

"I want that thing removed as soon as possible. Tell Fabian he can have it, on condition it is out of my sight within twenty-four hours." He glowered his eyes full of anger.

"You don't want to sell it to him?"

"No – it sounds like ill-gotten gains to me."

Charles nodded, pursing his lips tightly.

"Let's go and see how the children are doing. We can finish this another day." Gerald didn't need Alexander reaching out from the grave with even more aggravation he thought, as they made their way to the stables.

Sam called to them. "Look Granddad, look Uncle Charles. I'm going to be a show jumper when I get bigger. Bob says I can."

Bob gave a humorous smile as he kept pace holding her rein. "She's a natural, sir," he said quietly. "Afraid of nothing; just like Pickles."

"And Tim?" Gerald asked, highly amused by the way Sam's curls danced as she bumped along on Pickles.

"Happy to take things in his stride."

Tim's pony was walking sedately round the yard without a lead rein.

"You seem to have matched the ponies and their riders well," Charles observed.

"Yes, sir. Skipper is steady. You're doing well, Tim," he encouraged, bringing Pickles to a halt. Sam dug her heels in and clicked her tongue, protesting as Bob lifted her easily out of the saddle, saying firmly, "Pickles needs a rest, Sam. Come and groom him."

"I want to groom Skipper as well," Tim called. Bob lifted him down and gave them a brush each.

Gerald turned his chair, smiling at their enthusiasm, confiding to Charles that he had wanted to make their first birthday with him memorable.

"Let's take a turn round the garden, shall we?" Charles suggested.

The summer was drawing to a close – September next week. It was good to have Charles and Felicity in the house again. On impulse, Gerald said wistfully, "Christmas will be good again. Will you and the family join us?"

"Don't know what has been arranged yet. We went to America last year – so they might come here this one. I will speak to Felicity."

"Gerald would like us all to spend Christmas at Anders Folly." Charles said later to Felicity. She smiled contentedly.

It was a happy week, with Sam and Tim getting to know their ponies in the mornings, and afternoons on the beach with Fran and Mike, making the most of what was left of the summer. Fran thought regretfully of returning to London. Her excuses had run out. Abigail was organised; the children went to bed early and slept soundly, after active days in the open air – there wasn't any reason for her to stay on longer. And then, something incredible happened.

It was Friday afternoon. Fran and Felicity were looking through old photographs in the sitting room; Gerald and Charles were going through Alexander's papers again.

"I could do with a cup of tea, could you?" Felicity struggled up, piling albums onto Fran's lap. "Shan't be long."

She went into the hall, just as a crunch of tyres sounded on the gravel drive. The front doors were wide open and thinking it was Mike, expected him to just come in as always, so she continued on her way and was nearly to the kitchen when an anxious voice called, "Excuse me."

She turned and went back. "I understand, Fran Anderson is staying here," the voice said, as she drew nearer. His face came in to focus and she stopped dead, letting out a shrill scream, as she went running to the study, calling to Gerald and Charles to come quickly.

Hearing her cries Fran ran to the hall and also let out a scream, before flying into outstretched arms. By this time the other three were in the hall, watching in amazement, as Fran hugged the familiar looking figure. Tears streaming down her face, she managed to say, "This is Darren," drawing him forward. "Darren, this is your grandfather – and, oh – it's a long story," she said in answer to his bewildered look. "I must fetch the children." She ran upstairs two at a time.

Gerald sat thunderstruck, until Charles said, "Are we going to keep the boy on the doorstep all day? Come in. Come in," he said leading the way. Felicity was convinced it was Robert standing there. Then the children, followed closely by Fran, stampeded down the stairs and threw themselves at him.

Sam talked non-stop about things they found in the attic – all *sorts* of games and a *gigantic* picture of a lovely lady, she spread her arms. "Nanny says she was the loveliest lady in the world."

Tim just snuggled against him. "You won't go away again, will you, Daddy?"

Darren clutched them both tightly. "No, son. I'm going to look after you."

Bewildered by everything that had happened in his absence, Darren told of how he had been on a routine test flight when his engine failed and he had crashed in to the sea off the coast of Italy. He had drifted for two days before being picked up by a fishing boat. The crew took him to the nearest village, but he had hit his head and couldn't remember anything. All of his papers were in the pocket of his missing jacket and it took time to discover the location of his base, where a telephone number to Fran's flat was produced, but there was no reply, so he was kept in hospital, until a week ago when he started to remember the odd thing.

"I remembered Mike's address but his flat was empty, with a sold sign on it. I thought you must have got married and taken the children to America with you. My only hope then was the newspaper where you worked – but I couldn't remember the name. Heaven only knows how long it would have taken if I hadn't regained my memory."

He suddenly looked exhausted.

"You shouldn't have driven all this way on your own," Gerald said.

"You need rest and food," Felicity said. Fran got to her feet.

"You stay with Darren. I will help." Charles pushed her gently back on to the settee.

"Don't know how you found your way," Felicity tutted.

"Well amongst other things, navigation is part of flying," Darren smiled weakly, amused by her slightly vague air.

"Get Maisie to prepare Laurie's old room," Gerald said as she reached the door.

He had said very little. Fear of losing the children cast a shadow over his joy and Darren's uncanny likeness to Robert wrung his heart.

Mike arrived later to take Fran out and was filled with fresh hope when he heard the news. He was getting restless; his leave was running out and there were things he had to do in London, before taking up his post in America; besides which, the quiet life in Cornwall was beginning to pall. He had done his level best to discover the identity of Fran's miscreant father but had come to the reluctant conclusion, that if anyone did know they weren't saying. What did it matter anyway, after all this time, he thought gloomily, his natural good humour affected by his need to be doing something lively.

They were sitting in the car on the headland. Neither of them had spoken for several minutes and the silence was getting to him.

"I would just like to be sitting in a London nightclub, making plans for our wedding. Come on, Fran; you can't give up a wonderful opportunity like America, for a fellow who might not even want you."

His eyes looked hopefully in to hers but there was no answering light, as there would have been not so long ago. He opened the car door and got out. His patience snapped.

"Well I am going back to London tomorrow – with or without you. If you come to your senses in the next few days, you know where to find me – if I had any sense I would say it's now or never, but you might think more clearly when I've gone."

Fran stared at him, remembering the last similar scene in her flat, only this time there were no extenuating circumstances, no agonising decisions to make.

She knew for sure now, come what may, she didn't want to marry Mike and it had to be said. She spoke slowly, searching for the right words.

"Mike, it's got nothing to do with how I feel about someone else, or who my father is, or even how I feel about this part of the world. If I had really cared, I would have found a way round my problems before."

"By the same token, you could argue I should have married you, kids and all."

"Exactly," she agreed softly.

He sat beside her again, his anger evaporating.

"I can't altogether agree – but I see what you mean." He gave her a sidelong glance. "A definite thumbs down then? In that case I shall make haste, back to 'the Big Smoke' and pack my bags for the good ole US of A," he said with a twang and a jocular smile to hide his disappointment.

She nodded and gave a tremulous smile.

"You're absobloominlutely sure?" he said whimsically.

"Absobloominlutely," she assured him, blinking rapidly.

Arriving back at the house they went straight to the study, walking in with their arms entwined. Mike held his hand out to Gerald.

"Just came to say thank you for your hospitality, sir. It's time I returned to London."

Gerald's face fell as he took the proffered hand. "Look after her, m' boy, and bring her back to see us soon."

"I'm not going," Fran smiled happily.

"But?" Gerald spread his hands indicating their smiles and linked arms.

"She has decided not to spoil a beautiful friendship by marrying me," Mike said in a resigned voice.

"I hoped she would make the right decision. You are both lovely people, but you want very different things from life: better to find out now."

Fran laughed at Mike's crestfallen expression and pulled him towards the door.

"Come on, I'll help you to pack." They still held hands. "And you make sure you write; do you hear?"

"Stop nagging woman. People will think we're married."

Their voices faded; Gerald gave a contented smile.

"One step closer," he murmured.

Lorna and George arrived home from the Scilly Isles on Saturday. It was nine o'clock but the children were still sleeping after a very late night. Darren was wandering around admiring the house and had reached the library, when

Lorna first caught sight of him. He was sitting in the wing chair (Robert's favourite spot). As she passed the door, she froze – he smiled – she fainted – he jumped to his feet calling for help. She came round to a sea of anxious faces looking down. George was kneeling beside her patting her hand, and Felicity was holding a glass of water to her lips.

Her eyes wandered from Gerald to Fran to Charles and then – Darren. She clutched George and pointed at Darren. Darren moved away.

"He's gone! No. No, there he is again."

Darren came forward again and she cringed against George.

"It's alright, I'm not a ghost. I'm Robert's son."

They laughed later, but it took an hour and two cups of tea, before Lorna felt herself again.

The day was perfect. Darren and Fran took the children into the town to buy them belated birthday gifts and came home with big, bouncy space hoppers.

There was great hilarity as they showed them how to use them.

"Good substitute when they can't go riding," Gerald said, laughing at their antics around the furniture.

Darren and Fran looked at each other. He wasn't sure about the children staying at Anders Folly. It was clear they were happy and Fran had said they were heirs to this wondrous place but, after coming close to death himself, he didn't want to be parted from them or Fran, ever again.

"Keep them here for when they come to visit, sir." Darren hadn't yet been able to bring himself to say 'grandfather'.

"I'm hoping we can come to a better arrangement than that, m' boy," Gerald said heartily. "When you are fully recovered we will talk. This is their home now."

The twins came over, clamouring for their father to play and he was dragged off with Fran's words echoing in his mind, 'They are Anders – nothing else matters to your grandfather.'

CHAPTER THIRTY

Marcia wandered restlessly from room to room, persistently returning to Tamara's airy bedroom. Standing on the wide balcony with its panoramic view of the sea, she felt she would go mad if she didn't talk to someone, but who? She sat on the king size bed, plucking at the pale green sprigged duvet cover with nervous fingers, her tormented thoughts reliving her last meeting with Bob.

A week ago, she watched his face change as hopes of ever owning the stables were dashed, but he had assured her nothing would change between them. Later he had been evasive about his next visit and since then, she had telephoned the stables every day without reply. Desperate for reassurance, she had overcome her dread of bumping into Gerald and eventually gone for an early morning ride.

A strange groom was working about the yard. He said Bob was on holiday and wouldn't be back for ten days. Angry and bewildered she had ridden her little mare hard, spurring her on until the gentle animal was lathered up. Bob had never taken his holidays, preferring to collect an optional wage packet. It had to be because of the bad news. He could at least have had the gumption to tell her. Seething with fury, she had caught the surprised animal a sharp whack with her riding crop, causing her to whinny and shy in protest; only then, contrite for her treatment of the gentle creature, she calmed down and allowed her to drop to a walk.

Bitter reflection told her, as she swayed to the rhythm of the horse, that Bob was only attracted to her position and wealth. In her heart, perhaps she had always known; but he was such a wonderfully tender lover, she had happily deceived herself. Now the moment of truth had come – just when she needed him most. By the time she reached the stables she had come to the devastating conclusion that Bob had finished with her. She had shattered his dreams.

Now, as she moved around Tamara's room, touching the paraphernalia on the glass topped dressing table and idly sliding back the wardrobe doors, she searched in her mind for someone to confide in; mentally ticking off friends, for one reason or another. When it came down to it she didn't have a soul to share her innermost secrets with. She ran her fingers along the row of exclusive outfits, hanging still and lifeless like their lovely owner, picturing her daughter as she had last seen her, leaning against the rail of the yacht. Then she wept body-wracking sobs that forced her to her knees.

In her desolation, she didn't hear the doorbell, or the voice that called to her a few minutes later.

Finding the door unlocked and hearing her distress Adam quickly investigated. She seemed almost unaware, as he gently raised her to her feet, guided her downstairs to a chair and fetched a glass of brandy. She took a sip and looked at him vaguely.

"You're in Scotland."

"I was on my way home and popped in to see how you are. Good job I did by the look of things. I'll ring Sir Gerald and drive you over."

"No, I can't go there," she whimpered.

"Well you can't stay here on your own. You look as if you haven't slept for a week. I'm not leaving you on your own," he said firmly.

"I'll be alright – really. I'll ring a friend," she assured him.

"You aren't in a fit state to drive. I will take you."

Minutes later, having arranged to stay with a friend four miles away, she went upstairs; shortly afterwards she leant over the banister, calling to him to reach her case down for her. The case was on top of Tamara's wardrobe and pulling it down he commented that it had things in it.

"Just empty it on the bed 'til later," she called.

He snapped the locks back and raised the lid. A gasp left his lips and he stood motionless – seeking an explanation, before taking the case in one hand and holding his briefcase out in the other, he went into Marcia's room.

"This will have to be explained," he said, seriously.

"Sorry?" She stared at it blankly.

"This briefcase is mine; it was stolen by the person who attacked me in London."

Without warning, she slipped to the floor.

*

Gerald faced his wife angrily. "I demand an explanation Marcia."

She denied any knowledge of the briefcase and sat ashen faced as Gerald asked again and again how it came to be there.

"Would I have asked Adam for help, if I had known it was there?" she argued logically.

"Perhaps not, so why did you faint when you saw it."

"I was shocked," she insisted.

He was unconvinced but could see she was at the end of her tether.

"You will come home. The doctor says you are not to be left alone," he said brusquely. "I intend to get to the bottom of this though and by golly if you…" He left the sentence unfinished and rotated his chair.

"I have arranged to stay with Angela," she objected, knowing she would rather die than go home with him at that moment.

He continued on his way to the door. "Until this matter is settled to my satisfaction, you aren't going anywhere. You are making yourself ill; it's obvious you know more than you are admitting – and I don't want to involve the police unless it becomes absolutely necessary."

He turned to Adam, who was standing by in embarrassed silence, regretting he had been the one to cause Marcia further distress.

"Be good enough to help my wife into the car."

With a resigned shrug, she allowed him to assist her, deserted by her strong will, her whole body trembled.

On the way to the car Adam said quietly, "You don't have to shield Tamara and put yourself through all of this; nothing can hurt her now. We both know Sir Gerald won't give up until he gets to the truth – and I'm certain you aren't involved, are you?"

"No!" She protested loudly, causing Gerald to glance round suspiciously.

"So tell him everything you know," Adam breathed.

"It could kill him," she whispered shakily.

Surprised by her concern he said, "I don't think so," as he helped her into the car, adding as she slumped into the corner, "He is a tough old bird and the children have put new life into him." Aloud he said, "I will contact you in the morning sir."

As he watched the car disappear in to the dusk Adam's thoughts returned to that night in London. He was convinced now; his attacker *had* been Tamara. He knew she held a black belt in Judo, but what ever had possessed her? He had suspected for some time she was emotionally unstable and had even suggested she should see a doctor, to which she had reacted with extreme violence.

There were also the two occasions when he tried to break their engagement; she had become wildly passionate, protesting her love for him, threatening to kill herself if he left her; she had finally gone as far as to stand on the edge of the cliff, swaying dangerously until he had pulled her back – and then she laughed.

In the past week he had walked for miles over the Scottish hills turning things over in his mind – feeling guilty for not loving her, until finally realising that all of the scenes had been contrived. *He* had never been her problem.

His thoughts turned to Fran. She would be gone by now, maybe even married. For a little while he could have sworn she cared for him. Wishful thinking, he thought wryly. It was obvious from the way her wonderful eyes danced when she was with this character that she was madly in love with him, and he had proven *his* feelings by coming to find her.

329

He had driven along the cliff road mechanically; now as he drove up to his cottage and switched the engine off, he sat staring out to sea in the gathering dusk – the resolution built up over the past week, crumbling at the thought of Fran being lost to him.

A telephone call from Gerald the following morning saved him a trip to Anders Folly. Apparently, Marcia had collapsed again that same evening and the doctor had ordered complete bed rest for at least a week.

"He says she is suffering from nervous exhaustion," Gerald exploded down the phone. "More likely avoiding my questions," he ranted on. "Well she can't stay sedated forever – and then by golly…" he spluttered, leaving the sentence unfinished.

Adam replaced his receiver feeling slightly weary of the Anders family problems and also relieved. He still had four days left out of his fortnight's holiday, and on the spur of the moment he decided to motor down to his parents' home in Penzance. His case was still packed so in less than half-an-hour he was on his way. Consequently, when Fran (after inwardly debating with herself) plucked up courage and drove along the cliff road to the solitary house, she found it shuttered and deserted.

CHAPTER THIRTY-ONE

With Nanny Spence to supervise the twins, Fran found herself with time on her hands. She felt she was staying under false pretences but dreaded returning to her empty London flat. Darren was very pre-occupied. He and Gerald spent a lot of time locked in the study. She was glad Darren was getting on well with his grandfather, but she felt left out. It was time for her to go. There was no possible reason for her to stay now.

She brought the subject up at dinner that evening and Gerald said, "Are you anxious to get away?"

"I must try and get my job back."

"Your job is safe," Gerald assured her adding casually, "if you aren't in any *particular* hurry to get back, there are some rare reference books I have been planning to get catalogued for some time; the problem is finding someone suitable for the task. They were your father's."

He looked her straight in the eyes and she nodded furiously, not trusting herself to speak. The meal ended and Gerald and Darren made straight for the study, leaving her alone again, but feeling less left out. He had actually said 'your father'. Oh well, no time like the present.

It was going to be a lengthy task, involving a list of perhaps two hundred books. After an hour of making notes, she went back to the sitting room, wishing she could join them and wondering what they would be talking about?

As if in answer to her thoughts, Darren appeared in the doorway.

"Come to the study." He couldn't conceal his excitement and held his hand out urging her to hurry. She went, consumed with curiosity, and Gerald beckoned her to sit by him. His dark eyes gleamed as he waited for Darren to pour Fran a glass of wine and settle in a chair opposite. Then he raised his glass.

"A toast to Anders Enterprises."

They clinked glasses, Fran looked mystified, Gerald nodded happily and Darren sat back looking bewildered.

"I can see, I will have to enlighten you," Gerald said gripping her hand tightly.

"Darren is going to leave the Air Force and start his own charter business right here in Cornwall, which means he and the children will live at Anders Folly. What do you think?"

"I, I don't know. It's a bit out of the blue. Is that what you have been talking about all of this time?"

"It took time to convince Darren he could do it."

331

"And now?" She directed the question at Darren.

"It's a dream come true, Sis. I can be around for the kids and you needn't worry about them. Sorry about Mike; I feel it was my fault."

"I have no regrets. This idea is wonderful; when will you start?"

"Grandfather will look for an airstrip, while I resign my commission. He thinks six to nine months."

It was late when they finally retired, after discussing everything in minute detail. Of course, Darren was now heir to Anders Folly; Gerald was happy beyond measure.

"Thank God he's not a book worm," he beamed at Fran.

She smiled mischievously. "I think you might have one more in the pipeline."

Gerald groaned in mock despair.

*

Fran made an early start the next morning, climbing up the long stepladders to reach down the heavy, leather bound volumes, then dusting, cataloguing and returning them in their new order. Excitingly, she recognised her father's handwriting in some of the margins and pointed out the notes to Gerald, who had come to watch.

"He must have been the last one to touch them; I know no one else ever has," he said nostalgically, his blue veined hand smoothing the page.

They shared a moment of intense sorrow and joy, and Fran felt an aching pity for the proud old man who had relented his harsh decision too late.

The job was absorbing and took up most of her day but she made a point of stopping at three o'clock, to spend time with Sam and Tim. It was a time also when Abigail could be found in her room, knitting or sewing. Today she was mending.

"Let me help," Fran offered, selecting a needle from the big workbasket and threading it with cotton as they sat talking companionably. They had become good friends and Fran found the room with its sloping ceilings cosy and inviting. With three bedrooms and a big old-fashioned bathroom all on the same floor, it was an orderly, complete little world of its own, quite remote from the rest of the house, where nothing disturbed the routine. She compared it to the warm, slightly cluttered home she and Darren had been brought up in, and knew she wouldn't have changed it – in spite of all the advantages the twins were enjoying.

"Don't you find it quiet here, after London?"

Fran looked up and met the bright, enquiring eyes studying her over the top of gold-rimmed spectacles.

"No, I love it."

"Will you stay then?"

"No. I shall leave when I have catalogued the reference books. Sir Gerald has invited me to stay, but it isn't as if I belong. The children are settled and happy. They adore their great grandfather – and you. Their father has come back, everything is perfect."

"They will still miss you."

"Not for long," Fran smiled tremulously.

"Why didn't you marry that young man of yours?"

"Oh, at first I made the excuse of not knowing who my real father was, followed by other similar excuses, which he saw through. Then I realised I didn't love him in the right way. We had known each other for so long I accepted it as love – but now I know it wasn't."

She spoke matter-of-factly to hide her real feelings. She had become used to the bird-like little woman's pert questions, mostly finding they helped to clarify her thoughts, but right now they were on sensitive ground.

"Why is it so important, after all of this time, to find out who your father is?"

Fran considered before answering, "Because I don't belong anywhere any more. Even Sam and Tim aren't as closely related as I thought. I feel as if I have been living a lie."

"Let's have a cup of tea, shall we? All this talk is making me thirsty."

Abigail got up and plugged the kettle in with quick, positive movements. "Cottage pie and pineapple upside down pudding, for nursery tea," she said approvingly, deftly changing the subject.

Each engrossed in their own, very different, thoughts, they drank tea from Abigail's rosebud patterned china cups and sewed until they heard the twins climbing the stairs.

She was impressed at how quickly they had adapted to the highly organised nursery routine. At the same time, she recognised what a curiously remote environment it was. She couldn't picture her father living here as a boy. A small, still voice asked, 'Had he ever got over the hurt?' She would never know!

She helped with tea, read them a story, stayed for bath time, then realising, with a start, she would be late for dinner, kissed the children and said goodnight.

As she was leaving, Abigail said, "Go forward my dear, don't let this business spoil your life. It's robbed you of enough already." And she gave Fran a fond hug.

Marcia was at dinner, looking pale. The atmosphere was strained and Fran, although unaware of the reasons, could tell by her nervous glances that something was terribly wrong. Afterwards Gerald asked Fran and Darren to excuse them, and they went into the study. Darren said he had phone calls to make, and Fran decided to go for a drive.

On her way downstairs, after collecting a warm jacket, she saw George show Bob Johnson into the study.

Curious, Fran mused, forgetting the incident as soon as she stepped out into the beautiful September evening. The sun was setting low over a perfectly calm sea, creating a rose coloured world. A feeling of absolute peace filled her mind and body; again, there was a marvellous awareness of being at one with her surroundings. Automatically she turned the car towards the headland, feebly denying to herself it was because she could see Adam's house from there. It was four days since she had called to find his cottage empty; each day since, she had waited, hoping he would come, deciding when he didn't, he must still be in Scotland. Now as she peered across the bay she could see lights shining from the house and her pulses leapt painfully.

Heart beating loudly in her ears, she steered the car back to the road and drove on round the coast, slowing down as she neared the cottage. His car was in the shallow, semi-circular drive and she could see quite clearly into the small sitting room. As she watched, another light went on – this time upstairs. Adam appeared, carrying in his arms, a slight figure, in blue. The two blonde heads were close as they laughed together, before he lowered her gently to the floor and kissed her forehead. Suddenly becoming aware of the un-drawn curtains and the car driving slowly past, he moved to the window and drew the curtains, blocking the view.

Guiltily, as if having been discovered spying, Fran put her foot down and the car gathered speed. She drove on, not knowing where the road led, just wanting to get as far away as possible. How could she have been such a fool as to think there wouldn't be anyone else, when in spite of his engagement to Tamara, he had made his interest in her so clear.

Well he didn't waste any time she fumed, scalding tears forcing her to stop the car. The dark road was deserted and she felt completely alone, nothing mattered, not even staying in this part of the world, where she felt so right. She would go back to London in the morning, anything rather than staying here, now she knew how shallow he was. She sat for a long time crying out the hurt, until calm and dry eyed she felt ready to turn the car around and drive back the way she had come.

His house was in darkness as she drove past this time and she swallowed hard, resolutely fighting back the tears that threatened again at the thought of Adam and the slight blonde figure together.

In spite of the late hour, all of the lights were blazing at Anders Folly and George was still on duty. Aware of her swollen eyes she put her hand to her forehead and hurried past him to the stairs.

"Tell Sir Gerald I've gone straight to my room with a really bad headache, would you, George?"

"Yes, Miss, but he did say he wasn't to be disturbed anyway; shall I mention it?"

"Oh no. Goodnight."

A murmur of voices reached her from behind the double doors of the study, as she reached the wide landing over looking the hallway; then the doors opened and she was taken-a-back to see Adam emerge, dressed, unusually for a visit to Gerald, in casual slacks and sweater. Called-out unexpectedly, Fran thought bitterly, as he glanced up and did a double take. Closing the door quickly behind him he started up the stairs.

"I thought you had gone!" he exclaimed incredulously, his gaze never leaving her face.

She looked scornful as he drew level.

"Does this mean …?" he asked, hardly daring to hope.

"No, I am not going to marry Mike," she said with a hostile stare.

"His choice or yours?" Adam demanded.

"Mine – if it matters." She turned away, telling herself she hated him but he caught her arm.

"Let me go!" she demanded angrily, trying to pull away.

He gave her a puzzled look. "Not until you tell me why you are so angry with me."

"I'm not angry with *you*; I'm angry with *myself* for believing you cared. Now will you *please* let go of my arm?" She demanded, trying again to free herself from his firm but gentle grip.

"I love you, Fran," he said gently, moving closer, trapping her against the broad banister. She stopped struggling and stared at him.

"You expect me to believe you love me, when the woman I saw you with earlier is probably waiting for you to return to her?" she cried accusingly. Adam recoiled as a look of understanding crossed his face. He released her arm but his eyes still bored into hers.

"Yes, I do expect you to believe me," he said quietly.

"I suppose you are going to say she means nothing to you?" Fran stormed scathingly.

"I wouldn't dream of it," he replied coldly.

"I suppose she also believes you care. How will she feel? Or is she more understanding than I am?" Fran challenged sarcastically.

"The young lady in question and I are both aware of our feelings for one another – and yes, she will understand."

There was a glint in the blue eyes, that warned her he was losing patience, but something drove her on heedlessly. "Well then, you had better go back to her, because I'm going back to London, first thing in the morning. I don't intend to spend my life being part of a queue, thank you very much."

Dismay registered before he demanded, "Already planned, or decided this minute?"

"While I was out driving this evening; I shall tell Sir Gerald first thing in the morning; he is busy right now and doesn't wish to be disturbed."

"Too late on both counts, you have already disturbed me and I heard your intentions loud and clear," Gerald's voice floated up. "Now will you please finish this discussion somewhere more private and let me have peace. Further more, you have contracted to catalogue my library, so let's hear no more about leaving." And with an imperious wave of his hand he went back in to the study.

They hadn't heard the study door open, but now Fran became embarrassingly aware that Marcia and Bob Johnson had also heard their heated conversation.

"I'm sorry, Sir Gerald," she called over the banister. "We've finished," she snapped, glaring at Adam.

"Oh no we haven't," Adam contradicted vehemently, catching her by the arm and dragging her – protesting loudly – downstairs.

"A key please George; no need for you to wait up."

George produced a key from his pocket, saying cheerfully, "Goodnight, sir. Goodnight, Miss."

Still protesting, Fran was bundled into the car, where she sat, unable to escape due to the child safety lock, whilst *he* walked round and climbed into the driver's seat. He drove with an intensity that would have done justice to landing a jumbo jet, whilst she, after mentally letting off a round of machine gun bullets and driving a tank over him, did her best to muster what was left of her injured dignity.

They were obviously going to his home; with great difficulty, she kept silent until his purpose was made clear – another reason of course, was there was no choice – a fact which did not improve her frame of mind.

At the cottage, he opened the front door before letting her out of the car, then, without a word, led her to the door and stood aside for her to enter. There was just time to take an inquisitive look at her surroundings. A square, plainly decorated hall, leading to a kitchen beyond and the sitting room she had seen from the road, on the left, before he led her to the stairs, where a banister in

336

gleaming white paint stretched up to the darkened landing above. She resisted, giving him an indignant look.

"Come along," he urged. "I'm going to convince you that I really do love you."

She snatched her hand away and had started to march to the door when a sleepy, feminine voice called from upstairs, "Is that you, Adam?"

"Coming," Adam called back, giving Fran a wicked grin.

At last it began to dawn that he was playing a game with her. Overcome with curiosity she retraced her steps, looking at him with narrowed eyes. This time when he held out his hand, she put hers into it and allowed him to lead her up the pale grey, carpeted staircase and into the bedroom she had seen from the road. The bedside lamp was on and half sitting up in bed, in a pale blue nightdress was a very pretty fair-haired girl in her teens.

"Melissa," he said, drawing Fran into the circle of his arm, "this is Fran, and I'm going to marry her."

The girl pouted reproachfully: "You always promised to wait for me. Hello, Fran."

She had a lovely smile.

Adam grinned. "I told you she would understand."

"He's never stopped talking about you for four days: he's nearly driven Mum, Dad *and* me crazy! Thank goodness you have decided to put us all out of our misery and marry my besotted brother. Adam, how about a cup of tea, now that you have woken me up *thoroughly*?"

He went off muttering something about bossy women and Melissa patted the side of the bed. "Forgive me for not getting up, I broke my ankle three weeks ago so walking is painful – that's why I'm here," she explained ruefully.

"Dad had to go to Plymouth on business, and so that Mum could go with him for a break, Adam brought me back with him; they are going to pick me up on the way home in a couple of days. Hope I'm not in the way," she said anxiously.

Fran shook her head. "I've never been so pleased to meet anyone in my whole life."

An hour later as he drove her home, Adam teased: "Well, what do you think of the other woman in my life then?"

"She is beautiful, but why didn't you tell me it was your sister?" Fran reproached. "Why did you let me go on so?"

"Would you have believed me? Even supposing I could have got a word in edgeways."

337

Fran sheepishly admitted, "Probably not, I had just spent an hour awash with tears."

He pulled in to a lay-by and switched off the engine. "I'm sorry you were so unhappy, sweetheart," he said taking her into his arms and kissing her gently, "but when we are married I shall expect a fair hearing – innocent until proven guilty and all that stuff? As a solicitors wife…"

"Are you trying to say something?" she interrupted dreamily.

In the velvety darkness he put her hand to his lips and kissed the palm, saying gently, "I'm asking you to share my life."

"Willingly," she murmured, her lips against his. She was in his arms and he was smothering her with gentle kisses, her eyes, the corners of her mouth, her neck, down to the warm v and finally her lips. She gave herself up to the sheer pleasure of his exploring touch, moaning softly as his long, gentle fingers caressed her small, full breasts, arching her back in ecstasy, surrendering to his passionate yet tender, demanding kisses, which drove all other thoughts from her mind. Still in a dream she felt him draw away and disappointed, asked softly, "Must we go yet?"

There was a pause before his voice came back in the darkness and she could sense him fighting his desire.

"I want you, Fran, and if we stay – but this is no place to make love to you for the first time. It's going to be so very special," he vowed, taking her face between his hands and kissing her lips tenderly again.

"Let's get married soon," she urged breathlessly.

"I'll get a special licence. How long do you need? Two? Three days? A week?" She gave a light laugh, as a sobering thought struck her. "Won't your family be shocked, so soon after Tamara's death?"

"They knew I would never marry Tamara, but of course, you didn't. I tried twice to end the engagement but she threatened to kill herself each time. On the afternoon you and I spent together, I went straight to the house, determined to end it once and for all, but as you know, she was very drunk when we got there."

Fran shuddered. "Thank God you were there but why haven't you told me?"

"Sir Gerald was convinced you were nursing a broken heart and sent me to inform your employer of your whereabouts. I didn't want to go but he insisted you needed to get things sorted. When Mike arrived, my worst fears were confirmed; you looked so happy together."

Fran murmured, "And I thought you were devastated at losing Tamara."

"If it hadn't been for Bob Johnson, the truth might never have come out. He persuaded Marcia to make a clean breast of things. Oddly enough, it was Sir Gerald she was concerned about; thought it would kill him to find out *Alexander* was Tamara's *father*, and that *Tamara* was responsible for attacking me and stealing my brief case. Then Bob confessed he had gone to the cottage and found it deserted. Then he heard from Lorna that Marcia was in trouble. Apparently he took his holiday, to go looking for somewhere to start a stud farm, in the hope that Marcia would join him. It was at that point Sir Gerald sent for me; luckily as it happened, because one of the things Marcia explained with my being there, was how I became engaged to Tamara. Apparently, her over-zealous friends spiked my drinks at the yacht club 'do' and the rest was lies. So the engagement never existed – except in Tamara's mind and nothing ever happened between us that need give you a moments concern – I promise."

It was early dawn before he eventually opened the heavy front door and she noted, thankfully, that apart from the small lamp at the foot of the stairs, no other lights were on. Nothing was going to spoil this night. Adam took her tenderly into his arms again and they clung together in a lingering, timeless embrace. She had never imagined such happiness could exist.

The following morning Gerald was already sitting at the breakfast table reading his newspaper, when Fran appeared.

"Good morning, Francesca. I don't need to ask how last evening went," he commented, noting her bright eyes and happy flushed cheeks.

"Is it that obvious?" she beamed.

"You *could* say that," he answered dryly. "And, as you have probably dismissed the idea of rushing off to London – *and* if you can possibly come down to earth long enough, I would like to see you in the study, around ten o'clock – please?"

Fran nodded with a faraway smile, and Gerald retreated behind his newspaper, grunting.

After breakfast, she stood on the wide steps with Lorna and waved Sam and Tim off, as George drove them, with Nanny Spence, to nursery school for the first time.

"Isn't it a lovely day, Lorna?" she said with a dreamy smile, as they turned back in to the house.

Lorna gave a frown, looked back at the misty rain and heavy clouds and shrugged. Later, as she was walking through the hall, Adam arrived dressed for business and carrying a briefcase.

"Morning, Lorna. Lovely day," he called cheerily.

In amazement, she went to the front door and looked out; it was still raining and the mist was still rolling in from the sea, blotting out the view.

"Must be me," she muttered, shaking her head.

At ten o'clock Fran went to the study. Adam was going over papers with Gerald and he put them to one side as she entered. They exchanged smiles as he took her hand.

"I gather Fran hasn't told you, we are going to be married very soon, sir."

"I did rather gather that her air of preoccupation at breakfast, might be due to something like that. Congratulations to you both," he said with an approving nod.

"I thought it would be nice to tell you together," she explained shyly, smiling up at Adam adoringly.

Gerald cleared his throat, seeing signs of their concentration being air-born again.

"Let's get the serious business over, then we can return to pleasanter subjects."

Gerald guided his chair away from the paper-strewn desk and indicated to them to sit down.

"Well now," he began, uncertain where to start. "This news changes things, yet again."

"I told Fran the main details," Adam volunteered.

"Right!" Gerald cleared his throat again and contemplated his frail, blue-veined hands as he always did when he was thinking deeply.

"I am giving my wife a divorce, so that she can marry Bob."

Fran heard a sigh of relief from Adam as she murmured: "I'm sorry."

Gerald put his hand up. "Marcia has had a lot to bear for many years; add to that the events of late, it's small wonder she is in such a nervous state. I only hope she finds happiness at last. I cannot condemn my son too strongly for the misery he has caused her and others but at least I can try to make amends. I intend giving them Forest End. It will be ideal for an equestrian centre."

They listened with growing sympathy.

"I think your son was more than justly punished in the end," Fran said in the poignant pause. "And poor Tamara never knew she had a proper family. It would have made such a difference to her, if she had known she belonged. At least I grew up believing in a background, even if it wasn't true."

"Hold on to that, child. But for another ironic twist of fate, you would have been an Anders. At least you and Darren were brought up by one – and a fine job he made of it too."

Gerald's head went up, reminding Fran of her first stormy encounters with the proud old man; this time though, instead of feeling antagonised, she met the proud look in his eyes and lifted her own chin.

"Have you thought about the name?" she asked quizzically. "It wasn't really changed at all. He was saying he was still Anders' son."

"I would like to think he meant it that way," Gerald said sadly, reaching for the bell rope. "Now, let's return to happier things."

George appeared with a tray of sparkling, cut glass flutes and a bottle of champagne.

"May you always be as happy as you are today; your gain is our loss, m' boy. I intended keeping Francesca with us permanently, even though I hadn't told her." He raised his glass. "To you both."

"What's that? What's that?" Abigail poked her head round the door, her face beaming. "When's the wedding then?" Lorna followed with a tray of delicacies and they raised the glasses that George handed them. Obviously prearranged.

"As soon as possible," Adam said firmly, tucking Fran's arm through his. She nodded, alight with happiness.

George stood behind Gerald's chair, like a faithful watchdog, knowing the previous evening had exhausted him. He caught Adam's attention discreetly and Adam stood up, saying, with an apologetic smile, that if he didn't go home soon, he would be accused of child neglect.

"Come with me Fran. It would give you and Melly a chance to get to know one another. We might even celebrate over a corned beef sandwich, which is about her limit when it comes to food." He smiled tolerantly. "Not the most domesticated of creatures, our Melly. She feels she is better suited to the ski slopes, with a macho instructor in tow."

He shook Gerald's hand, thanked everyone for their good wishes and drew Fran to the door.

She turned and Gerald raised his fingers slightly; his eyes were already hooded, as they said a last goodbye from the doorway. Once outside she turned anxiously. "Will he be alright?"

He nodded reassuringly. "Charles says he was a real dynamo before his accident. He also says, and I quote: 'If anything is going to kill him it will be that damned pride of his'." The imitation of Charles was not good, but it made her feel better.

Melissa was delighted to see them and eventually asked the inevitable, "How did you meet?" Fran realised there was a lot of explaining to do to account for her being at Anders Folly, but Adam came to her rescue.

"It's a long story. Let's skip the questions for now and drink another toast. Cheers!"

They had a lovely day that ended with Fran cooking dinner in the evening.

"I'm really, really glad you came," Adam said with a contented grin. "Melly's a rotten cook."

A cushion hit him squarely on the head, followed by another from the other direction.

"Was it something I said, girls?"

"Just for that, *you* can make the coffee," Melly scolded. She was propped up on the settee in front of the window and gave a surprised "Oh!" as a car pulled onto the drive. "Better make that coffee for five; Mum and Dad are here."

He eased himself lazily out of the armchair. "They weren't expected until tomorrow; what's the betting something, or even everything didn't suit Mother?" he said with a sly grin in Melly's direction.

Fran fingered her necklace nervously; listening as Adam opened the door, then found herself being introduced to a tall couple. Ronald Wesley shook her hand warmly, giving Adam an approving look. They had the same startling blue eyes and his hair could have been blonde or silver; there was no mistaking they were father and son. Jane, his wife, in complete contrast, was dark haired, over tall (which caused her to stoop) and had a rather supercilious air. She was nothing like Fran would have imagined, and the hand now resting in hers, was surprisingly small for such a large woman. The handshake was brief, accompanied by an equally brief, "Hello," before she launched into a detailed description of a wretched journey: a hotel lacking everything – in spite of being five stars, and a migraine headache, which was a result of both.

"Why don't you go and lie down, dear, and I'll bring you a nice cup of tea?" her husband suggested solicitously.

"Ronald, we have a guest! I wouldn't dream of doing such a thing – no matter how bad I feel. You should know that," she complained in a long-suffering voice.

"I must be going anyway," Fran said quickly.

"Nonsense, my dear, come and tell me all about yourself." She motioned her to sit down and settled herself opposite, with a martyred expression.

The palms of Fran's hands were sticky and her eyes sought Adam's. He was making signs behind his mother's chair, to relax and not worry. She saw Melly toss her eyes and turn away to look out of the window and Ronald Wesley excused himself, saying he must check the car.

"I'll make that coffee," Adam said with unnecessary gusto.

"You know I can't drink coffee with my migraine, dear," his mother rebuked.

"Sorry, Mother, one tea coming up," he bowed deeply and backed through the door, smiling mischievously at Fran, who gave him a nervous smile, feeling she had been left in the lion's den, as he disappeared.

At the end of ten minutes she was squirming with embarrassment. She had to admit the questions were normal and could have been easily answered until recently, but Adam's mother waffled on, completely unaware of any discomfort on Fran's part.

"I expect I knew your mother if she came from these parts; what was her name?"

"Celina Edyvean," Fran answered quietly, her face burning.

"Mother, does it really matter?" Melly interrupted, puzzled by Fran's embarrassment, trying to come to her rescue – but at the same time, curious.

"Be quiet, Melissa; I'm trying to think." Her mother waved a dismissive hand at her, continuing to test her memory for the elusive facts. "I'm sure I know the name – I just can't put a face to it – isn't that annoying? But I *will* remember; I'm very good on names and faces as a rule."

Adam and his father brought the coffee in, and much to Fran's relief, the subject was dropped.

Adam perched on the arm of her chair and put an arm around her shoulders.

"We plan to marry very soon and quietly," he said firmly. "Just you three, Sir Gerald, Fran's brother, Darren, and his two children.

"Why so secretive?" his mother asked.

"Not secretive, Mother, private," Adam corrected her in the same, firm voice.

"Surely Fran would like to invite some relatives or friends, wouldn't you, dear?"

"Fran hasn't any family apart from those I have mentioned and her nearest friends would have to travel from London. That is why – no fuss," he emphasised.

"Well I don't know what Aunt Heather and Uncle John will think or Saul and Megan, and Peter and Sandy. And what about Great Uncle Toby – you really can't get married without asking him and that means asking…"

Adam held up his hand, eyes closed. "Exactly Mother, if you have your way, half of Cornwall will come and Fran won't know any of them – and I daresay the majority would be strangers to me as well. No! It's been decided – no fuss."

Jane Wesley gave a disapproving sniff, knowing when her son spoke in that tone, she couldn't bulldoze him. All very unsatisfactory in her view; he should have found himself a nice Cornish girl – that's where the controversy lay, she decided, missing the point that the only controversy was of *her* making.

"Can I be your bridesmaid?" Melly piped up, introducing a lighter note in to what threatened to become a major issue.

Fran threw her a grateful smile and nodded.

"I think it would be wise to get you home before the fog gets any thicker," Adam said, peering out of the window at the rolling clouds of sea mist. Fran rose, lly they would shop together for their dresses, as soon as she could

Jane and Ronald followed them into the hall, and Adam had opened the front door when Jane gave a triumphant cry.

"I've got it! I remember your mother."

"You do?" Fran asked, apprehensive yet still eager for information.

"You said she came from Padstow, didn't you? They were a really old Cornish family but her father died and she and her mother went to live in – Plymouth, if my memory serves me right. Yes, yes it was definitely Plymouth. Then her mother became ill I believe, and Celina came back here and took a job as a secretary in one of the big, local houses. The last we heard was she had left because of some kafuffle. Yes, it was something to do with..." She paused, her memory clouded momentarily. "Of course! That was it: rumour had it she was pregnant and the eldest son married her against his father's wishes."

Until that moment, she had been excited by her own successful recall, now she stopped suddenly and stared at Fran, saying slowly, as it dawned on her.

"But Adam said you haven't any family – and yet, surely?" The question hung, as she stared from one to the other of them. Fran stared back and slowly felt the colour drain from her face.

"Jane, for goodness sake!" her husband exploded and without a word, Adam took Fran's arm and led her to the car.

Jane ran after them. "Adam, I'm really sorry. I didn't mean to upset her – please don't leave like this, Fran dear."

Fran turned. "It's alright Mrs Wesley," she said in a small, flat voice. "Please don't blame yourself. I really do understand, you see it's all quite new to me as well but Adam will explain when he gets back."

All the way home, Adam kept assuring her how unimportant it was; they loved each other – end of story. She nodded and agreed with everything he said, but went straight to her room, wanting to be alone with her battered thoughts.

He went to discuss the unfortunate incident with Gerald and explain her drastic change of spirits since leaving that morning.

"Is there no way of discovering who her father is? It will haunt her until she knows."

Gerald gave a hopeless shrug. "I tried desperately at the time, because I didn't want Robert to marry her mother. I don't hold out much hope after all this time."

"I'm so afraid she will call the wedding off," Adam said gloomily, as he left.

After much thought, Gerald rang for George and asked him to fetch Abigail, who listened with a worried frown and said she would speak to Fran.

As expected, she found her packing.

"Running away?" she challenged.

"It's no good, Abigail, I'm just an embarrassment to myself and everyone else – at least in London nobody knows my past."

"What nonsense! You make it sound as if you have committed a crime," came the brisk retort.

"You don't understand," Fran said wearily.

"I understand it's time to put it all behind you and get on with building a family of your own," she advised gently.

"That's what I intended and then I met Adam's parents today and realised even a quiet wedding will cause speculation and I just can't live with it." She shrugged miserably.

Abigail studied the forlorn droop of her shoulders for a long minute, then said decisively, "Come along; stop that packing. I want you to come to the study with me."

"Not tonight," Fran implored.

"Yes tonight. Right now in fact. The time has come for us to have a talk; Sir Gerald must hear as well."

Reluctantly Fran allowed herself to be led down to the study where Gerald was sitting alone, staring pensively into the fire; he brightened as she entered.

True to character, Abigail came straight to the point. "It is time for me to speak out, even though it means breaking a solemn promise I made years ago to your dear wife – God rest her soul. I know she will forgive me because it can do no harm now to the one she was protecting and I am the last one alive to know the truth."

They waited, realising what it must be costing her to break her word but neither were prepared for her next statement.

"Alexander was your father."

Her words met with stunned silence and she prayed the news wouldn't prove too much for Gerald, on top of recent events.

"Are you certain?" he asked incredulously, finding his voice at last.

"Beyond a shadow of doubt and I can only hope I am right to speak out now."

He nodded wordlessly, stretching out his hand to Fran.

Still too stunned to take it in, she sat on the footstool, her hand in his, whilst the rest of the story unfolded.

It all started one lunchtime when Pamela returned home to find Celina with torn clothes and bruises; she sobbed as she named Alexander as her attacker.

n, Pamela went to his room and found him in a drunken stupor, ̱npty whisky bottle. Her one thought was to keep the incident from ̗er husband, knowing how severely Alexander would be dealt with. Even knowing him to be reckless and wild, she still idolised her youngest son and would go to any lengths to protect him. Celina was persuaded to say nothing, but three weeks later, she discovered she was pregnant. Beside herself, Pamela told Abigail, saying the only solution was an abortion and although horrified she agreed to help. However, Pamela had reckoned without Celina's strong, moral views on murder, as she saw it, and scathingly assured Pamela she would rather die than reveal the name of her child's father, or the way in which it was conceived.

The proudly delivered words had so enraged Alexander, that instead of being grateful, he took delight in telling Robert, even boasting of *his* child she was expecting.

"At first I thought attacking her was his way of evening up the score. He was such a loving child to me, but as well as fun loving and mischievous, he did have a malicious streak, and apparently it was his mother he was furious at, for going to London without him. As a boy, he could always twist us around his little finger; so we were both to blame really."

She faltered and gave Gerald an apologetic look before continuing. "Robert was persuaded to keep quiet, on the understanding Pamela would support him in his wish to marry Celina, because he wouldn't hear of Celina bearing the stigma of an illegitimate child alone and – well you know the rest."

She spread her hands. "I'm not proud of my part in it and our actions, *most certainly* came home to roost with a vengeance, when you think, Robert wouldn't have been in Oxford but for his brother's actions."

Gerald remembered Alexander's treacherous allegations; he had known the truth all along and allowed him to blame Robert.

Fran turned to Gerald. "But how did you know I wasn't Robert's child then?"

"I overheard Robert saying he would always treat the child like his own. To be fair she told him she couldn't allow him to make such a sacrifice for something he wasn't responsible for. We both said things and they ran away together. I thought I could force him to give up such a foolish waste of his life. I don't know how he supported her. He had no money, no job and yet you tell me he was able to buy a substantial property in Oxford. I never gave him a penny."

Gerald was so overcome that Fran cried quietly for him and Abigail took up the story.

"Robert didn't care that Alexander got off scot-free. His only thought was he could marry Celina. Lady Anders financed them."

She gave a sad, reminiscent smile. "It solved everything at the time, but I can't stand by and see more lives ruined; it's time you two made up for lost time," she ended briskly, more than a little overcome now she had unburdened herself.

"I'm truly sorry you have been encumbered with my family's indiscretions, and thank you for being so loyal to them, but most of all, thank you for speaking up now and introducing my granddaughter to me, before it was too late again."

He hesitated, then said, "I know it's late, but ask George if he would bring Lady Anders's portrait down. It's time to heal old wounds."

Abigail beamed through her tears and hurried from the room.

Fran looked at him questioningly, and he said, "I was very annoyed when Samantha saw the picture."

Fran shook her head. "Sorry?"

"Don't you remember? The day Darren returned, Sam came downstairs talking about a picture of a beautiful lady. It was the portrait, you will see shortly."

"I assumed she had seen a picture in a book. I don't think I was really listening at the time."

He smiled, before explaining, "By standing on a chair, Samantha managed to unbolt the connecting door to the unused part of the attic, where the portrait is kept. It's alright, there is a padlock on it now," he assured her, seeing her alarm.

"She is a very adventurous child," Fran apologised.

"I have great hopes for Samantha," he confessed quietly. Timothy already has the faraway look of a book worm; as you yourself pointed out," he said dryly. "I won't make that mistake again. There are going to be no more secrets or unfulfilled dreams in this house."

There was a tap at the door and a large picture frame entered, with a pair of shoes at the bottom and a hand either side. Fran laughed and leapt up to help George; they struggled to free a space, turned it around and stood back to view it.

Fran gave a gentle gasp. "That is my grandmother. My parents used to show us her picture; it was in black and white, so I never realised she had red hair and green eyes, but Dad would often say, 'you are just like your grandmother', when I lost my temper."

Gerald watched her, as she stood transfixed. She was indeed like Pamela. Abigail crept in, eyes brimming and hugged her.

"That isn't the only time you are like her," she said and hurried away. George went to tell Lorna the news, leaving Gerald and Fran to their memories.

"By the way, Darren telephoned earlier. He will be home for Christmas! It's going to be a wonderful Christmas. Did I tell you Charles, Felicity, Sophie,

the children will be staying with us? I heard today." Fran gave a
⌐ss, tearing her gaze away from the portrait.

Wonderful! Almost like old times, as Felicity would say. She certainly
believes in serendipity, doesn't she? It has been another long day; you must be
tired." She walked with him to the lift and pressed the bell for George.

"Goodnight – Grandfather." She kissed his cheek.

"Goodnight, my child."

She watched the lift ascend and heard George excitedly telling Gerald about
his father. The portrait confirmed Joe Watts *had* stayed at Forest End, because he
still had a group photograph of Lady Anders with a number of patients, and his
father was one of them. As their voices faded along the landing she heard him
say, "And Lorna says to tell you, she has made a start on the Christmas puddings.
She says they have to be very special if Mr Charles is coming. I'm quite jealous."

She waited long enough to hear Gerald give a low chuckle, then turned
away for just one more look at the portrait. It had been a day that would start a
new life. The feeling of coming home hadn't been just wishful thinking after all.

In spite of the late hour, she rang Adam. They had parted unhappily and she
needed to put things right as soon as possible.

He had been waiting for her call and arrived ten minutes later, looking
anxious and uncertain. One look at her face though, as she met him at the door,
told him everything he needed to know.

"Let's drive up to the headland," she whispered, her eyes full of the love
and longing she felt for him. He took her hand and they walked out into the night
together. Miraculously, the fog had cleared; stars shone from a clear sky and the
moon hung low over a calm sea. They sat listening to the waves breaking gently
on the shore far below and across the bay, a single light shone.

"It's like sitting on the edge of the world," Fran whispered. "And it became
even more special when I discovered I could see your house from here – sort of
like a bonus to something already perfect."

"I know what you mean. *My house* is waiting for *you*. Together we will turn
it in to our home."

Wrapped in their own world, they sat huddled together, watching the moon
disappear as the dawn crept slowly over the horizon. It was a time to stop and
stare – a memory to cherish.

"I'm so happy," she murmured sleepily. "I want everyone to be happy.
Shall we have a big wedding just before Christmas, when Charles and Felicity's
family are over? It would please Grandfather. And shall we let your mother invite
whoever she wants to?"

Adam looked at her with tender amusement and kissed her upturned mouth.

348

"She will be your friend for life, but are you sure you know what it means to give Mother a free rein? You could end up meeting the whole population of Cornwall in one fell swoop."

He spoke drowsily and Fran snuggled closer, enjoying the firm warmth of him through his wool sweater, as his encircling arm drew her closer again and as the rest of the countryside was waking up – they slept, basking in the early morning sunshine slanting through the car windows. Fran was home, at last.